PRAISE FOR MICHELE ISRAEL HARPER

"Ro is back, and I am here for it. Battered from her previous adventures, she launches headfirst into a new one full of excitement, betrayal, and numerous twists. I absolutely loved the tie-ins from various fairytales and Harper's unique spins on classic stories. If you want a story full of blooming romance, friendship, and sacrificial love, you'll want to dive head-first into this book."

—Hope Bolinger, author of the Blaze trilogy and the Dear Hero duology

"*Silence the Siren* is a fresh take on a classic fairy tale that I did not see coming! Michele Israel Harper weaves a wildly creative tale that will have your heart beating fast with excitement one moment and then breaking the next. Ro is the heroine we've all been waiting for. You'll be rooting for her as she takes on man and sea in this odyssey-esque adventure. Can't wait to see what Harper does with the rest of the series!"

—Julie Hall, *USA Today* Bestselling author of the multiple award-winning Life After series

"Michele Israel Harper continues her unique spin on fairy tales well-loved. While the Huntress dives into waters unknown, there is enough familiar and new to keep readers invested in this intricate and expanding world that feels almost as real as our own history."

—Derrick Elchers, author of *The Battle for Art*

"*Silence the Siren* takes readers on a high seas adventure that sets personalities from all over the fairytale spectrum on a crash course with peril and betrayal. Michele Israel Harper offers a delightful cast of characters who struggle with complex emotions, tight dilemmas, the very real frustrations of their own limitations. The story's deft weaving of resonant retelling and original twists will keep readers enthralled to the last page."
—Rebecca P. Minor, fantasy author, artist, and Realm Makers founder

"*Silence the Siren* does not fall into the fairy tale trap of simple good and evil, but features a protagonist who insists there are two sides to a story—and then is frustrated when neither is as honorable and noble as pretended. Perseverance and honesty are as important as strength and ferocity (although we get those, too!). And it's all in a fascinating world where multiple fairy tales mingle and tangle."
—Laura VanArendonk Baugh, award-winning author of *The Songweaver's Vow* and the Shard of Elan series

"Michele Harper creates a marvelous world in *Silence the Siren*, where French fairy tales are spun into something new, their golden story-threads woven into lavish, compelling tapestries. From pirates to princesses to sirens, things are never quite what they seem. Enemies become friends and vice versa, magic turns up in the most unexpected places, and the promise of true love hovers on the horizon."
—Merrie Destefano, award-winning author of *Shade: The Complete Trilogy*

Praise for other books in the Beast Hunter series:

"Beast Hunter sweeps you up in a rousing tale that twists the fairy tale world on its head. Quick to read, but sticks with you and makes you eager for more."
—H.L. Burke, award-winning and bestselling author of over twenty eclectic fantasy novels

"Beast Hunter captivated me! From the first page, I was sucked in, unaware of all sense of time, and *had* to know what was going to happen next (even if it took reading into the wee hours of the morning to find out). Ro is such an admirable character, and seeing her courage through all the plot twists Michele wove into this engaging story, it left me desperate to get my hands on its sequel, *Kill the Beast*, as soon as possible to continue Ro's adventures!"
—Laura A. Grace, author of *Dear Author* and *Team Lines* and *Gathering Faith*

Silence the Siren

Silence the Siren

Book Two of the Beast Hunters

Michele Israel Harper

Love2ReadLove2Write Publishing, LLC
Indianapolis, Indiana

ALSO BY MICHELE ISRAEL HARPER

Wisdom & Folly Sisters:
The Complete Story

The Candace Marshall Chronicles:
Ghostly Vendetta
Zombie Takeover
(Coming Soon)
Vampire Feud
Mummy Resurrection

The Beast Hunter Series:
Beast Hunter
Kill the Beast
Silence the Siren
(Coming Soon)
Quell the Nightingale
Slay the Wolf
Stop the Snow Queen
End the Fey

Coming Soon:

Altered Time Saga:
The Lady Bodyguard
The Lady Spy
The Lady Assassin

Standalones:

Queen of the Moon

Dreamworld

Stars Collide

Tales of the Cousin Kingdoms:

Ruby Dragon Kingdom

Diamond Unicorn Kingdom

Sapphire Griffin Kingdom

Emerald Pegasus Kingdom

Time of the Dragons

To Cam, Savannah, and Alicia,

A critique group is every writer's secret for success,
And you are mine.
Thank you for embarking on this journey with me!

PART ONE

Elles avaient de belles voix, plus délicieuses que la plus
magnifique voix humaine ; et quand une tempête se préparait,
et elles pensaient qu'un bateau pourrait être perdu, elles
nageaient devant le navire, et chantaient les délices sous la mer,
et disaient aux marins de ne pas avoir peur de descendre là.
Mais les marins n'ont jamais compris les sirènes, et ils n'ont
jamais vu les merveilles sous la mer ; car quand le bateau
descendit, les hommes se noyèrent, et leurs cadavres seuls sont
arrivés au palais du roi de la mer.
~Hans Christian Anderson, *La Petite Sirène*

They had beautiful voices, more beautiful than any human; and
when a storm was brewing, and they thought a ship might be
lost, they would swim in front of the vessel, and sing of the
delights below the sea, and tell the sailors not to be afraid. But
the sailors never understood, and they never saw the wonders
below the sea; for when the ship went down the men drowned,
and their corpses alone reached the palace of the sea king.
~Hans Christian Anderson, *The Little Mermaid*

1

*K*ing Wilhelm rose shakily to his feet, a vein pulsing in his forehead. "You will do as I say! And I'll not hear another word about an all-female crew. Either you accept my terms, or you may return to that God-forsaken land from whence you came!"

Ro shouted back, "And I'll not die because the English king is too bête to heed my warning! Maybe I will go back to France."

The king pointed a meaty finger at her. "And good riddance."

The words washed over Ro, bringing with them rage, embarrassment, and a pinprick of light as the vast throne room closed around her. How dare he?

He was the one who had dragged her all this way. *He* was the one who had begged for her help. Now *he* was dismissing *her*?

Not a sound was heard from the many courtiers swiveling their heads at the volley of heated words flung between the English King Wilhelm and the French huntress Ro LeFèvre.

"Well?" the king demanded. "Are you going to do as I say?

Or shall I bid thee farewell and send you back to your father for punishment?"

Punishment? *Punishment?* As if she were a child young enough to be placed over her père's knee?

Ro instinctively reached for an arrow that thankfully wasn't there, and the king's eyes widened at the movement. Ro covered the move with a stiff bow and a hand flourish, feeling absolutely ridiculous doing so.

"As you wish, votre Majesté."

She turned without waiting to be dismissed and stormed away from the throne, every footfall thunderous in the cavernous space.

Just as she reached the carved double doors, King Wilhelm shouted, "Wait!"

Ro paused but didn't turn.

"You will have your ship, with the crew I choose, and you will leave when I say and not before. Am I clear?"

Ro turned and stared at him, arms crossed, eyebrow raised.

The king sighed, long and deep. "In return for your service, I will sign the trade agreement with your king."

Something Ro was certain he never would've agreed to—the terms were outrageous, in his opinion, and far too lenient, in Ro's—had he not been desperate to rid himself of the sirens sinking his ships, and therefore, his wealth.

It wasn't enough. Ro didn't budge.

He sighed even louder. "And I will allow negotiations with the sirens first."

Ro masked her surprise. Negotiate? He'd insisted hunting was the only way. And she'd insisted she wanted the full story before she started killing things.

If he could compromise, well then, so could she. Perhaps.

Ro grinned, more a baring of her teeth than a true smile. "Once you sign both agreements, I will set sail."

King Wilhelm spluttered, his face turning purple, and Ro thought he was going to have a stroke right then and there.

He controlled whatever he clearly wanted to shout and gritted his teeth. "Very well. You agree to my terms, then?"

She nodded once and gave another stiff bow. "As you wish."

He opened his mouth—Ro heard something about "trousers" and "don't wear them in my presence again"—but she heaved closed the impossibly heavy doors, their screech covering most of what the king said.

And good riddance.

Ro blindly made her way outside and gripped the banister overlooking the English king's gardens.

The insufferable maggot!

Fury danced a clanging step within her, urging her to go back in there and tell him exactly what she thought of him. Without being flogged and thrown in the dungeon.

Ro closed her eyes. Deep breaths. In, out.

She tried to think of something else, something other than the debacle she'd just gone through, but the only thing that came to mind was what had haunted her with every hoofbeat from Champagne, France to the port, what had taunted her with every rock of the boat across the English Channel, and what had badgered her with every carriage shift from the English port to London. And the many stops in between.

Cosette wasn't her sister.

Non, her little sister was dead somewhere, replaced by a well-meaning fairy. Something Ro was very much going to confront the immortal Queen of the Fairies over, should they ever meet again.

Her little sister had already been dead when the fairy had replaced her with her own fey daughter in order to hide her, to save her daughter's life. The Fairy Queen had only done what any desperate mère would've done. Someone had been hunting to end the child's life, after all.

But she had no right!

Thoughts flew through Ro's head as quickly as she shot arrows.

What would her sister's name have been? For that matter, what would Cosette's name have been, had she not been placed in Ro's family? Where was her real sister buried? Was she even buried, or simply forgotten somewhere? Drifting in the ether as some unknown, unloved mortal?

Well Ro would've loved her, had she been given the chance.

Ro gripped the stone banister harder and ducked her head. A groan wrenched up and out of her soul, so deep and full of anguish, Ro had no idea how someone she'd never even met could affect her so deeply.

"My lady?"

Ro groaned again—this time in annoyance—and turned to the intolerable messenger who'd dogged her every step for the last three months.

He'd paraded her before every noble across the English countryside, and not one of her urgings to be taken directly to the king had made the slightest difference.

An entire summer, wasted.

Almost as if Cosette was standing next to her, Ro felt her sister's admonition before the thought fully formed. Cosette would urge her to get to know him, to think the best. To never make snap judgments.

Ro thrust the voice out of her head. It hurt too much.

The king's messenger stood next to her at the banister, overlooking the king's garden as she'd been doing. "Well, that didn't go as expected, did it?"

"Oh, really? It's no wonder after receiving that ridiculous letter of his. No one can know he hired me, indeed. That pompous, arrogant—"

"Choose your next words wisely, my lady. He may be your employer, but he is my king. Not to mention your words may get you locked in the tower, should someone overhear." Though not said unkindly, there was a measure of steel in his voice that brooked no argument.

Ro snapped her mouth closed. *Insufferable, egotistical . . . pompous windbag!*

She finished the diatribe in her head and nodded in agreement with herself. She might not be able to say it aloud, but oh, it felt good to think it!

No matter what Cosette might say.

She went back to gripping the stone banister with a vengeance. Each squeeze of her fingers held back yet another thing she wanted to say about the English king. And she wasn't thinking about Cosette right now.

"Will you do it? Find the siren, I mean."

"I said I would, didn't I?" Ro snapped. She took a deep breath and scrubbed a hand down her face. "Désolé—I mean —I'm sorry, truly. I just can't believe he couldn't see the wisdom of my plan. What good will I be if my ship crashes and I go down with the rest of a men-only crew?"

Ro wanted to throw back her head and scream her frustrations at the top of her lungs, but there were already enough rumors of her taking on the beast's characteristics after spending so much time in his château. How were they to know she'd had this temper as long as she could remember?

The messenger's gaze bored into the side of Ro's face, but she kept her eyes on the garden. She was pretty sure she'd snarl if she looked his way.

He held something out, and she glanced down at it. A folded square of paper.

"This came for you while you were with King Wilhelm."

Ro didn't touch it. She recognized that handwriting. Madame LaChance. Excitement warred with trepidation.

The messenger continued. "I think you will find a great

7

many things yet to do to prepare for your journey. Who knows when the king will acquire a ship and crew for your voyage? Perhaps you should ensure you have everything you need."

Ro's eyes slammed into his. A slight smile graced his face. He laid the scrap on the banister and walked away as she stared after him.

Was he condoning her wild plan? Against the king's wishes? Or was he simply relaying Madame LaChance's message?

Tired of conjecture after three years of it in the beast's château, Ro snatched up the missive and unfolded it.

2

"*M*adame LaChance will be with you in a moment."

Ro nodded, and the young Mademoiselle left her where she stood in the foyer of an opulent boarding school. Ro stared around her in wonder. Her feet sank into the plushest of carpets. Rich, patterned wallpaper in deep rouge lined the walls, and the molding on the walls and ceilings—surrounding masterful paintings—was gilded vibrant gold.

Every piece of furniture spoke of wealth, and every decorative piece was essential to the room's décor, artfully arranged.

So this was where Cosette would've lived had she escaped the curse and come to Madame LaChance's school as Ro had arranged.

A smile found its way to Ro's lips. She was rather glad it hadn't worked out as planned. Then Ro would be married to Prince Trêve—King Trêve, would she never get used to that? —and subject to the French court, stifling dresses, and far-too-much attention.

She wouldn't be here, now. She wouldn't have her freedom.

Ro ignored the pang in her heart, the whisper that all those things might not have been so terrible, not with Trêve at her side.

Ro lifted her chin. Non, Cosette was exactly where she should be. Even if they weren't actually sisters. Ro frowned and moved in front of a portrait, hardly seeing it.

Her hands flitted over her bodice, and for the thousandth time, she questioned wearing her hunting gear. But she would have felt exposed without her fitted trousers, tall leather boots, leather jerkin, and tailored blouse. The cuffs of her leather jacket—once belonging to her brother—were worn smooth from her constantly rubbing them, and she kept flicking a glance at her mère's red cape, hung by the doorway. She smoothed her dark hair, self-conscious about the strands just now long enough to put back in a queue, then clasped her hands tightly together.

She hated to admit it, but she was nervous.

She'd never met Madame LaChance. She'd only written to her and heard her praises sung by that old bat of a priest, when he wasn't trying to convince Ro to get out of France and take her sorcery with her. Ro scowled at the opulent oil painting she'd taken to examining. She'd hoped restoring the rightful king to power and breaking France's curse would've smoothed out their differences, but Père Guise still couldn't stand her.

Not that it bothered her much. The feeling was mutual.

She moved on to a tapestry, woven in tones of robin's-egg blue, the exact shade of Beau Alexandre Trêve's eyes.

Good heavens! She wasn't thinking about her sister's husband's eyes! Not again. What was done was done. They were married, and she was not.

Ro's fingers ached as she twisted them. Would Madame LaChance see her already and rescue her from these insufferable thoughts?

Her gaze flitted to the red wallpaper, the shade reminding her of the beast's eyes when they glowed red—a much better image to keep in mind when thinking of Trêve—and she began to pace.

What kind of woman was Madame LaChance? What kind of woman would Ro have sent Cosette to?

Footsteps brushed against thick carpet directly behind her, and Ro turned. She was about to find out.

"This way, please, Mademoiselle."

Ro followed the same young woman down the hallway and into an ornate office. It was just as lavish as the foyer, except this room was decorated in tones of rose and vert—a virtual rose garden of colors.

Madame LaChance stood from her desk and spoke English in a thick French accent. "Welcome to England, Mademoiselle. Won't you please come in?"

The first thing that struck Ro was how young she looked for a woman in her forties. The second? Madame LaChance was positively intimidating.

Dressed in a vibrant-purple gown with a lavender underskirt, Madame LaChance was a living portrait of French nobility. Snow-white lace decorated her décolletage and dripped from her elbows in elegant layers. Her perfectly coifed and powdered curls were piled atop her head, one curl elegantly draped over her shoulder, and the beauty mark on her cheek only rounded out the picture.

Ro tried not to stumble over the plush rose-pink rug as she approached the ash-wood desk. She felt like an awkward, gawking colt. What was she even doing here?

One thing was certain: Her hunting gear was clearly the wrong choice.

The young Mademoiselle closed the door as she left, and Ro had half a mind to follow her out. Anyone with an office this lavish was in for an unmitigated disaster with Ro in it.

Madame LaChance gave Ro a demure smile and switched to French. "Ah, the huntress I have heard so much about, n'est-ce pas?"

She moved out from behind her ornate desk and held out her hand. Ro took her fingertips and bowed over them, as she'd seen others do to royalty. The action seemed appropriate, and it seemed to please Madame LaChance.

"Sit, oui?"

Ro sat. She hoped words would present themselves when she needed them, but for now, rien. Nothing.

Madame LaChance moved back to her seat, every movement demanding Ro pay attention. It was like being in the presence of a goddess of old. Mesmerizing, intimidating, not meant to be in the presence of mortal man. Er, uh, woman.

Ro shook off the ridiculous thoughts. Her imagination was getting the best of her and carrying her right along with it. As always.

Madame LaChance settled behind the massive piece of furniture and smiled kindly. "So you have come to me because the English king is a bête, non?"

Ro blinked.

"My time is precious, Mademoiselle."

"Oh, ah, oui."

Madame LaChance waited with hands folded atop her desk.

Ro jumped a little when she realized she was still expected to speak. "And, uh, your note. Your missive. You sent me a letter."

A servant slipped into the room with a tray bearing an ornate coffee service, interrupting Ro's pitiful attempt at conversation. The servant left it on a table and exited without a word. Ro stared longingly after her.

"Ah." Madame LaChance rose and poured them both café, adding sugar and milk to Ro's without asking. She then placed three raspberry-filled macarons on Ro's plate, their deep rose color matching the luxurious rug. Ro's favorite. She couldn't get enough of the newly invented treat.

Ro was dumbfounded that Madame LaChance had taken

the time to find out her preferences. Such a thought would've never occurred to her.

Madame LaChance placed it all flawlessly in front of Ro. "But I knew exactly how it would go, and that you would need my help."

A thought struck Ro as she sipped her perfectly enhanced café and then took a bite of only the best dessert in all the realms. A request for mounds of gold usually followed such a declaration. She swallowed. "The king has not yet paid me . . ."

Madame LaChance waved away the statement with a graceful hand. "I will consider the chests of gold and precious jewels you sent me payment enough. Especially since your sister did not require my services."

Ro frowned. Chests of gold . . . ? Oh! She'd forgotten about the treasure the beast had sent Madame LaChance at Ro's request, while Ro was trapped in his château.

Although, from what she'd heard of Madame LaChance, this was not how she conducted business. At all. Ro raised an eyebrow as she polished off a second macaron.

Madame LaChance shrugged, the movement delicate. "I do not make this my habit, non. But you were quite insistent in your payment. You purchased this entire school, you know."

Ro nearly choked on her final macaron. She hastily dabbed a few crumbs off her mouth. "All of it?"

Had she truly sent enough wealth from the beast's chests of gold and the Mesdemoiselles of the Mountain's payments to purchase a place such as this?

"Oui. But that is not why I asked you here. I will help you this once, and my debt to you is fulfilled. Understood?"

Ro nodded dumbly. Why, oh why wasn't she silver-tongued like Cosette? Bitterness filled her. Right. Because her sister was half-fairy, and not her sister.

And she needed to move past it.

"I will provide a second ship, contacts of whom I recommend for captain and crew, and payment—half before they leave, half when they return—and you will set it all up, under your name, of course." Her smile, though friendly, showed considerable distaste. "Non, I do not wish to be tied to such a venture."

Ro tried not to be offended, but . . . well, she was. "Then why do it?"

Madame LaChance smiled. "I cannot imagine your success without my aid, oui?"

Ro deflated a little. "Oui."

She didn't have a chance of defeating the sirens if she did the same thing as every other hunter who'd failed. Besides, she was in a strange country with strange money and strange habits. At least she didn't struggle *too* much with the language . . .

Ro needed the help.

Her mind spun, but something didn't feel quite right. She squinted at Madame LaChance. "I can't imagine that will be inexpensive. Surely you must want something in return?"

"Oh, my dear, don't do that."

Ro blinked. "Pardon?"

"Uncrinkle your forehead. Oui, there you are. Don't want wrinkles before you're thirty, after all."

Ro's mouth hung open for a second, then she rubbed her forehead. "All right, so if you are willing to pay—"

"Good heavens, arrête!"

Ro froze, fingers still on her forehead.

"Has no one taught you not to touch your face?"

What in all the realms? Ro couldn't help her glare as she dropped her hand. "Non. My mère died when I was young."

Sympathy filled her eyes. "You poor, sad thing. Then you should know the oils from your fingers will cause blemishes. A Mademoiselle ought never touch her face."

Ro's glare deepened, and she spoke through gritted teeth. "We were discussing what you wanted in exchange for providing me with what the king expressly forbid?"

Madame LaChance sighed, the sound full of sorrow. "And that glare—oh dear. I can't imagine what your sister would have been like, what ungodly habits she might have possessed, had she been anything like you. I'm not sure I would've been up for the task." She tisked and shook her head.

Ro snapped upright, just shy of jumping to her feet. "My sister is the most graceful, polished, lovely, *gentle* soul I know, and she would have put any of your girls to shame." She bit back her next words, just in time: *She would have put you to shame.*

The quiet smile was back on Madame LaChance's face. "Is she? Indeed."

Ro sniffed. "Indeed."

"And she is now—?"

Ro just stared at her. *What?*

Madame LaChance had a look of extreme patience about her. "Her position, chérie. What is her position?"

Ro somehow stopped herself from rolling her eyes. "The queen of France."

"Ah." Madame LaChance sat back and twirled a ruby-encrusted pen knife with her fingertips, a pleased smile on her rouge-painted lips. "I very much look forward to meeting her."

Ro gritted her teeth. Didn't everyone who found out her sister was queen? "The details of our arrangement?"

Madame LaChance clucked her tongue. "Your poor face. I suppose it cannot be helped. Who can unlearn such dreadful habits when one is so old?"

Ro choked a little. One's twenties was not old!

Madame LaChance spoke right over her spluttering. "All I ask is, when you meet the Siren Queen, you request something of her for me."

Ro raised an eyebrow. The siren what now?

Madame LaChance's smile was full of delicious secrets. "You see, you will discover a great many things on this voyage"—she raised her hand at Ro's opening mouth—"things

I do not know nor care to know, but of this I am certain: You shall meet the Siren Queen, and you shall ask a favor for me."

Ro's mind spun. The Siren Queen? That would imply structure, a people—one with governing and rules, not mindless monsters as the king had implied . . .

She realized Madame LaChance had stopped talking, allowing Ro space to think.

"And that favor would be . . . ?" Ro prompted.

Madame LaChance's entire demeanor changed. Gone was her smile, intensity in its place. "Her coral and pearl hair combs. There are three—one coral, the other two pearl. I want them."

Ro blinked. *That's it?* "What do they do? The combs, I mean." They must contain some kind of magical enchantment for her to want them so badly.

"That is not of import. You see, one of the ships that sank was mine, a mistake she dare not make again, and something very precious to me was onboard. She took it."

Ro tilted her head. "What was it?"

Madame LaChance kept speaking as if Ro had not. "All I ask, in return for financing your alter voyage, and for my discretion, is that you ask her for the combs after you mention the item she took from me. That is all."

"And she'll give them to me," Ro deadpanned. "Just like that."

Her smile returned, holding even more secrets. "Just like that."

There had to be more to it. "And if she doesn't? What if I don't meet her? The ocean is a vast place, after all." Her thoughts circled back to the thing she was stuck on: The sirens had a *queen*?

"Then I trust you to find it for me."

Ro couldn't wrap her mind around it. At the bottom of the *ocean*? What in all the realms? Fairy creatures were one thing, but creatures at the bottom of the sea . . .

Ah, she should be used to it all by now.

She rubbed her forehead, snatching her hand away before Madame LaChance could reprimand her again. "What do they look like? The combs."

"She wears them in her hair. You'll remember my words when you see them."

Something snapped in the atmosphere, and Ro jolted a little. Fog filled her head and cleared just as quickly. How kind of Madame LaChance to invite her here to offer aid! The king could take a lesson or three from her in diplomacy. But did she want nothing in return?

Madame LaChance stood and picked up a little bell. It tinkled merrily. "That will be all, huntress."

Ro scrambled to her feet, mouth ajar. She felt like she was missing something. She snapped her mouth closed, Cosette's words ringing in her ears. *It isn't ladylike, Rosette.*

No need to give Madame LaChance one more thing to scold her over.

"My assistant will provide you with all the details you require. Bon voyage, Mademoiselle Rosette Jacqueline Reynard."

Ro tried to stutter out a response, but before she could, she was ushered out of the office, down the hallway, and back into the empty foyer.

It took Ro a moment to realize Madame LaChance had used her real name, not her mère's maiden name, LeFèvre, which Ro used to distance herself from her family. To keep them safe.

Ro gritted her teeth. Apparently her efforts had been in vain. Again.

Scraps of paper were thrust at her at a rapid-fire pace. "The location of the ship, its captain, first mate, and the rest of the crew, and a few additional hands Madame LaChance thinks might be an asset to you."

Ro stared at them dumbly, not even sure where to begin.

The assistant eyed her. "You can read, can't you?"

Ro snatched the papers away. "But of course I can read."

The young Mademoiselle nodded and went back to shoving bits of paper with elegantly scrawled script into her hands.

"The banker, to settle all debts before you leave and after you return. The captain will know where best to supply the ship, but if you choose to supply it yourself . . ."

At her questioning look, Ro adamantly shook her head. She wouldn't even begin to know how to supply a ship. Her père had taken care of all such details when he'd owned a fleet of merchant vessels.

"Then here are the names of the grocer, ship repair yard, and butcher, already paid for. Do you need anything else?"

Ro swallowed, hard. "Oui, um . . . where do I start?"

The assistant gave her a momentary, sympathetic smile before she was back to all business. She gently tugged one of the papers from Ro's hand and set it on top, slipping a folded letter under it. "Start with the captain. She'll help with the rest. Here, a letter from Madame LaChance, explaining the situation. Though she won't like her crew being selected for her."

Ro raised an eyebrow. "Shouldn't I trust her to choose her own crew?"

"Not for this voyage. Madame LaChance has chosen this crew specifically for their, how shall I say, specialties? Now, off with you. You haven't much time to set this up without the king's knowledge. Be wary, for surely he'll have men watching you."

She eyed Ro's red cloak, still hanging by the door, most pointedly.

A bit of offense filtered through Ro. Was nothing sacred? It was her mère's cloak, the only thing Ro had left of her, and she hadn't yet seen a hunt without it.

Ro slipped it on as the woman showed her to the door. So far she seemed to be the only one who wore a bright-red cloak in all of Angleterre, or England. Nothing like being conspicuous. She should probably wear drab brown or green like everyone else.

"Oh, and huntress?"

Ro paused just on the other side of the threshold.

The Mademoiselle offered her a kind smile. "Be sure to burn each scrap as you see to its completion, oui?"

Ro nodded her assent, and the door closed. She didn't want the king knowing of her plans, either. A jolt of pure thrill trickled through her. Thanks to Madame LaChance, her mission now had a chance of succeeding.

She slipped off into the night and headed for the first address.

In an area she was told never to go.

3

*R*o wished she hadn't come. She'd been in some rough places, but this place was *rough*. Sewage sat stagnant in narrow streets, buildings crumbled all around her, and ladies in red dresses that covered little stared at her with hungry, empty eyes as she passed.

She knew what it was like to be shunned, to be judged for her choice to hunt. To pull herself from poverty by her fingertips, never knowing if she'd end up tumbling back in. She only wished she knew how to better help those like her.

She met each woman's eyes and gave a nod. Most didn't return it.

Trying to keep her cape out of the filth, she drew it a little tighter around her and walked with resolute steps toward the tavern. Anxiety twisted her stomach in knots.

She'd just been all over London, switching transportation until she was dizzy—until she was sure no one was following her. She'd even stopped for a late dinner at a questionable establishment. It wasn't sitting well at the moment.

She could do this. She could. She was only doing everything King Wilhelm forbade her to do.

She shivered at the thought of being thrown in a

dungeon. Again. No light, no fresh air, heavy manacles and bloodied wrists . . . she took a deep breath and pushed away the memories. She would just ask a few questions, get a feel for how receptive the female captain was . . . how hard could it be?

She could always walk away. But then what chance would she have against the sirens?

She pushed past some very drunk and very gawking men and entered the place she didn't want to go. The first thing that hit her was the *smell*. Unwashed bodies and putrid breath and sour liquor. The second? So much noise. Her head throbbed with it. And third, her stomach was threatening to empty itself on the nearest bystander.

Ro kept from retching by the sheerest of willpower, her senses thrown off by so much stimulation all at once. Good grief, was everyone shouting just for fun?

She missed her quiet forest, especially now that it was green, for more reasons than one.

And the taverns in curse-laden France. Somber, quiet, sparsely populated things—no one spent more time outside their homes than strictly necessary. Ro rarely saw anyone in them other than her fellow huntsmen.

In other words, they were nothing like this.

Vertigo hit her, and Ro pushed more desperately through the crush of people. She mustn't show weakness. She mustn't heave her dinner all over those closest to her. She must get her bearings.

Drunken men jostled her—a few taking liberties Ro normally would've used her fist for—but she hardly noticed as her senses overloaded.

Who went to a place like this? On purpose? And how would she ever find whom she was looking for? She kept pushing through the mass of humanity, not one for giving up, even if she desperately wanted to.

She'd almost reached the long, high table where everyone

was ordering spirits when a hand wrapped around her elbow and started dragging her the other way.

Ro swung around to fight off her assailant, but the motion sent her stomach to swirling, and she staggered under the onslaught of nausea. Air. She needed air. She was suddenly so thankful to be heading toward the exit, she didn't even put up a fuss as the person pulled her along.

A flamboyant hat blocked her view of the person's face, and a burgundy frock coat disguised gender.

Once outside and away from the door a few paces, the hand released her, and Ro scrambled back a few steps, her back to the tavern wall. Her stomach heaved. The person cupped gloved hands around an unlit cheroot, the hat's brim keeping her rescuer a mystery.

Ro bent over her knees, taking deep breaths. She sincerely hoped she wasn't about to get clobbered over the head and robbed blind. But she was *not* going to lose her dinner like some weakling.

A flare of a match and a few puffs later, sweet smoke drifted by her nostrils, and Ro coughed. It reminded her enough of her père that Ro straightened and tried to take control of herself.

That's when she noticed she was clammy, shaky, and the smoke hadn't helped calm the roiling meal in her stomach. Had the food she'd eaten gone bad?

A soft-like-pearl voice, its rough edge reminding her of a blade, soothed her. "That's right. Take a moment, love. Then we can talk."

Ro nodded and bent over her knees again, hating how unstable she felt.

The woman purred, "You must be the huntress who put France back on our maps, eh?"

Ro choked out a laugh. "That's me." She hated how feeble her voice sounded.

"You don't look like much."

Ro was too sick to be offended. "To be honest, I don't feel like much."

"No taverns where you come from?"

Ro shook her head. "Not since . . . most of the spirits . . . and food . . . ran out. Not like this, anyway."

"Who you be lookin' fer, dearie?"

"Captain — Lady — Captain Red?"

"Is that so?" The woman chuckled, a pleased sound.

At that moment, Ro's eyes lifted to meet her rescuer's, and the Mademoiselle in men's clothing grinned, her expression satisfied like a cat's, predatory like a wolf's.

She spoke in flawless French. "It seems you've found her, love."

Ro nodded, bent over her knees, and lost her dinner all over the place.

Some time later, they were seated at a respectable inn's table, the captain giving Ro plenty of time and space to recover. They'd been bustled to the back of the room, near an exit, where both Ro and the captain had a clear view of the room.

Food had come quicker than any other service Ro had experienced in Angleterre so far, and the room seemed to create a bubble around them, each person showing deference and not coming too close.

The captain was clearly a regular.

Ro studied the woman across from her. A flamboyant captain's hat, tilted to one side, perched over dark-red curls that spilled over sturdy shoulders. Her boots were propped up on the table, and she had a strong face that wore an almost constant smirk. She was beautiful, curvy in all the right places — quite unlike Ro's tall, willowy frame — and seemed instantly liked by all she met.

Ro even liked her, and she didn't even know the captain.

Ro dug in to her meal gratefully. A short while ago, she was certain she'd never want to eat again. But now she felt more like herself, especially after some hard cider and the surprisingly good soup and bread the inn had to offer.

She was never eating slop in some random back-hole inn again.

Whatever was in that cider the captain had ordered her had worked like magic. She still drank it cautiously, however. No need waking up in a ditch somewhere. Or worse.

"There now. Your color's a wee bit better. What can I do for you, huntress?" The captain's voice had a slight rasp to it, memorable and soothing, all at once.

Ro found herself relaxing. Something about the woman put her at ease—something she instantly liked. Ro told herself to be cautious. Someone like that was used to getting what she wanted.

Wordlessly, Ro took out and handed over the letter from Madame LaChance. Captain Red unfolded it. The woman's deep, throaty chuckle caressed Ro and made her like the woman that much more. Ro definitely needed to be cautious.

"Interesting." The captain folded the missive and tapped it once on the table's surface. "What's your offer?"

Ro froze, spoon halfway to her mouth, and blinked. "Pardon?"

"I see her offer. What's yours?"

The spoon lowered toward the bowl, and Ro sat there like an idiot, trying to come up with a response that made sense.

"Surely you understand how this works." Captain Red spelled it out slowly, as if to a small child. "I see Madame LaChance's offer; now I want to know what you will give me."

"But—isn't what she offered enough?" It sounded ridiculous even to her own ears. But of course a captain accepting such a dangerous commission would want more. Even though she was receiving an outrageous amount already.

The woman's smile stretched over perfectly white, glimmering teeth, a rarity in Angleterre. "Oh, love. Surely you must know: A pirate can never have too much gold."

Ro dropped her spoon. "A pirate?" she hissed.

Her eyes darted around the room. Would the woman be arrested—hanged—for her words? And more importantly, what had Madame LaChance been thinking, having Ro hire a *pirate*?

Captain Red's throaty laugh somehow calmed Ro and set her on edge, all at once. "Surely you must see we are among friends."

Ro's smile was fleeting, and she met the woman's eyes without a flinch. "I've learned most by that name aren't. Not really."

The woman saluted Ro with her ale. "A hard lesson to learn, but a valuable one. Back to my original question." She dropped her boots off the table and leaned forward, an eager light to her eyes. "How much?"

Ro didn't hesitate. "I'll match it."

Captain Red leaned back, her grin full of delight. "Oh my. Straight to the point. No haggling. I like it."

"But the same as Madame LaChance's offer. Half up front, half when you complete your mission and return us to Angleterre, if need be."

The woman seemed to be speaking to the bottom of her pint. "Oh, if you're sailing with the king's men, you'll definitely need us to bring you home. Might need us to take you there, too."

"Out of the question."

The pirate captain raised an eyebrow and met Ro's gaze.

Ro scowled, hating the king's words even as she repeated them. "Not allowed. I shall sail with the king's men or not at all." Bitterness filled her, and she took a deep breath and tried to let it go.

Captain Red grinned and raised her tankard. "Long live King Wilhelm."

"So about this group of sirènes attacking the king's ships —"

"Groups."

The word echoed in the stillness that followed. "What?"

"Though technically, it's a muse of sirens, a pod of mermaids."

Ro slashed her hand through the air. "Non, wait, go back. What do you mean, groups, plural? Or muses. Or whatever."

Captain Red gave her a mild look. "Huntress. Surely you don't think only one siren muse is causing such destruction? Sinking so many ships? The king may be blind to the bigger problem at hand, but surely you are not."

Ro blinked. "Of course not." She licked her suddenly dry lips. "How many muses are we talking here?"

The captain's smile stretched her full, red lips wide. "Many, many more than one."

"Oh." Ro didn't know what else to say. She fingered her mug, spinning it in place and staring into its mostly empty contents.

The king had been adamant there were only a few sirens hunting down his ships and picking them off one by one. Ro should've known better than to outright believe him. It wasn't as if the king had been forthcoming about anything else.

Ro looked up. "Madame LaChance mentioned a queen. Am I dealing with more of those too?"

"One queen rules the creatures."

Ro let out her breath. At least she wouldn't be chasing down multiple rulers. "Is the Caribbean the correct location?"

Captain Red abandoned the letter on the table to wave down a refill of her ale. "I believe the king's information is solid. He hasn't heard from his island colonies for quite some time, any ships sent there have not returned, and most of the attacks seem to originate from that location. So . . . yes. It's a good place to start."

Ro nodded. "Very well." The serving girl came and went,

and still Ro hesitated over her next question. "Do you—have any further information for me? Their customs, history, any legends . . . ?"

The pirate captain shrugged. "It is, of course, considered contraband, what with the king's fear of the creatures, but I can send you what I have."

Ro sagged, a huge weight lifting from her shoulders. One less thing to scrounge up before she set sail with the king's men. "Très bon. I mean, very good. Merci. Uh, thank you."

"Je parle un peu français, huntress."

Ro wilted a little. Then why had they been struggling through English this whole time? Oh, right. Because the captain only spoke a little French. How was Ro to know which words she knew and which she didn't?

Ro flipped over the letter from Madame LaChance and scratched out her residence in the English king's palais. "Send it here, s'il vous plaît."

Captain Red accepted the letter without comment and tucked it away.

Ro pulled out the rest of the papers from Madame LaChance and shuffled through them. "The ship's location, grocer, repair yard . . ." Ro noticed the captain's smile had turned positively indulgent. "What? What is it?"

Captain Red just laughed. "I think I know how to outfit my own ship, huntress."

Ro eased the papers to the table, wishing she could sink through the floor. "These are, um, already paid for?"

Something like greed glinted in Captain Red's eyes. "I see."

Still, she made no move to lift them from the table. Ro left them there.

Ro swallowed. The captain definitely wouldn't like this next bit, then. "Regarding the crew . . ."

The pirate waved away her words. "You needn't worry. I have it covered."

Ro took a deep breath. She wasn't sure what she was

getting herself into, but in for a penny, in for a pound as the English say, non?

"Mademoiselle, I'm trusting you, perhaps with my life, if it comes to that. I have to, for what choice do I have? But I also trust Madame LaChance, and if she says I need these women to complete my mission, then I need these women." She slid the paper with the suggested crew across the table. "You may choose whomever else you like, but I will have these as part of your crew. *My* crew."

"Ah, then you aren't as intelligent as you appear."

Ro started to object, but the woman kept talking.

"The first lesson you must learn in this new land, ma chérie, is this: Trust no one. Especially me. The second?" She leaned closer, her magnetic eyes drawing Ro in as if she were the puppeteer, and Ro, only a puppet to be directed at whim. "Do not place your trust in Madame LaChance. Not ever."

The captain leaned back, breaking the spell she'd woven with a shrug.

"And pay me, of course." She took her time lighting another cheroot, the action absolutely mesmerizing. "Things will go well for you if you take my words to heart." Her teeth flashed brilliant white.

Ro felt a little shaken, a little unsure of herself, but she was running out of time . . . and options. She nodded toward the untouched paper. "I'm afraid I must insist. If I send them to you, will you allow them on your vessel?"

The woman shrugged. "I cannot say."

Ro sat back, tucking the crew list away and taking another sip of her cider. She hated things being out of her control, but what else could she do? It seemed to be the theme of her entire journey through life. Nothing was under her control.

And she hated it.

As if on cue, the serving maid came to clear their dishes now that their meeting was over. Although Ro barely spared her a glance, Captain Red nodded at the girl.

"Thank you, love." The captain jerked her head in the girl's direction. "Huntress, if you want someone more than capable on *your* crew, you should ask the Cendre girl here."

The girl's face took on a healthy glow of pleasure, and she dipped a curtsey. "Thank you, miss."

Ro frowned and flashed the girl a once-over. Long golden-blonde curls were pulled back under a headscarf, she was so thin she was almost waif-like, and wide aquamarine eyes gave the girl an appearance of childlike innocence.

Why on earth would they need a cinder girl? The only fire on the ship would be in the galley, and the cook would fiercely guard that. No one wanted a ship going up in flames in the middle of the ocean.

Both women stared at Ro expectantly, a mischievous smile lingering around the pirate's mouth, a hopeful expression making the girl's blue eyes dance.

Ro stuttered out her reply, not thrilled about disappointing both of them at once. "D-désolé, mais I do not think we have need for une fille cendre." Flustered, Ro wasn't exactly sure of the right English words, but it was clear both women understood.

The girl paled a little, lips thinning, and she dropped her eyes and dipped another curtsey. "Of course. Excuse me."

Ro stared after her. Did she detect a slight French accent?

She reluctantly glanced back at the captain. Captain Red's smirk never wavered as she dipped her head, sending the dark feather in her hat quivering. "Good evening, Mademoiselle. I look forward to doing business with you."

Ro scrambled to her feet as the pirate remained seated. "And I you."

She hoped.

Ro hurried out into the night. She'd start on her list first thing in the morning.

And if Captain Red refused the crew Ro sent her, well, she'd just deal with that later.

4

*C*endre tripped lightly through the inn, delivering mugs of ale, hot meals, and clearing tables. It was good, honest, hard work, no grasping princes in sight.

Well—she eyed the customers—there may have been a few patrons who didn't keep their hands to themselves, but at least she wasn't employed by any of them.

"Hey, new girl!"

Cendre's head popped up at the tavern owner's shout, even as she gritted her teeth. She hated being called that, even if she was new. But how could she be called anything else? She'd never been anywhere long enough to be anything but that.

"Watch the bar for me, will ya?"

Cendre nodded, dropped off two mugs of ale, and headed to the bar. The woman who owned the place gave her a hard look before disappearing into the back.

Cendre most likely wouldn't see her again for a few hours.

And good riddance.

The end-of-lunch crowd was hardly the high-paying drinking crowd that would come after dinner.

Another patron came in and plopped himself at the bar.

Cendre called without looking, "Be with you in a moment, good sir."

She was rather proud of her English accent, not a hint of the French she was born with or the German she'd acquired. She'd mastered this new language quickly, and a part of her yearned to learn others. To travel. To explore. To be more than a serving maid.

She finished serving her patron and turned to the one who'd just entered. And her heart dropped.

Him. Again.

He grinned and offered a friendly wave. "Afternoon, cinder girl. How're you this fine day?"

Cendre dropped her gaze at the title the owner had given him when he'd asked her name, thinking Cendre couldn't hear. The owner's response still rang in her head, so many months later. "Wot, the cinder girl? Why would ya want ta know her name when me own daughter's right over there?"

And she'd pointed to the pudgy, dirty thing lazier than any cat, to whom the young man had given a smile, tipped his head, and gone whistling out into the day.

Sabine had mooned over him ever since.

And Cendre most certainly had not.

There was no sign of her today. Probably wasn't even up yet.

And Cendre was taking far too long to respond.

She tried to answer, but the words stuck in her throat. She tried again. "Can I get you something, sailor?" She surreptitiously scanned the room for Sabine.

"How many times do I have to say it? Call me Olt."

The words were said with the same cheerfulness this man seemed to exude from every pore. She wasn't about to be swindled by cheerfulness. Yet a shy smile peeked through without her consent. She ducked her head so he wouldn't see.

When she didn't respond, he glanced behind her to the

hand-sketched slate board. "I'll take the day's special, cinder girl."

Cendre was glad she couldn't flush as embarrassed heat built within her with nowhere to go. One of the few oddities about her she was most thankful for. The nickname, said with so much warmth it made her head spin, was endearing coming from him.

But she didn't want him to know that.

She hurried to get his order from the back. With the cook's back to her, she dipped her hands in fresh seawater, iced and ready to store the day's catch of eels, and splashed her face, steeling herself to go back out there and face him.

When she returned, patrons had already started to leave, and she dropped off Olt's food as quickly as possible without being accused of throwing it at him. Then she was off and clearing tables from the lunch rush and staying as busy as she could, short of volunteering to wash dishes.

Even he couldn't make her run to the back for that.

She was scrubbing the bar, pointedly ignoring him, her heart dropping with every customer that left, when he did what she was hoping he wouldn't.

He started talking to her. As he always did.

"So what's your story, cinder girl?"

Cendre scrubbed the bar that much harder and tried not to meet his eyes. She peeked anyway. They sparkled with so much warmth, it chased away the chill of the room and promised better days. Days she'd best not hope for.

"You said you'd tell me, remember?"

She did remember. And she'd only said it to put him off. "Why you'd want to hear my story . . ."

"I do. Trust me."

She continued to scrub furiously at the countertop, refusing to make eye contact with the far-too-handsome-for-his-own-good sailor. The last customer left, leaving no more excuses. Might as well get it over with.

Her sigh was heavy, and words poured from her lips without her being able to stop the flow this time. "I worked at a château in France. As a cinder girl. Kept the fires lit, emptied chamber pots. Hardly glamorous."

She peeked at him. Still listening. Her glance darted away from warm brown eyes that watched her attentively, made her feel special. Wanted.

"He—the prince—didn't have a good reputation, but anytime he saw me, I was covered in soot and ash, and he turned up his nose at me. I was told to stay away from him, never to be out of my room alone, after my duties were done." She shrugged one shoulder. "The pay was good, the bed was warm, the king and queen were kind and generous, and I had one day off a month. It was bliss."

"Bliss?"

She scrubbed harder, scraping her knuckles raw. "I was young and on my own for the first time. Away from . . . everything. Yes. Bliss."

He wrinkled his perfect nose, and a dark swatch of hair fell over one eye. He tossed it back with a flick of his head—must happen often. "But chamber pots?"

She shrugged. "It was work. And food. And pay. I couldn't have asked for more."

"All right."

His smile sent her heart tumbling off a cliff into a freefall. She jerked her gaze away. "I disregarded the warnings. I felt safe. Then one night, he noticed me." The memory raised gooseflesh.

He stiffened. The smile was still on his face, but it was tight, frozen.

"He—he would've forced me—"

His hands, arms crossed on the bar, clenched into fists.

"But an old woman saved me. She distracted him, and I fled. Didn't look back, didn't take anything with me. Apparently I got out just in time. The curse fell not long after that. Now here I am."

She met his gaze defiantly, daring him to make light of her story. To say that's just how noblemen were.

That it was somehow her fault.

His smile turned gentle. Twin dimples sent her heart galloping away. "And I for one am glad you're here, cinder girl."

The words burrowed deep in her heart and threatened to overflow in tears. She wasn't about to let that happen, but one rogue tear escaped.

He took his napkin and dabbed her cheek. She couldn't move. Didn't want to move, if she were being honest. The yellowed cloth came away with a wet smudge.

And Cendre's heart was no longer her own.

The door behind her burst open, and in her peripheral, she saw Sabine frame herself in the doorway, hungry eyes devouring the handsome stranger, tousled hair and bleary eyes stating just how recently she'd scrambled out of bed.

Cendre blinked, gave him a curt nod, and went to tend to a few newly arriving customers, late for their midday meal.

He grabbed her hand as she passed. "You know, I still don't know your name."

Cendre paused, his touch like fire. Her eyes flitted to Sabine. Based on her glare, there'd be the devil to pay later, but Cendre couldn't help her answer.

"Cendrillon, but my friends call me Cendre."

Understanding dawned, and his eyes sparkled. "Ah. Cendre." His smile was delicious. "Perfect."

She pulled away, her steps swift as she fled Sabine's glare and Olt's touch, but both followed her across the room.

There. She'd talked to him. Now she'd never have to do it again.

❧

Ro's coach pulled up in front of an inn. Last stop. Ro stretched her weary neck and got out, flipping the driver a coin. She'd spent the past few days gathering the female crew and sending them to Captain Red.

She only hoped her efforts hadn't been in vain.

The horse and carriage rumbled away, and Ro turned to the inn, ready for lunch. When her eyes settled on the building, her heart dropped right down to her toes.

Non. It couldn't be.

She took a deep breath and entered the same tavern Captain Red had taken her to the other night. She wondered if she'd be talking to the same girl who'd served them. Hopefully not. No way would she consider working for Ro after she'd dismissed her so swiftly . . .

As the sparsely populated room echoed with her footfalls, Ro dug in her pocket for the slip of paper with the final crew-woman's name and a few details about her.

"You again."

Ro's head came up. She hadn't made it halfway across the room, and the same girl who'd served them the other night— but of course it was—blocked her path.

"Oh, ah, bonjour. I mean, hello." *Smooth, Ro, very smooth.* "Um, might I eat something?"

The cinder girl sighed, deep and heavy and decidedly annoyed. "Very well. Follow me."

Ro settled at the rough table shown to her. She couldn't help but notice it wasn't as nice, nor was it in a strategic position, not like the other night.

"Wot can I get you?"

The girl's English accent was just off, but Ro wasn't about to blurt that out and make the situation worse.

"Um . . ."

Ro almost let the girl choose, but then Ro was afraid she'd pick something like blood pie or a fish head. Ro had already had those particular experiences—in the same meal. Her eyes flitted over the menu board, far across the room and almost impossible to read.

It lit slightly, each letter illuminating, and Ro jumped a little.

That weird thing her eyesight did usually only happened at night. While she was hunting. Or in danger.

The girl jolted, and Ro met wide, startled eyes.

"Oh, um," Ro stammered, "I'll take eel pie, s'il vous plaît. I mean, please."

The English were rather proud of their eel pies, a local delicacy, and Ro hoped they were more delicious than they sounded. Then again, the French considered escargot a delicacy, so far be it from her to pass judgment.

And her mind was wandering again and the girl was still staring at her as though she'd seen a phantom.

Ro waved a hand in front of the girl's face. "Allô?"

Wrong move. The girl slapped Ro's hand away, shot Ro a rather vicious glare, and disappeared into the back.

Ro finally found and pulled out the paper she was after, the only one left in her deep pocket, but her hands shook so badly, she couldn't read the blasted thing.

Could she control her eyesight now? Use it at whim? She glanced at the board again, but rien. Nothing. It remained as indistinct as ever.

Ro forced her hands to steady. There. Madame LaChance had written *Cendre*. Not because the waif was a cinder girl. Because her *name* was Cendre.

Ro groaned and started to plunk her head on the grimy surface, then thought better of it. Why hadn't she taken Captain Red's suggestion in the first place? And if the captain wanted this Cendre on her ship so badly, why hadn't she asked the girl instead of baiting Ro with the decision?

The serving girl was heading back, tray laden with food, leaving filled dishes in her wake. It was now or never.

The girl paused for half a beat, delivering Ro's mug and pie tin, and Ro spoke before the girl could dance away. "Are you the one called Cendre?"

The girl flicked her a glance. "Who's asking?" She passed out the last of the food to a nearby customer.

Not quite as friendly without the captain about.

Food delivered, the girl set the tray on an empty table and picked up a wash bucket and a rag. Ro tried to show her the paper, but the girl didn't even glance at it, though she started cleaning a table right next to Ro's.

Ro lowered her voice. "It's a job, aboard a ship." She didn't miss the girl's pulse jump at her throat, or the hitch in her busy hands, but those were the only indications she'd heard. "Madame LaChance said—"

The girl slammed a wet rag down on the table, sloshing Ro and only Ro in the process. "Désolé." The girl didn't look sorry. "Madame LaChance, huh? I wouldn't trust that woman with my slop bucket."

Ro almost groaned. Right. Madame LaChance didn't want her name thrown about. Just the pirate captain's.

Cendre finished wiping down the table next to Ro's and started to move away. Still sitting, Ro caught her wrist. Their eyes clashed, and Ro dropped the girl's arm.

Not from the glare, non, but just for a second, there was something familiar about her. Something that reminded Ro of Yvette, only a much younger version of her older sister.

Ro shook off the feeling and spoke before the girl could turn away. "Look, you don't have to like her. Or trust her. By going on this voyage, you won't be indebted to her in any way."

The girl moved her bucket. "Bon. Because I'll never be indebted to that witch again. I'd rather starve."

Ro blinked. "She's a witch?"

The girl shrugged and bent to scrub another table. "Might as well be. And you know what? If you're involved with Madame LaChance, you're no good either."

Ro had had enough. She jumped to her feet and got in the girl's face, a head shorter than her own. The younger girl straightened and got right back in her face, though Ro was certain she'd stretched up on her tiptoes to do so. Ro felt a flash of admiration before words started pouring from her lips.

"Look, I don't care what you think, and quite frankly, I don't need you. But Madame LaChance said you loved the sea, you'd be an asset to my crew, *and* you were about to lose your position here—"

The girl's chin quivered, but she jutted out her jaw and refused to let the glassy sheen in her eyes form into tears. Ro admired her pluck.

"—then Captain Red suggested you. Let me tell you, you are the *only* thing those women have agreed upon. I'm not going to force you, but if you come, *I'll* pay you, you'll be working for *me*, and you needn't deal with Madame LaChance. At all. Ever. You'll be under Captain Red." She softened her voice. "I know what it's like to be indebted to someone who, well, you shouldn't. I won't do that to you."

Cendre blinked. "And why would you care?"

Ro shrugged. "I don't, not really. I just know what it's like."

When the girl didn't say anything more, Ro scratched down directions and held it out. "If you change your mind, here's the address. We leave soon." *I hope.*

Cendre raised her chin a hair higher. "Can't read."

"Oh for the love." Ro closed her eyes and took a deep breath. After counting to ten, she stepped close to the girl and spoke low, so the others in the inn's dining room—who were watching the exchange with open interest—couldn't hear. "Fisherman's quarter, east dock. Ask for Mary McSimmons, and tell her the huntress sent you. Think about it."

When the girl made no move to take the paper, Ro shoved the scrap in the girl's apron pocket and stormed out of the inn, washing her hands of the whole affair. She hailed a hackney and gave directions to the palais.

If the girl wanted to show up, bon. If not, bon. It was time she prepared for her own journey. Captain Red had everything else under control.

It wasn't until she was halfway to the palais, when she was debating whether to be disappointed about not sampling eel pie, that she realized they'd both switched to French once the conversation had become heated, and the girl hadn't even blinked.

Ro sat up in the carriage. What was a French girl doing living in Angleterre, and how long had she been there? Ro was enough of a rarity—were any more French people hidden away in this land?

Ro groaned, realizing she'd probably never see the serving maid again.

❧

Shaking, Cendre lowered herself to the table where the force of nature had just been sitting, eel pie and mug of ale untouched.

Non, it couldn't be.

She'd thought the huntress looked familiar the other night, but now, in daylight, there was no doubt.

The woman, the one who'd gotten in her face and looked like she wanted to throttle her, the woman she'd felt a distinct flare of magic from, had looked just like the one portrait Grandmère kept of Cendre's parents. The one she didn't know Cendre had seen.

The one that had sent Cendre fleeing the old woman to find them.

True, the huntress had Père's dark hair, crystal-blue eyes, and his lanky, willowy build, but she also had the elegant neck of her mère, the same distinguished nose, and the same graceful, feminine slope to her lips.

Could it be—? Was it possible . . . that Cendre had a sister?

Cendre covered her mouth with her hand. Why hadn't her grandmère told her? Did she even know? Or was Cendre assuming too much?

Something hit the side of her head, and Cendre slammed to the floor. Before she could even comprehend what was happening, she was lifted by the back of her dress and hauled toward the inn's door.

"Lazy, selfish, stupid girl! Think ya can laze about and get paid? I think not. Out with ya like the rest of the garbage!" Then the innkeeper dropped her voice, and her putrid breath wafted over Cendre's face as she spoke low and hot in her ear. "Don't think I didn't see what ye was doing. Trying to win the lad for yerself?" She laughed, and Cendre went dizzy from the smell. "Well good luck finding 'im now that he don't know where ye be."

A man opened the front door for the inn's matron, and Cendre was thrown into the streets to a guffaw of laughter. Sewage soaked her skirts.

"And stay out!"

The noise died down as the door slammed, and Cendre choked back any sobs that dared show themselves. She glanced back at the inn.

Sabine's smug face peeked out of a window, and she smirked.

Cendre jerked her gaze away. Hauling herself to her feet, she marched away from the hateful inn and its hateful owner and its hateful people.

It wouldn't be the first time she had to leave everything behind and start afresh.

5

"*M*ilady?"

Ro jerked upright and crumpled the half-finished letter she'd been writing. "Oui?"

The servant flicked a glance to Ro's hand before she curtsied. "Pardon the intrusion, miss, but this came for you." The servant held up a paper-wrapped parcel. "And I have news."

Ro casually tossed the crumpled letter into the fireplace, feeling the servant's inquisitive gaze like a burn. "Go on."

The servant rushed over, words pouring out of her lips as she placed the parcel on the little writing desk in front of Ro and stepped back. Ro tried to remember her name. Elise? Eloise? Elsie?

She really should pay more attention to all the people she was introduced to.

"My lady, the ship you are leaving in has just arrived! The king has sent instructions to the captain, the ship is being supplied, and the moment the Marquis Valère arrives, you'll be off!" Her eyes sparkled. "Isn't that exciting?"

Ro forced a stiff smile. "Oui. Exciting." She'd only been waiting months for the king to do *something*. It was a good thing she'd spent the last few days getting her own plans in place.

A sly look entered the servant's eyes. "Now, you didn't hear this from me, but if you happened to take a leisurely carriage ride down by the wharf, you might catch a glimpse of it before your official tour." She winked. "But again, you didn't hear that from me."

Casting one last glance at the fireplace and the letter that was fully ash now, the servant headed for the door.

Ro couldn't help the frustration that spilled over. What, was King Wilhelm going to wait until the ship set sail and inform her she'd missed it? If not for the nosy servant girl . . .

Ro's head shot up. The door was almost closed. "Wait!"

Elsie, Elise, Eloise—whatever her name was—popped her head back in. "Yes, miss?"

Ro hoped her smile looked far more genuine this time. "Merci beaucoup."

The servant grinned. "Of course, milady." Then she was gone.

Ro seized the parcel, slipped off the string, and carefully unfolded the wrapping paper. Three slim books, a few folded news sheets, and a letter fell into her hand.

She unfolded the letter.

Mademoiselle:

My agents have procured as much information regarding legends of the sirènes as possible, all written in or translated into French, as you have requested of Captain R.R.

May your journey be gratifying for us both.

M. LaChance

Ro smiled and jumped to her feet. She hid the parcel in her bags—bags that had been packed for weeks—and started getting ready. She needed to meet with Captain Red one last time before they set sail.

The stack of half-started and scratched-out letters stopped her cold.

Should she try one last time to write to Cosette? She possibly wouldn't see her for another year or two—maybe not ever again, depending on how the voyage went.

Ro settled on the edge of her chair. She pulled out yet another blank page, dipped her quill in ink, and tried again.

Cosette. (No darling or dearest this time.)

The ship is here, I am about to leave, and . . . (*I miss you,* she thought but did not write.) She moved on to the next line.

The English king is a beast. He has wasted much of my time, only just now acquiring a ship, and parading me before witless nobles while demeaning me at every step. (She couldn't write that! What if her letter were intercepted?)

She growled, crossed it out, and tried again.

So much has happened. I wish I could tell you more, but . . . (Trite. Boring. Why was she putting herself through this?)

And I love you.

Ro stared at the words. Did she? So much heartache flooded her chest, the pain was physical. Her eyes burned, and she couldn't look away.

She still loved Cosette, didn't she? Whether they were sisters or not, they still had a bond no Fairy Queen had forced upon them, oui?

She crumpled her latest attempt and chucked it into the fire. She needed to see Captain Red, and it would soon be dark enough to meet the captain in secret.

Ro grabbed her red cape, slipped a few more knives in a few more secret places, and stalked toward the door. Halfway there, she turned, marched back, grabbed the pile of mistake-ridden letters, and threw the whole stack into the fireplace.

She waited just long enough for the edges to catch before she left.

She'd write Cosette. She would. She just had to wait until it didn't hurt so much.

❧

Ro stared up at the ship, eyes wide. "*This* is the ship Madame LaChance acquired for your voyage?"

Just enough moonlight glanced off the fog-shrouded ship to highlight it in all the right places. It. Was. Glorious.

Captain Red looked positively smug. "As you would say, oui."

Ro counted eight decks, painted alternating black and tan. Three masts towered so high above her head, she almost fell over looking up at them. Everything gleamed fresh and new, and wood and lines creaked in welcome. This ship could house hundreds of sailors. Hundreds. Her père, when he had been a wealthy merchant, hadn't even owned ships this exquisite. Or enormous.

Ro couldn't help her open mouth. "C'est magnifique!"

The pirate captain chuckled. "That it is, love. That it is. Incidentally, have you see the ship you'll be sailing on?"

A bitter taste filled Ro's mouth. "Oui." She'd seen it. In passing. And had asked her driver if he was mistaken.

That was one quick way to get on the wrong side of a driver who prided himself on knowing all the latest gossip. And a good way to keep him from speaking to her the rest of the ride. Ro had a gift with people. Not.

"Ah." The captain gave her a sympathetic look. "Such an important mission, yet the king treats it as though it's below his notice."

Ro couldn't agree harder.

"You've hurt his pride, you know."

Ro's head whipped toward the captain. "Quoi? I mean, what?"

Captain Red's smile was gentle. "I knew Wilhelm once, when we were children."

Ro had so many questions.

"Even then, he was as chauvinistic as his father. I very

44

much liked to put him in his place, but he was stubborn. Determined that boys—men—could do everything better." She shrugged in a very French manner. "I had hoped he'd outgrow it, but how could he with such an example?"

Again, so many questions, but Ro held her tongue and let the woman talk.

Captain Red sent an admiring look Ro's way. "And then there's you. You've done what even Monsieur Gautier could not, though our king had such hopes he would. Broke a curse holding an entire kingdom. And Wilhelm can find no one else to break his own curse." Her eyes went back to the ship, her gaze caressing it as one would a lover. "He doesn't know what to make of you, chérie. Be kind to him."

At Ro's sharp look, she amended her words.

"Kind yet firm. His pride is about to take a mighty fall, what when you return and the merchants and their families sing your praises in the streets."

Ro barked a laugh. "You are so certain of our outcome?" She couldn't say she was.

Captain Red dropped a hand on Ro's shoulder and squeezed. "If I were not, I would not have joined you in such a dangerous venture."

With that, the captain moved up the wide, railed plank aboard her ship, now able to caress its rails lovingly with her hands.

"Oh, ma capitaine!"

Captain Red paused, her eyes on Ro.

"Has the cinder girl joined you?" Ro's voice echoed in the stillness of the moonlit docks, and her eyesight lit everything slightly so she could see the captain.

A brief flash of disappointment crossed the captain's face, then it was gone. "I yet have faith, huntress." She gave Ro a nod and moved on, disappearing into the heavy fog lying like a cloak upon the ship and the surrounding water.

Ro almost went aboard, then thought better of it. Its

captain had not invited her, and no more words needed to be said between them. Plans were in place, and now they would be carried out.

Besides, no need to draw further attention to this particular ship.

She wrapped her bright-red cloak tighter around her, huddling in the white-fur-lined satin against damp fog, and made her way into the night, hoping against hope that the pirate captain and her crew would be at the end of her long voyage.

Especially when she needed them most.

6

*R*o eyed the king's finest ship with a sinking heart.

It was just so darn small. A sloop made for speed but not much else. She'd expected something much bigger. Huge, even. Something like Captain Red's ship. A galleon of the highest order.

They were crossing the ocean in *that*?

Her eyes drifted across the masthead of a woman to the letters engraved on the side. *King's Ransom*. It was small and delicate, more like the women gracing the English king's court than the king it was named after. It would barely fit a hundred sailors. Half that, perhaps, comfortably.

Just when Ro thought her opinion of the king couldn't plummet any further . . . this. An obvious slap in the face. Did he mean for her to fail?

Then why hire her to take care of his problem in the first place?

"It's fast and can turn on a hair. Just what you need for hunting, non?"

Ro turned to the voice that was far too close for comfort and took a step back. "Excusez-moi?"

The first thing she noticed was his rash grin. One that

made her heart trip over a beat. The second? He was actually clean, unlike most of the sailors—well, *any* of the sailors she'd seen so far.

Her eyes flitted over him, categorizing everything in a hot second.

Tailored, well-fitted clothes, combed dark hair tied back neatly in a queue. Perfectly muscled—she had no idea where *that* thought came from—and he spoke flawless French.

Before he could answer, she blurted, "Êtes-vous le Marquis de la Valère?"

His eyes—a warm brown, flecked with the smallest spattering of gold—widened for a split second. "Am I the marquis?" He burst into laughter. White, even teeth—something else she hadn't seen in a sailor yet—made his tanned face even darker, and his laugh reminded her of the warmth of a fireplace and the safety of home.

Ro blinked. What in all the realms? Had she gone mad?

She definitely needed to watch this one. Closely. Her eyes flitted over his form, all masculine, and heat crept across her face.

On second thought, she needed to ignore him. Completely.

"Oh, that's rich. Probably the best thing I've heard all month. All year, even." He mimed sweeping off a hat and gave her a gallant bow. "Olt, at your service, milady. Nothing but a lowly deckhand."

He straightened and settled the imaginary hat on his head. His movements were so smooth, so believable, she could almost imagine he truly held a hat.

He leaned closer and winked. "Were I the marquis, Mademoiselle, you would have no need to ask. He's quite, how shall I say, flamboyant?"

Sweat popped up in places Ro wasn't thrilled about, and warning bells clanged in her head as his masculine scent invaded her personal space.

He stepped back, taking all oxygen with him, and offered

one more bow before striding toward the boat, his laughter floating behind him.

Ro watched him go, amazed at the way his muscles moved under his white shirt, almost a cadence to them, like a dance. Such confidence, too.

Ro snapped her eyes away and fanned her face, taking deep, steady breaths, just wanting the heat to go away.

Oui, she'd definitely be ignoring that one.

"Mademoiselle Ro LeFèvre?"

Ro jumped and spun toward the new voice, a bit on the gruff side and not as pleasant as the one she'd just heard. "Oui?"

The tall, thickly muscled and older man tilted his head her way. "I am Captain Montrose. May I escort you aboard, my lady?"

"Oh, ah, oui. Merci."

He slid the bag from her hand. She reluctantly let go. "Is this all your cargo, milady?"

Ro nodded dumbly, then pointed to the crates she'd had delivered earlier. They were full of weapons.

He glanced at them, then at the slight satchel he held in his hands, his thick beard and moustache disguising his expression. "Yet—will you need anything else on your voyage? From the crates, perhaps?"

Ro jerked her chin in the negative. What was wrong with needing little? She thought he'd protest if she brought too much.

He handed it off to a passing sailor. "See that this makes it to my quarters." Ro raised an eyebrow as he gestured to the ship. "This way, milady."

She started walking, more than a little panicked that her things were being stowed in the captain's chambres. "Votre quarters?"

"Yes. I will bunk with my men."

Ro eyed the plank, then pranced across it to the waiting

ship. Once the gently rocking deck was under her feet, she turned to the captain, taking in his neatly trimmed beard and meticulous appearance. "That isn't necessary, I assure you."

"It's completely necessary if you want to be on my ship."

Ro propped her fists on her hips. "Have you no petite chambre? What is the word—smaller room? I needn't much space."

"Milady, it would be an insult to give you any other room."

"What of the Marquis de la Valère?"

His jaw visibly tightened. "The marquis will take whatever room I assign him, or he'll bunk below with my men. This way."

He gestured to the back of the ship, toward the stern, and Ro trailed him to a trio of doors. The captain opened the center door and led her into a good-sized chamber. A bed was tucked in the corner, and an ornate cherry-wood desk stood proud in the middle of the room, nautical charts and navigating instruments strewn all over its surface.

Thick-paned glass covered the whole of the back wall in hand-sized squares, allowing feeble sunlight in, and a window seat lined with books underneath huddled into the wall opposite the bed. A bar of wood across the bookshelf kept books from tumbling across the floor with the rock of the ship.

Ro swallowed. "C'est trop grand . . . it's too big."

She turned to the captain, whose brows were most definitely raised.

"S'il vous plaît, what is la chambre, the room, next door? Surely there is a smaller room for just me." Her voice turned pleading. "Please, mon capitaine, this is not for me. I would feel—lost—in here." Not to mention she'd feel guilty the entire voyage for commandeering his chambre.

The captain considered her a moment before heading back outside. There were two doors on either side of his, and he opened the one to his left. Ro peeked in as he held it open. It was small, neat, and tidy. Bunk beds nestled in the corner, and a small desk, round mirror, and porthole made up the rest of the room.

"This is my first mate's quarters."

He turned and made his way to the other door. Ro shuffled a few extra steps to keep up with his long, confident strides.

"And this is my quartermaster's."

He opened the door to an identical room, everything placed opposite the other. Though it looked somewhat clean, there was an odd smell, a few things were thrown on the top bunk, which sagged, and something was smeared across the mirror. Ro cast a furtive glance at the captain, whose jaw tightened as he took in the quarters.

"Which will most certainly be tidied."

Ro nodded and stepped back, allowing him to close the door. "I would love the first mate's chambre, s'il vous plaît, Monsieur. I mean, if you please, sir."

The captain grunted, but he looked somewhat pleased and maybe a bit relieved under his gruff scowl. "Then the first mate's room is yours, milady. I will inform him of the change. Until then, if you will wait in my chamber while we cast off, I will inform you when it is acceptable to tour my ship."

Ro nodded and followed him back to his room.

He gestured to the strewn charts. "Normally these would be in their proper places," he said a bit apologetically, "but I was informed by the king's man that you wished to know our route. I can show you how to read the navigation lines later, but for now, they are available for your perusal."

"He will not be joining us?"

"No, milady. He is needed elsewhere. But if you need anything, do not hesitate to ask me or one of my men."

A warm glow filled Ro. The respect in his voice and his consideration of her — Ro couldn't even name the last time that had happened. Not since she'd been in Angleterre.

And she'd finally be rid of the pesky messenger.

"Merci beaucoup, Monsieur. You have made me feel most welcome, and I truly appreciate it."

He looked surprised for a moment before covering it with a bow. "It is a pleasure to have you aboard my ship, milady. Until the tour." He turned and walked toward the door.

Ro moved behind his desk and bent over the charts far more detailed than regular maps, fascinated by the lovely things.

"Lady Ro?"

She glanced up.

Standing in the open doorway, Captain Montrose hesitated before he spoke. "I have looked forward to meeting you for quite some time. Father Guise has brought us many stories of your feats, and I am eager to hear them from your own lips."

Ro had no idea how to respond. Père Guise had something good to say about *her*?

"Perhaps, once we are underway, you can share a few of your stories with my men and myself?"

Ro's stomach dropped. He'd soon find out she enjoyed storytelling as much as being the center of attention. "Peut-être. Perhaps. If it pleases you."

He nodded once, that gratified look again crossing his face, then he was gone.

Ro groaned and dropped her forehead on the desk. Yet one more person she'd disappoint when they learned she wasn't a great orator as well as a mighty huntress.

Ugh.

Hair shorn, in boy's clothing, dirt smudged across her face, Cendre watched the *King's Ransom*. It was a fine ship, sleek and made for speed. She itched to climb aboard and see where it would take her.

And the huntress had boarded not that long ago.

If she could just get on that ship, find out if the huntress was truly her sister, find the family she'd been looking so long for—her chest tightened.

What if they weren't sisters? Well, Cendre would simply disembark at another port and start a new life all over again. Maybe travel with another crew.

She took a deep breath of the salty air, and calm filled her. She loved nothing more than the ocean. It sang of freedom.

"You there, new boy! Get the cargo loaded."

How would she get onboard? Could she fool them into getting a position?

"Are you listening ta me?"

Once again, she was sent sprawling, and she looked up at the scariest man she'd ever laid eyes on: huge, muscular, covered in tattoos, thick black ropes for hair, skin weathered by the sun, ugly scowl directed at her.

"What're ye, deaf?"

She shook her head furiously, reached for her cap, and wedged it back on.

He hauled her to her feet and pointed to a load of cargo. "Get that on the ship, stash your bag somewheres below, and get to it!" He shoved her toward the ship.

Cendre stumbled but came up running. She hauled up a crate, used to doing heavy labor at the inn, the palace, the cottage—anywhere she worked, really—and headed toward the plank leading into the ship's belly.

The man yelled after her. "And don't drop that! It belongs to the huntress."

She crossed nimbly and found her sea legs. She couldn't help her grin.

It couldn't be this easy, could it?

Angry voices awakened Ro. The rock of the boat reminded her of where she was, and she began untangling herself from her hammock. She should be used to the blasted thing after three days, but she could barely get out of it each morning.

While they were waiting for the marquis to arrive, they'd been asked to move to the middle of the port to allow other ships access to the wharves, and Ro had begun the process of getting used to life aboard a working ship.

The Port of London was a busy place, and Ro thought to herself more than once that they could do with a better system to accommodate the many ships that came and went. She tired of rowing to shore every time something was needed.

She untangled herself at last.

Although she preferred the hammock, it was a chore to get out of every morning. Yet it wrapped her nice and tight and swayed with the ship's motions, rocking her to sleep without fear of rolling out of the small, flat bed, with a large wooden lip that liked to take a swing at her shins—and often left shining bruises. She loved the coziness of the room, the rock of the boat, and not feeling guilty for taking the captain's quarters.

And she'd just slip the hammock from one hook over the other, freeing up space for attempting more letters to Cosette at the small desk, pouring through siren legends, or practicing with the short sword that had been a reluctant gift from the king at her send-off.

Ro wondered if he thought the sirens would climb aboard for a rousing swordfight before or after they sank the ship.

Another shout reminded Ro why she was getting up in the first place.

She pulled on her boots, stuffed the sword under the top bunk's mattress, and made sure she was presentable before stumbling out on deck to find out what was going on.

She blinked. They were back alongside the wharf, plank extended.

"You there! Come back here. What do you mean the

marquis will not be joining us?" the captain bellowed at a messenger boy.

Ro's eyes flitted over the boy. It seemed as though he got yelled at quite often. It didn't seem to faze him, though he kept his distance.

"We have delayed our trip and tempted the weather and the gods for no reason?"

The captain cut off the most colorful string of curse words Ro had ever heard when his first mate nodded in her direction. The captain turned.

Ro tried her best not to be smug. So the marquis wasn't joining them? Well that worked out perfectly for her. She could hunt in peace, her way, without anyone stealing her credit.

Not that she truly cared about such things.

And suddenly the small ship made that much more sense. Were the king and the marquis sequestered somewhere, toasting themselves and laughing at abandoning the huntress to a doomed voyage? All smugness disappeared, and she let out a little growl.

The conniving, pompous, insufferable . . .

The captain stomped toward her. "Huntress, I'm sorry you had to hear that."

"The marquis will not be joining us?"

"No." He bit out the word on a growl.

Ro raised an eyebrow. "Oh? How will he then take my credit?"

The captain's tight smile was more of a grimace. "As he always does. Through falsehood and misdirection."

"And lots and lots of boasting," someone muttered off to the side.

Sounded like the marquis was a stand-up fellow, as the English would say.

The captain turned and started barking out orders. "Cast off! Untie the sails. Unfurl the mainsail. We are away!"

55

The boy scrambled down the plank and jumped over the gap as the plank started to move under his feet, and Ro watched with wide eyes as the ship came to life under the most beautifully orchestrated dance—one she hadn't seen since childhood.

The captain shouted a few more orders before his measured steps brought him back her way. "My lady, I ask that you remain in your room until we are underway."

The first mate cast her a sullen glance at the words "in your room." She offered him an apologetic smile, but he turned away as if he hadn't seen.

She'd be sullen too if she'd been forced to share bunks with the unkempt quartermaster. The captain ran a tight ship, demanded everything be kept clean and in its place, but there was only so much he could do about the grisly man.

Ro scanned the crew, fascinated as the seemingly lowest of humanity—well over half looked as though they'd been begging on street corners mere seconds before being dragged aboard—did what they did best: brought a ship to life. It was incroyable.

"My lady, I'll not ask again."

Ro's startled eyes met the captain's unflinching gaze. "And I'll not be in your way, Monsieur." She turned to go, wishing she could stay and watch.

"See that you aren't," he snapped.

A bit of temper filtered through Ro, but she clamped her mouth tight and marched away. She reminded herself he was most likely upset with the marquis, not her. Not that it helped.

Her eyes met those of the clean, handsome sailor she was ignoring for the entirety of the trip—Olt, was it?—and his warm smile soothed the beast inside, if only a little.

She jerked her eyes away and kept herself from fleeing by using precise, measured steps to carry herself to the captain's quarters, hoping her face wasn't as hot as it felt.

If she had to stay out of the way, she might as well go over his charts, especially now that she could read the Tradewinds route east to west and the strong currents that would carry them back home.

She still wasn't sure what the line of dots marching alongside the coasts of the Americas was, but she would soon find out.

They would travel first to the Canary Islands, off the westernmost tip of Africa, then on to the Caribbean from there.

Excitement filled her. Finally, they were off.

She risked one more peek behind her. She might be going to the captain's room now, but she intended to spend every free moment that she possibly could on deck.

7

*C*endre's heart pounded wildly as she sought shelter in the ship's storeroom. She covered her face with shaking hands.

She'd just come face to face with Olt, the handsome, impossible customer she'd poured her heart out to, and he hadn't even recognized her.

What was he even doing on this ship? She groaned. He wasn't supposed to be here. She wasn't supposed to see him again.

Yet a tiny part of her heart thrilled that he was.

His grin had been friendly, open, but not a hint of recognition had touched his eyes, even though she'd lost her cap to the sea on a particularly strong gust of wind.

He'd stuck out his hand. "Olt."

"Cen." She'd barely touched her hand to his before jerking away.

It didn't seem to bother him. "Welcome aboard, Cen."

Cen had nodded and fled.

That meant her disguise worked. It also meant he no longer looked at her in a way that sent her heart trying to flee her chest.

The loss was acute.

She took a shuddering breath. She hadn't been counting on having to deceive both the huntress and Olt—both of whom she'd already met—as well as a full crew. Now she had to be even more careful.

Although, the entire crew had already accepted her as a crewmember, for some reason, and Olt had been so incredibly clueless . . .

Her eyes opened slowly as her hands slipped away from her face. It was a risk, perhaps too great a risk, but would the huntress even recognize her?

Decision made, she strode from the hold. She was going to find out.

Then maybe she wouldn't have to avoid her for the entirety of the voyage.

Ro took a deep breath and closed her eyes, thankful to be allowed on deck. Finally. Ocean stretched endlessly in every direction but one, and it was glorious.

"'Scuse me, miss."

Ro flicked a glance at the scrawny boy beside her. She did a double take. Something about him looked familiar. But that feeling of familiarity slipped away as soon as she'd thought it.

She nodded for him to continue when he started to squirm under her thoughtful gaze.

"Cap'ain gave me permission ta give you a tour. Now that we're underway and all."

Something about that didn't feel right. Wasn't the captain quite clear that he wanted to give her a tour? Ro's eyes sought the captain, but he was behind the wheel, wholly absorbed in his task, not giving them any mind.

"Miss?"

Ro's eyes found the lad's, and her forehead scrunched.

What was it about him? Again, the feeling left as soon as it came. "Oui?"

"If you're ready?"

Ro nodded and followed. Perhaps the captain had changed his mind. He had far more important things to do than show her his ship, after all.

She only half-listened as the boy showed her every inch of the craft, including the galley, the brig, and the storerooms belowdecks. He peppered off nautical terms as if he'd been born on a ship, and Ro didn't bother to tell him that her père had owned a fleet of merchant vessels before the curse. She could probably name a few terms he couldn't.

His enthusiasm was contagious, but something niggled at Ro that she couldn't let go of. Or figure out.

Every once in a while, the boy slipped in a personal question, but Ro deflected. As she always did when someone wanted her to talk about herself.

She battled with the feeling of familiarity, trying to hold on to it. To let her mind tell her what she was trying so hard to figure out. Not being able to grasp it bothered her more than she could say.

"Désolé," she interrupted. "Do I know you?"

The boy froze and met her squinting eyes with his wide ones.

"I swear there is something familiar about you, but I cannot place it. Did we meet in Angleterre, perhaps?"

Again, wide eyes held hers, and the boy seemed unable to string two words together. Ro waited, more than a little impatient.

He finally stuttered, "I'm s-sorry, milady, but I have d-duties to attend to."

And with that he was off, running from the storeroom in his dirty, bare feet. Ro shook her head and followed, not necessarily wanting to be caught alone in the darkened storeroom on a ship full of men.

Her jaw tightened. The captain had been more than accommodating—pleasant, even—but why, oh why hadn't the king listened to her and given her the ship she'd requested? One with a crew immune to the siren's song?

And how many would die because of it?

₰

Cendre circled around and ran back to the storeroom after the huntress left, heart beating madly. Bête! She was so bête! Why had she talked to the huntress? Why had she spent time with her alone?

Why hadn't she just stuck to her plan and watched from afar? Avoided the huntress at all costs? She no longer had any doubt. The huntress looked just like Cendre's Mère and Père, but Grandmère had never mentioned Cendre had living family. Not once.

She thought she was the only one.

Well, besides the cranky old woman she couldn't get away from fast enough.

Hands shaking, Cendre found a nook deep within the ship, away from the bustling crew, and stuffed her small frame into it, taking slow breaths to calm down. She needed to calm down. If she didn't, she wouldn't be able to breathe.

And if she couldn't breathe, she might pass out, and the men might discover her secret. She could *not* let that happen.

The space was just big enough to rock herself in, so under her breath, she started reciting a portion of the nursery chant Grandmère had taught her.

"The magic that holds you

"Shall not undo you.

"This I vow

"To ease you from this curse, somehow.

"Though trapped, one day, free,

"If you love her more than self . . ."

Her voice trailed off. This first part had captured Cendre's heart, and it was those words she recited to herself, over and over.

The rest had to do with some castle and sorceress and thorns, and while Cendre didn't mind it, even enjoyed saying the full thing sometimes, the first six lines punched her in the gut every single time. Made her think they were meant for her and her alone.

But this time, it wasn't working.

Cendre closed her eyes and forced herself to breathe, reciting the way her grandmère had taught her. For once missing the soft, bony arms that would hold her tight when her episodes left her weak and shaking.

The cadence of the words rose and fell, and she let the hope they inspired fill her. She could do this. She had to do this. The words soothed something deep inside, and her vision, which had started to close to a pinhole, began to clear.

She finally took a full, deep breath, then sagged against the rough plank wall, her sweat-soaked clothes sticking to her skin. She lifted shaking hands to her eyes. It was getting worse. And it couldn't get worse. Not now.

Not when she was this close to finding out the truth—to finding the rest of her family.

8

*R*o wandered the deck, loving absolutely everything about sailing the coasts south, especially as the air turned warmer and she saw new sights and lands for the first time.

She'd forgotten how much she loved the sea.

And thanks to the captain's overprotectiveness, the sailors stayed out of her way. Something she couldn't thank him enough for. Silently. In her head. Because she'd just butcher it if she tried to say it aloud.

After moving from starboard to the port side and the turquoise that rimmed the sliver of land on the horizon—either Spain or perhaps Portugal by now—she stilled. The hairs on the back of her neck prickled. Someone was watching her.

Slowly, cautiously, she turned, eyes sweeping the deck. There. A leering grin full of rotting teeth. The same man she'd caught watching her several times on this voyage. Ro gave him a cool look and turned away. A snub.

The brush of bare footsteps headed her way, and Ro just barely kept from groaning aloud. How was she supposed to know a snub would encourage the vile creature?

Hoping she wasn't being too obvious, Ro glanced around for the captain.

She stiffened. Since when had she started relying on him? She should know by now she could rely on no one but herself. Ro squared off with the approaching sailor.

He stopped right next to her and whistled. "Woo-ie, but ain't you a sight. Purtiest thing I ever did see. The stories don't do ya justice."

Ro gave him a cold glare. "Excusez-moi?"

The sailor looked her up and down, eyes slightly yellowed and crazed looking. "No need ta get high 'n mighty with me, missy. I gave ye a compliment. The proper response is a thank ye."

Ro's eyes widened. As if. He let fly a glob of chew over the rail, and she instantly felt sorry for the fish below.

The infuriating man continued. "And how 'bout you smile while ye're at it? I always say a woman looks better with a smile on her lips or a laugh at the ready. C'mon, lovie, for me?"

Ro held his gaze just long enough for him to see her disdain, then lifted her chin and turned mostly away. She was acutely aware of the stillness of the entire deck, watching them.

She didn't care if she'd come to rely on him—where was the bloody captain?

The sailor chuckled low and moved past her, boldly brushing his hand along her backside.

Ro spun, stuck out her foot, and swung her fist, all at once.

Her fist met someone else's open hand, and the leering sailor was caught mid-trip and roughly jerked away from her.

Olt held her fist while another sailor pinned the man's arms to his sides.

"I think you have duties to attend to, don't ya, mate?" Olt said affably, though his nonchalance seemed a bit forced.

The sailor sneered. "And what's it to you, new boy? You don't outrank me."

Ro flushed hot and cold at Olt's hand around her own and

pulled away. He let go. But then he stepped between them. Ro scowled. It wasn't like she was going to haul off and hit the vile sailor while he wasn't paying attention. Maybe.

Ro stepped to the side so she had plenty of room to defend herself.

"No," Olt continued, "but the captain does, and he said ta leave the huntress be."

"Again, I don't answer to you." The unkempt crewman jerked away from the sailor holding him.

Ro stayed open, settling into her center, ready to drive him back if need be.

He moved close to Olt, and Ro found herself thankful he'd stood up for her, else the sailor would be breathing in her face instead.

She stilled. Thankful? What was *wrong* with her this voyage?

"You gonna squeal on me, deckhand?"

Olt grinned, though it held something dangerous this time, and flicked a glance past Ro. "I won't have to." He lifted his hands and stepped back, next to Ro, shrugging in a "there's nothing more I can do" manner. "Just remember I tried to warn you, mate."

Olt's eyes started to twinkle. Literally twinkle. Ro refused to be captivated by them. Sailors were the scum of the earth, or so her père had emphasized repeatedly, and she'd never be taken in by one. Especially not this one.

Ro crouched slightly, readying herself to fight. The sailor grinned and took a step forward.

"What's the meaning of this?"

The sailor scrambled away from Ro faster than a rabbit from a wolf.

Ro straightened and relaxed her stance. She couldn't say she'd hold back if he accosted her again, but she was thankful the captain hadn't caught her in the midst of a brawl on his ship.

She blinked. She actually cared what he thought. Weird.

"Atten-hut!" Everyone stood at attention—except Ro—as the captain paced before them. "I realize this is not a military crew. I understand we have hired on hands from every walk of life, but that does not mean I will tolerate mean behavior."

He stopped in front of Ro, though he did not look at her.

"The huntress is our guest. And I specifically stated she is not to be harassed, disturbed, bothered, or mistreated in any way." He eyed each sailor in turn, again skipping Ro. "If I so much as suspect an inkling of mistreatment, the lot of you will spend time in the brig. Do I make myself clear?"

"Aye, aye, Cap'ain."

"What was that?"

"Aye, aye, Cap'ain!"

He nodded once. "Now, back to your posts, on the double!"

Everyone scattered, including Olt, though Ro couldn't exactly say why her gaze tracked him and him alone. The captain waited until they were well away and busy before turning to her.

She held up a hand before he could speak. "I know, I know. I'll go to ma chambre."

She was beginning to feel like he sent her to her room every time he saw her. Maybe the man didn't know what to do with those of the female persuasion.

His eyes gleamed, and a slight smile could barely be seen through his thick beard and moustache. "Actually, I was going to say: If he bothers you again, do what you need to do."

Ro blinked. "Um . . ."

"Although you are more than welcome to read in my room or retire to yours?"

Ro held up both hands and backed away. "Non, merci. I'm quite enjoying the fresh air and the . . . freedom . . . if you will."

He nodded. "Enjoy your day."

Ro didn't know what to make of him. "Merci, Monsieur."

He stalked away, and Ro watched him go. She felt eyes on her and turned. Olt had been watching their exchange, and he raised his eyebrows. She shrugged, and they shared a chuckle, which warmed Ro more than it should have.

Something about him put her at ease, and she didn't like it one bit.

A little flustered, Ro went back to watching the open water.

A pod of dolphins swam alongside the ship for a bit before swimming away. A few birds floating in the middle of the sea fooled her into thinking they were shark fins, then finally, a true shark fin poked through the water. She gasped and pointed, looking around to share her find, but—she knew no one.

And she wasn't about to be more friendly with Olt than necessary.

She sighed and went back to watching the sliver of land trailing past on the port side, vowing to one day return and experience Portugal and Spain for herself.

9

*R*o panted a little and bent over, wishing it were a thousand degrees cooler. Why was it so *hot*? And humid?

They were nearly to the Canaries, and the cooling breezes had evaporated and left sweltering heat behind. The end of summer was brutal. Especially this far south.

She'd changed her mind. She hated the sea.

Ro lifted her face to find a breeze, wishing it were stronger, as it had been for most of the trip. Now the air just settled hot and heavy around the ship, like it was trying to weigh everyone down.

Mon Dieu, it's almost worse than wearing a corset!

"Milady, might I have a moment of your time?"

Ro straightened and turned to Captain Montrose, attempting a smile. "But of course, Monsieur."

A trail of sweat slid down the middle of her back.

Surreptitiously, she tried to pry the thick, sticky material from her skin, all while wishing she could take off her leather hunting vest without her white under-blouse being completely see-through.

"We are almost to the Canaries . . ." he began.

She nodded, her mind instantly on all she had to do to prepare for the sirens. "I brought weapons to outfit your ship. Harpoons, net traps, and more. Also, I need to begin training your men . . ."

The captain shook his head. "There will be time for that once we are upon the great sea. For now, I must ask you to retire to your room, milady. We are about to dock."

Ro lifted her short queue of dark hair off the back of her neck and tried not to look like a bedraggled mess. "Am I really that much in the way?"

Captain Montrose didn't bother to address that particular subject. "I'm afraid there's more."

Ro groaned. How could it possibly get worse? There was no air, it was a thousand degrees, and her lightest clothing was designed to keep France's previously endless winter at bay. This was the first time she could remember being so uncomfortable in trousers.

"I'm afraid you'll need to stay in your room while we wait for good crossing."

Ro lifted bleary eyes to his. "If you keep me in my cabin in this heat, I will die."

He coughed, and Ro was almost certain he was disguising a chuckle. "Your porthole window and door can be opened, and of course you can walk the deck at night, but I must insist you remain in your cabin during the day."

"For how long?" Ro snapped her mouth closed at the whine that escaped. Was she an enfant?

"Until we depart Las Palmas de Gran Canaria, huntress. I am sorry."

Ro fanned herself, doing everything in her power not to snap at him. She rubbed at her neckline.

The captain's eyes tracked her movements briefly. "You know, in the Canaries and the Caribbean, most people wear a light linen material, perfect for the warmer weather. I'll have a few pieces made for you while we're in port."

Ro brightened—perhaps she could go on land, explore—but the captain cut off her hopeful expression before it could turn into a request.

"I will have the seamstress come to you."

Ro took a deep breath, counted to ten, and said, "Merci, mon capitaine."

Captain Montrose inclined his head, then walked away before she could think of a valid excuse to disembark and explore the last stop before their three-month voyage across the sea.

Just wait till the breeze returns, she thought. *Then I'll have the realm's greatest retort for you.*

Ro glanced at the approaching port, still in the distance, palm trees and lush vegetation overflowing on the islands.

Why couldn't she be on the other ship? *They* wouldn't keep sending her to her room. Probably.

"I'm telling you, if we leave now, that storm'll hit us broadside and sink us faster'n you can blink!" A pause. "Sir."

Ro rolled her eyes at the first mate's familiar argument and flipped a page in her book.

"And I'm telling you," came Captain Montrose's strained response, "if we don't leave now, we'll hit nothing but storms for the entire journey. Three months of storms! Even you don't have the stamina for that. Nor does the ship, I might add."

Ro lost her place in her book and covered her ears, missing the first mate's response.

Through the wall.

Not that she hadn't heard one form of it or another during their constant arguing.

Now that they'd been docked in the Canaries for the last three weeks, waiting for safer weather, she'd done the only thing she could do: escape into her book worlds.

It was no longer helping.

The captain's and first mate's voices pounded relentlessly through the bulkhead into Ro's cabin, and she groaned. She couldn't take their going at it one more time.

Apparently all the delays had placed them close to storm season, and most ships would not set sail until it was over. In several months.

Just one more thing to be most grateful to the king for.

"And what of the huntress?" the first mate demanded.

Ro perked up. She hadn't heard this one yet.

"Do you truly want to sentence her to puking her guts out over the side for the entirety of the voyage?"

Ro bristled. Her père was a *merchant*. How dare he?

"She handled the journey down here just fine," Captain Montrose rejoined calmly.

Ro gave him a nod he couldn't see and grumbled, "That's right I did."

The silence was brief before the captain came up with another argument of why they should leave right away.

The truth was, they'd already missed good sailing, both men knew it, and neither wanted to sail. But they had their orders from the king.

Now if only they would admit it to each other, Ro could have a few moments of peace. And maybe they could be on their way.

She'd still rather be on deck, looking out over the bustling docks, or on the island, exploring a new land for the first time, but the captain still wouldn't let her off the ship or on deck, where she could be seen. And she had no idea why.

Ro slumped against the rough-hewn bulkhead, too weary to fan herself or wish one more time for a strong breeze to sweep the room. She wondered if the ship would survive the inevitable storms.

The first tendrils of fear wended their way around her heart.

All of her père's ships had sunk in a storm whipped up by the curse that had fallen on France, leaving her family destitute. She'd had nightmares for years, thinking of the men she'd known floating in an endless sleep.

They often drifted above her in her dreams, backlit by flashes of lightning, staring at her with sightless eyes. She shuddered and shook herself out of it.

She couldn't let herself go there. Their journey across the great sea would take roughly three months, and she would not allow herself to be wracked by fear the entire time.

Besides, she was only trying to distract herself from her greatest concern: Would the crew she'd hired follow her? Or would they take the money and flee?

She cursed and smacked the wall, earning momentary silence from next door. They started at it again far too soon, and it didn't take long for them to forget to keep their voices down.

Ro jumped up and began to pace. She didn't want to sink in the middle of the ocean if blasted by a hurricane, but at this very moment, it was favorable to hearing endless pros and cons through her wall while sweltering.

She slid to the floor and clamped her hands over her ears. Taking several deep, calming breaths, she made a promise to herself. She wasn't going to obsess over it, not for the whole voyage. If she only had herself to come to her rescue, then so be it.

Ro crawled to her feet, snatched up one of the siren legends from Madame LaChance, and flopped onto the bottom bunk. She'd already read it twice, but perhaps she'd missed something.

Sirène Oceanus was a scientific defense of the sirens' existence, taken from firsthand accounts of survivors—of which there were few—tales of sailors being sung to and beckoned by such creatures—however, sailors loved to spin and stretch a good tale—and other historical sources, all of whose validity Ro sincerely doubted.

The unnamed scientist called the siren a "champion of the water," said that due to its structure, the siren "exhibited greater agility and speed than any other sea creature," and repeatedly emphasized that to come in contact with one of the creatures meant "sudden and swift death."

A chill crept through Ro, which she welcomed against the oppressive heat. She took the warning to heart to treat this hunt with the caution it was due.

Ro turned the book sideways to better view sketches of the skeletal, muscular, and possible physical structures of the creatures, all half women, half fish.

One was spotted and striped with spiny protrusions all over that made it look a close cousin to the lionfish.

One squat specimen with a dolphin's tail and thick torso had two fins coming out of its spine, spread out behind her like wings, making the creature look like a demented angel.

Ro snorted.

All were as far-fetched as the sailor's fictional tales. How was she to take any of these stories seriously? It was all speculation and fairy tales.

Ro adjusted her position for what felt like the fifteenth time and played with the hem of her new shirt, thankful one good thing had come out of her imprisonment in the Canaries. Her new clothes were functional, simple, and at least attempted to keep her cool.

Someone rapped on her open door. "Milady?"

Ro's head came up, and it took her a moment to focus on the captain. Had they finished arguing already?

Thank heavens—she was ready to relocate to his room. Not only did he have an extensive library for a ship—nearly thirty books—the captain's quarters somehow got more of a breeze than hers ever did.

"It is time," Captain Montrose said.

The first mate stomped rather loudly by the open door.

Ro held her place in her book with a pointed finger. "Time? For what?"

The captain gave her a small smile, most likely used to her brusque manner by now. "We have taken on our cargo, and the winds be right. It's time to cross the great sea."

Excitement filled Ro, and she bounced up, tossing the book aside. "Très bien!"

Although he seemed pleased by her reaction, his eyes followed the book she'd so carelessly tossed.

Ro retrieved the book and smoothed its cover. "Oh, please let me watch! I'll stay out of the way, I promise. I'm so fascinated by everything on this ship, and I love when you cast off. I'll stand exactly where you want me to and do exactly as you ask, I promise. Please."

She apparently wasn't above begging.

The captain's eyes twinkled, and Ro felt her mouth curve into an answering smile.

"Aye. Wait for my signal, then join me at the wheel."

Ro froze midstep, then her shoulders slumped.

The captain let out a deep belly laugh. "I won't make you wait long, milady. Just until we're out of port."

He closed the door behind him, and Ro sank onto the desk's little chair. "Wait until we're out of port. Of course."

She snapped upright. *Did the king—?* Had the king ordered her out of sight while among civilization?

Rage threatened to boil over. "Are you *kidding* me?"

Ro jumped to her feet and stormed toward the door, but she froze with her hand on the latch. Be that it may, the captain was following orders. He'd been nothing but pleasant this entire trip.

And not only that, he was the captain. He deserved her respect. Even if she didn't agree.

Grumbling the whole way, Ro returned to her reading nook, grabbed her book, and read the same paragraph over and over while she waited for the ship to tug away from the noisy port.

As they slid away from the dock, Ro tossed the book on her bunk and rushed out into the open, not even caring if the captain bodily carried her back to her room. She couldn't take one more second of being cooped up.

Her eyes slid closed, and she took a deep breath of the salty air, tinged with too much fish and bustling life and humanity, with only a hint of a breeze. But she was so excited to see a snippet of the Canaries, her eyes didn't stay closed long.

Lush, verdant green, everywhere. Boats, all being prepared for a lengthy stay in port.

They were the only ones setting out across the great sea.

She pushed away the slight drop in her stomach at that.

People swarmed the docks, chattering in multiple languages and pointing at the *King's Ransom*. The ship rapidly left the teeming port behind, and the water changed from light green to deep turquoise to vibrant blue, then to the loveliest, deepest blue.

Ro couldn't help but soak in the ocean. The way the waves splashed against the hull. The gentle rise and fall of the deck.

The *freedom* of being above deck.

Once land could no longer be seen, the captain approached her. "Thank you for your patience, milady. Are you enjoying your voyage so far?"

Apparently he hadn't noticed her early escape. Guilt tried to make an appearance, but she brushed it off. She wasn't about to feel guilty over something so ridiculous.

Even then, she couldn't help her full smile. She hadn't realized how much she'd missed the open sea, it'd been so long since she'd been on one of her père's ships. It was completely different than being able to see a sliver of land, a measure of safety, on one side or the other.

The edge of danger sent a thrill through her.

"C'est magnifique. I mean, it is glorious."

"I'm glad." A pause. "If you would be so kind . . ."

Ro sighed. "I know, I know. Retournez à ma chambre." Ro turned toward the part of the ship she was beginning to loathe more than any other.

"Actually, milady."

Ro stopped.

"Perhaps now would be a good time for a tour?"

Ro's brow crinkled. She slowly turned to the captain. "A —tour?"

"Yes."

"Of your ship."

"Yes."

"With you?"

Another pause. "Yes." It looked like it pained him to say the word.

"But I thought—" Her gaze swept the deck. The lad who'd given her a tour a few weeks ago was ducking out of sight, a panicked look on his face.

"You thought what, milady?"

Her eyes returned to his. He had no idea. She blinked. What did the lad want from her that he would disobey his captain's orders? "Nothing. Never mind."

Although he looked frustrated by their exchange, he graciously offered his arm. "Perhaps we should start belowdecks and work our way up?"

Ro took it hesitantly, her face heating, not used to being treated as a Mademoiselle. He smoothly moved to the stairs leading below and began the tour.

She slipped her hand from his arm the moment she could do so without appearing rude.

After the most uncomfortable tour of her life—when she passed the boy, he wouldn't look at her, and instead of pumping her for personal information, as the boy had, the captain filled her in on every detail of the ship's construction and the many voyages it had seen, his voice full of pride — Ro was grateful when they returned to the fresh air above.

Ro couldn't help thinking he looked at his ship the same way Captain Red had.

The captain moved away, whistling, leading her up a short flight of steps to the wheel above the three rooms aft, including hers. Apparently talking about his ship cheered him up as much as it made Ro need a moment to herself in complete silence.

They ended the tour at the wheel. Ro watched in fascination as the captain took over for the first mate, piloting the vessel as a master, making it look easy and seamless.

"Teach me."

The captain and first mate looked up.

Ro flushed. She hadn't meant to sound so demanding. "Désolé. Might I learn how to pilot the ship?" When they didn't respond, she kept explaining. "You see, I would love to be able to know how to do this. In case you need me, n'est-ce pas? Or, even if you don't! I would just love to learn. I —"

She snapped her mouth closed as heat burned up her neck. Sometimes her mouth took over without her brain having any say in the matter.

The first mate snorted and stalked away, still not speaking to her since she'd commandeered his chambre. She hadn't yet found a way to apologize that worked.

She peeked at the captain, not wanting to know what he thought of her tirade.

"Very well. Come here."

Ro scrambled over, still not meeting his gaze.

He had her stand in front of the wheel. "Place your hands here and here."

Then he let go. The wheel was nearly ripped out of her hands. Ro gasped and hung on for dear life. It was far different than when her père had held the wheel for her, letting her think she was steering.

He chuckled. "Steady on."

He helped her right it, then he stepped back and explained how although they were going against the current, the winds in their sails more than made up for it. On the way back, the opposite would be true.

Realization dawned as Ro listened to his patient explanations and followed his coaching. He was everything she'd wished for in a père—everything her père had once been—everything he now lacked.

Except the constantly being sent to her chambre part. That she could do without.

Her heart stuttered, and she choked back a flood of emotion. Certain the captain would be aghast were he privy to her thoughts, Ro kept them to herself and threw herself into learning everything she could about piloting a vessel.

10

"*B*eautiful, isn't it?"

Ro startled at the voice next to her, then tried to pretend she hadn't. She hated being caught off guard.

She sneaked a sidelong glance at the man beside her, then her gaze pinged away.

"Oliver, was it?" She knew it was Olt.

His grin was breathtaking even in her peripheral. She needed to get a grip.

"Olt, actually."

"Ah. Désolé."

"De rien."

Her head came around. "Parlez-vous français?"

"Oui, I speak a little French, but I'm afraid not very well."

"Oh." She turned back to the open water, heart pounding wildly for some reason. "Been a deckhand long, Olt?"

So much for not speaking to him. It was maddening enough that one grin could send her stomach whirling and her mind spiraling to thoughts of what his lips tasted like. Ugh.

She didn't have time for this.

Of course, being on a small ship for the next three months, she might want to make friends. Emphasis on *friends*.

His grin threatened to send her heart galloping away, and she reined it roughly back in. She was not about to lose her head or her heart to some handsome stranger.

"Actually, only a few other voyages. I liked them enough that when I heard about this one, I jumped at the chance to go again."

The words soured in Ro's stomach. She studied the white caps that made their going a bit rougher today. "Aren't you afraid you might die?"

The words carried more bitterness than she would've liked. Maybe he hadn't picked up on it? She felt him studying her profile, but she refused to look his way.

"Are you afraid I might die?"

The words were said quietly, intimately, and Ro felt tears threaten. She swallowed hard against the burn in her throat. She didn't want to be responsible for a full crew's deaths. Why hadn't the stubborn king listened to her?

Why hadn't she insisted just a little harder?

"Oui," she whispered.

After a heartbeat, he shifted, and Ro couldn't help looking at him. A grin spread across his face, and he placed one hand over his heart. Ro lifted both eyebrows.

"Why, huntress, I didn't know you cared. I'm touched, truly."

Ro stared at him, mouth parted, mind whirling. She swiftly recovered. "Not just you, you idiot! Everyone. Don't you care that every person on this ship might lose their life because of a terrible decision? Don't you care that this ship will most likely splinter to pieces like every other ship the sirènes attacked? Don't you care we're heading into storms most are smart enough to avoid? How dare you make light of it!"

Heat crawled up Ro's neck and spilled onto her face, and now she was facing him and two steps away from throttling him. How dare he make light of this situation! The one she would solely be responsible for if she couldn't figure out a way to keep everyone onboard from being sirened and sinking the ship themselves.

Olt studied her face, his grin growing. "Whoa, you really do have an explosive temper, don't you?"

Several heartbeats passed before Ro could speak. "Was that all this was?" she demanded. "Taunting me to see how I would react? To see if the stories about me were true?"

Rage simmered just under the surface, and Ro took deep breaths to try to stay rational.

"Actually, I wanted to get to know the woman who has so thoroughly wrapped our gruff captain around her finger." He chuckled. "I hear that's impossible to do."

Ro blushed even more hotly and tried to protest.

His voice dropped so she could barely hear it below the sweep of wind. "Who seems to have captivated me as well."

She stood frozen, not believing she'd heard those words, certain he hadn't meant her to. Or had he? Ro clenched the rail. Insufferable man. Did he flirt with every woman like this?

He wasn't the first to try to flatter her, nor would he be the last, but she most certainly didn't have to fall for it. He could take his charms and go use them on some other poor, unsuspecting female.

Ro pointed a finger at him. "Let me make one thing clear, sailor. I am not here to flirt, laze about, or enchant some captain, or whatever it is you think I'm doing. I'm here to save lives, and if you can't respect that, leave me alone."

Olt's eyes widened, and he floundered a moment, losing that infernal grin. "I meant no harm, huntress, truly. I apologize. I—sometimes I make light of a situation, when I ought not. It's—I just do. I'm sorry. Je suis désolé."

Ro nodded once, too miffed to say anything kind. She thought about walking away, but she stood her ground, silently daring him to retreat first with a steady glare.

"That was something, huh?"

She blinked. Couldn't he take a hint and leave her alone?

Ro gave him a mildly irritated look. "If you want me to read your mind, I can't."

He grinned, his cockiness flowing back in spades. "All those people coming to see the ship? Our dock was so crowded, it was hard to get anything done."

Ro grumbled, more to herself, "Now that would've been nice to see." She leaned a hip against the railing and crossed her arms.

Olt nodded, his look sympathetic. "Yeah, sorry about that."

She shrugged. "It wasn't your fault."

"No, but I wouldn't have liked to be stuck below the whole time, either."

Ro slapped the railing. "But why? *Why* couldn't I go above deck when we were in the Canaries?" Angry tears burned the back of Ro's throat, but she didn't let them loose. Never, and never in front of Olt. "I've always wanted to see them," she said, hoping she didn't sound as petulant as she felt.

Olt rubbed the back of his neck, looking like he didn't want to answer. "Well, the rumors are that the Marquis de la Valère is on a voyage to silence the sirens, so . . ."

Ro's eyes widened. "So that's why all those people were pointing at the ship when we left."

Olt nodded. "And why you couldn't be seen above deck. What would they say, if the huntress was seen onboard, but the Marquis was not? Especially since he so dearly loves to be seen."

Ro had half a mind to shoot the king in the buttocks with an arrow next she saw him. She relished the thought a moment before forcing herself to act her age. She took a deep breath. "Tell me about the Marquis."

Olt shrugged. "There's not much to tell, really."

"You've met him though, non?" Ro prodded.

"I have. And as I said, never was there a more pretentious peacock."

Ro tilted her head. "But I heard he's a great hunter. A

wordsmith. One to call when one needs out of sticky situations."

"Nothing could be further from the truth." Olt rolled his eyes and barked a laugh.

Ro rested her chin in her hand, gaze on Olt. "Not the most cunning and devious of men? A man to be admired and feared?"

Olt snorted. "Hardly. For once, the rumors are not true." He flicked a glance her way. "Unlike the stories about you, of course."

Now Ro rolled her eyes. "You have no way of knowing that. For all you know, my legends could be as false as the Marquis de la Valère's."

Olt's grin hinted at teasing. He crossed his arms and pretended to be deep in thought. "Hmm. You know, you're absolutely right."

Ro straightened and smacked his arm, falling into teasing as she'd done a hundred times with her brothers, only this time, without meaning to. "Watch it. I just may have to prove to you how legendary my hunting skills truly are."

Enjoyment leapt to Olt's eyes. "Now that I would like to see."

Ro sobered instantly, her gaze drifting away to stare at the endless tapestry of blue. "I truly hope you don't have to."

A heartbeat of silence. Olt leaned on the rail, moving into her peripheral vision. "Now that's interesting."

Ro blinked and looked at him. "What?"

When her gaze met his, attraction welled deep in her belly and trembled there. She backed up a little.

"A huntress who doesn't show off. Isn't seeking a fight for the sake of fighting."

Although Ro's heart raced, seriousness took over, and she took a moment to answer. "I've learned that not everything is as it seems. I have the king's point of view, and now I want the sirènes'. If they'll speak with me."

Olt's eyes widened. "So you're going to try to talk to them?"

Ro hesitated, then decided it wasn't much of a secret. "Oui. Why start a war—one I'm not certain we can finish—when it can be prevented? The casualties will be far worse for us than for them. They can sink a ship, drown all the men aboard, and stay underneath the surface, silent, deadly, unseen, when we cannot. We've already seen a preview of what they can do. Can you imagine if we go to war?"

Olt nodded, thoughtful. "Forgive me, but what good will talking to them do? Can't they just go back on whatever they say?"

"Non, as magical creatures, they are bound by the laws of the fey. Once given, their word cannot be undone without their power draining away, weakening them and making them more susceptible to disease or being killed by hunters."

Olt looked impressed. Ro tried not to let that distract her.

Ro shrugged. "Besides, the king will start offering a bounty for each sirène body brought in if I cannot stop them myself." Her voice quieted. "I would not wish that on any people."

A comfortable silence settled between them.

Olt smacked the rail. "That's it!"

Ro jumped at his outburst. "What? What's it?"

His warm gaze sent a swarm of papillons trying to fly away with her heart. Ridiculous, fluttery things. She shot them all down as if with arrows.

"I've decided I like you, huntress." He held out his hand. "If you are who you say you are, you can count on me. For anything. Just say the word, and I'll help."

Ro stared between his hand and his captivating brown eyes flecked with gold. "Why? You don't even know me."

Even though Olt was trying to look serious, that ridiculous twinkle danced in his eyes. Ro found it fascinating, and she shouldn't. Not at all.

"I pride myself on being able to tell the mettle of a man—or in your case, a woman—right away. I don't always get it right, I admit, but I've got a feeling about you. I think we'll get along just fine."

And then he quirked another grin, and Ro fought not to catch her breath, blush, or give any other hint of what he was doing to her racing pulse. His smile made the entire world around them stop.

"If you need anything, anything at all, you need only ask." His hand was still outstretched, waiting for her to clasp it.

She took a deep breath. "Merci." And grabbed his hand.

Lightning didn't physically spark, but the sensation jolted her nonetheless. And from the look on Olt's face, he felt it as well. Their gazes caught and held, and Ro panicked. She didn't know what to do.

"Huntress!"

Ro jerked away, already moving toward the voice, though she had no idea who'd called her.

"Oui?" she asked, and a heartbeat later, her eyes settled on Captain Montrose.

"May I have a word with you?" He may have been speaking to her, but his glare was firmly settled on Olt.

Ro's heart dropped. "But of course."

She followed the captain, but her mind—her heart, even—stayed behind with the sailor whose easy grin and twinkling gaze she could get lost in, were she not careful.

She needed to stay far, far away from Olt.

Ro grumbled to herself and quickened her steps. Now to avoid him on a three-month voyage on a small ship.

Ro groaned. She had to make things awkward between them right away, didn't she? And of course the captain would notice.

The captain turned on her the moment they were in his cabin, door closed. "I cannot have you distracting my men."

Ro's head came up. "Pardon?"

"I'll not have you distracting my men."

Ro's mouth dropped open. "Excusez-moi, Monsieur, but I seem to recall you pressing me to get to know your crew, to make a few friends."

"I run a God-fearing ship, milady, and I'll have no onboard romances here." His jaw tightened.

Ro spluttered, her face on fire, her temper in full swing. "I can assure you, I am not interested in romance! I simply asked the sailor what to expect, and he was kind enough to answer a few questions. Nothing more."

And Ro hated having to explain herself.

The captain opened his mouth, but Ro moved closer and spoke firmly. "Non, I'll not be sequestered in my room any longer. If you want me out of the way, then give me something to do. Allow me to help in some way."

His gaze turned flinty. "Absolutely not."

Ro's head jerked back. "And why on earth not? You'll find I'm as hard a worker as any of your crew."

The look on his face made her feel as though she'd just requested to take up dancing lessons on his head. Or something equally ridiculous. "You are my guest. As my guest, you'll not be relegated to hard labor. Not on my ship."

Both of Ro's eyebrows climbed her forehead. "And you think I'm not used to hard labor? As a huntress—"

"My decision isn't up for debate."

"But—"

"That's all I have to say on the matter."

Ro scowled. The man was impossible. Apparently now wasn't the time to bring up the topic of outfitting his ship to defend against sirens, though it needed to happen sooner rather than later.

"Then allow me the courtesy of a few acquaintances." Ro

held up a hand at his hard look. "I'll not distract them from their tasks."

Captain Montrose nodded curtly. "Aye. But I'll be watching."

Ro didn't even try to hide her eye roll. She opened her mouth.

"That will be all." He opened a ledger and dipped a quill pen in an inkwell.

Ro snapped her mouth closed. Dismissed. Just like that. Ro stormed away, giving the door a harder shove than necessary on her way out.

Moving to the opposite side of the ship from where Olt worked, she gripped the railing and took deep, calming breaths.

How she'd survive the stupidity of this voyage, she'd never know.

PART TWO

<< Lorsque tu auras quinze ans, dit sa grand-mère, tu auras la permission de monter à la surface de la mer et de t'asseoir au clair de la lune sur les rochers et de regarder passer les grands navires des hommes. >>
<< Oh ! si seulement j'avais quinze ans ! disait-elle. Je sens que j'aimerai bien le monde de là-haut, et les hommes qui y habitent. >>
~Hans Christian Anderson, *La Petite Sirène*

"When you are fifteen years old," said her grandmother, "you will be allowed to rise to the surface of the sea and sit on the rocks in the moonlight and watch the great ships sail by."
"Oh! If only I were fifteen!" she said. "I know I shall love the world above, and all who dwell there."
~Hans Christian Anderson, *The Little Mermaid*

11

*R*o groaned and shifted in her hammock. Something teased her toward wakefulness. Something not quite right, yet not invasive enough to wake her just yet.

She snuggled deeper into her hammock.

She was back in the forest. With the English king's messenger who had fetched her from her sister's summer palace in France, the reason for this entire foolhardy voyage.

Then the forest changed. A shroud of fog separated her from the messenger.

A fairy, soon to be queen and under the threat of her human husband and half-human child being killed by the fey court, stretched tight the fabric between realms and stepped through.

It snapped closed behind her.

Ro gasped as the nightmare unfolded.

The fairy—no wings, tall, lithe, and stunning in her beauty—reeked of desperation. She cradled her child close as snowflakes drifted down her cheeks as though they were tears.

Ro could only watch as she rushed to the small village— where Ro's family had once lived in a hovel—to a poor merchant and his wife. Five little girls and two boys slept upstairs. One dark-haired girl had fallen asleep on the stairs, not willing to leave her youngest sister's side.

It could have been contagious. So the stairs were as close as she was allowed.

One shriveled old woman sat before the fireplace in a shawl and nightcap, her face turned away from Ro. Before the fire, a babe in a cradle struggled for every breath. Ro's mère sat on the floor beside the cradle, fast asleep. Her hair was a mess, rosary clutched in her fingers, dried tear trails streaked down her cheeks.

All this Ro saw before the fairy reached the cottage.

The fairy found the house she was looking for, one Ro knew well, and paused at the front door. An iron cross made of two long nails hung over the door to protect those within from evil spirits and unwanted fey.

The fairy lifted her face to the sky. "Please, Mighty King, allow me passage this one night." She hastily made the sign of the cross, hunched her shoulders, and forced her way over the threshold with a hiss of pain.

The cross burned a deep orange color before settling back into its disguise of cold iron, blackened shadow seared into the wood behind it.

The old woman alone stirred.

Just as she was lifting her head, turning so Ro could see who she was, the fairy waved a hand and put her to sleep. The old woman slumped in her rocking chair. The fairy leaned over the cradle, took in the human child, whose chest had gone achingly still, and breathed out her relief.

"Oh, thank you. Thank you, little one, for giving your life for my daughter. Your sacrifice will not be forgotten."

With one last kiss for her babe, she switched the bodies and fled into the night.

The old woman stood and followed her, face hidden. Always hidden.

And Ro wept in her sleep, reaching one hand toward her

mère, longing to comfort her, to hug her just one more time, stretching the other toward the sister she'd never known.

Her hammock slammed her just past the rim of the bunk beds, then hurled her the other way, barely missing the wall. Ro woke with a cry.

The nightmare lurched away, its memory dissipating under a crash of thunder.

Ro gasped and sat up, watching the room pitch crazily around her, the hammock making it so much worse. Then, a pounding at her door.

"Coming!" she called as she tried to untangle herself from the hammock. She growled as the twisty thing kept her in its grip. "What is it?"

Lightning filled the room through the small porthole, illuminating mountains of waves outside, and one giant dip they were headed straight toward. Another boom of thunder drowned out the man's words, but Ro wasn't paying him any attention.

Her eyes were riveted on the now-darkness as a lingering image of the trench they were about to plunge into stayed like a flash before her eyes.

"Huntress!"

The word jolted her back into action, and she fell hands first to the floor, taking one leg out of her hammock at a time, her heart in her throat. Out of habit, she took just long enough to pull on her boots and tuck her shirt into her trousers before opening the door. Well, before trying to open the door. The maelstrom outside fought her.

One giant heave, and her door flew open. The planks under her feet tipped.

A figure stumbled into her, and her door slammed shut. Ro cried out as the ship dropped and they both crashed to the floor. She would've hit her head had the stranger's hands not cradled her just in time.

The sudden fall jolted to a stop, and a wave slammed into

the ship, knocking it to the side. She could hear a bell ringing over and over and felt the ship lurch madly to head off the next wave. The stranger's arms held her steady.

First, a pleasant scent filled her senses. So masculine and strong and breathe-deep worthy. Second, his weight settled on her just right. She started thrashing. She didn't care how good he smelled; she just wanted him off!

He tried to get up, just as a wave lifted the boat high and sent them tumbling to the other side of the room.

Something crashed into the door outside. Something huge.

"What's going on?" Ro shouted, not liking the way her voice rose in pitch—in terror. She could've sworn she'd seen the sandy bottom of the ocean floor in that last lightning flash. Would the ship topple sideways? Would they drown? Trapped in her room, unable to get out?

The man again tried to separate himself from her as he shouted to be heard over the tempest. "Storm, Mademoiselle! Cap'ain wants you to stay in your chambers—wanted me to check if you were all right."

Ro gave him a sour look, one illuminated by another lighting flash. Olt grinned in response right before the light went out.

"That's exactly what I was doing until you barged in here!" she shouted.

"Yes, but he didn't want you to be scared, and—are you all right?"

Ro elbowed his side as mirth flooded his voice. "I was until your bony body started throwing me around my chambers." It wasn't bony at all. Strong, muscular—perfection.

What was *wrong* with her?

"Scared or all right?"

She huffed. "All right, of course!"

Olt laughed outright. "My apologies, Mademoiselle."

He staggered to a crouched position and helped her do the same.

"How long will the storm last?" She stumbled as the boards under her feet refused to remain still.

He shrugged, again only visible from the glaring flash of light. Ro shuddered at the roar of thunder that followed. "Only Poseidon knows."

Ro cut him a sharp look. "You're a believer in Poseidon?"

She'd heard of them, worshippers of the false god of the sea. Some were said to throw gifts overboard while crossing, though throwing people overboard was now expressly forbidden, thank the Creator.

Not that that mattered to some sailors.

Olt helped her to the bed. He plopped next to her, their backs propped up by the wall. "In the Creator, actually, but I've seen some crazy stuff in my lifetime. I'm almost certain something else rules the sea. A lesser power, sure, but another ruler nonetheless."

Ro frowned. "Besides the Creator?"

"Aye. Something underwater. A king of sorts." Olt grinned. "I've been on too many voyages to think otherwise."

"Or a queen," Ro shot back, not about to believe the entire world was ruled by kings.

"Or a queen," Olt conceded with a grin. He was far too happy at times. All the time, actually.

Again, Ro shouted to be heard over the storm. "As stirring as this conversation is, shouldn't you be out there helping?"

"Naw." Olt folded his hands behind his head and struck a pose of utter carefreeness. "Captain wanted me to check on you, help you if need be."

Ro glared at him. "In my bedchamber." She glanced down. "On my bed."

A double flash illuminated dusky red suffusing his neck, and he straightened. "Oh, uh . . ."

The ship bucked, and his body slammed into hers. They tumbled from the bed onto the floor. Ro's heart flew up past the ceiling as the entire ship dropped.

Ro cringed against the heart-stopping thunder. "Maybe we should go help . . ." Anything to put distance between her and the handsome sailor.

Olt caged her body with his arms as the ship pitched the other way. He held her in place just barely, and the room got a thousand degrees hotter. Would he get away from her already?

"Can you imagine being on deck when the ship dips like this? Pitch you right over the edge, it will. Captain was having the crew tie themselves off when he sent me in here."

Ro struggled to get away from those absolutely delicious arms. A little voice said to enjoy them since these could quite possibly be her last few moments on earth, but Ro slammed a door on such thoughts. She wasn't about to die now, thank you very much.

Olt pulled away, propped himself up on his knees, and raised his hands. "Easy now. I won't hurt you, I—"

A double flash of lightning interrupted him. His words ground to a halt. He reached for her in the darkness, something Ro could see but was too frozen to do anything about. His fingers brushed her cheek.

"Tears?"

Ro crawled toward the door. Great. Now he thought she was crying over the storm. What had she been crying about? She'd been dreaming . . . something . . .

"What are you doing?" Olt asked.

She tried to open the door, but it wouldn't budge.

"It's not safe out there!"

She slammed her shoulder into it. Rational or not, she wasn't staying in this cabin with this man a moment longer. Her instinct was to flee from things that scared her, and Olt most definitely scared her.

"Huntress!"

"It's Ro!" she snapped. "Help me get this door open."

Olt came close and turned her face to his, the touch so surprisingly gentle, Ro stilled. "And if you fall overboard?

On my watch? After the captain ordered me to keep you safe?"

Ro clenched her jaw. "I can take care of myself."

Olt's smile was kind. "I have no doubt of that."

She rattled the door, pushing on it with all her might. "They might need my help."

Olt looked dubious as the lightning flashes came faster, but he helped her push against the door anyway. It wouldn't budge.

Olt frowned. "Perhaps something fell against it." He lowered his voice, almost speaking to himself, right as thunder cracked. "I hope it wasn't the mainmast."

Ro strained to hear him. "What did you say?"

"The mainmast. That supports the other sails? If it's the mizzenmast, we can repair it and limp along." He glanced at her. "The mizzenmast is the smaller mast at the aft of the ship, right outside these doors."

Ro scowled. "I know what and where the mizzenmast is."

"But if the mainmast comes down, we're dead in the water until we can get another."

Ro knew that too, but cold filled her gut anyway and sank like a cannonball. "Creator, please, don't let us sink."

Olt shot her a half-grin, half-puzzled look as he tugged her away from the door. "Thought you didn't believe in the Creator."

Ro lifted her chin. "A Mademoiselle's beliefs are her own, and none of yours. Now, be quiet. It looks as though neither of us are going anywhere."

Olt gave her a mock salute. "Aye, aye, Cap'ain."

Ro bumped his shoulder with hers. "Watch your words, crewman. Can you imagine if the captain heard you call me that?"

Olt just laughed. "What? I could see you as a captain. Taking charge, barking orders . . ."

The ship dipped again, and Ro grabbed her stomach as she

staggered about like a drunken sailor. It felt as though she'd jumped off a cliff and was still falling.

All of a sudden, Olt's carefree grin shifted to concern. He inched away the smallest bit. "Shall I get you a bucket?"

Ro glared at him, even though he couldn't see it in the dark cabin. "I'm not about to lose my dinner. It feels like I'm falling."

She didn't miss Olt's long look—he didn't quite believe her. The ship juddered at the end of another long dive and was immediately popped back into the air by another wave.

Olt caged her against the wall with his arms, holding on to the hammock straps until his muscles bulged. Which Ro was most certainly not noticing.

Ro pushed him away, but it didn't do much good. The next wave had them both clinging to the unsteady hammock. "I'm fine," she insisted. "So what are we supposed to do now that we can't get out of my room?"

A sparkle leapt to his eyes, and Ro immediately wished she hadn't asked.

"Oh, I don't know. Can you think of anything?"

Ro just glared, and Olt gave a deep belly laugh.

"I'm jesting, huntress. Surely you know that about me by now."

"Ro."

He startled. "Excuse me?"

"My name is Ro. You can call me that. If you want."

A smile, one that made Ro's heart skip a beat, found its way to his lips, and he looked genuinely pleased. "Ro." His voice deepened. "Thank you for the honor of your name, huntress."

Ro nodded and pretended wild horses weren't dragging her heart far, far away while trampling it to death. And then she realized she could see him. Had been able to for a while now. She squinted at the porthole. "Is it getting lighter out?"

Olt snorted. "I wish. With a storm this black, we might not be able to tell when it's daylight."

Ro blinked. Oh. Her eyesight must be doing that thing again. She looked around the room. Yep, she could see everything quite clearly.

It never ceased to amaze her how objects lit up all on their own and sparkled with glittering light as she focused on them. It was quite possibly the most beautiful thing she'd ever seen. But it often came on so slowly, she didn't notice at first.

Unless she was in danger. Then things blazed to light like the sunniest midday ever.

The ship dipped, and Ro lost her footing. She stumbled into Olt. He caught her, and they both went perfectly still—in each other's arms, clinging to the hammock.

Ro cleared her throat. "Um, ah . . ."

The ship pitched and they slammed into the wall, but Olt held on. "Look, I don't mean to be forward, but the bed is probably best."

Ro stiffened.

"I'll be the perfect gentleman, I promise, but I don't want either of us to break any bones. I need those."

He didn't see Ro's sharp look, but she didn't miss his cringe, heightened color, or the way he raised his eyes to the ceiling.

"I need those?" he mouthed. "Really?"

Ro bit back a chuckle and allowed him to help her to the bed, hating that she needed even the smallest amount of help. As before, they propped their backs against the bulkhead and braced their feet against the bunk's deep edge, Ro as far from him as she could get.

After a moment of twiddling his thumbs against his knees and looking like he didn't know what to do with himself, Olt broke the silence. In the cabin, anyway. The storm still raged outside. "Tell me a story?"

Ro raised an eyebrow, then realized he couldn't see it. "Excusez-moi?"

He grinned, and Ro studied his face, especially since he couldn't see her doing so.

"One of your hunts. I haven't been able to hear one yet. I always seem to be busy or belowdecks when the men ask for a story. Tell me your favorite." A long pause. "Unless you don't want to, of course."

Deep liking overtook Ro, and she shied away from it. She told herself the same thing she always did when a handsome hunter, like Liam or one of the others, showed her a smidgeon of interest.

Her père had been kind, attentive, wildly in love with her mère. Yet nine children and wealth had turned his affection toward wagering at the boîte de jeu tables, and his wife's death had turned him hopelessly to drink.

He hadn't kept his promise to care for them. He hadn't been the man he should've been. And Ro wasn't about to trust her heart to someone who could do the same. Who *would* do the same.

"Huntress?"

Ro jolted, realizing she'd been quiet for far too long. "My père promised me to a beast in exchange for his own life."

She hadn't meant to say it; the words just came out.

A heartbreaking moment of silence, chased closely by a boom of thunder, followed. Both Olt and Ro had to brace their feet and cling to opposite wooden posts as two waves hit the ship at once, one bouncing it to the side, the other, straight up.

Olt's quiet voice cut through the tumult outside. And in her heart. "Ro, I'm so sorry."

Ro lifted one shoulder and let it fall. "C'est comme ça. It is what it is."

"What happened?"

And so Ro told him. Of accepting a contract to hunt and kill the beast, fulfilling her père's promise and her word to her employer. Of being trapped. Of nearly succeeding in killing the beast and escaping, until the wounded creature kidnapped her sister to take Ro's place.

Of Ro's promise to stay in her sister's stead.

That's where she meant to stop. Truly. But Gautier's lies, his secrets, came out. Along with so much more. The whole story.

Well, except the little detail that Cosette wasn't truly her sister.

Yet Cosette's marriage to Prince Trêve, the beast Ro's sister had set free with her unconditional love—Ro's secret heartbreak of which she had not yet spoken, to anyone—came prancing out of her lips as if the words had a mind of their own.

A gentle pause followed. One she desperately needed.

"Did you love him?"

The questions felt like a slap. Ro sat there, stunned. "I—I —perhaps. I mean, I thought I did. I—"

Ro didn't know how to finish.

He waited patiently, silently—the expectant space gentle between them.

She said, "I promised to marry him. To break the curse. But he wanted her instead."

Ro choked a little, and she hoped he hadn't heard the strangled sound over the waves crashing against the hull.

He touched her arm in the darkness. "Ro, I'm so sorry for your loss. Your heartache. I have to believe something good will come of it. That you're here, at this moment in time, in this place, for a reason." His voice dropped an octave. "That the Creator will make something good come from it all."

Olt's quiet voice felt like a lifeline, and Ro clung to it. When had she begun to care so deeply what he thought? Had one little conversation changed her mind so drastically?

She shook it off. She couldn't let it.

She shrugged again, and the motion brought with it the

painful memory of how elegant Mère looked when she shrugged and said, "C'est comme ça."

So lovely. So graceful. So French.

Ro whispered her mère's words. "C'est comme ça."

It is what it is.

Olt reached over and took her hand. And Ro couldn't say why, but she let him keep it.

The hours stretched on. The sea calmed, rain poured, and choppy waters bounced the ship around, as if in reminder that the sea could do whatever it wanted to the ship.

At some point, Olt shifted and Ro slipped her hand from his.

She hated the steady yet gentle insistence in her heart that said she could trust him. The peace that merely being in his presence brought her. She found herself believing it, no matter how hard she tried to deny it.

Ro started to relax, if only a little. "I'd love to hear one of yours."

Olt yelped and smacked his head on the top bunk. Half a heartbeat passed, and Ro burst into laughter.

Olt's cheeks, a dusky red, lifted into a half-smile even as he rubbed his head. "Hey, now, it wasn't *that* funny. You startled me, is all."

But Ro couldn't stop laughing. It felt so *good* to laugh. She clamped a hand over her mouth, but a snort-giggle escaped anyway.

"I'm so sorry," Ro gasped, trying to stop the onslaught.

Olt grinned. "Don't be. Pretty sure this is the first time I've heard you laugh." A pause. "One of mine?"

When Ro had control of herself, she said, "Stories. You said you've been on other voyages. Tell me about them?"

Ro wiped her eyes and took a deep breath, not even sure why she was still laughing. The release was bliss.

Olt chuckled, the pleasant sound filling Ro with warmth. He told her about his last voyage sailing to the southernmost tip of South Africa, fighting pirates, evading mermaids who wanted to drown the sailors for fun—unlike sirens, who made sailors drown themselves for vengeance—and nearly being marooned thanks to a vast misunderstanding.

One that took a duel, a slap, and three caskets of rum to rectify.

Ro was still snickering over his almost-marriage to a pirate's daughter when he changed subjects.

"What made you become a huntress?"

Ro wasn't so sure about his near-miss marooning story—she'd love to hear the other side—but she easily fell into her tale. About the wolf that had nearly killed Cosette. How she'd found a way to earn livres to feed her family. Though she kept her tone light, her throat burned with every mention of her not-sister's name.

And Olt was uncustomarily silent through it all. His face serious. Hanging on to every word. "Do you miss your sister?"

Ro didn't know what to say to that. He was far too astute. "But of course."

"I am truly sorry, Ro."

Ro looked at him. "For what? You did nothing."

"I am sorry you had to go through that, too. The curse— your father—" She'd never seen him look so serious. "I wish you hadn't."

Ro shrugged, realizing too late he couldn't see the motion. "I'm not. As you said, I wouldn't be here today if I hadn't. France wouldn't be free, and I wouldn't be seeing the world."

A wry grin lit Olt's face. "Or the bottom of the ocean."

Ro grabbed her stomach, the memory—or maybe the current bounce by a rogue wave—making everything lurch. "You saw it too?"

"Aye. In the worst storms, the waves become mountains and pull away from the sand at the bottom. I've only seen it a few times, but it's something I'll never forget."

"Me neither. So another story of yours?"

Olt grinned. "Oh, you're gonna love this."

Ro rolled her eyes, but she couldn't help her smile as Olt plunged into captivating tale after captivating tale of impossible things and far-reaching voyages, nearly making her forget the storm outside.

Now what to do with the storm that raged within her chest.

12

Gradually, consciousness found Ro. Ah, bon. The ship was rocking more than its usual, gentle motion, but nowhere near as terrible as last night. Ro snuggled deeper into the blankets and the arms that held her.

Her eyes flew wide. Arms that held her?

She peeked down, terrified to do so, and found sturdy, masculine arms holding tightly to her, keeping her steady near the cabin's wall.

She quickly did a check. Fully clothed, solid chest at her back, Olt's mesmerizing scent just strong enough to know exactly who it was. As if she had any doubt in the first place. She bit her lip to keep from groaning and tried to figure out what to do.

She pulled away a little, trying not to move too much. She didn't want to wake him, for heaven's sake! What would he say? What would he tell others? Panic built. What if someone found them like this? They would surely think the worst.

She was thinking the worst.

Just when Ro was ready to scream, his breathing changed, and she slammed her eyes shut, holding perfectly still. He moaned and stretched a little, then snuggled deeper into the blankets with her, sending her heart into overdrive.

Then every muscle in his body tightened.

He lifted his arm in a steady, gentle motion, then untangled himself from the blankets. He slipped from the bed and eased onto the floor, his breathing quick.

Ro waited until someone pounded on the door to even pretend to be awake.

She stretched and yawned and sat up. "Who is it?"

Her voice sounded too high-pitched, even to her, and she refused to look at where Olt was sitting on her floor. She could, however, feel his steady gaze like a burn.

"It's the quartermaster and the ship's physician, ma'am. We'll get you out of there soon. Part of the mizzenmast seems to be wedged in front of your door."

Ro stumbled out of bed and over to the door, nearly tripping in front of Olt. Her face burned, but at least the quartermaster couldn't see it. "Can it not be moved?"

"Working on it, ma'am. It's also partially wedged into the captain's quarters. Through the wall."

Ro sighed. "I'll be here."

An oily voice she didn't recognize came next. "Are you hurt, Mademoiselle?"

Ro recoiled and stared at the door. For the life of her, she couldn't place the physician. Had she met him? After a moment, she said, "I am unharmed, Monsieur. Merci."

"Very good," the quartermaster replied. "We'll get you out of there as soon as we can."

"Merci beaucoup." Ro took a deep breath, shook off the crawling feeling the physician left with her, and turned. She was relieved to find Olt was having as much trouble looking at her as she was him. It gave her confidence a boost. "No breakfast for some time yet, I suppose."

Olt nodded and fiddled with the silver buckles on his boots. "I sure hope everyone made it through all right."

"As do I," Ro said quietly. "And the ship. I hope the damage isn't too bad."

He quirked a smile at her then. "Same." Then a full-fledged grin. "It's gonna be something to see the looks on their faces when we both come out, 'tisn't it?"

Ro's stomach plunged harder than it had all night, but she gave him a scowl worthy of the LeFèvre name.

He laughed weakly and held up both hands. "I jest, I jest."

She glanced around the small cabin. No place for him to hide. No way out but the door at her back. The porthole was far too small, though she had half a mind to try to shove him through it anyway.

She sighed and turned away. Well this was magnifique.

Cendre scrambled through the barely pried-open door into the huntress's chamber. She was the only one onboard who fit. Her heart stalled in her chest when she saw Olt sitting on the floor. She gave him a surprised look but didn't comment.

Instead, she held out a bag. "Breakfast."

"Merci, garçon," the huntress said.

Cendre blinked. Boy? Not that she'd forgotten her disguise, but sometimes it amazed even her that it worked so well. "Right. Anyway, it's not the mainmast, so we'll be underway soon, and we have materials onboard for most of the repairs." Her eyes landed on Olt. "Once we get the mast moved, I'll come back for you." Her eyes shifted to Ro. "Then you can come out later."

Her words sounded harsh even to her own ears.

Cendre caught the huntress's frown as she turned without another word and slipped through the slit in the door.

She couldn't get out of there fast enough.

Her heart pounded wildly, and she clasped the bucket held

out to her and ducked belowdecks. She left it in the galley and fled for her safe place.

"Cen!"

She tripped and spun around.

The cook was staring at her, head poking out of the galley. "All hands on deck. You know that."

She changed directions and tried to slip past the burly cook.

"Here."

He shoved a length of coiled rope in her hands, and she ran it back upstairs. She set her jaw. Very well. She'd throw herself into work and not think about any of it. About Olt being in the huntresses' room. About the rumpled bed. The guilty expressions on both of their faces. Their mussed hair.

Cendre bent over the sails and gasped, her hands fumbling to tie the right knots. Why did it hurt so much?

Startling clarity washed over her. The stranger who'd come into her pub with sparkling eyes, ready grin, his full attention on her, had slowly worn down her defenses. He'd talked to her, listened to her, showed her kindness for the first time in her life.

She'd fallen for him, hard, and she hadn't even known it.

Yet she couldn't deny the way he looked at the huntress. Or where she'd just found him. Her heart cracked just a little deeper.

Curses! Why did she have to fall for someone she couldn't have?

Cendre threw herself into cleaning up the deck, repairing the ship, and raising the repaired mizzenmast.

Yet her thoughts remained on the small cabin and the two lovers sequestered therein.

§

They did as the boy had said, only in the opposite order.

When the beam was finally moved just enough, Ro slipped out, shutting the door behind her, and later, when no one was paying attention—she hoped—Olt slipped out and into the midst of on-deck duties.

His quick wink in her direction set her face on fire, but she soundly ignored him. Cheeky bête.

She glanced around, but no one else seemed to notice.

Ro breathed a deep sigh of relief. As long as the cabin boy didn't say anything—would he say anything?—maybe the only person she would have to be humiliated around was Olt. And the boy. And perhaps the captain with his eagle eyes.

Ro groaned and rubbed her forehead. Why, oh why was she forever getting herself into scrapes, and why did this have to be one of them?

"Are you all right, milady?" Captain Montrose asked, right next to her.

Ro yelped and spun around. "Oh! Oui, mon capitaine. I am fine. How are you?" She crossed her arms, then placed her hands on her hips, then swiftly changed to leaning both elbows on the rail at her back. None of it felt natural, but that's the one she stuck with.

It wobbled a little under her weight.

Captain Montrose eyed her, just long enough to make it awkward. For her. "And how did you fare last night?"

Ro flushed bright red, and she popped upright and crossed her arms. "What? Just fine. Who told you? I mean, it's nothing. We—I'm fine." She snapped her mouth closed.

The captain didn't stop eyeing her. "And did Olt find you?"

"Olt? Who said anything about Olt?" *Normal, Ro, act normal.* "Ah, I mean, oui, he did, and I was fine, so that was that." She laughed, a strangled-sounding thing, then swallowed. Hard.

He nodded briskly, once, his eyes already on the bustle around them, not questioning her inept attempt at conversation. Thank Dieu.

Then Ro said without thinking, "Though I was surprised you sent him." She snapped her mouth closed.

He looked faintly annoyed. "At the time, I had no other choice. Now that you're finally out of your cabin, I'm going to have roll called."

Ro barely had a chance to acknowledge his words before he was striding away.

"All hands on deck!"

Once again, Ro was amazed at how quickly everyone responded to the captain's booming voice. Sailors poured out of the hold, carrying supplies they'd been sent to fetch, and everyone working feverishly on the quarterdeck or main deck paused or moved closer to the captain.

"Muster for roll call!" Captain Montrose widened his stance and nodded at the first mate.

As the men pressed in closer or climbed down rigging or up the stairs, the first mate unfurled a scroll and starting listing off names. "Anders. Ezra. Hank. Jamar."

After each name, the man in question called "Here!" or "Aye."

"Olt."

Ro stiffened. She wasn't going to look.

"Here."

Her eyes slid to Olt, who was standing at attention. He towered a good fifteen centimètres or more over her, and she was repeatedly told she was tall for a woman. How tall was he really? She tilted her head.

His eyes skimmed to hers as other names were called, and he winked.

Ro jerked her gaze away.

As the list went on, Ro starting counting. Anything to get her mind off that impossible sailor. While Captain Red's ship could easily hold a crew of three hundred—though Ro was positive she hadn't sailed with near that many—this one seemed maxed out at about fifty. Maybe fifty-two? Fifty-five?

Ro started recounting when an awkward pause fell on her ears. She froze, numbers forgotten.

The first mate cleared his throat and read the name again. "Huntress Ro LeFèvre."

Face aflame, yet again, Ro struggled to speak. On the third try, her "oui" could just barely be heard.

The first mate gave the captain a longsuffering look that once again made Ro feel guilty for taking his chambre, then he snapped the scroll closed and marched away.

"Return to yer duties!" the quartermaster called.

The ship burst into movement.

Captain Montrose stopped next to her, a pleased look on his face. "Not one hand lost. 'Tis a good day."

Ro hoped he could say the same after their encounter with the sirens. She eyed the busy crew. "Is there something I can do to help, mon capitaine?"

He glanced around the deck. "Actually, come with me."

Ro followed him half a beat later, and her gaze pinged away from each person who looked at her. Blast it all, she cared far too much what others thought.

As she passed Olt, the sear of embarrassment came back, hot and swift. She refused to look at him, but she could feel his gaze on her the whole way up the stairs to the captain's quarters.

Ro stopped when the captain walked into his room, past two crewmen who were rebuilding the portion of the wall the mast had smashed through. She hoped they repaired the wobbly rail next.

Ro eased after him, heartbeat pounding wildly. Surely he wouldn't confront her with half a wall and witnesses, would he?

But of course he would. He'd been kind, but he was the captain, and a rather strict one at that. She stepped gingerly into his cabin, glass crunching underfoot.

The captain gestured to the room. "As you can see, my

MICHELE ISRAEL HARPER

cabin is a mess. Unfortunately, I must focus on getting my ship underway before the next storm blindsides us. If you truly wish to help—and please know you are under no obligation to do so—perhaps you can straighten up in here?"

Ro just blinked at him. He hadn't called her in here to reprimand her?

"You don't have to, of course, but I would be more comfortable with you in here than elsewhere. And my men can clean up the glass, and pick up the books if there are too many for you, or anything else dangerous . . ."

Ro barked a laugh, half giddy from relief, half incredulous. "And what then would I do, mon capitaine? This may surprise you, but I did not become a huntress by sitting on my hands and doing nothing. Non, I earned every ridiculous title to my name by working hard and cleaning up messy situations." She raised one eyebrow. "If you consider this difficult, I invite you on a hunt to see what I can really do."

The captain looked like he'd swallowed something distasteful, but he nodded solemnly. "Now that I would like to see."

Ro didn't quite believe him. What kind of women did the captain know, anyway? This was getting beyond ridiculous. "I'm sure you will, soon enough."

He nodded again and looked around the room. If she waited any longer, he'd most likely start cleaning up every shard of glass and leave her with nothing to do.

"Believe me, mon capitaine, I am grateful for the work. And I would like to get started, so if you please . . ." She swept her hand toward the door.

The captain looked startled for half a heartbeat, but then he regained his composure and stepped smartly out the door and past his men. Ro was certain she hadn't imagined the slight smile on his face or the twinkle in his eye.

The moment the door closed behind him, Ro lunged for the broom. Finally! Something to do. She'd never enjoyed cleaning more.

13

$\mathcal{R}$o knocked her forehead against the wooden post of her bunk. For good measure, she thumped her head one more time. She couldn't read one more word. Not one more blasted word.

She tossed one of the legends of the sirens aside. Flying bird women, her foot.

They'd only been a month at sea, and Ro could recall every nuance of the captain's charts, even if he never would tell her what those strange markings were. She'd read every book in his library and hers, multiple times.

And she still wasn't allowed to do anything useful.

Not work for a lady, the captain had said.

Well if she just had to sit here and do nothing for the next few months, she'd go stark-raving mad.

She jumped up and headed to the wheel of the ship, looking for the captain.

"Captain Montrose!"

He turned at her shout, surprise on his face. Warmness crept onto her face. She hadn't meant to screech like a banshee. Someone else took the wheel. His face fell into its normal stoic lines as he moved toward her, his steps swift.

"Yes, milady. All is well?"

She realized with a start that she'd been avoiding him. That insufferable Olt had made her self-conscious around him, and she had no need to be. Wrapped around her finger indeed.

"Forgive me for bothering you, mon capitaine . . ."

His teeth gleamed against his tanned face. "It is never a bother, milady."

Ro paused. Maybe Olt was right . . . she shook off the thought. Non. She wasn't going to think like that. "I need something to do. Anything."

He cocked his head slightly, a hint of obstinacy filtering into his expression. "My charts and books are at your disposal."

"Non, something active, Monsieur. I must stay in shape if I am going to defeat the sirènes."

He waited for her to continue.

"Perhaps I could target practice? Or swab the deck. Or mend sails. I really do not mind—"

"Out of the question. You are a guest on my ship, and you will be treated as such. Swabbing the deck is not for young ladies."

If she had a livre for every time she was told something she did was inappropriate . . .

She tried to bite back a retort, but it escaped anyway. "And neither is hunting, mon capitaine, but that is why I am here. And for me to do my job, the job the *king* hired me for, I must keep up my strength—non, build my strength—by any means possible." She looked around her. "I can set up a target against the rail. Shoot with the wind so I do not endanger your men."

"To say nothing of distracting them."

She shot him a disgruntled look. "Everything I do distracts them. I might as well do something useful." She held up a hand against his protest. "If not for you, then for me."

He thought about it for a minute. "You will waste your arrows."

Ro cocked her head. "Not if they all make it in the target."

His slight grin was back. "Shooting at sea is much different, milady. You must account for the wind and the rise and fall of the ship."

Ro's eyebrows climbed her forehead. "Then I certainly need to start shooting now. How else will I prepare for when it counts most?"

He nodded smartly. "I'll see to it you have everything you need." A pause. "I hope you won't lose many of your arrows."

Ro shrugged. "I won't. But believe me, I brought plenty."

The captain just looked amused as he called for the cabin boy—the one who'd been avoiding her since he'd found Olt in her cabin—and asked him to take her belowdecks to retrieve her weapons.

Ro followed the lad below, and when he unlocked the armory, Ro entered first and headed straight for her weapons. She snatched up a metal pry bar and wedged it under the marked crate's lid, eager to hold her new bow. The top popped off with little effort.

She picked up her recurve bow, loving its slight weight and silky-soft texture. She checked it over carefully, but the light ash wood had been stored well against salty air. She returned it to its crate and reached for several sheaves of arrows.

"Do you truly love killing things so much?"

Ro startled and glanced toward the voice. Oh, the cabin boy. She'd forgotten he was in here with her. "Excusez-moi?"

"Killing things. Do you love it?"

"Oh." Her hand lingered over her bow, and she ran her fingers down the length of wood. "Non, not exactement, but oui, also. I can't explain it."

"Then try." A current of emotion swept through the words.

Ro sighed. Probably someone close to the lad or a favorite pet had been killed needlessly. She looked directly into his eyes and made every word a promise. "I do not take life for the enjoyment of it. Only when it is necessary."

A scowl marred the lad's face. "How can taking life be necessary?"

"Do you not eat? Fowl. Fish. Game?"

The lad's scowl just deepened.

"Right. Not the same in this situation." Ro pulled out several belts and geared up. "How much do you know about what happened to France in the last fifteen years or so?"

The lad shrugged and looked away.

"When the curse fell and food became scarce, wolves overran my country, preying on the weak and the helpless. One attacked my sister. It was the first time I killed anything. I did it to protect her."

When the lad said nothing, she glanced at him.

The lad stood frozen, every muscle in his body rigid, eyes wide. "You—you have a sister?"

Ro frowned and shot him a look. What did that have to do with anything? "Oui. Cosette—my best friend—she's married to the king of France now . . ."

The words soured in her mouth, and she didn't pay much attention when the lad sank onto the nearest barrel, gripping its rim until his fingers turned white.

"You have a sister," the lad whispered. He looked up after both were lost in their thoughts awhile. "And your mère? Your père? They live?"

Ro came out of her trance and looked closer at the lad. "Why do you ask?"

He ducked his head. "Just want to know more about the mighty huntress."

Ro shrugged. Didn't they all. She turned back to her weapons. "My mère died before the curse fell. My père, well, he might as well have. As soon as he lost my mère, he lost himself to drink." Ro's voice quieted. "I miss them both."

The lad hesitated, then said, "I'm sorry."

Ro snapped herself back to the present and started attaching quivers to her belts, dropping two sheaves of arrows in each one. "C'est comme ça. And so I hunt, not to take life, but to protect those I love." She turned, bow in hand. "And now I hunt the sirènes, not to take life, but to protect sons and husbands and fathers and give them a chance to come home."

Though Ro hoped with everything she had it wouldn't come to that.

The lad still didn't look convinced, but he gave a brief jerk of his chin.

Ro nodded toward the door. "Are you helping me set up the target?"

The lad bounded off his barrel and shot out the door. Ro followed, but all she saw was his dirty feet leaving the top few steps as she rounded the corner.

She shook her head and chuckled. She had to admit she liked the lad. She just hoped he understood why she hunted. And didn't hold it against her.

Ro couldn't help but wonder why he cared so much. Maybe one day she would ask him, but for now, her fingers itched to let arrows fly.

Ro growled and pulled another arrow from her quiver. She'd truly brought enough—crates and crates of them—but she hated wasting even one.

Another arrow flew up and over the target only to be lost in the rich blue depths. Ro growled and pulled out another arrow. She let it fly.

This one embedded itself into the deck.

Now the captain let out a growl.

Ro turned toward his voice, heat crawling up her face. "Désolé, mon capitaine."

He grunted and jerked his chin to the cabin boy, who rushed over, removed the arrow, and smoothed the puckered wood the best he could.

"Milady, if I may?"

Ro handed off the bow and an arrow, face burning. She was a huntress. This is what she did for a living. What she was good at. It was absolutely humiliating to fail with an audience.

Maybe that was the problem.

"Brace your feet. Bend your knees slightly. Don't hold them so stiffly. Yes, like that. Allow your body to move with the rocking of the ship. That's it. Don't fight it. There you are. And when the timing is right . . ." He aimed, held it steady, his body moving as one with the ship.

The arrow flew, embedding itself just off-center of the bullseye.

"You will know."

He handed her the bow, and Ro took it, certain her face was as red as the setting sun. At least he hadn't put his arms around her and treated her as an enfant, learning for the first time.

Ro softened her stance, matching the cadence of the ship. She'd been staggering around the boat for weeks now, still not used to the sudden, jerky movements made by the rough seas or a rogue wave.

Hurricane season was brutal.

She mimicked the captain, reaching out, learning the waves. Not fighting them. Reminding herself it had been over fifteen years since she'd been on a vessel, and she'd never hunted on one before.

There was nothing wrong with learning something new.

She took a deep breath, let it out—and let the arrow fly.

It hit the rim of the target, safe from the sea this time. And keeping Ro safe from the captain, as long as she didn't put any more holes in his ship.

The captain nodded. "Very good. Now . . ."

"Cap'ain!"

He turned.

"Ship sighted, sir."

The first mate handed him his spyglass. Captain Montrose took it and was at the ship's starboard side in three swift steps. "Pirates." He spat the word. "Baker, turn about."

Ro's heart jumped into her throat. They weren't her pirates, were they?

She rushed to his side. "May I see?"

The captain wordlessly handed her the spyglass. She lifted it to her eye, and her heart dropped right down to her toes.

Though a mere speck on the horizon, it was a gorgeous, shining galleon, the favored ship of pirates in the Atlantic and Caribbean. Not just any galleon, however. *Her* galleon.

She was sure of it.

The quartermaster came alongside the captain as the rest of the ship jumped to follow his commands. It was the first time she'd seen such a smile on his grisly face. "We going after them, sir?"

"Aye. We can't let that plague continue upon our seas."

Ro stepped closer. "Won't that delay our voyage, Captain Montrose?"

He was already moving toward the wheel, and Ro dogged his steps, dodging sailors running every which way.

"Not enough to cause any concern, milady. I suggest you sequester yourself in your room. The fighting may get —rough."

He kindly didn't mention her lackluster archery skills. Which were just fine on land, she likewise did not point out.

Panic clogged her throat. "I don't care the slightest about that, mon capitaine. What I care about is delaying my job."

"They be fleeing like the rats they are, Cap'ain!" the quartermaster called with a shout, sword raised.

The captain grinned, the gesture carefree, rash—an inner light making his eyes sparkle. "Turn about! Give chase!"

Apparently Ro wasn't the only one who enjoyed the hunt. "You mean, go back the way we came?" Did she sound as panicked as she felt?

"It won't be enough of a delay for you to even notice. Now, your quarters?" He moved to take the wheel.

Ro stepped in front of him, blocking his path. Even though she was considered tall by most standards, she barely came to his chin. It didn't stop her from adopting a commanding, wide stance.

"I'm afraid I must insist, mon capitaine. I have been hired by your king to do a job, and to do it right away. A delay of days or even hours may cost even more lives. I can't allow that." He tried to sidestep her, but she matched him step for step. "They are, after all, fleeing like rats, as your quarter-master so delicately put it, n'est-ce pas?"

He stared at her, his look not exactly cold, but not warm and welcoming either. "Let's make one thing clear, milady. You may be in the employ of my king, but on my ship, out on the open seas, my word is law. Quarters. Now."

His tone bordered on hostile.

"Unacceptable." Ro stepped closer, hating herself for the way her heart trembled, yet with every ounce of her being, she needed him to stay away from that ship. "Shall I have to explain to the king that more died because of you?"

He paused halfway through another sidestep.

Ro lowered her voice. "Captain, I beg of you. I do not wish to engage an enemy on open seas if I do not have to. Repairs, wounded men, resources used or gone—mon Dieu, even the ship sinking if things go terribly wrong. The storms have been bad enough."

Ro swallowed hard when she noticed he was listening.

"You're a good man. A king's man. Of course you must eradicate pirates. But I beg of you, get me to the Caribbean as quickly as you can, without loss of time, life, or precious resources. Before the next storm hits. Please."

He studied her for too long as the ship started to swing in a wide arc.

"Please. We've wasted enough time as it is."

She jumped half a kilomètre when his voice boomed right in her face. "Return to your course! Leave off pursuit!"

Ro jumped again when his hand clamped down on her arm.

"I'll not have you question me again, huntress," he said in a low voice of steel. "You may be under the king's command, but here, at sea, you'll do as I say."

"Oui, mon capitaine. Of course, mon capitaine. Merci, mon capitaine."

She didn't know why his sudden hostility unnerved her, but it did. Completely, utterly, unnerved her.

He leaned closer, and Ro fought not to shrink back. "I suggest you retire to your chambers for the remainder of the evening, milady."

Ro started to protest, but his icy stare stopped her cold. Ro nodded, too quickly. "But of course."

He released her. He waited half a second before jerking his chin toward the cabins. "Then go."

Ro fled. Berating herself as she did so.

Ro paced, hating herself for being so weak in front of the captain. Hated that once again, she was sequestered in her cabin while bustling life danced right outside her door. Hated that her ship had almost been discovered.

Thankfully, they continued on their course, pirates abandoned if not forgotten.

She took another small lap, brushing her fingertips on the rough canvas of her hammock with every pass.

Why had his sudden hostility unnerved her so? Was it because she considered him a friend, had thought she'd earned his trust, only to lose it?

She batted the hammock away and stumbled a little as the rough boards beneath her feet bounced unsteadily. She paused. Had the water gotten rougher?

And then the word she'd been hoping never to hear again this entire voyage made its way through her door, the call distinct and clear.

"Storm!"

Ro groaned. Not again.

She walked over and barred the door to ensure Olt wouldn't get in this time.

14

The water was rough for so many days after that storm, Ro was more than concerned she'd be sick. But she needn't have worried. Her stomach, apparently, was like steel.

Something she was unaccountably grateful for as she had the pleasure of watching several of the sailors heave their guts over the edge. Thankfully it wasn't her, Olt, or the boy.

Once the water was calm enough, she got out her arrows and target once more, thankful for this haven in the midst of the ship.

Ro flung arrow after arrow at the painted target, each *thwack* matching the stabbing worry in her gut. Her ship had almost been discovered. They'd almost fought her hired crew. And she had no idea how she would've explained that.

Her mind latched on to another subject: the captain.

Of all the bête, ridiculous things in the entire world. Her, scared of the captain! She'd faced down larger, more commanding men than he without batting an eye. She must be losing her touch.

Another arrow flew.

"Um, Ro? Huntress?"

Ro tried to find a calm that wasn't there. When she was almost certain she wouldn't snap his head off, she turned to the cabin boy. "Oui?"

He shifted and looked at his feet as he mumbled something.

Ro closed her eyes and sighed. "Pardon?"

He looked up. "Can you teach me? To shoot?"

Ro wanted to bark out a harsh, "Non! Leave me alone!" but the boy had nothing to do with her problems, and teaching him might distract her from them.

"D'accord."

"D'accord? You mean all right? Yes?"

"Oui. Yes."

The boy whooped and jumped up and down, fist in the air. A smile found its way to Ro's face. Maybe this wouldn't be too terrible after all.

More than a few hours later, Ro was rather pleased with herself. Teaching the lad had been therapeutic. She'd not once worried about the pirate ship. Or her troubles with the captain.

And with the focus off her, she was able to relax, get used to the feel of her new bow, and hit the target most every time.

The boy had a sharp eye, she'd give him that. And he handled the toss of the sea like a pro, something Ro envied. Ro found herself liking him more and more as time passed. He still reminded her of someone, though she couldn't say whom.

"Lad! Be about yer duties."

The lad scurried away as the sailor who'd assaulted Ro before came close. Ro squared off with him, still wary, yet nearly certain he wouldn't attempt anything in the middle of the day, on deck where everyone could see.

He leered at her. "Giving lessons, are we? Got any more to give?"

Ro couldn't help her wide smile. "Oh, plenty, but I'm not sure you'd like them."

A round of laughter let her know their conversation was being listened to—and enjoyed—by others. She cast a quick glance at the men slowly gathering. A little of her tension filtered away as Olt made his way toward them.

At least she'd have one person on her side. Especially since she didn't know where she stood with the captain. Bitterness filled her belly.

The antagonistic sailor came closer, his putrid breath upsetting everything she'd eaten for the past few days. He leaned close. "Maybe I should be the judge of that."

Ro raised her fists and squared off with him. "Gladly."

She grinned, and for a second, the man looked startled. Ro was more than ready for a fight, a way to exorcise her frustration. He would regret baiting her, or her name wasn't Rosette Jacqueline Reynard.

His grin morphed into a sneer. "You think you can take me? You're nothing but a no-good fake, one the good king wouldn't even give his best ship or his best crew to." He looked her up and down. "I've seen you shoot arrows; I bet you can't even fight."

Ro sucked in a breath and jerked back, his words like a slap, then started to swing.

Her fist froze. As did the entire ship around her.

Images presented themselves to her in rapid succession.

In a flash, she saw the man come at her, past her guard, and punch her in the face, breaking a tooth. It was enough to throw her off. He pummeled her. Olt jumped into the fray, but men swarmed him, the captain only stepping in once Olt had been beaten senseless. Then the three of them were in the brig, murder in the sailor's eyes, directed at her and Olt. A knife jammed into Olt's ribs as soon as they were alone.

All possibilities, all real, all her future, if she didn't take the situation in hand. If she didn't change something. Ro's temper fled, cold fear taking its place.

Time hiccuped, and the man was leering at her all over again, her fists where they were before she started to swing.

The sailor was still running his mouth. "The king should've

tossed ya in the tower, not sent ya across the sea to get us all drowned."

Panic swelled. She hadn't seen time slow, reveal its secrets to her, and then reverse itself in so long, she just reacted.

In a move so sudden he didn't see it coming, Ro dropped her shoulder and plowed into him. She caught him off guard as she drove him back, and his legs tangled in a coil of rope.

With a swift lift from her center, she sent him up and over the railing. A mighty splash sounded far below.

Ro's mouth popped open. She hadn't meant to do that. Not exactly.

One of the sailors next to her shouted, "Man overboard!" A fair amount of panic ran through his voice.

The shout was quickly echoed. "Hoist the sails! Turn about! Man overboard!"

Ro couldn't believe how swiftly they left the man behind. She hadn't realized how fast they were moving.

But then a rope trailed in the water, and a billow of waves spoke to something dragging under the surface.

The ship burst to life, men scurrying every which way, as the ship slowly lumbered in a wide arc to head back the way they'd come.

The captain burst from his quarters. "Update!"

"Man overboard, Cap'ain."

He shouted a plethora of orders before asking, "Which one?"

"Hank, sir."

He let loose a string of curse words Ro could honestly say she'd never heard before. And she'd heard quite a few in her line of work.

The ship made its lazy arc, and men stood at every part of the ship, looking for Hank.

The first mate spoke to the captain in a low voice. "You know we ain't going to find him."

The captain's only was response was a tighter jaw.

"There! There he be, Cap'ain! He's dragging behind the ship!"

Captain Montrose dashed to the sailor's side and extended his spyglass. "Pull him aboard!"

The men scurried to obey. The ship had barely turned off its course in all this time.

Ro leaned toward Olt, who was standing next to her, tying off a line as he helped secure the mainsail. "The ship can turn on a hair, can it?"

Olt's neck went a dusky red. "Well, faster'n most ships, it can."

Ro just rolled her eyes.

Once the man was safely onboard, an eternity later as far as Ro was concerned, the captain marched with angry steps toward him. "Explain what happened. Now."

Hank's watery eyes found Ro's, and her heart sank. Would she ever learn to control her temper? And—she'd prevented something worse, hadn't she?

"Nothin', Cap'ain."

Ro blinked. What?

Hank's words were echoed by everyone else the captain turned to.

"I see." Captain Montrose marched back and forth, hands folded behind his back. "Would anyone on this bloody ship care to divulge why I leave the bridge for two seconds, one of my men ends up in the water—with a black eye, no less—and I find you all lying through your teeth about what happened?"

Not one person replied. Ro was clenching her jaw so tight, she thought she might crack a tooth. Someone was going to blame her any second now, she just knew it. A brig stay could still be a thing.

"Honest, Cap'ain, 'twas nothing. I just slipped." His eye was starting to swell shut.

The captain came up to Hank and stared him down, eye to eye. "Slipped. You."

Hank stared straight ahead, standing at attention. "Aye, Cap'ain."

"I see. Perhaps you need to be reminded of how dangerous it is to be unsure of your footing at sea. Inspect the rigging. By your lonesome. The lot of you sorry landlubbers get us back on course." He turned to Olt and the cabin boy. "And you two. Swab the decks."

The boy groaned, and the captain's eyes snapped to him.

"And you swab the lower deck. By yourself."

The lad's lips went white. "Yes, sir." The words were so soft and strangled sounding, Ro barely heard them.

Ro almost felt sorry for him. Almost. She was a bit too concerned with what was going to happen to her.

"And the rest of you—back on course!"

Captain Montrose marched away, not even calling for her to follow, and Hank's eyes swung toward her. They promised retribution, murder—everything unpleasant—and Ro forced herself not to squirm.

When the captain found out what had really happened, what would he do to her?

And worse, what was Hank planning?

As he passed her, he dropped a few words for her ears only. "Ye may've tried to murder me, huntress, but I don't go easy."

Ro's eyes widened. Murder him?

He chuckled at her startled look. "What else do ye think happens to those lost at sea?"

Ro's heart dropped to her toes. That wasn't what she'd meant to do at all—just teach him a lesson.

Hank turned away, and she caught Olt staring at the lad with sharp eyes, brows lowered. Ro glanced at the boy. His lips were turning blue. She did a double take, but he darted belowdecks, not even bothering to grab a bucket of pitch.

Ro's eyes met Olt's, and at his nod, she followed the cabin boy belowdecks. He moved swiftly, his steps light and sure, and Ro struggled to keep up.

The lad went to a part of the storeroom they weren't allowed to go in, and then he was gone. Ro frowned. What in the realms?

She moved on silent feet all around the storeroom, trying to figure out where he could've gone. A slight wheeze caught her ear. She froze. Again. A struggle for breath.

Ro eased toward the sound, then passed it. She came back. There. But where was it coming from? Ro got down on her knees, looked all around, then got up and peeked over stored goods and barrels of who knew what.

The ship wasn't as loaded down as her père's cargo ships had been, since this one needed to move light and fast, but there were still plenty of hiding places in a room this full of stored goods.

She heard another gasping noise, and it nearly broke her heart. Was the lad—was he dying?

Ro started moving crates, rolling barrels out of the way, taking care to be quiet. A barrel bumped the back wall. She froze. A strangled gasp, then nothing.

She cursed under her breath. Stealth was no longer an option—he needed help right away. "Garçon? Where are you?"

Nothing. Then the tiniest wheeze. Was he even breathing?

"Look, you're not in trouble. I can help."

A footstep behind her. She spun, and Olt held a finger to his lips. Ro breathed a sigh of relief. He spread his hands in a "where is he?" motion, and Ro shrugged. "I have no idea," she mouthed.

Again that gasp, that struggle for life-giving oxygen. Olt's wide eyes met hers, and they both started moving barrels and crates.

"Here he is! Cen, are you all right?"

Ro blinked as she realized she'd never even asked the boy's name.

Olt dragged Cen's slim frame from a crevice Ro had passed

without seeing. Twice. *Way to fail me, magical eyesight*, Ro grumbled to herself.

Cen's face was tinged with blue, and the little wheezing noises he made broke Ro's heart.

"Quick, lay him here," Ro said needlessly, because Olt was doing exactly that.

Olt covered the lad's mouth with his, slowly forcing air into his lungs. Something Ro hadn't seen before. Olt's eyes widened, and he jerked back. Cen's head flopped to the side.

Ro jumped toward Cen and cradled him. "What are you doing? Here—" She stared down at the lad, eyes wide. "Oh. Oh! He's a—he's a . . . girl."

"Yeah," Olt said miserably.

Ro's eyes shot to his. "You knew?"

"I suspected."

"How?"

"She reminded me of my sister."

Ro jerked back, her eyes wide. "You have a sister?"

His eyes took on that teasing glint. "Can't sailors have sisters, huntress?"

"Well, of course, they can. I just never thought—" She looked down at the boy—er, girl. "We need to help him. Her."

Olt's stormy eyes met hers. "Him. For her sake, she is always a him. Always."

Ro nodded, and Olt went back to forcing air past her blue lips.

❧

It was some time before Cen began breathing on his—her—own. Covered in sweat, shaking, and leaning weakly against Olt, her eyes found Olt's.

"Thank you," she barely managed to get out.

He nodded solemnly.

Her gaze shifted to Ro. "Are you . . . are you . . . going to tell anyone?"

It was painful how long it took her to get the words out.

Olt gave her a gentle shake. "Rest now, talk later."

Cen nodded wearily and closed her eyes, her gentle breathing soon filling the space around them.

Ro's eyes stayed on the girl. "Have you ever seen anything like it?"

Olt nodded. "Once. My, uh, a childhood friend had fits similar to this, only it never got so bad." He looked genuinely worried.

"What did they do to help him?"

"Her." Olt shook his head. "Keeping her calm was important. They also warmed water and had her breathe in the steam, then they'd bundle her in warm clothes and take her outside to breathe cold air, if the time of the year was right."

"What was it?"

Olt shook his head. "I have no idea."

"Did it worsen over time? Get better?"

Olt stretched out his legs. "Actually, it went away with age. As I said, it never got this bad." His voice quieted as he stared down at Cen, her slight weight against his shoulder. "I was so scared she wouldn't take another breath."

"Me too." Ro kept her voice low. "Do you recognize her?"

Olt studied the girl's face. "Now that you mention it, I think so. I think she was a barmaid at a tavern that has the best eel pies in the city."

Ro's heart dropped, and she rubbed her forehead. "But of course." No wonder she kept thinking the lad looked so familiar. It had nothing to do with similarities to her older sister.

"Do you know her?" Olt asked.

Ro peeked at his openly curious face. "I—she—perhaps. I think I had the pleasure of ordering an eel pie there." Just not the pleasure of tasting it.

Olt accepted her answer, his attention back on the girl. Cendre. Who was supposed to be on the other ship.

"What are we going to do?" Ro whispered, trying not to wake the exhausted girl.

"We're going to keep her safe," Olt said fiercely.

"I agree," Ro was quick to add. "But how?"

He looked down at the girl slumped against his side. "I have no idea. Especially if she has another breathing fit."

Ro nodded. "I don't like the idea of her sleeping in the bunks with all the men. If they were to find out . . ."

Olt visibly paled.

Ro shrugged. "We could tell the captain. I could let her stay in my room."

"The penalty for stowaways is death, huntress. You would be doing her no favors."

Ro's brows lowered. "She's part of the crew. She's not a stowaway."

Olt's expression didn't budge. "She lied. She's female. Pretended to be a male. They will not hesitate to throw her overboard for her crime. Or lock her in the brig and do who knows what to her while she awaits trial in England."

"Why, that's just . . . that's just ridiculous!" Cendre stirred, so Ro dropped her voice. "Are you certain? You'd rather risk rape than the captain's good graces?"

"Ro, you don't understand."

"Then help me understand."

"She. Will. Die." She'd never seen him look so stubborn. "I've seen it before. If no one knows she's a girl, she won't risk ravishment or death. Her disguise is good—one of the best I've seen. Leave her be."

Ro slowly nodded, and his fierce expression eased.

They sat in silence for some time.

Ro finally broke it. "Do you think they'll miss us? You were supposed to swab the decks. And Cendr—Cen—the lower deck."

Olt looked like he didn't want to leave. "You'll be gentle with her, won't you? Things had to be pretty bad at home for her to run away like this."

Ro eyed him. "Why, I think there's a soft heart under that crusty exterior, sailor."

"Crusty?" Olt sniffed under his arm. "I'll have you know I bathed last week, huntress."

Ro wrinkled her nose and then smirked. "Softy."

With a smile, he transferred the girl's weight to Ro's shoulder. He paused at the door. "Roll a barrel in front of the door until she wakes up?"

Ro looked from the girl starting to drool on her shoulder to a barrel to Olt. He chuckled and moved back into the room, dragging two barrels as close as he could to the door.

"What will you tell them when they cannot find her?" she asked.

Those sparkling brown and gold-speckled eyes sent her heart zinging in ways she wasn't exactly thrilled about. She squashed the elation and tried to focus on what he was saying.

He winked, shattering her resolve not to let him affect her. "I'll think of something."

Then he slipped out, reached in, and pulled one of the barrels as close as he could to the door.

As his footsteps receded, she said softly, "I have no doubt you will."

Some time later, as the room was growing dim and Ro was starting to worry about needing a lantern, the girl stirred. Ro moved slightly, easing the pressure on her tailbone and right leg. Pain shot through her leg, the unfeeling limb waking with a vengeance. She couldn't help her groan.

Cendre shot straight up and gasped.

Ro raised her hands in a placating manner. "Easy, Cen. It's

just me."

Panic dilated the girl's eyes, turning them almost black. She grasped at her open collar, opening and shutting her mouth like a fish on dry land.

"Do you—did I—have you—?" the girl sputtered.

Ro offered a gentle smile. "If you're asking if I know your secret, then oui, I'm afraid I do."

The girl gave another little gasp, and the sound sent panic galloping through Ro.

"Easy, Cen. Steady breaths. I don't want you to go through another episode." Ro shuddered. "It was terrifying."

"Olt . . ." the girl said weakly.

"Said your secret was safe with him as well."

Her pale face took on a greenish tinge, giving her even more of a sickly glow. "Is anyone looking for me?"

Ro glanced toward the closed door and the barrel not exactly close enough to bar entrance, but hopefully close enough to alert them in time to hide. "Olt said he would stall them, but we've been down here for quite some time." She grinned. "Perhaps they'll believe I've been in my room, and you, getting ready to swab the lower deck?"

The girl didn't respond, just starting adjusting her rumpled clothing.

"What's your name? Your full name, I mean," Ro asked gently, trying to ease the truth from her.

The girl paused for so long, Ro thought she wasn't going to answer.

"Cendre," she finally said.

"Ah. The girl from the tavern? The one Captain Red recommended?"

The girl just scowled, but she didn't have to respond for Ro to see the confirmation in her eyes. She looked so different as a boy!

"And what are you doing on this ship, Cendre, instead of the one you're supposed to be on?"

15

*C*endre froze, then slowly met the huntresses' gaze. She was smiling in a way she probably thought was kind, but it felt more condescending than anything. Cendre gave her a moment more, but the huntress still didn't recognize her.

Not as anything more than the tavern maid the huntress had so easily dismissed.

Ro continued that inane smile, like she was talking to an imbecile. "Did you want to see the sirènes? Go on a grand adventure, perhaps? Without being indebted to Madame LaChance?" When Cendre didn't answer, Ro continued. "You do realize you would've been safer on the other ship, don't you?"

The last question was too much. Her own sister didn't recognize her! Cendre no longer had any doubts, not after scrutinizing the huntress for over a month and gathering any information the huntress let slip. Yet questions still plagued her.

Questions she daren't ask the confident huntress before her. She'd think Cendre mad. She had no proof.

Yet how could this knowledge be burning in Cendre's soul

and not a spark of it light the huntress's? Surely something deep down recognized they had a connection.

But, no. Nothing. The huntress just smiled at her blithely, unaware that Cendre's whole world revolved around her. That Ro was the key to finding the rest of her family.

And she couldn't even tell her.

Cendre snapped on her jacket and tousled the shorn blonde strands stuck flat to one side of her head. "Look, I appreciate your help. I'm not sure I would've survived this one without whatever you and Olt did." Her voice still sounded feeble, so she tried to strengthen it. "But you haven't the right to any of those answers."

She stood to leave, but the huntress reached up and caught her arm. Cendre spun around, and the huntresses' eyes went wide, just as they had in the tavern. She let go as though burned, a strange light in her eyes.

Cendre immediately wanted to hide, and the huntress blinked like she couldn't remember what she'd begun to think.

Ro shook her head. "I beg to differ, Cen. You see, I'm now responsible for you. If anything happens to you—"

"Responsible for me?" Cendre stepped back, fire lighting up her insides. "What, because you feel sorry for me? Because you think I can't take care of myself?" She spun and marched toward the door. "Don't bother. I've been taking care of myself for as long as I can remember."

Ro stumbled to her feet and hobbled after her, grabbing Cendre's arm before she reached the door. "Arrête! I'm not trying to tell you what to do. I'm not trying to mother you or boss you or whatever you think I'm doing."

Cendre snorted and crossed her arms, dislodging Ro's hand. Some of her fire seemed to leap into the huntress's eyes.

"But Olt said the penalty for what you've done is death. Instant death, at sea, no trial."

Some of Cen's fire died out, and the huntress pounced on what she saw.

"I can beg for the captain's mercy, move you to my chambers—"

Elation and horror warred within Cendre. She'd learn everything she wanted to know!

"Or as Olt said, since the captain is not the merciful sort, we keep up this charade, and Olt and I take turns watching your back."

Cold fear stirred in Cen's belly. He was the last one she wanted noticing who she was. The thought stilled her. Panic threatened to claw its way out of where she'd stuffed it. What if he thought she was on this voyage because of him? Heat gave way to lightheadedness. What if he wasn't as kind as he'd appeared, and now that he knew . . .

"Hey, where'd you go?"

Cendre slapped the hand Ro waved in front of her face. "I don't need you, and I don't need Olt looking out for me."

She hauled one barrel away from the door and reached for the other.

"And if you have another episode?"

Cendre peeked over her shoulder at the woman who shattered her heart every time she looked at her. How could she not recognize her own sister? Didn't something deep inside say, "I know who you are," just as it did for her?

The huntress leaned against the barrel, then reached down and rubbed her leg. "I don't want to tell you what to do, truly, but, well, I have a little sister. About your age. If she were in your situation . . ."

She looked down and cleared her throat. Her voice came out husky.

"If she were in your situation, I would give anything for someone to look out for her. To keep her safe." She spoke over Cendre's objection. "To give her aid, should she need any. We're stronger together. That's all."

Cendre faced her fully, hoping the last sparks from the setting sun would illuminate what she wanted the huntress to see. Fear of discovery still trembled inside, however, left over from hiding from her grandmère for so long. When the huntress didn't react, Cendre shoved the second barrel aside.

"Merci, but non. I don't want your help, and I don't want to hear another word about this." She turned right before she stepped into the hallway. "And I swear to Dieu, should you disclose my secret, should you cost me my life or my position here, I will take you down with me."

Cendre stomped away, her heart breaking with every footfall, which only made her angrier.

When she returned to her little cabin in the woods one day —if she ever returned—she was going to ask her grandmère what right she had to keep her sister from her.

And her from her sister.

Ro immediately went looking for Olt. He was busy swabbing the deck with some nasty-smelling substance, and Ro took to moving the bucket for him—after glancing around for the captain, of course.

She tilted her head. "Did you already swab the lower deck?"

"Of course. Did you talk to Cen?"

It was amazing how he could speak while barely moving his mouth. Ro relocated the bucket before answering.

"I did. She"—Olt shot her a stern look, and Ro startled —"*he* doesn't want our help."

"I figured as much."

"But . . . what should we do?"

He shrugged. "Not much we can do except respect his wishes."

"But, but—" Ro spluttered.

Olt chuckled and spread more of the nasty-smelling goo

over a new section of deck. "You're used to getting your way, aren't you?"

Ro scowled. "That's beside the point. Not helping—him—is unacceptable."

Olt moved on, and Ro moved the bucket automatically, without checking. "I thought you might say that."

"Then what should we do?" Ro persisted.

"We can't—"

"And what's the meaning of this? Where's the cabin boy?"

Ro froze, smelly bucket in hand. Olt plucked it from her fingers and set it far out of her reach. Captain Montrose stood over them both, chest heaving, scowl black, fists clenched. Ro wouldn't have been surprised had fire spewed out of his mouth at any second.

Olt spoke quickly. "I believe he just finished below and will join me shortly." He scanned the quarterdeck. "Ah, there he is."

The three glanced to where Cen was busily swabbing her side of the deck.

"And why is the huntress helping you when I expressly forbid it?"

"It's my fault, sir. She was concerned speaking to me would keep me from my duties, and I didn't move the bucket as I should've."

Ro glanced at Olt and snorted. "As if." Her gaze sought the captain's. "I'm feeling utterly useless, Captain. I'm used to hard work; it's all I do elsewhere. Give me something to do, please."

His eyes blazed a warning. One Ro didn't heed.

"Perhaps now would be a good time to outfit the ship, begin training the men—"

The captain leaned forward, annunciating every word. "Let me be clear, huntress. On my ship, my orders are absolute. Should you disobey them again . . ."

His voice trailed off, and Ro squirmed a little, uncomfortable with the silent tongue lashing she was getting. The silence stretched on for eons.

"Well, then, I leave it up to you. A flogging or time in the brig."

Ro gasped. "You wouldn't!"

He nodded solemnly. "I would. My word is law, and it's past time you discovered that."

Ro gritted her teeth. "Noted."

He nodded and walked away.

Ro watched him go, fists clenched, eyes spitting fire.

Olt, who began busily swabbing the deck the moment the captain departed, whispered, "Huntress, you may want to wipe that glare off your face. You know, look less like you want to kill him?"

Now Ro glared at Olt.

He just grinned. "That's better."

The next morning, Ro's temper had considerably calmed. She still didn't know what to do about Cen, but Olt was right. What could she do? Nothing. Not as long as the girl kept her secret and Ro was stuck on this ship.

And now she was avoiding the captain on purpose. When would he allow her to do her blasted job? She'd wait a few days and ask again. Insufferable man.

Ro came up alongside Olt and propped her hands on the rail, in full view of the captain in case he cared to look. Stopping for brief moments to chat with Olt had become a daily routine. And, if she were being completely honest, the moments weren't all that brief.

"So tell me what you know of the sirènes. Why doesn't plugging one's ears work?"

Olt, who looked beyond exhausted, perked up. "I don't know—something to do with the vibrations they make. As in, not sound exactly, but it moves through the water like ripples. I only felt it once, and even though we were far away, it was hard to ignore. I felt it more than heard it. Thankfully, the lookout saw the ripples coming, and the first mate, a tenacious old soul, wouldn't let us veer off course."

"What did it feel like? The sirènes' waves."

Olt stared out over the water. "It's hard to explain. It was like an instinct. I *needed* to go toward that sound. And it was hard to resist because it wasn't a conscious thought. More like a habit that overtakes your steps without your realizing it."

Ro let that soak in. "But it's different with those who are close?"

"Absolutely." Olt took out a length of rope and started tying and retying various knots, his shoulders sagging. "Then it becomes more of an obsession, a compulsion that cannot be denied, and sailors will kill each other to get to the sirens. They'll run a ship straight into a barricade of rocks, drown themselves, do anything the sirens ask. The crew will go absolutely, utterly insane and take the ship down right along with them."

A shudder snaked through Ro, and Olt bumped her shoulder with his.

"Hey, now, none of that. That's why you're here."

Ro couldn't help her incredulous look. "And you honestly think I can do anything against full crew? There are fifty-something of you and one of me. What if we get too close? What if the crew feel the vibrations? What if the crew are sirened? What if there's nothing I can do!"

"Huntress . . ."

Ro dropped her head, clutching the rail, and groaned. "I feel so helpless. And this is why I insisted on a crew of women."

Olt made a slight noise, one of surprise. "Did you really?"

She gave him a scathing look. "But of course I did. I don't want anyone else to die, I don't want innocent blood on my hands, and I don't want my mission to fail simply because some man who happened to be born king decided women can't do anything but give birth and make food to fill his fat belly."

Olt choked on a laugh and dropped his voice. "Uh, you may not want to say such things. This is a loyal king's crew, after all."

She eyed him. "I have nothing to worry about from you, do I?"

Olt gave her a tight smile. "Listen, just . . . don't say that on this ship, all right? I don't know what your king's like, but this one likes to hang people for treason."

Ro rubbed her neck without realizing she'd done so.

"Exactly. So though I'd never say anything, it's quite possible I'd join you if someone reported us both. And neither of us wants that."

Ro threw her hands in the air. "What is wrong with the world? You cannot even say what you think?"

"Sure you can." Olt winked at her, and her stomach did a funny little flip. "Just make it kind and above reproach, and you'll have nothing to worry about."

Ro gave him a deadpan look. "Have you even met me?"

Olt startled a little, then burst into laughter.

"It wasn't *that* funny," Ro grumbled when the laugh stretched on and on . . . and on.

"Ro," Olt gasped out mid-laugh. "You are amazing, you know that?"

And Ro's world went completely still. No one had ever said that to her. Not ever. And she didn't know what to do with it.

So she shrugged it off. "Not really."

"No, really. You are. I never know what you're going to say, and whatever it is, I'm so pleased I listened. I can honestly say I've never met anyone like you."

Come home with me and you can meet five other grumpy sisters just like me, she didn't say aloud. Thinking of her sisters made her think of Cosette, and she was staying far away from that particular subject. Besides, she'd never take a man home in a million years. Not to her family.

"What? What is it?"

Ro glanced up. "Pardon?"

"You looked really sad just then." He leaned forward and stared straight into her eyes, as if her eyes would give him answers all on their own.

Ro wasn't thrilled with the invasion of personal space, but she didn't move. She wasn't about to retreat or show discomfort. If she could help it.

She tried to gentle her words, but they came out harsh anyway. "It's really none of your concern, crewman."

He flinched, just a little, and regret swelled inside. But she'd never been more thankful when he backed off.

She changed the subject, desperate to get away from her harsh words. "You said you're not afraid to die. Why?"

He hesitated a moment but answered anyway. "Because when I breathe my last, I'll see my parents again. My—the rest of my family. And the Creator, of course."

"Oh." Ro blinked. She hadn't expected him to say something so . . . personal.

Sure, Mère had made them all go to mass when she was still alive, but Ro hadn't thought of that time in an age. And his family . . . should she ask? She wasn't sure.

And . . . one day . . . would she meet her little sister, her true sister? Her eyes widened. She would see Mère again! Aching hope stirred in her chest, but she pushed it down. She couldn't think about it now. Not in front of Olt.

Later, when she was alone.

So she turned the conversation back to things she was comfortable discussing. "Have you heard other stories of ships that crashed? Because of the sirènes?"

"Aye, I have."

Ro folded her hands atop the rail and ducked her head. "Tell them to me?" She peeked at him when he didn't respond.

"S'il vous plait? I keep reading these ridiculous legends, and I haven't gotten a straight answer from anyone else I've asked."

He took a deep breath. "If you're sure . . ."

"I need to know."

"As you wish." He studied the waves for far too long before he spoke. "The stories have been grossly understated to keep panic from spreading. To keep sailors from refusing to sail the open sea."

Cold crept through Ro's veins.

"It hasn't been just a few ships; it has been hundreds of ships. And not just in the area we're sailing to." The words seemed to rattle calm, even-keel Olt. "Trade between the American colonies and Europe has halted. Ships can't get past what they're calling the Ring of Death. Ships are being destroyed off the coast of Africa, in the northern seas, even as far away as the Orient. More and more, captains are refusing to sail."

"What?" The word struggled past Ro's lips. "But . . . how can that be? Why have I not heard more about this?"

Olt's smile was sad. "Most rulers keep it under wraps. They don't want all trade halted. And France is not yet a viable trading partner. How could you have known?"

"Oh." Ro didn't realize she was wringing the rail until he covered her hands with his and stilled her frantic motions. Ro didn't move away.

"If anyone can stop this madness, it's you."

Her eyes met his, desperately. "How can you know that?"

He shrugged, breaking some of the tension with a gentle smile. "Because of what you said. Because you do not plan to kill them. Because you'll try for peace before you resort to killing."

Ro sagged. "How do you know it's going to work?"

He grinned, the movement lighting up his whole face. "Because it was what you did with the beast, and it's what you'll do with the sirens. It's not in you to kill without reason."

Ro had no idea what to say to that. How did he know exactly how to comfort her? "Thank you for that, Olt."

His smile was delicious to behold. "Of course," he said simply.

Ro turned away, every fiber of her being aware of the man standing next to her. They both stared out over the water, neither saying a word, the tension between them so thick and just . . . *there*.

"Well." He pushed off from the railing. "I should get below and get some shut-eye."

Ro blinked. "Sleep? But it's the start of your shift."

She flushed hotly when Olt looked far too pleased that she knew that.

He shoved his hands in his pockets. "Ah, there's been a bit of a change."

Ro's eyes narrowed. "He didn't make you work all night, too, did he?"

That's when Ro noticed how tired he looked, the bags under his eyes, and the swaying that was a bit more than the rocking ship called for.

"What better way for me not to distract the mighty huntress?"

She clenched her fists. "Just wait till I talk —"

"Don't," Olt cut in. "It'll just make it worse."

Ro floundered. She felt so . . . helpless. And she hated feeling that way. She thought about her harsh words when Olt had been nothing but kind.

"Olt . . . look, I'm sorry . . ."

"No hard feelings, promise. Your secrets are your own, and none of my business."

"I didn't mean —"

"You don't have to tell me anything you're not comfortable with. And you're welcome to talk to me, no matter how tired I look. I'd still like to get to know you, even if my shift has changed."

Ro tilted her head. Even though he was only working all night because of her?

Olt grinned, and Ro enjoyed it far too much. "I mean it. See you around."

And with a friendly wave, he walked off whistling, hands in his pockets. Ro watched him go, absolutely fascinated. The loping stride of his gait. How masculine and carefree he was. The way he never held anything against her, even when he should.

He disappeared belowdecks.

She might just be the slightest bit taken with him.

She wished with all her heart she wasn't.

16

A few days later, Ro uncurled one of the captain's charts. Based on her calculations, they had to be at least halfway there, depending on how far off course the storms had driven them. She started to let the map curl, then slapped the page open.

That couldn't be.

She studied the parchment, searching for what was different. It was the same map she'd seen many times before, yet something had changed.

She traced the continents. All there. All the same. Next the rivers and waterways and oceans. Still as they should be.

So what bothered her?

She traced the mysterious dots that lined the Americas' east coasts, from the tip of the northernmost continent to the southernmost tip. Her finger deviated from its path halfway down.

She froze. The dots had shifted. But . . . how? A few additional peaks in the middle of the ocean had been added, several erased. Ro's brow lowered. What in all the realms?

It wasn't the penciled-in sections the captain changed at will to adjust their route; it was changed on the inked base map. Something that shouldn't have been possible.

Clearly the captain had changed it, but how had he known to do so? No one had come aboard to deliver updates of new discoveries or shifting landscapes.

And even then, an intense surveying process usually came before changing the maps the charts were based on. Then an even longer process of distributing them and convincing folks to replace their well-loved maps.

She'd seen it all firsthand when her père had been a merchant, his life ruled by such things.

Captain Montrose entered his chambers. He startled. "I beg your pardon, milady." He started to back out.

Ro waved him in. "Not at all, Monsieur. Please, can you look at something for me?"

He warily approached the desk, and Ro felt the loss of their friendship as a short, stabbing pain. She lightened her voice, tried to act as before.

"These lines—here, here, and here—have you redrawn them?"

He flicked what could barely be considered a glance at the curled paper and didn't answer.

"See?" She traced the path her finger had taken on its own earlier. "It used to go this way. And this mark used to be here, not here." She looked up at him.

He avoided her gaze by looking at the map. "I see the same markings as before, milady. Perhaps you imagined it."

And without another word, he left.

Ro watched him go with her mouth parted. What in all the realms? If he thought he could make her think she imagined it, he would be most surprised.

She marched off to find Olt and Cen. *They* would believe her.

❦

As dusk settled around the ship like a comfortable blanket, Ro paced the cargo room, waiting for Olt and Cen.

This spot had become their own, perfect for clandestine meetings at the start of Olt's shift and the end of Cen's. And the creaky stairs gave plenty of warning if someone were coming so they could hide or escape without detection.

She liked having a spot to chat with Olt away from the captain's scrutiny.

And Ro's mind got stuck on the fact that the spot was theirs. For goodness' sake! It wasn't *theirs* theirs; it was Cendre's too. All of theirs.

She needed to get ahold of her thoughts before they carried her away to places she had no business going.

"Ro?"

Ro jumped and spun around. "Cen! You scared me."

Cen's grin was so carefree, something in Ro's chest eased. Cen often looked like she was trying to hide from everyone and everything—like she didn't want to be noticed, like she was trying to disappear. It made sense, but Ro treasured these moments when Cen felt free enough to be herself.

"Expecting someone else?" Cen asked.

Ro refused to answer the teasing barb in that one. She shrugged, pretending oblivion. "Concentrating too hard, I suppose."

Cen cocked her head. "On what?"

"Geez, but you guys are loud."

This time they both jumped, and Cen yelped a little. At least, Ro sincerely hoped Cen was the only one who'd yelped.

Olt burst into laughter. "You're both too much fun to scare."

Ro immediately went into glare mode, thanks to constant teasing from her brothers. "You could at least warn us. What good will our hiding spot be if you make us scream every time we come down here?"

He grinned and brushed past her, heading for the barrels they liked to sprawl on while they chatted.

Ro tracked his easy gait, distracted from why she'd come down here in the first place.

It was absolutely ridiculous how a simple grin from Olt could send her stomach fluttering or his walking by her could make her hyper-aware of his every move. The moment he appeared, she felt it like fire.

She was hopeless. If only Cosette could see her now.

The thought soured everything, and she jerked away from it. She'd have to deal with it at some point, but that moment was not now.

Ack! She'd spent so much time ogling him—to which he'd sent her a sly grin, as if he *knew*—she'd missed what he'd said to her.

Ro crossed her arms. "What was that?"

"I said," Olt repeated, "it's the shift change. No one'll hear us with all that racket on deck."

Ro pretended disdain. "Those sound like famous last words, Monsieur."

Olt laughed, and Cen watched them both with wide eyes, looking like she didn't know what to do. Not with Olt's teasing, not with Ro's saucy retorts, none of it.

Must not have any siblings.

Ro tried to rein in Olt's mirth. For Cen's sake. Not because she was enjoying his teasing far too much.

Olt noticed her exaggerated glance at Cen. He flicked back a swatch of hair that had fallen out of its queue and leaned against the bulkhead. "What did you want to talk to us about?"

Ro hopped up on a barrel and told them about the shifting map.

⁊⁊

Cen sat on a barrel, swinging her legs, as Olt and Ro bantered. It was amazing how at ease they were with each other.

How focused they were on each other.

Ro was currently complaining about the captain's dismissal of her. "I mean, really! Telling me I imagined it."

"Well, did you?" Olt asked affably. "Imagine it?"

Ro shot him a glare.

He laughed and held up his hands. "I retract the question."

Ro sniffed. "As you should."

Cen shifted, uncomfortable with their constant teasing. "I for one want to know what those markings are."

"Yeah," chimed in Olt. "Although . . ." He rubbed his chin and the scruff there. "You said they were along the coasts of the Americas?"

Ro nodded.

"Huh. That does seem to match some of the stories about the Ring of Death."

"Ring of Death?" Ro's back went ramrod straight. "What do you mean?"

Olt seemed lost in thought. "I'm not really sure . . ."

Ro huffed out a breath. "Fine. Be mysterious. It's not like I've had enough of that on this voyage."

Olt looked startled, then laughed. "Ro, I didn't mean—"

Cen interrupted. "Why's it called the Ring of Death?"

Olt looked grateful for the interruption, and he shot Cen a wink. "It's where all the ships are crashing. Well, mostly." His attention was back on Ro. "You say there are random peaks in the middle of the ocean as well?"

Ro nodded. "But only a few." She squinted at him. "That doesn't explain why they're moving."

"Perhaps they're moving because the sirens can move them. At whim. I mean, think of it." Olt looked like he couldn't quite believe what he was saying himself. "The siren attacks all have one thing in common: ships crashing on rocks. All of them. The rocks must be linked to the sirens somehow. And the map must somehow reflect that."

Ro rubbed her forehead. "Mon Dieu, protect us all."

"Exactly," Olt echoed. Then his eyes started to twinkle. "Think you can sneak one out so we can see it? Maybe something will shift while we're watching."

Ro's glare at Olt deepened. "What, and make the captain even more suspicious of me? I don't think so. Merely talking to you is enough of a threat."

Olt's smile dimmed a little. "Hey, sorry about that."

Ro shook her head, her frown easing. "Don't be. It's not your fault."

"Anyway," Cen interrupted, looking between the two of them, her irritation growing. "You should make another map."

They both looked at her.

Cen couldn't believe they hadn't thought of it already. "Then if the markings move again, you'll know for sure."

Ro smacked her forehead. "Of course! Why didn't I think of that?"

Olt grinned. "Because you were too busy thinking of ways to throw the captain overboard without anyone noticing?"

Ro gave him a mock glare. "Don't tempt me."

Cen spoke up quickly. Anything to make her sailor stop looking at her sister like that. "Also, it's clearly enchanted. You could always enchant your copy."

Now Cen held their rapt attention. She had trouble looking away from Olt.

Ro frowned. "First of all, I didn't know such a thing was possible. Second, how am I supposed to enchant a map?"

Cen shrugged. "It's in the ink. Look for purple ink that glows slightly. It's possible to mistake the glow for little flecks of mica, but if you put it in a dark place, you'll be able to tell the difference. If the captain deals in enchanted maps, he'll have some."

Grandmère had drawn a few of those herself, and Cen had helped.

"Whoa," Olt breathed out, his look of admiration doing funny things to Cen's stomach. Thank goodness she couldn't flush and pronounce her feelings to the world.

"Brilliant!" Ro jumped up and hugged her. Even though the huntress pulled back quickly and looked uncomfortable, her smile didn't waver. "Leave it to you to know about enchanted maps."

The unexpected hug had startled her so much, Cen couldn't even react.

Ro headed for the door.

"Hey, where're you going?" asked Olt.

"I'm going for my evening constitutional so I can be seen by the captain, then to get a good night's sleep, then I'm going to sequester myself in my room all day tomorrow and draw myself a map." She grinned at Cendre. "Perhaps use enchanted ink, if I can find it."

Olt chuckled. "Don't get caught."

Ro turned just enough to toss a wink his way. "Do I ever?"

"I don't know. Do you?" Even though the words were teasing, a touch of red heightened Olt's features.

Ro grinned. "Never."

Then she was gone.

Olt smiled to himself, staring after the huntress a moment before turning a friendly smile on Cen. He winked and wordlessly left the storage room.

And Cen's heart ached harder than ever.

Leave it to her to want something that was no longer available.

17

*R*o had no luck finding anything but ordinary brown ink. The charts hadn't changed again, and several weeks had passed without Ro working up the courage to ask the captain if she could outfit his ship.

Surely he was done being miffed at her. Surely she could find the courage to ask him.

But it hadn't happened yet.

Ro found herself looking for Olt and sighed. Would she never stop being so fascinated by him?

The lanterns were already lit, and a few stars graced the sky deepening to an indigo blue. She paced the main deck until the sky was too dark to see any color at all.

Ro hated to admit it, but she missed her daily chats with Olt. The few times she and Cen had caught him before his shift had become more and more infrequent as the captain worked him harder and longer than the rest of the crew.

And still Olt wouldn't let Ro say anything on his behalf. Not that it would do any good.

Anymore he was so tired, though he was far too polite to say anything, she could tell he longed for his hammock whenever he was upright. It made her feel guilty.

Just one more thing she'd messed up for somebody else.

"Thinking about me, huntress?"

Ro yelped and spun around, stopping herself from punching him at the last possible second. "Don't *do* that, Olt."

He just chuckled, staying just out of the glow of the closest lantern, eyeing the fist she dropped with a raised brow. "What are you doing up at this hour, anyway?"

"I, uh, well, I was just—thinking."

"Thinking. In the middle of the night."

Ro pretended great offense. "I do my best thinking at night, I'll have you know. Besides, it's cooler out here. And not as busy." She pointed to her room. "I'm usually wide awake in there at this hour, so I just decided to be wide awake out here instead."

She was *not* roaming the decks hoping to see him, no matter how it might seem.

Olt crossed his arms, his eyes twinkling in the vestiges of lantern light. "Is that so?"

Behind Olt, a man pale as death, with stringy, dark hair, came out of the forecastle and more oozed than walked toward the stern, slinking in and out of shadow. It may have been Ro's imagination, but the light set every few paces seemed to shy away from him.

Before Olt could say anything more, Ro gasped and used Olt's body to shield her. She couldn't say what instinct drove her to do it; she only knew she wanted to hide. "Who is that man?"

And how on earth had she never seen him before? It wasn't like this ship was all that enormous.

Olt glanced to where she was staring. The well-dressed gentleman in a suit that matched the shadows was joined by the captain, next to the three rooms under the ship's wheel. Where she was supposed to be sleeping right now. The man didn't look like he quite . . . fit in . . . with the rough-looking crew. Stringy hair aside.

Olt kept his eyes on the man as he and Ro instinctively backed away a few steps, where lantern light didn't reach. He said with a strained voice, "The ship's physician, I'm afraid. He only comes out at night."

"You don't like him."

Olt's smile lacked its usual brightness. "You are astute, huntress. Very astute."

Ro swallowed. "Care to share why you dislike the poor fellow so?" Though Ro wholeheartedly agreed.

Olt gave her a cheeky grin. "You're cute when you attempt English sayings."

He kept talking before Ro could transform her glare into a rant.

"The physician and I have a—history—shall we say?" He touched a finger to her lips to forestall any questions. "You have your secrets, and I have mine. All I know is he is not to be trusted. Not ever. With anything."

Ro's eyebrows climbed higher, and her face flamed as she tried not to think of how she'd almost kissed his finger out of pure reflex. What was *wrong* with her? "You? Not trust someone? Now I'm intrigued." Her eyes returned to the new passenger. "Why have I not seen him aboard before now?"

Olt shrugged. "He likes to stay in his infirmary, take strolls at night." He pinned Ro with the most serious expression she'd ever seen on his face. "Cen is not to go to him, do you understand? Not ever."

Ro couldn't think of a blasted thing to say to that. "Uh . . ."

"Just promise me, please? No matter what, you will not take Cen to him."

Ro's head spun as she wondered what could possibly make Olt hate the man so. "Even if sh—he is dying?"

Olt's stern expression didn't budge. "Even then. It would be better if Cen were dead than placed in his hands. Chances are, one means the other."

A chill washed over Ro. "You have my word."

Olt sagged, his breath leaving him a whoosh. "Merci, Ro. You have no idea how much that means to me."

Ro wanted to ask a thousand—no—a million questions, but she held them back. "De rien. You're welcome."

His grin was rather weak. "I suppose I should get back to my tasks before we're seen."

"I suppose you should." Ro couldn't smile back.

Olt left without another word, and Ro turned to the physician, not wanting the creature out of her sight.

At that moment, he shifted, and their eyes met. A bucket of ice-cold water splashed directly in her face couldn't have been more startling.

She stepped back, bumping into the rail, unable to break their gaze, wanting to separate herself from the crawling sensation his look left all over her skin. How had he seen her in the darkness?

He nodded at her—she never knew if she nodded back—then he shook the captain's hand and made his way to the forecastle via the other side of the ship. Her eyes tracked him, unable to look away, until he disappeared into the single cabin there. The infirmary, if Ro had to guess.

And she couldn't explain why she'd never ventured there, why it was never pointed out to her on either of her tours, why she'd shied away from it when she explored—why she'd never even noticed that room in the months she'd been on this ship.

As if it were veiled from her.

Who was he really, and what was he doing here?

The next day, Ro stood near the railing, watching the crew bustle around her and wishing for the thousandth time she could join in. Maybe she could just . . .

Her gaze wandered the captain's way. His eyes homed in

on her at the same time. Drat. She jerked her gaze away. It was as if he knew she was itching to disobey him. She daren't.

This particular captain had an available brig and wasn't afraid to use it.

Everything was mapped out in her head, to the best of her ability. Every siren lore read multiple times. Every siren legend wrung from each sailor willing to tell it.

Most weren't willing to speak of the creatures on the open sea, but it was more than she'd learned in London.

There was nothing left to plan.

Months of being forced to do nothing. And nearly a whole month to go. How had all the people who'd crossed the great sea before her borne it?

"Huntress?"

Ro yelped and jumped a kilomètre, spinning on the captain and grabbing her chest. "Oh, it's you!"

Captain Montrose looked slightly concerned. "Yes, it's me. Can I get you anything? Ale, perhaps?"

Ro eyed him suspiciously. He was talking to her now?

She sighed. "I'd rather have fresh water and fruit, if I'm being honest." She'd grown quite attached to such things after the curse in France had ended.

The captain smiled, though it was strained and each word was spoken as if to a small child. "Unfortunately, ale is the only way we can keep water fresh, and the last of our fruit has been eaten or molded."

Didn't Ro know it.

"But I can see what our cook has?"

Ro held up a hand. "Merci, but I can wait until dîner."

Ro jumped as the captain lightly touched her arm. "Is there anything else . . . ?"

"You know there is." Ro spread her hands in a helpless gesture. "Give me something to do! I'm going stark-raving mad, not being able to do more than look at fish."

"You could always help in the galley, you know."

Ro snorted. "If you want your food burnt to a crisp."

Captain Montrose looked mildly surprised, but Ro just shook her head.

"I'm serious, mon capitaine. I am not interested in working in any kitchen. I'd just as soon set fire to the place as be able to cook anything decent."

It was why she purchased her meals whenever possible. And why Cosette never let her near their kitchen while growing up.

The captain looked perplexed, as though he'd never heard of a woman who didn't like to cook. The whole idea rankled. "The men are used to doing their own mending, but a few have asked if you'd be willing to take on the task. I of course told them not to bother the great huntress, who surely had plenty of her own mending to attend to . . ."

Ro glanced down at her clothing. Just what was he implying? Most of her clothes were new!

"But if you'd truly like something to do . . ." He raised a brow.

Ro just scowled at him.

"Only a suggestion, Mademoiselle."

The scowl didn't leave her face. "I hire out my own mending when possible. Believe you me, your men would find their clothing in the ocean out of sheer frustration. I need something active, s'il vous plaît."

His smile was somewhat brittle. "Fair enough." He looked as though he didn't want to ask. "What hard labor would you be open to?"

Ro couldn't keep the light from her eyes. "I could swab a deck. Hoist and unfurl sails. Repair rigging. Practice navigating the ship, like you showed me. Or even better, I can start outfitting the ship and training the crew. Anything, mon capitaine. Show me what you need done, and I'll do it. That is all I ask."

One of his eyebrows went up. "*All* you ask? My girl, I run

a tight working ship. Everyone knows their place or has been on a ship before. I am not about to have someone untrained underfoot, getting in my men's way, not on such a small ship."

He held up a hand to cut off her protest, which may or may not have included a tirade on the smallness of their ship.

"Or in my way. Nor am I putting the great and mighty huntress in harm's way when the king personally asked me to ensure your safety while aboard my vessel."

Ro closed her eyes and counted to ten. Why had he bothered her, then?

"I apologize. I got distracted from why I came over here in the first place. Might I suggest . . ." Captain Montrose paused and rubbed his beard, as if thinking over his words.

Ro's eyes went wide as hope flared to life in her chest. She leaned forward a little, eager to hear what he had to say.

"Once, before passage across the great sea became . . . difficult . . . I had the pleasure of escorting a great orator and scientist for His Majesty."

Ro raised a brow. And that had to do with her because . . . ?

"He conducted experiments while onboard, and he also practiced his speeches in his cabin and . . . wrote."

Ro blinked. Wrote? A flood of pleasant memories swamped her of the one tale she'd penned, followed by embarrassment that Cosette now had it to laugh at at will. Why hadn't she burned the thing? Why had she felt the need to write a tale of a beast and his beauty?

"I believe I still have the parchment Mr. Seawell left. If you'd like, I can have it sent to your room and several pens trimmed for your use?"

Ro crossed her arms, intrigued in spite of herself. "What of outfitting your ship? Surely you want it done before we cross the sirènes."

He shook his head, looking weary. "It is not yet time, huntress. I have seen the heavy harpoons you wish to bolt to the rails of my ship. It will slow our journey, and I would wait until we are nearly there."

Ro blinked. And if the sirens attacked well before then?

"In the meantime, would you care to . . . write?"

Ro stared at him a moment before excitement filled her. "Oui, s'il vous plaît. That is . . . acceptable."

The captain nodded once. "Very well. I will have it done right away."

"Merci beaucoup, mon capitaine."

"It is my pleasure."

Once he'd turned away, Ro couldn't help her grin. Maybe she wouldn't go mad after all.

18

*R*o didn't know if it was her mood, Trêve's abdication to her sister's affections, or just the mounting frustration of not being allowed to do a blasted thing, but what she intended to be a sweet romantic tale, much like the one she'd written before, turned to tragedy.

A young mermaid—sirens were on her mind, after all—longed for the world above, something her sisters and grand-mère couldn't speak well enough of. It started out sweet and innocent, something Ro very much needed, as she imagined what it would be like to see the above world for the first time.

Then it changed.

Ro felt the change coming, but she didn't stop it. Couldn't stop writing.

The little mermaid fell in love. With someone she couldn't have. Someone from the above world. A prince.

Ro's pen froze midair. Why were they always princes? Why not sailors or tradesmen or huntsmen? She rubbed the quill's feathery tip on her chin as she thought. Probably because the idea of being poor or committing hard labor for the rest of one's life didn't make for a good fairy tale. She shrugged and went back to her story.

The mermaid saved his life, though he thought it was the human girl who found him on the beach. He then went back to his world, and the little mermaid went back to hers.

But her heart remained above the waves with her prince.

A bargain with a sea witch later, and the little mermaid gave up her lovely singing voice for a pair of legs and went to live in the prince's castle.

But he didn't love her. He loved the girl who'd saved him. The one with the lovely singing voice. The one who'd nursed him back to health. The one he couldn't find.

He thought they were one and the same.

The little mermaid could do nothing but cry pearls in silence. Nothing she did won the prince's affections. His heart belonged to another. Or so he thought.

The king arranged his marriage with a princess of a neighboring kingdom, and although both he and the little mermaid despaired, he couldn't go against the king's wishes.

When he met his bride-to-be, he found the girl who'd nursed him back to health, the girl he thought had saved him, and they fell deeply and irrevocably in love.

The little mermaid despaired further, because her bargain with the sea witch deemed that if the prince did not fall in love with her, on the eve of his wedding, she would turn to sea foam.

Desperate, her sisters sold their hair to the sea witch, who gave them a dagger and said the prince and his bride must be killed in order for the little mermaid to return to the sea.

But as she stood over them on their wedding night, dagger poised above their sleeping chests, she thought of her friendship with the prince, the kindness his bride had shown her, and their happiness at having found each other.

She couldn't do it. She couldn't kill them, even to save her own life.

Tears dripped onto the page, but Ro's quill flew faster, smearing ink in her haste. With each swirled letter, she released her grip slowly, surely on what she thought she'd had with Trêve, her sister's prince. He'd never been meant for her, and she's known that from the beginning. She'd just convinced herself otherwise.

So the little mermaid kissed her prince's forehead, wished many years of happiness and blessings on them both, and dropped the dagger into the sea.

And turned into sea foam.

But just as nothingness enveloped her, air sprites lifted her spirit from the waves and told her since she'd sacrificed her life for another . . .

A knock on the door made Ro yelp and throw the inkwell she'd just picked up.

"Huntress? Are you all right?"

Ro stared at the door, stared at the ink splatter on the wall, stared at her ink-spattered hands, and wondered what day it was.

"Huntress?"

She squinted at the door, the beginnings of a headache starting to pound. "Oui?"

"Can you open the door, Ro?"

Her eyes widened. Olt! "Un moment, s'il vous plaît!"

She started grabbing papers, looking for places to stow them, blowing on the few still wet to dry them quicker. Where was the shaker thing that dried the ink right away?

And for the love of Dieu, what day was it?

She moved several empty plates and stilled. When had those gotten there?

Although Olt didn't say another word, she could feel him waiting patiently on the other side of her door, and the pressure of making him wait mounted.

She blew harder on the ink. Oh, blast it all!

Ro took the dried sheets and stuffed them into her satchel, hoping they were in order. The others, spread all over her bed, desk, and now chair, she just couldn't put away yet. Drat.

She opened the door and barreled through, shutting it behind her. Olt took a step back when she almost ran into him.

"Oui?" she asked, far too breathlessly. She squinted around at the changing light. Was the sun rising? Or setting? And how many days had passed since she'd last been outside her chambre?

She rubbed her bleary eyes and looked up at Olt.

He took in her hair, his eyes strayed to the side of her face, then he glanced down to her fingers.

Drat, drat, drat. His eyes were twinkling again. But why?

"Huntress, I don't quite know how to say this, but . . . well . . . have you looked in a mirror lately?"

She just stared at him blankly.

His lips twitched. "Cause you might want to."

She scowled. "Is that why you interrupted me? To tell me to look in a mirror?"

Again, those twitching lips. Could he not be serious for half a heartbeat?

"Non, Mademoiselle. The captain wanted me to check on you since you haven't been out of your room for a few days. He may or may not have been worried." A grin broke free.

She smoothed back her hair, and it occurred to her it was rather fuzzier than normal.

"Oh, ah, I'm fine. Just fine. But now that you mention it, I am rather hungry."

She moved to go past him.

He put out a hand, stopping her. "Huntress, really. A mirror." He nodded to the room behind her.

Ro glared up at him. "Just say it already."

Olt trailed his hand down her arm, his face turning serious. He swallowed. The look on Olt's face burned past her haze, it was so intense.

Ro was too tired to attempt tact. "What?"

"You've got some ink"—he reached forward slowly, the tip

of his finger resting on her cheek—"there"—her nose—"there"—brushing her lip—"and there."

Her lips parted, and she sucked in a breath. What in all the realms?

He was staring at her lips. Panic clanged a warning signal in her brain, but she couldn't move. She needed to move!

As if he couldn't help it, he brushed her lip a second time, a mere graze, but it set off a fire in her belly that burned hot and swift.

She reached for him.

Cen popped up between them. "Cap'ain's looking for you, Olt."

Ro jerked back. Olt made a frustrated sound, his mesmerizing eyes not leaving Ro's face, and slowly backed away.

Ro sincerely hoped he hadn't noticed her reaching for him—Dieu, she hoped Cen hadn't noticed!

His gaze held hers until he rounded the corner, then Ro darted inside and shut the door, completely forgetting about Cen.

She slid down the door, face buried in her hands. The one thing she'd sworn she'd never do—chase a man, pursue romance, trust someone with her heart—and she'd almost thrown herself into Olt's arms from a mere brush of skin.

And he looked like he was quite willing to let that happen.

Had she learned nothing from her time with the beast?

Ro groaned and struggled to her feet. She checked pages, putting a few more away, then tore through everything in her room, looking for that blasted drying shaker.

She passed the mirror and did a double take. Oh merciful heavens. She went out looking like *that*?

She grabbed a brush and attacked her shoulder-length dark hair. Then she rubbed smudged ink off her cheek, lips, and nose and tried to ignore the purple splotches under her bloodshot eyes. She looked down at her hands.

Spattered with ink, fingernails stained.

She dropped her head, stopping herself at the last moment from rubbing her face. What on earth did Olt think of her, looking like a cinder girl streaked with ink instead of ash? Almost kissing him? Oh merciful heavens.

And more importantly, she was starving.

Her eyes drifted to her story. All she wanted was to get back to it. Give it a proper finish instead of the delirious one she'd just penned.

Soon, she promised herself. *Soon*.

First she needed a pitcher of water to wash with. She grabbed the stack of plates someone had apparently delivered and she'd apparently emptied and headed toward the galley. She didn't care if it was breakfast or dinner—she'd eat it.

Cen wedged herself into her not-so-secret hiding place and cried until she couldn't speak. Couldn't breathe. Past that, even. And she didn't care.

The huntress was her sister, for pity's sake. She should be happy for her. For Olt.

But she just couldn't make herself feel that way.

She'd fallen for Olt, hard, and she'd give anything for him to look at her like she was his entire world. Like he wanted to kiss her into oblivion and then past that. The way he looked at Ro.

The more she cried, the softer her cries became. As if her voice was drying up.

Cen's head drooped, and she cried until unconsciousness claimed her.

19

a bout a week later, Ro sat on a barrel next to Cen, both in a ring of sailors on the main deck, eating, laughing, and chatting as twilight descended upon them.

Ro found if she told a quick story, such as the time she'd run off a ghoul from an inn in Brittany—the particular story that had won them seats tonight—then didn't say much after that, the sailors didn't care if she joined them.

Of course, Cen never said anything, but that was normal.

After a while, Ro noticed Cen wasn't laughing. In fact, and it was somewhat hard to tell with the setting sun behind her, but she looked rather pale and shaky.

Ro leaned close. "Cen. Cendre, are you all right?"

The girl didn't answer, just stared vacantly at nothing, her gaze unfocused, a line of sweat at her brow.

She dropped her voice. "Cen, you don't look so good."

Ro glanced around frantically, but Olt was nowhere to be seen. Of course not. He wouldn't be on deck for a few hours more.

Her eyes rested on the physician, who was watching them closely, something he'd been doing more and more often lately.

She hated it. Right now, though, he was deep within the shadows until the sun went away completely.

She needed to get Cen out of there before he came over to investigate.

She let off a laugh she hoped didn't sound too strained. "That's enough rum for you, young sir. Seriously, you're letting him drink that?"

A round of laughter met her words, and one sailor called out, "It'll put some hair on his chest, won't it?"

Ro just laughed again, hoping it didn't sound as false to them as it did to her, and helped Cen stand.

"Look at that! The huntress is taking Cen to bed!"

Ro's face flamed at the laughter that followed.

"I'm drunk too, huntress. Can you take me to bed?"

The heckling continued while Ro waved off the words and guided a sagging Cen away, wanting her out of sight before she turned blue. No way could she keep the physician away from Cen then, sun or no sun. She sped up.

"May I be of assistance?"

Ro's head shot up, and she came face-to-face with the physician, who was far closer than she would've liked. An undercurrent that trembled far below the register of his words set Ro on edge. She edged into the light, shielding Cen as much as possible.

The physician regarded her with cool eyes as he stayed within shadows.

Ro regarded him closely as well. Composed, smooth voice, dapper air—he should be roaming the Opéras of Paris, dressed in a coat and tails and holding a flute of champagne—though he really should use less of the greasy hair pomade, especially if he wasn't going to powder it like a proper gentleman.

Yet Ro couldn't help thinking of a snake. An asp, to be exact. What was he doing on this ship?

Ro realized she was still staring and jumped a little. "Ah, non, merci. I mean, no, thank you."

She needed to get past him to the stairs leading belowdecks. Before Cen started wheezing or gasping.

He regarded Cen far too discerningly, but he stepped aside to let them pass.

Ro hurried Cen belowdecks, summoning Olt with her mind, urging him to find them before the physician did.

If only that would work.

Ro nodded at the cook, who stepped out of the galley to see who was coming his way. She rolled her eyes and made a drinking motion as he looked over Cen. He gave an understanding grin and went back into his sanctuary.

Ro hurried on by.

She turned down the next flight of narrow stairs instead of taking the girl into the men's sleeping area lined with bunks and hammocks.

Footsteps clambered above her head, and she pulled Cen into the little room behind the staircase. It was cramped, but Olt had found it and suggested they use it instead of the storage area. He'd said it was safer than risking getting caught out in the open, especially during Cen's episodes.

Ro rubbed Cendre's back and took deep breaths for her, wishing with all her heart there was more she could do.

Ro cracked open the door as a line of sweat slid down the middle of her back. She fanned her face. So, so gross. At least the storage room had a slight breeze from the portholes when they were open.

Hours passed with no word from Olt. And it took even longer for Cen to wake.

Ro trudged up to the lower deck once she'd seen the now-breathing Cen safely to her hammock. The girl was out cold, and the snoozing men were none the wiser.

She squinted at the horizon and the light that was making itself known by degrees. Olt's shift would be over soon.

"You looked exhausted."

Ro was too tired to shoot him a glare, but she tried.

Olt chuckled. "Long night? Working on those papers of yours?"

This time she managed a glare, though her heart hitched and then sped up. That was the *last* thing she wanted him thinking about.

Olt held up his hands. "I didn't look at them, I swear. I just happened to see you working on them that day you were covered in ink."

Ro's face flamed at the memory.

Olt shoved his hands in his pockets. "So what has you so tired today, ma chérie?"

Ro gave him a mild look. She certainly was not his darling. She wasn't anyone's darling. But she had to admire his persistence in always talking to her when she couldn't string two words together.

"Cen," she said simply.

Every muscle in his body tightened—far too much of a distraction for her tired mind—and his eyes searched her face. "Again? Is he all right?"

Ro nodded wearily and rubbed a hand down her face. "It took most of the night—I was too scared to leave her to find you—and I fear the physician is suspicious." Ro peered closely at him. "Are you certain it isn't better to tell him? I was afraid so many times Cen might not take another breath."

Olt was already shaking his head.

Ro sighed. "It's getting worse, Olt. So much worse."

He sobered and stared out over the water. His quiet voice came after the silence turned comfortable between them. "I know."

Ro lowered her voice. "He may be able to help her. I mean,

him. I fear—I fear, if something doesn't change, Cen may not last the voyage."

Olt's whole body sagged, and his eyes took on a haunted look as he ran his hand through his hair, over and over. Most distracting. "Ro?"

Ro waited a second. "Oui?"

"Ro, I haven't been completely honest with you."

That woke her up a little. Ro's eyes flashed. Not that she expected any less from most people, but the words coming from Olt especially stung. She braced herself. "Go on."

Again with the frantic hair combing, though this time Ro found it decidedly less attractive. "Cen, well, he's, he's . . ."

Ro kept from throttling him. Just barely. *Just say it already!* Her voice was tight, controlled. "I find it best, when telling the truth, to just say it."

He met her eyes. "He's wanted," Olt blurted, voice low.

Ro jolted, the words almost a physical slap. "What?" she hissed.

Olt glanced around, dropping his voice to ensure their conversation was their own. Ro wasn't worried. The wind picked up their words and tossed them overboard—away from the ship.

"Well, you know, the real Cen is."

Ro couldn't wrap her mind around it. "How long have you known?"

He now took to tugging on the ends of his hair, long enough to curl around his collar. "I saw the notice as we were loading the ship. Guards were patrolling the docks, searching ships, but not one of them glanced twice at Cen."

Ro tilted her head. "Because of, um, how he was dressed?"

At this rate, he wasn't going to have any hair left—he was going to tug it all out. She reached up to stop the frantic motion, certain it would draw undue attention, and he stilled the moment her hand touched his.

He stared at her. Didn't pull away. And Ro found herself

staring back. The longer hair made him even more attractive, if that were possible, and she found herself staring at his lips.

She wanted to taste them.

She jerked away and dropped his hand, her voice turning rough. "They weren't looking at everyone of the same age?"

It took him longer to recover. "I, uh, um, what?" He was still staring at her.

Ro sighed, the sound carrying all the exhaustion she felt. "Cen. Wanted. Why?"

Olt shook himself a little, his boisterous demeanor severely lacking. "Right. No, they were checking the lads too, but they seemed to look right over Cen and move on. I thought it strange."

Ro peered at him. "But you didn't say anything. Why?"

Olt shrugged and scowled, the expression so foreign to his usual laid-back manner, Ro couldn't help but wonder if his carefree demeanor was an act. Then again, she thought that about most people.

"Wasn't my place. Besides, most of the time I wonder if those things are accurate or if someone powerful is using them as a personal vendetta." The words were said with just enough bitterness to make Ro curious.

But Cen was more important. "So you think if the physician discovers who she is, he'll throw her in the brig for the reward."

His scowl turned darker. "Believe me, that would be the least of Cen's worries."

"But how would any of them know about Cen?"

Again, Olt ran a hand through deep-brown, slightly curled locks, being played with and tossed about quite freely by the breeze. Ro was slightly jealous. She'd gladly take over the breeze's job.

But his next words slammed into her.

"Because one of the guards handed her wanted poster to the captain."

20

*E*mergency meeting in the storeroom. Emphasis on *emergency.*

Ro tapped her foot impatiently. Did those words mean nothing? She'd been waiting for hours!

She took to pacing, sat on a sack of grain, sneezed, hoped it wasn't moldy, then went back to pacing.

After another hour came and went, possibly two, silent footsteps revealed themselves to her. It still amazed her how she often heard things no one else could.

She spun around as the door opened and eased closed without a sound. She stomped forward once she'd identified Cen.

"For the love of all the saints, what took you so long?"

Cen eyed her dubiously. "It hasn't been half an hour." Her voice was ragged, half the volume it normally was.

Ro opened her mouth, snapped it closed, then opened it again. "Truly?"

Cen nodded once, not looking thrilled. "Olt said it was too risky to come as well. What do you want?"

The words were said with just enough venom, Ro faltered. "I, uh, it's important . . ."

Cen crossed her arms. "Then tell me. Quickly. I need to get back to my post." Cen's glare was rather frosty. "I find there are quite a few rumors about the two of us after last night."

Ro flushed a little. "Désolé." Then she blurted, "The wanted poster."

Cen raised her chin a notch.

"Did you know of it?"

"I did."

Ro's mouth fell open. "And you didn't tell me?"

Cen's jaw tightened. "Why would I?"

Again, what Ro was planning to say just vanished. Fair point. "Listen, in order to protect you, I need to know the full situation, be given all the information—what?"

Cen's lips were white with rage. "Protect me?" Her voice had gotten even quieter, though she seemed to be trying to raise it. "I don't need you to protect me. You think just because you watched me struggle to breathe once or twice you get to say what I can and can't do? Let me make this clear, huntress: I don't need you."

Cen spun and marched toward the door. Ro beat her to it and stood in front of it.

"Wait! I didn't mean it like that."

Cen growled. "Let me pass."

"Non! I mean, just listen to me, and I will."

Cen shoved her, and Ro stumbled back, more from being caught off guard than from the feeble attempt.

"I don't need you, huntress, and I certainly don't answer to you. For anything."

She tried to open the door, but Ro blocked it. This time, she took a fist to the gut.

Ro *oomphed* and hunched over just a little. It struck her just how tiny Cen's fist was. Her hit, though solid, wasn't very powerful. It felt more like an elbow jab.

"You'd probably get more power out of an elbow jab . . ." Ro mused aloud.

"What?" Cen croaked.

"What?" Ro shook her head. "Nothing. Just tell me why. Why are you wanted?"

Cen's glare shot sparks. "Let me pass, or I'm going to yell at the top of my lungs!"

Ro's eyes widened. Was she serious? Ro's eyes narrowed as she gritted her teeth. "You do, and I'll show you what a real punch feels like."

Cen lost her composure for half a second, and Ro rolled her eyes.

"Oh, calm down. I just want your story. I won't turn you in. And I'm certainly not going to hit you." Not that a yell from her feeble voice would garner much attention. What was with her today?

Cen's fierce look was back, but it was brittle. Crumbling around the edges. "Why should you care?"

Ro leaned against the door and started to rub her face, pulling her hand away when Madame LaChance's "you'll ruin your face" tirade came to mind. "I get that it's none of my business, but so far Olt and I are the only ones who have your back on this ship. If anything happens, God forbid, we'll be able to help you."

Cen vacillated, just a little. "I don't need your help."

"Mon Dieu, will you just let it go? I want to help, not tear you to shreds!"

Cen eyed her, her look still disbelieving. "It was a misunderstanding."

Finally! Ro bit her lip, trying not to hurry the girl along like she wanted to.

Cen sighed. "I didn't know anything about it till the day we left."

Ro tilted her head. Was that why she'd come on this ship and not gone with the others? Maybe she'd run out of time.

"I was thrown out of my last place of employment—the pub you first met me in?" She continued when Ro nodded.

"But apparently that wasn't good enough for Mistress Mabel."

She sighed again at Ro's questioning look.

"The tavern owner, all right? Anyway, a snake-like client of hers accused me of stealing something valuable, and she backed him." Her voice turned even more bitter and raspy. "Probably because I wouldn't let him grope me."

Rage descended over Ro like a cloud. "Tell me who he is."

Cen's eyes searched Ro's face even as she smirked. "What, you think you'll confront him once you get back?"

"Oui. Or worse."

Cen rolled her eyes, and again, a pang of familiarity hit Ro, not strong enough for any lasting consequence.

Cen snorted, the sound barely making it to Ro. "Hardly. Then he'll have you thrown in the tower too."

"I'd like to see him try." Ro tilted her head. "The tower?"

Cen dismissed its importance with a flick of her wrist. "London's most formidable prison. Reserved for the worst crimes." She glanced toward the door.

It was Ro's turn to snort. As if Cen could be capable of that. She was all bluster and no bite.

Cen spun and pierced her with a glare. "Do you doubt me?"

Ro's answer was swift. "Non. I know what it's like to tell a story no one believes."

Cen's posture eased. "Oh."

"Now that wasn't so hard, was it?"

Cen gave her a mild look. "It's not like you can do anything about it. It's your word against his. You weren't there so it wouldn't matter, and if anyone onboard finds out, they'll hold me for questioning and imprisonment back in England." She swallowed. "Or like you said, death at sea."

Ro gave her a grim smile. "Not if I have anything to do with it."

Cen shook her head, but her smile peeked through, and Ro

couldn't help but think Cen looked much lighter than before. "Oh, huntress. Don't you know you can't solve all the world's problems?"

Cen moved past Ro, and this time, Ro didn't stop her. But she spoke anyway.

"Then what's the point of my being here? If I can't make the world a better place. Right the wrongs I find." Ro shrugged, though Cen couldn't see the motion. "I have to try."

Cen paused with her hand on the latch. As in, for so long, Ro almost asked her what was wrong.

"Huntress, it is an honor to know you."

Emotion trembled through the nearly silent words. Then Cen turned the latch and fled.

Ro just shook her head. Now that was something she didn't hear very often.

PART THREE

Oh ! que le jeune prince était beau ! Il a serré la main des
hommes, riant et souriant, tandis que la musique résonnait
dans la belle nuit.
Il était tard, mais la petite sirène ne pouvait pas se détourner le
regard du navire et du beau prince.
~Hans Christian Anderson, *La Petite Sirène*

Oh, how handsome the young prince was! He shook the hands
of the men, laughing and smiling, while the music rang out in
the beautiful night.
It was late, but the little mermaid could not turn her eyes away
from the ship and the handsome prince.
~Hans Christian Anderson, *The Little Mermaid*

21

*R*o's eyes constantly scanned the horizon for threats. Surely they were close to the sirens by now. Surely the captain would let her outfit his ship soon.

The unnecessary wait was making her nervous.

Cen hacked another cough, and Olt looked up in alarm. "Are you all right?"

Cen shot him a dirty look and mouthed, "I'm fine."

Olt looked around a bit wildly, only calming a fraction when he saw Ro watching them. "Ro! Can you check him out? Make sure he's feeling all right?"

Ro almost felt sorry for him with the daggers Cen was glaring his way. "Olt, it's just a cold. He'll be fine. He's been losing his voice for days now."

Olt was already shaking his head, his eyes on Cen. "In warm weather? In the middle of the ocean? Ro, I lost a baby sister to a hacking cough like that, and we can't trust the physician. Please?"

Ro was able to cover her surprise by the time he looked back at her. She didn't know whether he would want her to acknowledge his loss or talk about it. She never knew the right thing, the normal thing, to do around people.

"I am so sorry," she managed.

He nodded once, acknowledging it, not pursuing what was surely a painful topic. "Just make sure it doesn't happen to Cen."

As he walked away, every stride a statement, one that said he was upset but trying not to show it, both girls watched him go.

Ro turned to Cen the moment Olt was out of sight. Ro caught just a flash of Cen's sorrow-filled gaze as she watched Olt stomp away, but she covered it with a glare directed at Ro.

"Don't you dare," she mouthed.

Ro just laughed. "Do you really think I can go against Olt after that?" She rolled her shoulders. "Very well then. Just tell me where you'll be most comfortable. My cabin?"

Cen gave a fierce shake of her head and glared all the more. Right. Ro knew precisely what the other sailors, and the captain, would think. Not going there.

"Belowdecks?"

Cen still shook her head, crossing her arms, but it wasn't as fierce.

"Fine, then. Physician's cabin. While he isn't there, of course."

Cen tilted her head, her eyes asking a question.

Ro just shrugged. "If we're caught, I'll tell him my throat was scratchy and I wanted him to take a look. Deal?"

Cen still didn't look convinced.

Ro couldn't help her grin. "Or right here on deck where everyone and the Creator can see?"

Ro just laughed at Cen's attempt to look even fiercer.

"Come on, we'll wait till the physician goes to the galley for his meal or takes his nightly stroll."

Cen struggled to say something, but Ro held up her hand.

"Save your voice. It'll come back quicker that way."

Cen just shook her head and mouthed words all the harder,

but this time, without trying to force air through her nonexistent voice.

Ro squinted at her, trying to make out the words. Her meaning dawned. "Ah. Do I know what I'm doing?"

Cen looked relieved and rubbed her throat.

Ro smiled mischievously. "I cared for five older sisters, two older brothers, and a younger sister for most of my life, and they all lived."

Ro felt her words as a physical blow to her stomach. Cen's stricken face didn't help.

"Oh, Cen, I'm so sorry. I shouldn't have said that, not after Olt—" She looked around for Olt but didn't see him. "Was he here just now?"

Cen shook her head, but she still looked so distressed, Ro couldn't help beating herself up for her careless words. Her hand went to her forehead.

"I can't believe I said that. Please, forgive me, and please . . . don't tell Olt. I would never hurt him on purpose."

Cen dropped her eyes, though it looked like she had great difficulty doing so, and gave a brief nod.

"Merci," Ro whispered, feeling absolutely miserable.

Why, oh why was she forever saying the wrong thing? Especially when it came out so unfeeling. She cleared her throat and tried again.

"I cared for my brothers and sisters, almost exclusively, until Cosette was old enough to help. My older sisters were too lazy, my older brothers too carefree and rambunctious. If you're willing, I'd love to help."

Ro had trouble looking at Cen, wishing she could choke back her bête, bête words.

Cen still looked like she'd been run over by a horse, but she managed a small nod.

Ro nodded back, wondering if Cen had lost someone close to her. "Bon. Meet me there when he leaves?"

The physician rarely left his little room full of medicines, except for the occasional meal or stroll, and he always kept it locked. Though more often than not, the cook could be seen bringing a covered plate to the infirmary.

Ro hoped tonight was an evening the physician needed to stretch his legs.

Cen nodded her agreement, looking torn and lost and like she wanted to flee.

"Bon. See you then." Ro escaped to her cabin, unable to face Olt after her careless words, whether he'd overheard them or not.

Why didn't she *think* before words came pouring out of her mouth?

❦

Cen just barely made it to her hiding place before she burst into tears. Again.

She had seven sisters! And two brothers. And they all still lived! Not only was that extremely rare, she'd never been told about any of them. Not one. And she never would've met Ro had she not run away from her crabby old grandmère in the first place.

She no longer had any doubts about who the huntress was. That they were related.

Ro's mannerisms were too much like her grandmère's, which she tried not to hold against her, her looks too much like the portrait of Cen's parents, which made Cen long to meet them that much more.

Her family had just grown exponentially, and she might never get the chance to meet them.

It was all she'd ever wanted for her entire life: a family that loved her and wanted her and didn't treat her like a bothersome pest.

Cen sobbed harder, unable to make a single sound with her raw, scratchy throat.

Why did she have to get sick now of all times? Right when she was starting to know Ro and Olt better. To let down her guard. To possibly be brave enough to reveal who she was. And now she couldn't say a blasted word to either of them!

Why did Olt have to come into her inn? Why did he have to pay attention to her, talk to her, act like he wanted to know her? Just for her to realize he'd never looked at her the way he looked at the huntress.

What were Ro's sisters like? Her mère. Her père. And goodness, she had brothers! What were they like? Did they like to tease as Olt did? Or were they serious all the time?

Were *they* good men?

Things she may not have a chance to find out before they reached their destination. Time pressed upon Cen, a heavy weight.

Something told her she didn't have much time left with the huntress.

Well. Her grandmère may not have allowed her to hunt the wolves of the Black Forest at her side, but Cen would most certainly hunt the sirens at the huntress's side. Even if Ro never knew who she truly was.

It just made her cry all the harder, yet no sound accompanied her grief.

She felt the familiar tightening squeeze her chest and throat, and she forced herself to calm. All she wanted to do was to sob until she could cry no more, but that would kill her. It was a miracle she'd woken up at all last time.

But she could tell, even now, that she hadn't been able to shake the effects of crying till she passed out. Of not getting enough air.

And right now, feeling the way she did, the way her head hurt, the way she'd lost her voice as if something thick coated the back of her throat and made breathing nearly impossible, the last thing she wanted was to make it worse.

So she closed her eyes, forced her breathing to calm, and began reciting her poem silently.

The magic that holds you, shall not undo you.

This I vow, to ease you from this curse, somehow . . .

❦

Feeling weary deep in her soul, Cen sat across from Ro and squirmed. Ro had picked the lock in no time, and her fingers were swift and sure as she checked Cendre over. She'd certainly done this a time or two.

And Cen still couldn't ask any blasted questions.

They heard a noise, and both girls froze. A creak. Right outside the infirmary's door. After an eternity, whoever or whatever it was moved on, and they could breathe again.

Ro smirked, but the action was a little shaky as she adjusted the shuttered lantern. "Maybe I should've asked Olt to guard the door for us, non?"

Cen scowled at her and mouthed, "You didn't?"

Ro flushed and put away what she was using, exactly where she'd taken it from, and grabbed something else. "Open your mouth. Quickly."

Cen did so, though she wanted to chew out the huntress for not thinking of that. Of course, Cen hadn't either, but still! They needed the lookout, and Olt would've been more than happy to do so.

They were here at his insistence, after all.

Ro studied the back of Cendre's throat once more, then turned away and blew out the flame behind the little magnifying glass. She nodded, decided. "Looks like putrid throat, or strep."

Cen tilted her head. She'd never heard of that before.

"Raw throat, hacking cough, lots of thick yellow mucus that smells rather unpleasant . . ."

Cen gagged, and Ro just chuckled.

"Oh, calm yourself, mon chou. You've seen worse things working on this ship."

Cen just gave her a sour look.

"It's more uncomfortable than dangerous, especially since you're not a wee one, but it may be a few weeks yet before you'll be able to talk again. Especially since we don't have any citrons—what are they called, lemons?—onboard to help cut the mucus." She tilted her head. "Do you know if the cook has honey? Herbal tea? Cayenne pepper?"

Cen just shrugged. Most food was tasteless, so she didn't really pay attention to what she ate. Well, except seafood. That she could eat all day.

Ro went back to straightening instruments, setting things at perfect angles to make it look as though she'd never touched a thing. "Well then, I'll ask. I can't imagine how this would compound your breathing problem, but we don't want to find out."

Cen's eyes narrowed. We?

Ro's hand knocked against a strange-looking metal container. It tilted, and a clear ball filled with sickly greenish-yellow liquid rolled out of it and off the counter. As soon as the colors mixed, the ball made a hissing sound, and bright light flared to life.

Ro caught it right before it smashed into the floor.

"Ouch!" she yelped, dropping the little glass globe back into its metal container.

Lightning zapped, popped, and arched out of the metal wires that wrapped around the glass ball, cushioning it in the box, and Ro slammed the lid in place. She hissed and held her hand to her chest, taking deep breaths as tears filled her eyes.

They both waited with bated breaths, but no one came to investigate, and no more lightning leaked out of the cube-shaped box.

Cen grabbed her sister's hand, forcing it open. Burned, melted skin, like candlewax, coated Ro's palm and fingers. Cen gasped soundlessly and tried to jump up, but Ro held her in place.

"Just watch," she whispered.

Within a few seconds, new skin came back in layers, soon settling into place as if nothing had happened.

Cen's wide-eyed look met Ro's guilty one. "I, uh, don't know why that happens either. But ever since I was little . . ." A shadow passed over her face, and she shrugged. "It just happens that way. Most of the time." Her face turned bitter. "It's part of the powers the Queen of the Fairies gave me for watching over her daughter."

Cen wanted to ask so many questions, but the huntress moved on, starting to prowl and snoop.

"What in the realms?" Ro questioned, rummaging in the crates stacked all over the room. Each one was full of the little metal boxes, straw stuffed all around them so they wouldn't touch each other. "What are these?"

Ro reached for another crate, carefully this time.

Panic filled Cen's chest. She jumped off the table and tugged on Ro's arm. All she wanted to do was leave. Before they were caught.

Her hair still stood on end from the charge, and it left her with a strange feeling in the pit of her stomach. Plus, someone was approaching. She just knew it.

Ro allowed herself to be pulled away, but she looked rather reluctant about it.

They both sneaked out of the physician's cabin and ducked around the corner. Footsteps came up to the infirmary, paused, then faded into the room, the door shutting behind the person.

Ro let out her breath and elbowed Cen. "Good call." Then she led them away.

Cen followed and took deep breaths, wishing the pressure would just ease from her lungs already, perhaps heal as the huntress's hand had just done.

Ro gave her a sharp look once they were away from the

infirmary. "Can you bunk near Olt? Get on the same sleeping schedule?"

Cen's pulse pounded in her ears, and although she wasn't prone to flushing for some reason, never even really turned pink when she'd been working hard or had been in the sun too long, she wondered if her face was making an exception today.

The huntress was waiting for an answer, so she just shrugged.

"See if you can. If you have another breathing attack, I want him nearby so he can help."

Oh my. If Olt was nearby, Cen wouldn't be getting a wink of sleep for the rest of the voyage. As it was, she slept lightly and cautiously.

"And get as much extra rest as you can. Your body will heal itself if you but let it. Oh, and any extra broth Cook can spare. I'll ask him myself."

Cen's eyes widened in alarm, but Ro held up a hand.

"For me. We'll keep it quiet."

Cen's shoulders sagged. Perhaps. But the captain and physician would be furious if they found out a sick crewmember had kept his—or her—sickness a secret.

Especially if it was contagious.

Ro squeezed her hand. "We'll get through this, promise."

Again with the "we." Cen rolled her eyes but nodded, and true to her word, Ro wasted no time bothering the cook first thing.

And Ro being a particular favorite of his, he had no problem handing over anything and everything she batted her eyelashes at and asked for.

Were all her sisters outrageous flirts like Ro?

A pit settled deep in Cen's stomach.

And would she ever get the chance to find out?

Well, Cen followed everything the huntress had said to the best of her ability, somehow keeping her sickness a secret from the rest of the crew—apparently she rarely talked, so no one noticed when she couldn't talk—and now, about a week later, she felt one hundred percent better.

But she still had no voice.

She and Ro sneaked back into the physician's cabin once more—this time with Olt as lookout—and Ro peered at the back of her throat, light shuttered to draw as little attention as possible.

Ro made a frustrated sound. "I don't understand. Everything looks normal. You should be able to talk. Here, say something."

Cen tried to make a sound, but nothing came out. Ro grunted and went digging for something else.

As the huntress went over Cen thoroughly, Cen couldn't help but notice that Ro looked so sad. Troubled. As she had for most of the voyage. Though it had taken Cen forever to figure it out, since she hadn't known her any other way.

Cen poked Ro's shoulder as she was putting away the tongue depressor. Ro's eyes met hers.

"Hey. You all right?" Cen made exaggerated motions to convey her unspoken words.

It took Ro a moment to work out what she'd said, but she gave Cen a feeble grin, nodded, and turned to put back the lighted magnifying glass.

Cen poked her again, this time in the ribs. The huntress let out a little yelp and jumped away, juggling the glass instrument so she wouldn't drop and break it.

She gave Cen a look. "Really, Cen? What was that little matter about not getting caught?"

Cen bit back her grin. Must be ticklish. She reached out to poke her again, but Ro slapped her hand away and gave Cen an annoyed look.

Hey, she only had one chance to be a little sister. She was going to master it.

Hmm . . . "Your sister?" she mouthed.

Ro stared hard at Cen's lips. After a moment, "Am I thinking of my sister? Cosette?"

Cen nodded and rubbed her throat.

Ro started wiping fingerprints and any tell-tale smudges from metal instruments. "Oui. I guess I was thinking of her."

Hoping she wouldn't offend the huntress, Cen tapped her shoulder. "You miss her?"

Ro barked a laugh. "Miss her? Of course I miss her. I'm just angry, you know? The Fairy Queen lied to me. She's not even my real sister."

Cendre's eyes went huge.

Ro glanced at her and sighed. "She was placed in my family when my true little sister died."

Cen had no idea why the huntress was explaining it to her, but she wasn't about to stop her.

"My sister was sick, dying, and the Fairy Queen took it as an invitation to switch the bodies. Healthy for the weak. Her daughter for my sister."

Excitement filled Cen. That explained so much! Why she and her grandmère lived in the middle of nowhere, as if in hiding. Why Cen wasn't allowed to see anyone. Why Grandmère refused to let Cen leave their little cabin in the woods.

Just not why the huntress was so upset about it. She seemed to be close to Cosette. Why would their not being sisters matter?

Though, Cendre had to admit, she was pleased to no end that it did.

She got Ro's attention again and mouthed. "You love her?"

Ro ducked her head, her voice a little choked up. "Of course I do. I just—she's just—I wanted to know my real little sister, n'est-ce pas? Not have the choice taken away from me."

Ro's hands flew faster as she talked.

"You see, no matter what went wrong in my life, no matter who abandoned me, I always had Cosette. She was my best friend. My confidante. I went to her when my world was falling apart, and I fiercely loved her and protected her. Then I found out our closeness, our bond, was a compulsion put on us by her fairy mère to ensure I'd protect her. It was all a lie."

She blew out a breath.

"And now she has Trêve. She doesn't need me anymore."

Ro flicked a glance at Cen and let out a nervous laugh.

"Désolé. I found out not long before I left France. I . . . apparently am not taking it well. I just wish I could've known my real sister, had she lived. No compulsion. No pretending. See if we truly would've been friends, you know? I just wish I could've known her."

A chink fell out of Cendre's armor, and she melted a little. Just as she was reaching out a hand to rest on the huntress's arm and say, "And now you can," Olt opened the door.

"Hey! Time to go." He took in their expressions. "Whoa. Don't the two of you look somber."

Ro moved away, missing Cendre's hand by a mere brush. "Just talking about family. Someone coming?"

At the word "family," a strange look came over Olt's face. "Oh, uh, yeah. I mean, no. I mean . . . you should probably be done." He grinned, his carefree demeanor falling over him like a mask. "You should see this."

The pair hurried away, apparently expecting Cen to follow, but she just sat there. Should she tell the huntress? Who she was? And what in Olt's past would cause such heartbreak?

She rose slowly and followed, wondering how best to dig into two people's lives who were hiding everything and didn't want to give up their secrets — or their wounds.

Before it was too late.

22

*R*o couldn't sleep.

She wrapped her red cloak around her and tiptoed out to the ship's railing. She nodded to the night guard, and he nodded back, not breaking his stride. They were all used to seeing her out this late by now. She did her best thinking at night.

It had absolutely nothing to do with Olt being on night duties.

She tried to lose herself in the spray of saltwater and the splash of waves against the hull—sounds she could never get enough of—but a sound came to her that was just . . . wrong. Off. Not supposed to be there.

A scrape against the side of the ship.

Her eyes roved the dark waters, but only a sliver of moonlight peeked out from behind clouds—not enough to cast much light. By the time the moon fully waned, they would have reached their destination.

When nights were dark like this, the few torches lit up the ship like a beacon, the surrounding water nothing but dark emptiness, like they floated on the edge of the world and were about to fall off. Ro regretted reading those particular stories.

There. Again. A scrape.

Ro glanced around to see if anyone else had heard—no one had—then leaned out over the rail. She could see next to nothing in the darkness.

A splash, very slight, but different from the others. Ro moved farther away from the lantern's glow and strained to see anything. Anything at all.

My eyesight couldn't work now *of all times?* she grumbled to herself.

Lines creaked, and Ro scanned the nets draped all over the sides of the boat to dry. At least, that's why Ro assumed they were there. She hadn't been on a ship yet that left their nets out nonstop, and this one had since the Canaries. Which just brilliant if they were trying to keep sirens off the ship.

Another slight noise came. Like ropes creaking.

She leaned out even more. *Come on, eyesight, work already!*

She was so focused on trying to find the almost-not-there noise, she nearly fell overboard when someone hissed, "Huntress? Huntress!"

"Oui?" she asked in a harsh whisper. She glanced behind her, but the night watchman wasn't near, and the man in the lookout was gazing the other way.

"I thought that was you." There was a grin in the voice—a voice she didn't recognize.

Ro still couldn't see who it was. Blasted eyesight! "Where are you?"

"You see those barrels over here? No, the other way. Come here."

Ro was still on the unsettled side of things as she eased toward the barrels to her right.

"Right here, Mademoiselle."

Ro ducked into the relative privacy the ring of strapped-down barrels offered and peered once more over the edge. She just managed to contain her yelp as a face—painted to blend in with the night, teeth a dingy white in the not-there moonlight, belonging to a woman clinging to the side of the ship—peered back at her.

Ro gasped. "Who are you?"

The person grinned. "Merja, first mate. Captain Red sent me, ma'am."

Ro looked frantically around and lowered her voice. "I thought that was her ship! Where is she? Is she close? She isn't going to get caught, is she?"

A low, soft chuckle came. "She said you were a worrier, but I wasn't expecting this much worry."

Ro scowled. "Why did she send you?"

"To tell you not to fret, and that everything is on schedule to meet at the rendezvous point."

Ro nodded, once more scanning the horizon. "Bon." Panic threatened to choke her as she thought about coming upon them unawares. Again. "Is she—close?"

"Naw."

"But how did you get here?"

Again, a flash of those ghastly teeth. "I swam."

Ro's mouth dropped open. "All this way?"

The crewwoman shrugged. "'Twas only a few miles. We'd outpaced you quite a bit, thanks to your extended time in the Canaries, until that storm. We've been keeping somewhat abreast of your position, though it's taken some effort to remain out of sight and keep up." She flicked an admiring glance over the vessel. "She's fast, I'll give 'er that."

"But—how will you find your way back?"

She chuckled. "You let me worry about that. You have your gifts and I have mine. Speaking of finding my way back—can you swim, huntress?"

Ro blinked. "You can't possibly mean . . . ?"

"Oh, but I do."

"But, but—won't I be missed?"

Again, a flash of teeth against painted skin. "Not if we time it right, huntress. My captain wouldn't mind an update."

Ro grumbled a little, glancing around her to be certain they weren't being spied upon. "Wouldn't telling her you spoke to me suffice?"

"How about you stash that cloak of yours and your boots somewhere."

Ro gritted her teeth. Not only would she most likely be shot if they were caught, she'd be half undressed. Try explaining *that* to the captain.

Ro tried to be inconspicuous as she glanced at the woman's legs. Just barely, she could see the woman had two. The reports said the sirens were half-women, half-fish, though some claimed they flew like birds. Could she trust this woman?

"How do I know you are who you say you are?"

The woman wordlessly turned away and bared her shoulder, where an encircled R.R. was melted into her skin. "All of her crew are branded as such before we are allowed in her employ or on her ship."

Ro didn't know what to say to that. She didn't know how she felt about that, either.

"Hurry, huntress. The faster we leave, the faster we can have you back."

Ro crawled over to a water barrel she knew was empty—she sat on it when hanging out with the sailors in the evenings—and stashed her boots, stockings, and cape. She started unbuttoning her jerkin, then paused. Unwieldy or not, her undershirt would be see-through after being soaked. No need to be caught like *that*.

She scurried back over to the pirate. Ro hated it, hated the very thought of it—it could ruin everything—but she followed the pirate over the edge of the ship.

For once she was thankful for the nets they left over the sides. They made it incredibly easy to climb the side of the boat.

She rolled her eyes. Yeah, that would keep the sirens away.

Ro paused just before she reached the water. She could do this. She could. If she just didn't think about it . . .

A black, yawning emptiness stared back at her, and Ro could honestly say she'd never been so scared in all her life.

The pirate took her arm, and they slipped into the water together.

Ro expected it to be freezing. It wasn't. Warm, balmy—the night watchman passed on the deck above, and she went perfectly still, but it didn't matter. They were quickly left behind by the rapidly moving ship.

The pirate jerked her head, and Ro followed her into the deep, deep ocean.

Sharks, jellyfish, giant squid, sirens—Ro swallowed back panic. What else could possibly be dancing below her feet? Need for stealth or no, if something bumped her out here, she wouldn't be able to hold back her scream.

And the night was so dark, it felt like she was blinded.

Ro was just settling in to the pleasant burn of the swim, when something loomed over them against the backdrop of clouds. Her eyes widened as the pirate latched on to her jerkin.

"Hurray, huntress! Grab the rope before she passes by."

Even though Ro was certain she was about to meet her watery grave, she lunged at the same rope the pirate did and was immediately pulled alongside the passing vessel.

Water broke over her head and face in a constant wave, and Merja hauled her out of it and farther up the rope. Ro came up spluttering, but she dragged herself up after the pirate, shaking wet strands of hair out of her face.

When she could see, she stared up at the massive ship in awe. She'd forgotten how huge it was! How beautiful it was.

How vastly different it was from the king's ship.

Eight decks to their three, nearly twice the length, and three masts instead of two—Ro sighed as she took it in. What she wouldn't give to cross the ocean in that.

They probably couldn't even feel the choppy water under their feet.

"Huntress. Are you coming?"

Ro transferred her weight to the rope ladder that had been lowered at her companion's call and climbed after the crew-woman. They helped her aboard at the top of a long climb, and someone handed her a length of cloth to wrap herself in.

Exhilarated after her swim, Ro took the fabric with a wide grin. "Going to be kind of hard to hide the wet spot when I climb back aboard my ship, non?"

Merja laughed. "Oh, we have something for that. Believe me. Just wrap that cloth around yourself as you climb the side, and not a drop will reach the deck."

Ro glanced down, and her eyes widened. It was exactly as the pirate had said.

Merja spread her hands wide. "Welcome aboard the *Siren Hunter*."

Ro blinked and, mouth open, just stared at her.

"Yes, in honor of you, and yes, it was rechristened as such before we set sail."

Ro laughed and shook her head. "Incroyable."

Again that welcoming grin made Ro feel right at home. "Thought you might say that. Right this way."

Ro marveled at the beautiful, newly made ship as she followed the woman. The new boards with a high shine glistened, even in the darkness. She'd never seen a finer ship.

She made her way to the captain's quarters, pausing outside the door as Merja announced her, feeling momentary embarrassment at her barefoot, soaking-wet status.

Captain Red was not one to appear as a bedraggled mess before.

Merja caught Ro's glance at herself and offered the huntress an encouraging look. "She's expecting you as such, huntress. Nothing to be embarrassed about a'tall."

Ro returned her warm smile and entered the captain's

spacious quarters. And her jaw dropped, again, as her eyes roved the space.

It. Was. Huge.

Captain Montrose's quarters could fit within five times over.

She had no idea how they even had a space this big on the ship, and used for one person, at that.

The door closed behind her, and Ro tried so hard to tear her eyes away and focus on the captain, but she was tired, and gold gilded just about everything. Almost impossible to look away from in her tired, distracted, and ready-for-this-voyage-to-be-over state.

"I have to admit, I'm quite pleased you're so taken with my ready room, huntress."

Captain Red's sultry, pleasant voice cleared the fog Ro was in, and she turned her attention to the commanding woman.

"You mean, this isn't votre quarters?"

"My quarters?" She rumbled out a laugh. "Oh no, huntress, but those are quite luxuriant as well."

Ro shook her head, a smile playing about her lips. "Fantastique. Do I want to know how you attained this particular vessel?"

That warm smile graced her face, hinting at mystery and allure. "Non."

Ro sobered. "We won't, uh, have anyone seeking this ship when we return, will we?"

"Not with whatever bargain Madame LaChance called in, I presume."

The air left Ro in a whoosh. She'd momentarily forgotten Madame LaChance had secured the ship for this particular voyage.

"Relieved I didn't steal it, huntress?"

Ro gave a weak grin. "You could say that. I wasn't particularly looking forward to a battle for ownership later."

"Now that you mention business . . ." Captain Red folded

her hands atop her desk. "Sit, please. Is the captain of the *King's Ransom* open to your plans?"

"Non, not at all," Ro growled.

"Tell me everything."

The captain gestured to a wooden chair, next to a plush, red-velvet chair outlined in gold. Ro sat and did just that, taking a moment to trail her fingers on the other chair's gilt surface. Everything she could think of that would be even slightly of import to the pirate captain came tumbling out.

She ended with the shifting markings on the map and Olt's theory about the Ring of Death.

The pirate captain leaned forward. "If what you say is true, if this barrier cuts off the rest of the world so entirely, I need the most updated map of its position."

Ro shrugged. "If the legends are true, it can move at the sirènes' whim, though it mostly mimics the coasts of the Americas."

The captain sat back, jaw tight. "That presents a bit of a problem."

"Such as . . ." Ro prodded.

"Such as"—the pirate captain poured Ro, then herself, a drink—"running aground when we least expect it. Not knowing when to stop. Not being able to reach any of the Caribbean islands if we need repairs."

Ro sipped the proffered drink cautiously and was pleased to discover it was watered-down ale. Not something stronger.

Ro thought about it, the captain's many charts flitting through her mind. "I can bring you one of the captain's maps, and I can add any current markings." She spun the goblet in her fingers. "I have not been able to find the enchanted ink, though. I am sorry."

"The markings must be exact, huntress. I cannot stress this enough. The slightest error can be detrimental to my crew and my ship."

"But of course, ma capitaine. I'll do what I can."

Captain Red scowled. "How did he come to be in possession of such nautical charts? I have heard nothing of a barrier, and I like to think myself informed."

"I'm not sure . . . many of the rumors include the sirènes singing from such a barrier. Well, from rocks, anyway." Ro frowned. "In fact, all the legends include that. The ships are wrecked upon it."

Captain Red's eyes lit up. "Very astute, huntress. I'll look into that myself."

Ro nodded. "One more thing: There is a physician aboard, one I've only seen once or twice. He's . . . creepy."

The captain raised an eyebrow. "You can hardly fault a man for being odd."

"It's more than that. His infirmary—it's full of liquids and substances and gadgets such as I've never seen. This is going to sound outlandish . . ."

"Not much surprises me anymore, huntress." She struck a match and lit a cheroot, taking a few puffs.

Ro nodded, knowing the feeling all too well. "He has these clear cannonballs full of lightning."

Captain Red blinked. "Lightning?"

"Oui. Crates of them fill his infirmary. An infirmary he keeps under lock and key."

Captain Red stroked a beard she didn't have. Ro tilted her head, the motion wholly out of place and yet so fitting.

"Lightning," the captain repeated. "Interesting."

Ro shrugged. "I'm not sure of his role, or what those things do, and I can't get anyone else to talk about him."

"I see."

"I thought it was worth mentioning. Perhaps the captain's knowledge of the barrier is connected?"

"I will keep that in mind."

Ro nodded and sat back.

"I must ask, huntress. Are you sure you don't want to go with the king's original plan? Wipe them all out?"

Ro froze. Hunt the sirens and bring back as many bodies as possible, to be paid for each carcass as she had for the wolves that once overran France?

The captain burned her cheroot down to a nub, lit another, and took a few puffs before Ro could find the words. In that excruciating amount of time, Ro doubted herself, rethought her plan, tried to make a new one, and came to the same conclusion: She needed to gather facts before she simply accepted a job to kill someone. Or something.

She'd learned that much with the beast.

"I must try, ma capitaine. If there's even a chance I can prevent a war, I must do all in my power to do so. Besides, there is always another side to a story. I must know what it is."

Captain Red's smile said Ro's answer didn't surprise her. "I thought as much." She opened a small chest on her desk and pulled out a compass. She set it in front of Ro. "This is for you."

After a startled moment, Ro picked it up. "Merci."

She turned it over in her hands. An intricate rose was engraved on top, and the bottom had a fleur-de-lis carved into the metal case. Although Ro was certain it was brass, as most seafaring compasses were, its high shine made it look like pure gold.

She clicked it open. An intricate fleur-de-lis was the compass rose pointing north, another true rose painted in the center of the cardinal points. A glass bubble covered the floating arrow.

"It is lovely," Ro breathed.

"It does not point north, huntress."

Ro's head came up, and she snapped it closed, punctuating her words. "What? What good is it to me, then?"

Captain Red just smiled. She pulled out another compass, and after a slight hesitation, slid it over to Ro.

Ro picked it up and turned it over in awe. Silver to the other's gold, though the metal was so pure, it almost looked white, this one had a snowflake carved into the top and drawn in its center, the fleur-de-lis pattern opposite the other.

"They are both très belle. Very beautiful," Ro said.

Captain Red held out her hand, and Ro placed the silver one there. Captain Red's face was carefully blank as she hid it away. "They point to each other, huntress. This is how we rendezvous."

Ro couldn't help her question. "Why did you not give this to me before? And the swim back . . ." Ro swallowed. She didn't want to ruin the lovely thing.

Captain Red just smiled, but she didn't quite look herself. "It is waterproof, love. You cannot harm it." Her voice and face turned hard. "But I do expect it back."

Ro's reply was swift. "You have my word."

The captain passed over a strip of leather. "It floats, but this will help secure it."

Ro nodded gratefully. The last thing she wanted to be responsible for was losing something the pirate captain so obviously held dear.

Captain Red nodded to someone behind Ro. "Merja will take you back now and ensure you are not seen or heard returning."

Ro offered a smile. "Merci, ma capitaine."

She inclined her head. "De rien, huntress. Don't forget my map."

Ro returned the nod, then followed the crewwoman out of the captain's ready room and over the side of the *Siren Hunter* to begin the long swim back.

23

*O*nce again, they were almost run over by the *King's Ransom* coming up behind them, and Ro almost missed grabbing the nets because she was trying so hard to figure out the *Siren Hunter's* path.

For all the *King Ransom's* speed, it seemed as though the *Siren Hunter* was dancing figure eights around them.

Merja chuckled low at the look on Ro's face. "Don't try to figure it out, huntress. I have my contribution to Captain Red's crew, and you have yours."

Ro started to ask anyway, but Merja held a finger to her lips and pointed upward. Ro grumbled to herself as they climbed the side of the ship.

Ro and Merja took turns surveying for the night watch to pass before Ro slipped onboard. Ro carefully wrapped the blanket Merja handed her around her shoulders. It should be dripping wet, but it wasn't.

"See you at the rendezvous point?"

"But of course," Ro answered.

The pirate grinned. "It was lovely meeting you. Goodnight, huntress."

Ro nodded. "Bonne nuit, Merja."

Had she not known the pirate was there, she would have never seen her crawl back down the ship, slip into the water with only a slight disruption, and push off into the vast ocean. Her illuminating eyesight had utterly failed her, yet again.

Shaking her head, Ro turned to leave.

Wait.

Ro froze. She hadn't heard that voice—not once—since she'd left le Château de Champagne, the beast's castle. And it unnerved her to hear it now, of all times.

She started to move, but it came again.

Wait.

Ro waited. And waited. And waited.

And started to doubt she'd heard the voice at all. The night stretched on, and she started to feel ridiculous. Maybe she'd just gather her belongings . . .

Adjusting her borrowed blanket, she tiptoed over to the barrel, slipped out her cloak, and pulled out her boots.

"I knew it!"

Ro spun on the raised voice, dropping her boots in one swift move and covering them—and her feet—with her cloak.

Hank stood there, leering, two sailors flanking him.

"I knew you was in with them sirens. Cap'ain! Cap'ain!"

"What are you talking about?" Ro shushed him. "Will you be quiet?"

As the man continued to caterwaul for the captain, Ro cast a furtive glance over her shoulder. The pirate was nowhere in sight. Thank Dieu.

Though on full alert, the captain appeared less than pleased to be awakened. "What is it? Sirens?"

Hank looked positively smug. "Caught her red-handed, chatting it up with a siren. She's on their side, Cap'ain. Going to kill us all in our sleep."

Captain Montrose looked like he wanted to strangle Hank. In an extremely patient voice, he asked Ro, "Is this true?"

"What? Of course not!"

He just looked at Hank. Hank was too busy leering at Ro to notice the captain's look. "Course she'd deny it, Cap'ain. There she was, easy as you please, climbing up the edge of the boat and speakin' to something in the water. Sounds fishy to me."

Hank nudged the men on either side, cackling at his joke. Fortunately for Ro, Hank's companions were actually looking at the captain's irate face and therefore were rather subdued. Ro took the moment of distraction to step into her boots.

"Is that what happened?" he asked both of them.

One stammered. "Er, uh, she was talking ta something, sir."

"And did you see what that something was?" He looked to the other sailor.

"No, sir, Cap'ain, sir. We just heard talking, Cap'ain, sir."

Captain Montrose now looked to Ro. She noticed he hadn't pursued the climbing up the side of the ship bit.

She shrugged. "Ask any of the watchmen. I have an unfortunate habit of talking to myself."

"Don't I know it." The captain rubbed his forehead and turned the full brunt of his frustration on Hank. "Return to your hammock, sailor, and if you try to besmirch the good name of the huntress again, I'll throw you overboard myself. And believe me, we won't be coming back for you." When the three men stood there in stunned silence, he barked, "Dismissed."

The other two scrambled away, but Hank backed away, his furious glare directed at Ro. She held it until he was out of sight. Then reluctantly looked at the captain.

He took in her damp hair, the blanket still wrapped around her shoulders as she held her cloak in front of her, and then glanced down at her booted feet, which were thankfully *not* dripping water all over the deck.

Ro had never been so grateful for the blanket, for the voice telling her to wait, and for slipping on her boots, as the crewmen were claiming all sorts of things that were almost true. Then she wondered if she'd waited even longer if she would've missed the confrontation entirely.

"Do I have anything to worry about, huntress?"

Ro just gave him a look. "Hardly."

"I see. Don't make me regret defending you."

Ro shook her head. "Never."

"Goodnight, huntress."

"Bonne nuit, Captain Montrose."

Ro waited till he was safely in his cabin to make her way to her own, ignoring the night watch's curious glances the entire way, thankful she hadn't seen Olt once.

She couldn't wait to pull her crumpled stockings from the toes of her boots.

The next day, Ro stood at the railing, still on high alert. If they could swim to and from the ship, they were close. Too close.

Her eyes no longer roved the sea in lazy, wide arcs. Non, now she studied every dark shape, anything that could be a ship on the horizon, and prayed the lookout wouldn't call a warning.

The last thing she needed was her plans being discovered. Or her crew being taken out. Or this ship sinking before it got to the sirens.

She swiped a hand down her face, exhausted from the stress of constantly being on edge. Of doing nothing. She was tired of it all.

"Penny for your thoughts."

Ro jumped and sucked in a breath.

Olt let out a merry laugh, which bounced its way out to sea. "I'm sorry, I didn't mean to scare you."

Ro lifted her chin. "You did not."

"I see." His eyes twinkled. "I'm glad to hear it."

If only she didn't feel like he was laughing at her every time she saw him! "What did you ask me? A penny . . . ?"

His grin widened. "A penny for your thoughts."

Ro cocked her head. "What is a penny?"

"Oh, ah, money. A livre. Only worth much less."

"Oh." Ro flushed. How was she supposed to keep his odd English phrases straight? There was so much about the language to remember!

"So . . . late night?"

Ro's eyes flew to his.

Olt scuffed the toe of his boot. "A beautiful night for a swim, perhaps?"

"I'm not sure what you're talking about." Ro's gaze darted all around them.

Olt just looked at her. "Don't you think the time for games is past, huntress?"

"D'accord. Fine." Ro dropped her voice and moved close. "How in all the realms did you know that? I didn't see you last night."

Olt grinned, but there was a tightness to it. "Oh, you know, you see things as lookout."

Ro gasped. "That was you?"

His look didn't waver. "Yep."

She stared back. She'd come to enjoy his company, sure, but could she trust him?

He just waited.

She huffed and turned away, flustered. "It's none of your business."

Olt made a frustrated sound and jerked his hands to the side. "Can't you and Cen believe I'm just trying to be your friend? That I don't want to see you thrown in the brig or whatever else you both think I'm trying to do?"

Ro glanced at him and lifted an eyebrow.

"I haven't reported anything, have I?"

He had a point. Still, she hedged. "The captain doesn't need to know."

Olt leaned close, and heat flushed down Ro's whole body. He needed to back up. Right now. "I think you're missing the point: I do. And if I think the captain needs to investigate, I have to tell him."

Ro couldn't help gasping again. "You wouldn't."

"I would. If I thought you were putting us in danger."

Ro whirled away and grumbled. "Your *king* is the one putting us in danger."

"Huntress . . ."

"So I have a backup plan. So what? I need one on this godforsaken voyage."

"Ro—"

She spun and poked him in the chest. "Not a word, do you hear me? Not a word."

He blew out a breath and ran his hand through his hair. "Ro, you see, the thing is, I know something too. Something you don't."

Ro just stared at him.

"But I need to know I can trust you."

Ro lurched back. "But of course you can."

"Then prove it. What were you doing last night?"

Ro swallowed. "I was ensuring my other crew would be in place when I needed them."

His eyes widened. "You swam all the way to another ship? At night? How?"

"Doesn't matter. Now, what do you know?"

Again with all the agitated motions and hair combing. "You see, you may think you're here to speak with the sirens, broker a peace treaty, but we have our orders as well. We're here to kill the sirens. To wipe them out."

Ro nodded once. "I know. If I can't come to terms . . ."

"No!" He lowered his voice. Moved closer. So close Ro was having trouble focusing on his words. He ducked his head, and his breath brushed her cheek. "No. That's not it. Whether you reach a peace or not, our orders are to—"

"Sailor, desist!"

Ro spun, and Olt straightened slowly until he stood at attention.

Captain Montrose looked like he was ready to spew fire. "Back to your duties, sailor."

Olt saluted, then walked away after giving Ro a long look, one that said he wanted to say more. He didn't look half as terrified as Ro felt. Would they be thrown in the brig? Receive a beating? Or both.

"What did he tell you?" the captain demanded.

Ro stood lightly on the balls of her feet, ready to fight or flee—the captain looked that angry. And now Ro was getting an inkling of the real reason Captain Montrose had tried to keep them apart for the voyage. She took a deep breath and forced herself to relax.

"The truth. Were you going to?"

With a heavy sigh, the captain gestured behind him. "Will you join me in my quarters, milady?" She didn't miss the dagger-like look he shot at Olt's retreating back.

Olt was already on night duties; what would the captain do to him now?

Ro hesitated.

"What I have to say cannot be overheard. If you want answers, I have them."

Now he had answers?

Ro followed him to his chambers, temper starting to broil under the surface.

24

*S*he spun on him the moment the door closed. "When were you going to tell me?"

Captain Montrose walked around her and poured himself a glass of sherry.

"*Were* you going to tell me?"

He held out a second glass, but she shook her head. He always offered; she always refused. "Are you sure?" he asked. "This conversation might call for it."

She speared him with a hard glare. "I am certain. My père lost most of his life to drink. I'm not about to do the same."

He shrugged and downed a glass, refilling it before answering. "No, I was not going to tell you."

Frustration brimmed, pushed against her tightly controlled emotions, until it spilled over. She slammed her fist on the desk. "And why not?"

He met her eyes without balking. "I wasn't free to tell you. I needed you to go through with your mission of finding the creatures first."

Ro wanted to scream and throw things at him. She did neither. Her voice came out in a low growl. "I think, Monsieur, that I needed to be informed, prepared for my task, not have information hidden from me." Without thinking, she snatched up an inkwell and threw it at the window seat. "I am sick of people hiding things from me that I need to know to do my job!"

He mildly watched her tantrum and the splash of ink running down the upholstery as he took another sip. "I was under orders, milady."

"Orders? Whose orders?"

He didn't flinch. "My king's."

Fear tried to strangle Ro, but she pushed it back. What kind of game did the English king play, pitting them against each other like this? Handing out differing information to each player? And what were the players in his game of strategy poised to do? The marquis, the physician, the captain, his crew . . . and were her own players loaned from Madame LaChance evenly matched?

"I have my own orders from your king," Ro rejoined. "Written, signed, and sealed. Do you really want to squabble over whose orders will be obeyed? Because it won't be yours."

His startled eyes turned stormy. He leaned across the desk. "You *dare* to—"

"Of course I dare." Ro matched his stance, her knuckles white upon the desktop. "I speak on behalf of your king, on the mission your king hired me to complete. Do *you* dare to say otherwise?"

His right eye twitched. "You tend to bandy the king's name about at whim, huntress. I urge you to be more sparing in its use. I have my own orders from the king, and they may not match yours."

Ro made a frustrated sound. She'd expected some push-back, but she *would* remain calm. "I have a job to do, mon capitaine, and I must be free to do it. And that job includes negotiating with the sirènes first, if at all possible, not just killing them on sight. Mon Dieu, I'm trying to save your men!"

Give them a chance to go home to their families unmolested. Can you not understand that?"

The captain dropped his head, took a deep breath, and settled in his chair. "I never said you couldn't negotiate. Only that you have your job and I have mine."

Ro frowned. "Then you will wait to kill any of them until my part is complete? Until you know the outcome and if further action is needed?"

He raised the glass to his lips. "Of course."

"Oh." Ro frowned. Olt seemed to think otherwise. "Is there anything else I should know? Some other plan hidden from my knowledge?"

"Not that I am aware of." He took another swallow.

Which could mean anything.

Ro cursed and began to pace. Once she felt a measure of calm, she spun to face him. Not a fleck of emotion marred his face.

"Then tell me your plan. What you expect to do when we reach our destination."

He smiled then, and Ro knew she wasn't going to like what he was going to say.

"Why, my lady, I expect to do nothing."

Ro blinked. "What do you mean?"

He beckoned to the second chair that had been brought into the room for Ro's use. "Please, sit."

She sat.

"My men and I can go nowhere near the sirens. Not without risking being taken in by their call."

Ro nodded. That much she knew.

"We will anchor at a safe distance."

Ro cocked her head. "How will you know when to stop?"

"Have you studied none of the charts I gave you?"

"But of course I have."

"Good." He nodded once. "Then as soon as we determine

we are about a day's journey from the outcropping they inhabit, we will set anchor, and you will row on alone."

Ro couldn't help it—her mouth fell open. When she'd recovered enough to speak, she blurted. "For a full day?"

Panic seized Ro, and it was all she could do to fight it. She'd be out there alone, on all that open water . . .

She stuffed what she was feeling deep inside. The water hadn't bothered her for most of this journey, and she wasn't about to let it start worrying her now.

Even if the thought of being alone on all that endless blue threatened to strangle her with terror.

He nodded, his smile not as fatherly as before. "You will need to go at night to let the stars guide you, and you must not fall asleep, lest you be driven off course."

Ro bolted to her feet. "And you haven't let me do any hard labor why exactly? Because you don't wish me to succeed?"

He opened then closed his mouth, then tilted his head. "I hadn't thought of that."

And because he wasn't thinking, because he was so impossibly stubborn, Ro might not be able to do her job. Of course, she could have insisted harder . . .

He'd been an obstacle, surely, but too much of the blame rested squarely on her shoulders. She should've done something about it.

And now it may be too late.

She shoved her finger his way, not even caring that she was close to shouting. "I am not like other women, Monsieur. I have to work hard, keep my body strong, and do tasks others consider unpleasant. It is imperative you stop treating me like a fragile woman and start treating me like the huntress I am."

The look on his face slowly changed, as if he was seeing the huntress for the first time. "I see."

For the love of all the realms. "How many days do I have to prepare myself?"

He swallowed hard, and Ro didn't exactly enjoy watching

the captain realize he was wrong about something. "About a week, at most."

A string of curses poured out of Ro's mouth, and she paced, tugging at her hair in frustration. "Mon Dieu, what should I do now?"

"Might I suggest . . ."

"Non!" She spun on him. "I'll take no more suggestions from you, mon capitaine, not unless they are to work hard and prepare myself for my task. I am not happy right now."

He eyed her mildly. "Yes, I can see that."

She kept pacing, trying to figure out what to do. "I need a path. To run around the rim of the decks. Up and down the stairs."

"To . . . run?"

"And your sails. I want to hoist and unfurl them with your men. Climb the rigging. Repair it. In fact, I'd like to do it as much as possible, whatever won't slow us down."

He just looked at her, most likely thinking she was the craziest female he'd ever met. Which just made her madder.

"And I still need to outfit your ship, to say nothing of training the men. Mon Dieu, you wait till now to tell me this? And swabbing the deck . . ."

"No."

Ro jerked around, ready to tear into him.

He quelled her with a look. "That I will not budge on, huntress."

"It is water! To scrub excess salt from the deck. Why in all the realms not? It builds lovely strength in the arms."

His gaze just went flinty.

She marched over to his desk and slapped both hands down on it. "Then tell me why."

The captain hesitated.

She leaned closer. "You need to understand this about me, mon capitaine, and you need to understand it well. I can abide by most rules if I know why. If I am treated as a rational adult and given an explanation."

The captain nodded. "I can respect that."

Ro threw her hands in the air. "Why in the blazes couldn't you have respected that earlier?"

He ignored that. "The harsh substance we use for swabbing the deck will eat away your flesh, huntress, hurt your hands should you accidentally touch it, and quite possibly make it impossible to hunt."

Ro blinked. That wasn't what her père had used on his ships. But this . . . it had a strong smell, sure, but eat away flesh?

"But . . ."

"I will not budge, huntress."

Ro shook her head. "I'm not arguing. Well, not this time. Why do your men use it, then?"

He seemed to weigh his response. "It . . . is the substance needed to keep my ship's deck in repair."

Ro opened then closed her mouth. He'd given her that much; she wouldn't push for more. She nodded her thanks.

He nodded back.

Her mind swirled with all she needed to do. "I need to go shoot something."

That earned a phantom of a smile. "I thought you might."

Ro leaned across the desk one last time. "I want your word that you will not harm one sirène until my peace talks have failed. If they fail, I will require your assistance. Not before."

He had the same look about him he usually got when Ro mentioned talking to the sirens. The one Ro couldn't decipher.

Captain Montrose inclined his head. "You have my word. Unless defending my ship or my crew is necessary."

Ro whirled without another word and bolted for where she usually set up her target.

Olt took one look at her face and walked her way.

"My target, s'il vous plaît," she ground out when he came close enough.

He veered away and soon had her target set up. Cen appeared out of nowhere with her bow and arrows.

Ro immediately started shooting.

Arrow after arrow flew, and soon she had a gathering at her back, but she paid it no mind. She only paused when her target was full.

She moved toward it, but Cen was already there, yanking out arrow after arrow. Ro closed her eyes. She couldn't even take out her own arrows or practice without an audience.

She was so ready to be done with this blasted, smelly ship that held no privacy whatsoever.

Once the target was clear and she had her arrows back, she set to flinging them the target's way once more, and she mostly ignored the murmurs surrounding her that not one of them had seen an archer shoot as she did.

25

*O*n deck, Ro unpacked the crates containing the newly invented harpoon guns, much like giant crossbows. It made her miss her black walnut crossbow, stowed safely back in Angleterre, that much more.

The harpoons themselves were made of soft iron, able to twist without breaking so any sirens ensnared could be hauled aboard, no matter how hard they fought to get away.

Ro felt sick to her stomach. She sincerely hoped she wouldn't have to witness that.

She directed where all four harpoon guns should be attached to the rails, helping the men get them in place and secure them.

Slowing the ship or not, they needed to be in place well before the crew needed them.

The captain had plenty of shot and cannonballs for when things spiraled out of control—even though the sirens tended to dodge such things—but until then, she was in charge of the hunt. And that required capturing them neatly, if possible, not blowing them to bits.

Ro went below to find the other weapons she'd brought and direct the crew where to place everything. She opened crate after crate of carefully packed weapons. She'd brought enough harpoons, nets, and arrows to outfit a small army.

Olt whistled as he helped her go through it all. "I've never seen so many weapons all in one place. Reminds me of a well-stocked armory."

Ro offered him a smirk, but her tone was mirthless. "I just hope we don't have to use any of it."

He gave her a sympathetic smile.

She set aside another crate of arrows, waiting to speak again till it was just her, Cen, and Olt. "The captain wants me to go on alone."

Olt paled. "Alone? Is that wise?"

Ro gave Olt a long look. "Non, what would be wise is being with my other crew." Her eyes drifted to Cen, and Ro cocked her head. "Maybe I can ask if you can go with me?"

Olt snorted. "Not without giving it away. You should ask if we both can go."

Ro's head whipped back to him. "Absolutely not! There's no way I'm putting you in that kind of danger."

Olt didn't flinch. "I'll do it. For Cen."

Cen abruptly turned and left the room.

Ro watched her go. "I'm more worried about you strangling us or throwing us to the sirènes if they tell you to."

Olt frowned and looked down. "Oh."

A sailor entered for another load of cargo, and Ro and Olt went back to separating crates and organizing weapons.

More sailors came and went, and it was some time before it was just Ro and Olt again. Cen flitted into the room for another crate, not looking at either of them.

"One more thing." Olt wasted no time getting to the point. "You should ask the captain if Cen and I can help you with preparations."

Ro frowned, then glanced around pointedly. "Isn't that what you're doing?"

Cen paused, her slight body bowing under the crate about half her size and twice as heavy.

He gave Ro a cheeky grin. "More than that. Outright permission for the three of us to conspire whenever we like. We'll have the captain's scrutiny, sure, but we won't have to sneak around and have clandestine meetings in the storage room."

Cen brightened and nodded her agreement before darting out with her load.

Ro hesitated, thinking it through. "I just may do that."

Unable to stay in one place for long, Ro was soon back to directing the madness on deck as sailors practiced shooting the newly invented harpoon guns for the first time.

She handed a bundle of harpoons to a passing sailor. "Here. These need to be stored under each gun. Mount the water-proofed containers—oui, those—within easy reach of each cannon. There, there, there, and there."

The sailor nodded and moved away to do as told.

She turned to the stack of crates, which had dwindled to a single crate. Ro sighed in relief. Only one more to be unpacked. She hefted it open, the nails fighting her iron bar a little, and frowned.

It was full of scimitars.

Ro pulled out a curved blade and scowled at it. "Cen?"

The girl was at her elbow in a flash. Ro put the sword back and replaced the lid.

"It looks like we got this by accident. Can you put it back in the cargo room?"

Cen nodded and was gone before Ro could thank her.

Ro smirked, but she couldn't help her worry. Would Cen be safe on this ship without her? She scowled and threw herself back into her work. She was trying *not* to worry here.

Once Ro was mostly satisfied, she marched to the captain's quarters and knocked on the open door.

"Come in," Captain Montrose called.

Still miffed at him, Ro stood rigidly before the captain's desk. "I require the cabin boy Cen's and the deckhand Olt's assistance to prepare the men to face the sirènes."

The captain flicked her a glance. "At ease, huntress. I am no longer a captain in the king's navy, nor are you a king's man."

Ro blinked, her heart stalling in her chest. No longer a part of the king's fleet? This whole situation just kept getting better and better.

"Still," she said, "I require Olt's and Cen's assistance. May they be released from their regular duties to assist me?"

Pausing from whatever he was writing, he straightened and looked at her. "Why the lad Cen and the sailor Olt?"

Ro met his gaze. "Both are competent, Olt has an easy way with the men, and Cen is swift to obey. I need someone I trust at my back, and should I require help rowing ashore, they are whom I choose."

The captain's eyes widened. "You would risk both their lives? At such close quarters with the sirens?"

Ro's jaw clenched. "Let's not discuss risk and lives, unless you'd care to bring up this whole doomed voyage in the first place?"

The captain's look darkened. "This voyage is not doomed, milady. Not with you and . . . with you aboard."

Ro shook her head, her resolve to keep things civil slipping a notch further. "It will be if I cannot have the help I need, mon capitaine. Can Cen and Olt assist me?"

Captain Montrose studied her for too long a moment. "They can. Please have them report to me first."

Ro nodded and started to turn away, but he held up a hand.

"But I do not release them to row ashore with you. Even I cannot condemn them to such a fate."

Ro nodded once more and fled, only allowing relief to

stream through her once the door was firmly shut behind her. Just as Olt had said, now they'd have the captain's scrutiny, but at least they could work together without sneaking around to do so.

Now if she could think of a way to take Cen with her.

26

*R*o slammed the door of her cabin, tossed her bow on the bed, and fell beside it, not moving. She was exhausted. She wanted to sleep.

But they were almost there, and there was still so much to do. Her eyes flew open. Her whirling mind refused to let her rest, so she jumped up and began to pace.

One more day.

The captain estimated they would reach their destination in only one more day.

All of a sudden, after months of yearning to be there already, for her mission to be over, she wasn't ready. She wanted to go back. To change her mind.

Why did doubt always assault her right before a task?

She dropped onto the bed and buried her face in her hands. *Creator, help me. I don't know what to do. I don't know how to proceed. I don't know who to trust. I'm so very lost.*

Ro couldn't help chuckling at that. After months of planning, *that* was her prayer?

Look on the bed.

Ro froze, then slowly turned, staring at the bed where she

daren't sleep for fear of being pitched onto the floor with every rock of the ship. Storm season was brutal.

There, on the thin mattress, lay her bow, redone, and three gleaming arrows. They were silver from tip to fletching, and they looked far too short for her bow. Ro couldn't help missing her crossbow once more. They would've fit it perfectly.

But her bow . . . Ro's mouth fell open.

Gleaming, pitch-black wood, a sturdy darkwood of some kind with deep-red tones, her bow was now curvy and elegant instead of understated and functional, with fairy runes embedded along its length.

Ro inched her hand forward, fearing to take her eyes off it lest it disappear.

A white rose glimmered to life alongside it.

Ro's hand changed direction, and she picked it up first. It unraveled into a note.

The Queen of the Fairies' voice wafted out of the rose, like a sigh drifting on a breeze. *My arrows fly true and never miss their mark. Accept this gift of my favorite bow as well, a token of my faith in you. It shall return to me when the last arrow flies. The Mighty King said you were in need; I hope I have satiated it. Hunt well.*

Ro smirked. Clever.

The white rose began to glow, then it sank into the palm of her hand, melting like snow in warm sun, a reflection of the first time she'd met the Queen of the Fairies. A rush of peace invaded her.

Ro smiled, a measure of calm taking up residence in her heart. Although she'd felt unsettled since she took this job, the feeling fled as if it had been banished.

She stared down at her palm, where it still tingled from the rose's warmth. The Creator didn't always answer, but when He answered that swiftly, that surely—and used the Fairy Queen to do it, no less—it was astounding.

Ro hefted the bow in her hands, taking time to admire it

before seizing an arrow and pulling it back, getting a feel for the weapon. The arrow lengthened in her hand, fitting her draw exactly.

Surprised, Ro dropped it. The arrow clattered to the floor with a slight hum, shortened once more. Ro whistled. "Incroyable."

A knock had her in motion before she'd even thought to do so. She opened her door. One of the sailors she hadn't yet spoken to stood there. Lars? Hans? Anders?

His fair looks said he most likely hailed from the north.

"Oui?"

"Milady, the cap'ain would like to see you in the infirmary."

Ro nodded and followed him across the ship, and as she did, she looked over the bustle on deck and sighed. She'd done all she could to prepare the men. Now it was up to them to use her training.

Tomorrow was almost here.

Ro took in the cabin that was slightly bigger than the captain's, daylight struggling to get past the coverings over the portholes, and startled a little to find the first mate, quartermaster, and physician in the infirmary as well.

She nodded to each in turn, her gaze lingering longest on the physician.

His return stare was unrelenting.

Ro tore her gaze away, and her eyes settled on the captain. "You wished to see me, mon capitaine?"

Captain Montrose nodded. "I wish to discuss our plans with you."

Ro kept from rolling her eyes by the sheerest of willpower. But of course he would wait till the day before.

"Should your mission succeed, we will wait for you here."

"And should it not?" Ro crossed her arms and leaned against the doorframe.

Captain Montrose glanced to the physician, who had not yet taken his eyes from Ro. "Should your mission not succeed, should the sirens refuse to meet with you or refuse peaceful talks, or you do not return in a timely manner, then we have a way to protect ourselves."

Ro tilted her head. "Different from what I brought? Your cannons have not worked."

Captain Montrose rubbed the back of his neck. "Well . . ."

"Shall I continue, Captain Montrose?" The physician's quiet voice filled the room, and Ro almost staggered under its weight.

How could his voice hold such power? And why couldn't she sense anything magical from him?

The captain looked relieved and nodded, stepping back to give the physician plenty of room to speak. An odd move.

The physician moved forward fluidly, one of the metal containers in his hand, and set it gently on the workbench Ro had used twice to inspect Cen's throat. "I carry with me a way to keep the ship safe. You have seen it, no?" His softly accented voice lilted of Spanish origins.

Ro just stared back, arms crossed, neither confirming nor denying. Oui, she'd seen it, but that was no one else's business. She didn't miss the captain's questioning look.

The physician smiled and opened the box with great care. "I do not recommend you take one with you to your negotiations," the physician continued, "but you may use our possession of it to, shall we say, tip things in your favor?"

He pulled out the glowing, hissing, popping orb, lighting arcing wildly within. His hands were encased in thick leather gloves.

Ro's hand twitched in phantom pain. "What does it do?"

The physician nodded once, as if he approved of Ro's question. "It is a weapon that paralyzes any living substance in the water. The blast radius does not go far, not yet, but it is enough to protect this ship."

Ro tilted her head. "Why are you telling me this now? And why have you not used it before?"

"It is experimental." The physician's smile didn't come close to reaching his eyes as he carefully hid his weapon away. "I thought perhaps you would want to know, should the king offer a bounty on siren bodies. He now has a way to get them."

And she was on the vessel sent to test the new weapon. Lovely. "I see." Ro thought a moment. "How will you use them before being sirened? If the blast radius doesn't go far."

He looked pleased. "An astute question." He said nothing more.

Ro didn't push. For some reason. "But you won't use them unless absolutely necessary, non? You'll give me an opportunity to first negotiate?"

The physician tilted his head, the move graceful, alluring, and downright repulsive.

"Merci." Ro turned to leave.

Captain Montrose spoke. "I have one more thing to discuss with you regarding the sirens."

Ro glanced back.

"It is regarding your navigation. To where the sirens live."

Ro nodded and stood before them, feeling judged. She kept her arms firmly crossed to ward off their quiet stares. "How will I find it?"

His eyes briefly met the first mate's. "First of all, they will call to you."

Ro tilted her head. "But I am not a man."

"If the legends are correct, then the sound will be tantalizing and make you want to investigate, but not enchant you so far as losing yourself."

All that water . . . all alone . . . Ro forced the thought away.

She lifted her chin. "And if I miss it? Will I know I've done so or find myself at a tropical island in a few days?"

Again, he and his first mate exchanged a look. Ro wished they'd stop doing that and let her in on it already.

"Huntress, do you remember the strange markings on one of the charts? The ones you asked about, but I didn't quite answer?"

"The marks that run along the coasts of the Americas? The dots?"

The captain nodded gravely. "Such markings are new. Not on any other chart."

She knew that. "What are they?"

"Outcroppings. Rock formations. Ones that were not there before, ones that seem to form all on their own and overnight. When this all began, a ship could not pass from the great sea to the coast without being within hearing distance of at least one of them. Now there is no way to cross. At all."

Ro thought of the barrier on the map she'd so carefully memorized, and her stomach dropped.

"That particular map shows us their locations and if they change."

Ro just stared at the captain, her mind whirling with implications. Olt and Cen were right. But she needed to act clueless. "If they change?"

Captain Montrose nodded solemnly. "You of all people should know a map can be enchanted."

Well, she hadn't. Not until Cen had told her.

The physician had withdrawn to the background, a silent observer, his gaze fastened on Ro.

"It means, huntress," put in the first mate, speaking to her for the first time, "that the sirens have somehow made a barrier to ensure ships cannot pass. You couldn't reach the Caribbean, even if you wanted to. They have hemmed the Americas in, and us, out."

"In other words, if you follow the compass true, you cannot miss them," the captain continued.

Ro's stomach dropped, and it wasn't just the ship pitching in an uneven cadence. It wasn't just a rumor, then.

What kind of creatures had the power to create something so vast?

27

The air warmed and the water turned lighter in hue as they neared the Caribbean. Billowing clouds broiled in the distance.

Ro checked one of the net traps, folded and ready to toss over the edge of the ship, then drag underneath the hull, entangling any sirens trying to tear the ship apart from the bottom.

The men were antsy, casting furtive glances over the rails.

Ro could understand why, now that she knew more of the rumors. A siren stole a human's free will, sucking it from them as if they were drinking it. A sirened person would do anything the siren told them. Even kill themselves. Or run a ship aground.

And the sirens hated humans, men especially. The bloodthirsty creatures would stop at nothing to make them suffer in the most excruciating ways possible.

She only hoped she could find a way to help them move past the hate. Reach a compromise.

Ro moved on to a harpoon gun, swiveled harmlessly to the sky until they were pulled around and aimed, checking and rechecking the crew's work. They'd followed her instructions well.

She'd had nearly three months to plan, yet she hated how many variables still danced before her. How did one follow siren protocol? Would the sirens even speak with her?

Or would the killing start before Ro even found out?

She was jolted from her reverie when the captain's shout and his crew's answering shouts filled the air. Ro turned and watched the commotion, still mesmerized by the intricate dance that was a working ship.

"Full halt!"

"Full halt!" Crewmen echoed the captain's words.

Sails were furled, anchors were dropped, and men took up protective stances all over the ship.

Captain Montrose came over to her, solemn look in place. "Milady? It is time."

Ro nodded. That was rather obvious.

"Are you prepared?"

"But of course." As much as she could be.

The weathered skin around the captain's eyes creased, but only for a moment. "Bon voyage, Mademoiselle. Allez avec Dieu."

Go with God.

Ro's gaze flew to the captain's in surprise. It was the first time he'd spoken French in her presence. Ro realized with a start he thought it would be the last, too.

She squared her shoulders and asked the question she'd been dreading since meeting with Captain Red. "I need a map, mon capitaine. One of the enchanted ones."

His eyebrows lifted in surprise. "I can assure you that if you head due west, you'll reach the outcroppings. Follow the compass and the stars, as I showed you."

Ro would be following a different compass first.

She shook her head, firm and insistent. "And if the outcroppings shift in the night? They already have several times on this voyage alone."

He nodded thoughtfully. "I'll see what I can do."

Ro swallowed hard. "I'd like to take the lad, Cen, with me too. To row the boat."

The captain's brows lowered. "Do you care nothing for his life? He cannot be in the siren's presence, not unless you want him to die. You have an advantage the rest of us do not."

Ro flushed. There was no way she could out Cendre, not without putting her in danger. "I think I may have found a way . . ."

Captain Montrose cut her off. "Wax in the ears doesn't work. Nor cotton. Nor any other substance. Tying a person down doesn't work. They will tear off their own limbs before giving up." He eyed her suspiciously. "What have you found that we, who have tried so many things, have not?"

Ro's eyes found Olt's. He gave his head a slight shake. Ro looked back at the captain.

"Forgive me, Captain Montrose. I did not want to be alone on the open water."

The captain accepted her words, though he still looked suspicious. "Very well. Remember, row all night. Do not stop. Tie the boat down and wait at the rocks. We will stay here, out of their reach, and you will contact them. Find out where the rest of them are."

She nodded. "I'll retrieve my things."

Ro escaped as the captain headed to the forecastle, and presumably, the infirmary.

She quickly gathered her belongings and returned to the lower deck. Captain Montrose was coming back from the infirmary, a leather tube in his hands, brass caps shining in the end-of-the-day sunlight. He handed it to her with a slightly bewildered expression.

"He already had a map prepared for you, huntress."

Ro blinked at that. She hadn't found enchanted ink in the infirmary either, and she couldn't enchant her copy no matter how hard she'd tried. Her traced version stayed as still and lifeless as any normal map. What kind of power did the physician wield? And how could she possibly learn to wield her own powers?

She'd give anything to know how she worked.

The captain pulled her from her thoughts. "The time to leave is now, huntress."

Ro tucked the map's cylinder over her shoulder, settled her bow more firmly across her back, and climbed down the netting on the side of the ship.

They gave her a few small casks of rainwater, something they had in abundance with all the storms, as well as dried venison and hardtack, the only edible things left on this ship, and sent her on her way with all the enthusiasm of a funeral.

Which it very well might be.

She settled the oars in place and started rowing away, into the setting sun. She held Olt's gaze as long as she could. His eyes promised he'd watch after Cendre, keep her safe.

Ro had to trust him. What else could she do?

Ro neared the rendezvous point. Well, according to the compass Captain Red had given her, anyway. It now swiveled back and forth slightly, as if in anticipation.

The ocean was an endless fabric of blue, fathomless and unceasing. Ro found herself looking forward to seeing land once again.

A tiny speck on the horizon grew until it became clear. It was a ship. Captain Red's ship. Ro was certain her arms were going to fall off before she reached it.

As she moved into the shadow of the *Siren Hunter*, two more rowboats joined hers, and two members of her hired crew crawled into her boat. Captain Red sat tall in her own boat, flamboyant hat perched upon her head.

"Oh, Captain Red," Ro panted breathlessly. "You have no idea how happy I am to see you." It had been a *long* night.

The captain grinned, white teeth flashing. "I look forward to the second payment I'll receive at the end of this foolhardy voyage." She quirked an eyebrow. "Did you bring it with you?"

Ro nodded and pulled the map from the bottom of the boat, passing it over to the pirate. She wondered if Captain Montrose would be furious when she came back without it.

The pirate popped open an endcap and unfurled the map greedily, studying it while the rowboats bobbed in the water. The other pirates crowded around her.

"That's the sirens' points of attack, all right." Ro watched with interest as the pirate captain drew circles and lines all over the map with her finger, linking the attacks. "The concentrations seem to be here, here, and here. Oh, and look. The rocks to the north just shifted."

Her eyes glowed as she looked up at Ro.

"This is exactly what we need." Captain Red rolled the map and carefully returned it to its waterproof tube. "Thank you, huntress."

Ro nodded and relaxed a little. At least she'd finally done something right.

The captain glanced at the crew crowding into her rowboat and peering over her shoulders. "All right, all right, that's enough. Back to your posts."

They all whooped and scurried away. The rowboats rocked with their movements.

Captain Red pulled out a tin and opened it. She pinched something and offered it to Ro. "Here, huntress. Eat this."

Ro skeptically looked at the thin gray flake in the captain's hand. "And what is this?"

Captain Red smirked. "A siren scale."

Ro's eyes snapped up to hers. "Why in the realms would I want to eat it?" she demanded, horrified.

"It will make you immune to their song. Something I very much think you'll thank me for later. And stop looking at me like I kicked a baby. It doesn't harm the creatures. We trade for them."

Like that made Ro feel any better.

Captain Red gave a deep belly laugh. "From the sirens themselves, huntress. Your face can't hide a thing, can it?"

Ro grumbled at nothing in particular and peered at the flake closely. Now that Captain Red mentioned it, it did look rather like a large fish scale. Ro swallowed hard, trusting the captain more than she had on the entire voyage so far, and placed it on her tongue. It melted in her mouth with a sharp, salty flavor, much like dried seaweed.

"As long as it's in your system," continued the captain, "you won't be tempted to drown yourself or anything else they demand of you."

Captain Red nodded to her crew, and they began rowing. The three rowboats moved apart in the water, Captain Red in one, Ro in another.

She was more than willing to let the other crewmembers row for her.

Ro's jaw started to go numb, and the last vestiges swelled in her mouth and turned slimy. She made a face and tried to spit it out, but she couldn't. Her mouth wasn't working quite right.

The captain laughed at the look on her face. "You'll want to eat the whole thing, huntress, even the gross bits. Believe you me."

Ro couldn't say she agreed, but she worked her tongue until it went down. She shuddered. Once the numbness faded and she could talk without gagging, she asked, "How long does it last?"

"About three days. It's rather potent."

Ro nodded, trying not to think about it. Captain Red grinned, her eyes roving the water for unseen threats.

"I thought women were immune," Ro managed, trying not to think about the slime or the salty flavor coating her throat. Or heave it back out.

Captain Red's expression dimmed a little under her bright smile. "Ah, huntress, we all want to believe in a little magic, women most of all. The sirens can still drown us if they want to."

Ro wasn't convinced. "Can men not use it? The scales?"

Captain Red shrugged, her eyes on the water. "Sure they can. But men are addled by a fine figure and pretty face on most days. Add magic and allure to it, and the scales tend not to do much good."

Ro's look was sharp. "But they can use it? To survive?"

The captain eyed her. "Aye. Perhaps," she amended. "It *can* keep them from being enchanted, but it usually doesn't. It's not worth the waste of a scale, in my opinion."

"Any life saved is worth it to me."

Captain Red slid her a speculative glance. "But they have to want to be saved, now don't they?"

Ro frowned. Who wouldn't want to save their own life? But if she'd found a way to save Olt . . . "May I have another? Non, wait. Two more?"

The captain wordlessly took another small case from within her frock coat, as if she'd been expecting Ro to ask, and stretched between the boats to pass it to Ro. Ro slipped it into her pocket with a nod, gratefulness filling every pore.

Cen and Olt would've been able to come after all. But if the king's men found out . . . she shuddered as she thought of sirens being hunted for their scales, no matter what she might accomplish here. She tucked away the information for later. Cen and Olt would have to keep her secret.

Or never know of it in the first place.

Captain Red grinned, eyes back on the water. "Don't look so gratified, huntress. You paid for it. Quite handsomely, I might add. It is I who should be thanking you for the mounds of gold now in my coffers."

Ro shook her head as the other pirates laughed. Captain Red may be a formidable woman, a commanding leader, and a fearsome pirate, but she was a bit of a sweetheart underneath it all. No matter what she might say.

The *Siren Hunter* grew smaller in the distance, and Ro couldn't help but wish she could go onboard and just forget the whole hunt. Go home.

"And now for the best part. Huntress, catch."

Ro's hand went up instinctively, and Merja tossed Ro a golden fruit, oblong, leathery, and soft. Ro's eyes widened. "Mango?"

Captain Red grinned. "We've got coconuts and bananas too."

Ro's mouth watered embarrassingly, to where she was wiping drool off her chin before she'd even taken a bite. The tangy, sweet juice filled her mouth, and Ro groaned. The whole voyage had been four months too long. She'd never tasted fruit this good before.

"Told ya she wouldn't mind the scale much after that!" one of the pirates cackled.

Ro just grinned and polished off the fruit, ducking her hands in the water to clean them and her face. The mango had lasted maybe three seconds.

"How long till we're at the barrier?" Ro asked.

"Not long now, huntress," another random crewmember answered.

Ro frowned. They were far closer to the barrier than the *King's Ransom*. "Aren't you afraid of the sirènes finding your ship?"

Merja snorted. "The creatures only chase after men."

"Don't we all!" chortled one of the other crewmen, er, crewwomen.

After a round of laughter from the crew and a grin from the captain, Captain Red continued. "They leave us be without any male presence onboard. Madame LaChance has a vested interest in this as well, huntress. You see, we have an exclusive agreement with the sirens to let our cargo pass."

Ro's eyebrows climbed her forehead, and she wasn't sure they'd be coming back down anytime soon.

"Unlike the English king, we truly want a lasting peace with the sirens. Hence why our joint benefactress agreed to fund this venture in the first place."

Now Ro's mouth fell open. She spluttered out indignant words. "May I ask why you are just now telling me this? And why you asked me . . . what you did?"

Why had she pushed Ro to hunt the sirens without negotiations first if that's not what she wanted?

The captain's glance held a warning, though a smirk still danced around her lips. As always. "I'll tell you what you need to know, when you need to know it." She grinned. "And to test you, of course."

But of course. So if peace talks failed, not only would the sirens be hunted down, Ro very well may be hunted down by a disgruntled Madame LaChance. If the woman did such things.

Ro nodded, digesting the words, beyond grateful the captain's women had taken over rowing. She'd most certainly not done enough to stay in shape on the *King's Ransom*.

After a time, Captain Red asked, "What troubles you, huntress?"

Ro startled, her gaze shooting to the captain's. "Besides what you just told me?" She gave the captain a grim smile. "Nothing of import."

Captain Red raised her hand. "Halt!"

The pirates lifted their oars out of the water, and the boats slowed, swaying gently in the waters.

The captain propped her elbows on her knees and leaned forward. "You've been among king's men for months, I'll give you that, but the lie you just said to my face is not acceptable. So tell me what you're thinking, and I'll allow this venture to continue."

Ro swallowed back a retort about who was keeping information from whom. "The captain has orders to wipe out the sirens. All of them. No negotiation or treaty as the king reluctantly allowed me to pursue, and as I now find is the only acceptable outcome for Madame LaChance. I'm afraid they're going to attack while I'm gone. And I cannot help but think it all has something to do with the physician, with his lightning spheres and enchanted maps."

"Perhaps you've delayed their attack."

"Perhaps. Perhaps not." Her eyes fell on where the captain had tucked the map. "I pray I've not made a grave mistake, bringing you that."

"I see. Then we haven't much time. Is there anything more?"

Ro hesitated, then decided not to mention her fears for Cendre. Not here.

After a moment of no sound other than the gentle lapping of waves against the rowboats, Captain Red spoke quietly. "You have not told me everything."

Ro chose her words carefully. "Non, I have not. And I cannot. But I will." She let her eyes flick over the crew present. "When it is just the two of us."

"I can accept that." She eyed Ro. "As long as it will not endanger my life or that of my crew."

"It will not."

Captain Red nodded once, then straightened. "Move out!"

And Ro found herself immensely grateful once more that she'd hired them against the king's wishes.

28

The rocks came into view before the singing did.
Shiny like black obsidian, spires of blade-sharp
stone jutted into the sky from the water, creating an impossible
barrier. Ro's mouth fell open.

Captain Red spoke for them all. "Stories don't quite do it
justice, aye?"

"Aye," Ro and a few others echoed.

All three rowboats stilled, drifting in the water, as the occupants took in the sight before them.

The deep blue of the ocean faded into the pure black of the
obsidian, each spray of white foam upon the rocks highlighting
the disparate shades.

Ro tracked it along the horizon, as far as the eye could see
in either direction. The sirens had the power to create *this*? A
tiny niggle of fear wormed its way into her gut.

Ro squashed it flat. She didn't have time for that. Still, she
lifted the small silver cross, a gift from her père, from inside
her shirt and kissed it, muttering, "Saint Margaret, Saint
Catherine, and Saint Jeanne preserve us all," in honor of her
mère.

A few of the crew eyed her, while a few others hastily made

the sign of the cross or echoed her words with their own patron saints.

Ro cleared her throat. "May we proceed, ma capitaine?"

Without a word, the pirates resumed rowing, the mood now somber and intense.

Suddenly, when they weren't that far from the dark stones, the most beautiful singing in the world came to them. The boats jerked out of rhythm.

Captain Red slashed her hand. "Keep rowing, lasses. Don't let it distract you."

They tried to obey. The rowing was no longer smooth, and the rowers looked like a group of adolescents learning to do so for the first time.

But how could Ro blame them? Even she was distracted. Ro was beyond thankful for the siren scale. How would they have reacted without it?

But the enchanting voice was hesitant, unsure. It started and stopped a few times before giving up altogether.

They all breathed a collective sigh of relief and cut toward the outcropping.

Ro signaled that she wanted to go away from the fading strains of music, and the captain nodded her agreement. They found a little grotto in the black stone, perfect for mooring all three rowboats.

The captain signaled for them to stay put and started to get out of the boat, but Ro stopped her.

"Ma capitaine, this is my mission. If they do not welcome me, I do not want you to pay for it."

Captain Red got a stubborn bent to her jaw. "And we're here to back you, no matter how this plays out."

Ro hesitated, then nodded when she saw the pirate would not be budged. "D'accord. But do allow me to go first, s'il vous plaît."

The captain looked a little disgruntled, but she sat back and waved Ro on.

She moved to get out. Up close, the rock looked like slick, dark-gray glass. Ro startled a little when she touched it. It. Was. Huge. It went for kilomètres upon kilomètres—she snatched her hand back. Its vastness snuffed out.

Perfect. Now she was connected with *rocks* of all things.

She tentatively grabbed hold and stepped out of her boat.

Not only was it huge, it thrummed with magic, singing a melody of its own. Ro paused. Non, not a melody. It harmonized. But with what?

The rock was slick like glass, and Ro's heart plunged as she stepped onto the glistening surface.

The stone wasn't a solid color at all—it was completely see-through, all the way to the ocean floor, though Ro couldn't see a thing in the dark-blue water caressing it. Ro swayed, and the captain was at her elbow, holding her upright.

"Steady, huntress. Are you all right?"

Ro nodded, still woozy, and tore her eyes from the fathoms of emptiness below. "Oui, Madame. Merci."

The captain barked a laugh, steering her farther up the rock, her feet somehow steady though Ro's were off-kilter. "Whoa, there, huntress. I'm not a 'Madame' yet. Give me a few years before you start slinging such terms about."

Ro chuckled and found her footing. "But of course, Mademoiselle."

Every step was treacherous, but the entire pirate crew climbed onto the rocks behind her, trusting her to lead. She fumbled through every step until the singing came again.

The haunting melody stopped and started again—the rocks definitely harmonized with the siren's voice—and Ro homed in on the sound as if it were a fairy light. Unable to resist its pull, she swiftly found her way to a place behind the siren.

Ro and the pirate crew knelt behind a sheaf of jagged rocks, its thrumming zipping through Ro's fingers as she clutched the spires from where she crouched.

Ro's mouth dropped open as her eyes fell upon the most

beautiful woman she'd ever seen. Stark naked, her skin so pale it had a gray-blue tinge to it—which didn't strike Ro as odd for some reason—jet-black hair shimmering with hints of iridescent blue, turquoise, and purple that fell past her waist, her back to them—Ro couldn't help but be mesmerized.

A head popped out of the water. "Merida! Is someone coming?"

The siren on the rock frowned. "I don't know. I thought I felt something, but now I'm not sure. Did you see anything?"

The siren in the water shook her head. "No, nothing. But you're the faster swimmer. Want to switch places?"

The siren on the rock, Merida, her profile to them, gave a feral grin that chilled Ro to her bones—it made the creature look otherworldly and completely inhuman—and plunged into the water.

The other siren climbed out, billowing dark curls springing around her shoulders, pale legs replacing midnight scales of moments before. Ro blinked. Incroyable.

The siren began a haunting melody that had Ro closing her eyes and leaning weakly against the rocks. The whole of the Opéras of Paris hadn't a singer who could compare.

"Huntress, what did they say?"

Ro's eyes flew wide at the whispered question. She'd forgotten anyone was with her. She quickly relayed the sirens' conversation.

Captain Red got a grim set to her mouth. "Then we haven't any time to waste, huntress. They may discover your ship soon."

If nothing else broke the trance, that did it. Ro's eyes flew wide, and she began picking her way to the siren. Though she realized belatedly the pirate captain had said nothing about her own ship.

Ro stood a distance behind the siren, not sure what to say. Not wanting her to stop singing. She took a deep breath. "Your voice is lovely."

The siren startled, and in one smooth flipping motion, all her scales turned from the palest blue-gray to the darkest gray-black. She blended in perfectly with the stones. She crouched and aimed her body toward the water.

"Wait, please!" Ro cried.

The stones echoed her cry.

The siren jerked around and stared at Ro with wide eyes—that were completely black. No other color touched them, not even white.

"Please, don't go," Ro said again. "I must speak with you."

The fear in the siren's eyes warred with curiosity. After a moment of startled silence, the siren asked, "How do you speak my language?"

The siren's sultry tones washed over Ro, and she shivered at the voice that was not human yet . . . was so much better. She shook off the thought.

Ro made herself answer. "French?"

The stunning siren gave one shake of her head, sending her curling hair glistening like black silk and shimmering with hidden rainbows. "Non, you are speaking my language. The language of the sea. Impossible for humans to know."

Ro grunted. But of course her maddening gift would show up now, and without her knowledge. "Your language?" She listened closely to the cadence of her words, but they sounded like regular old French to her. Ro tilted her head. "I hear only French."

The siren just stared at her.

Ro rushed on, not wanting to lose the moment. "I must speak with your queen. I have an urgent matter to discuss with her. Will you ask her? If I may hold an audience with her?"

The siren didn't respond.

"It is of the utmost importance that I speak with her. Please."

Still nothing.

"What is your name?" Ro asked.

Ro waited an eternity before the siren spoke.

"Llyr."

Ro blew out the breath she'd been holding. At least the siren hadn't left yet, oui? "Llyr, I seek peace with your queen. I wish to prevent more human deaths. Can you understand that? I want them to stop harming you, and I want you to stop harming us."

Confusion filtered over the cold, precisely beautiful yet not-quite-human face. "We wish womankind no harm."

Oh, dear. Here came the tricky part. "Oui, but we suffer as our trade and as our men suffer." Ro shifted a little. "Might you ask your queen if she will see me? Just to talk?"

"Who else is with you?"

Ro started to turn, thought better of it on the slick surface, and waved a hand instead. "I brought a crew of women with me."

Maybe mentioning the king's crew wasn't wise. Though if later the sirens thought she was deceiving them . . . Ro rubbed her temples. This was why she didn't want to be the negotiator. What was the right thing to do?

Ro made up her mind. "I come on behalf of the English King Wilhelm and"—she swallowed, hoping she wouldn't regret her next words—"Madame LaChance."

The siren, who was glancing past her, whipped her eyes back to Ro. After a long moment full of tense speculation, she said, "I will ask, but I promise nothing."

Ro smiled. "Merci beaucoup, Llyr."

The siren gave her a startled look, then without warning, she plunged in a perfect arc into the water. Right before she hit, her legs fused together in a midnight tail that matched her hair perfectly, fins flaring out like fluttering sails, iridescent glimmers of all spectrums of the rainbow throwing light into Ro's eyes.

Ro shielded her face as a thought occurred to her. "Oh, wait!"

But the creature was gone. A slight ripple echoed out from where she'd disappeared, and the rocks did not amplify Ro's cry.

Ro sighed. Should they wait here, on the pirate ship, what? And for how long? All questions Ro should've asked when she'd had the chance.

Ro carefully made her way back to the crew. The rest of the women looked fearful, but Captain Red was giving her a steady, speculative look.

"What did she say?"

Ro replayed the conversation as she carefully settled in a dip that wasn't unbearably jagged.

"So we wait," the pirate concluded.

Ro nodded. "We wait."

29

*R*o paced the little island. What if the Siren Queen refused to see her? It wasn't like she could go underwater and demand to speak with her. Was it demeaning to ask her to meet above water? How did one discover siren etiquette, for heaven's sake?

The books and legends and news sheets she'd brought with her contained fanciful stories, wild speculation, and fear-mongering, not cold, hard facts that Ro could readily use.

The bow across her back hummed, as if saying all would be well.

Ro stilled in one of her laps. First rocks, now a bow. She was beginning to question her sanity.

She looped around for another lap of frustrated pacing. Fortunately for her, and thanks to a pebble in her boot, she'd discovered the rocks were no longer treacherous while walking barefoot. Power thrummed through her, settling her nerves a little. But just a little.

There were so many ways she could mess this up.

Goodness gracious, she should've asked the siren how long they'd have to wait.

The sun trekked across the sky, and the ocean bustled

beneath her feet. She stilled, reaching out with her senses. Ocean life teemed there, and she reveled in the thrill that coursed through her at the wholly new sensations. Something reached back out to her, inviting her to be a part of it all. Ro jerked away from it.

A slight ripple in the water caught her attention.

A half-face peeked out of the water, waterline just under its eyes. Ro went still, stuffing her anxiety deep inside. She watched it steadily, then inclined her head.

And that's what got the siren moving. Or should she say, sirens?

They came out of the water, a few at a time, hardly causing a ripple, their feet—human-looking feet—not leaving a trace of their passage on the slick obsidian outcropping.

Ro counted twenty-two of them, and they looked nearly identical. Raven-black hair came past their waists in all textures and shapes. Many different nationalities stood before her, yet all had gray-tinted skin, as if they'd been drained of any color. Human legs, covered in nearly colorless scales. Yet they were so entirely foreign, Ro couldn't have mistaken them for humans. They were flawless. Too flawless.

And completely naked.

Ro struggled to keep her eyes above the creature's neckline, scandalized that they so obviously didn't care to cover themselves. No wonder men ran their ships aground!

"You asked to see me, huntress?"

Ro startled a little and instantly regretted it. One moment the siren was at the edge of the rocks, and the next, standing in front of her. It was uncanny.

And impossible.

Ro bowed deeply and spread her hands in a gesture of peace, hoping her neck wasn't about to be slashed. Not that she could stop it with their speed.

"Oui, Madame. I thank you with all of my heart for agreeing to see me. You are the Sirène Queen?"

When she came out of her bow, she was glad to see the siren looked pleased. And hadn't moved any closer.

"Well at least the mighty huntress has some manners. Yes, I am the queen of all sirens." She studied Ro a moment. "Ah, I see you are uncomfortable with the female form. My sisters?"

Scales the color of pitch flipped over on their bodies, clothing them in tightly woven scales that looked like fish skin, slightly iridescent in the sunlight, full of dancing blues, purples, and greens.

Ro couldn't have been more thankful. She had sisters, sure, and she may have skinny-dipped once or twice on a dare, but she'd grown up in a strict Catholic home. Being naked . . . in public . . . was just not done.

"Now tell me, why have you come? My siren told me you came on a ship of men?" Her nose wrinkled in disgust as her eyes trailed over the female pirates at Ro's back.

Ro couldn't help the annoyance that flashed through her, nor her sense of helplessness. Perhaps the Siren Queen would understand?

"Oui, I have. Though my colleagues"—she waved a hand to those behind her—"have agreed to assist me with negotiations."

The Siren's Queen's lip curled to show her disdain, dismissing Ro's crew with a cutting glance. "Have you no other method of transport? Could you not have found another way to traverse my waters?"

Ro winced a little. "I tried, votre Majesté, but the English king seeks peace with you and your people. I suppose he wanted his people represented as well."

"A pity. You would have had more credibility with me had you chosen another way."

Didn't Ro know it.

"That may be, votre Majesté, but I am here anyway, and I seek a peaceful resolution to our conflict."

The Siren Queen raised an eyebrow, and Ro hesitated,

choosing her words carefully. A negotiator she was not, yet here she was. Her hesitation was just long enough for the Siren Queen to derail Ro's carefully formed words.

"And what know you of our conflict? Have you lived under the glistening seas with my people? Have you watched your sisters be kidnapped and gutted like fish or taken as slaves to entertain men until they are used up like dry husks and die from lack of ocean water?"

When she put it that way . . .

Ro bowed, just a little. "I am truly sorry for your losses, I cannot begin to say how sorry, and I'm here to prevent further losses. I not only want my people to live, I want yours to live as well, votre Majesté. I want to stop both sides of the killing."

The queen studied her a moment. "And why should you possibly care, huntress? You know nothing of my people."

"I care about all life, votre Majesté. What some crews have done to your people is unforgivable, and I would never say you can't defend yourselves. Never," she repeated, at the obvious skepticism from the Siren Queen and her entourage. "If someone attacks you, defend yourselves, but against your attackers and your attackers only."

The queen's smile was brittle. "Ah, but my sirens are curious. Explorers. Some range far and wide, discovering new waters, learning of new vessels. They do not often travel in muses."

"But of course, votre Majesté. And I do not want harm to come to them. But surely you must know that not every sirène attack is sanctioned by the king. He wants to end this as much as you do."

She spread her hands wide. "Then where is he? Why has he not come himself to reason with me?"

Wouldn't you like that. Ro kept her thoughts to herself and raised her chin. "I am his representative, Madame. I speak for him, and anything we agree upon, he will honor. He wishes to protect his people as well."

The Siren Queen snorted. "He wishes to protect his coffers, nothing more. Tell me, huntress, do you know the main trade on these waters? The main cargo of these ships that glide across my ceiling?"

"Uh . . ." Ro thought back to the books she'd read in the beast's library about the water trade routes of France. "Goods, spices, cloth, sugarcane, cotton . . ."

"Wrong." The Siren Queen smiled when Ro startled. She leaned forward, and she was so captivating, Ro leaned forward a little as well. "They trade in human flesh, huntress. Slaves. Prostitutes. Prisoners. Ah, I see this surprises you."

"I—I don't understand." Ro's mind scrambled. "Perhaps—"

The queen's smile turned coy. "Have you no slaves where you live, huntress?"

Ro blinked. "Slaves? Non, not anymore." At the siren's look, she felt she had to explain. "A curse was recently lifted from my kingdom, and it was a great equalizer. Those trapped in its clutches were unable to die, and they were poor, starving, hopeless. Those with servants no longer could afford them, and soon, master and servant were alike." Ro noticed she was rambling. "But I did notice quite a few in England. Servants, I mean. Not slaves. I mean—there were a few. That I saw."

Ro bit her lip. *Will you please be silent already?* She didn't want to know what the pirates at her back or the sirens before her were thinking of her prattling.

The Siren Queen continued to stare at her, unblinking. "Not servants. Slaves, huntress. Not working for money. Forced to work. Against their will. Kidnapped from their homes, taken against their will, shipped across the great seas, most dying in route and being thrown in my waters to pollute them. And you want to enable this to continue?"

Ro hesitated. Of course she didn't want that to continue, but surely the queen was exaggerating . . .

"Ah, I see. You knew nothing. Cannot be held responsible.

It isn't your problem. Perhaps the king will keep you better informed next time?"

Ro snapped her mouth closed. Her voice was far too hoarse when it came out. "I do not want that to continue, non."

"Then we are done here." The beautiful woman-like creature started to turn away.

"But I also do not want any more humans to die who do not deserve to do so."

The queen sighed heavily and turned back. "Oh, huntress, how little you know of the world."

Ro clenched her jaw. She may have been trapped in her kingdom for most of her lifetime, but she'd been on her own long enough. She knew more than the siren could possibly imagine.

But her mission was to make peace before the king sent his best huntsmen to wipe them all out and called other nations to do the same. She couldn't let the maddening queen rile her. Of course, the king had sent a huntress with an explosive temper to do what diplomats daren't. Wasn't that just like him?

"Votre Majesté, please, work with me here. What are you willing to negotiate? What can we do to broker peace?"

The Siren Queen blurred and was suddenly inches from Ro's face. Ro couldn't have breathed if she'd wanted to. Captain Red, just visible in Ro's peripheral, shifted within sword distance.

A siren to Ro's left matched the pirate captain's steps.

The Siren Queen hissed through clenched teeth. "These men are mine, huntress. They became mine when they captured my sisters and sold them off as curiosities, only to die a slow and painful death as they suffocated in your world. They became mine the moment they passed my sisters from man to man to ravish, then gutted them like fish or threw them back once they tired of their sport, pregnant with their spawn that cannot survive in our waters or on their land. They became mine when humans chose to declare war on me and mine, all while they threw disease-ridden bodies, human lives wasted, into my waters. They *made* it my problem. They are mine, huntress, and nothing you can do will separate me from my prey."

After a pause, the Siren Queen reached toward Ro's face. Ro stiffened, but she didn't back away.

"Curious." She lifted a tear from Ro's cheek that Ro didn't know was there. The siren jerked when the liquid came in contact with her skin and stared at Ro with wide eyes. "Curious indeed," she whispered.

"What is it, Your Majesty?" one of the other sirens asked.

The queen didn't acknowledge her, just continued to stare at Ro. "You are a mighty huntress indeed. The things you've seen. The things you've done. I've underestimated you."

Ro didn't know what to make of that. Had she seen everything in Ro's entire life through just one tear?

Slightly unnerving to say the least. And it reminded her of the beast. Able to read her thoughts with one touch.

The Siren Queen rubbed the tear between her fingers, then flicked it away. "Tell me, huntress, would you consider joining us?"

Ro blinked rapidly, as startled as most of the sirens surrounding their queen. The siren who'd taken her message to the queen, Llyr, watched Ro with open curiosity, a slight frown on her face.

"Join you? I—you—what do you mean?"

The Siren Queen's smile was rather cat-like. "Exactly what I said. You would be a great asset to my people." One regal eyebrow lifted. "Perhaps it would enable you to better broker peace as well."

Ro very much doubted that. The sirens weren't even a little bit human. If Ro joined them, she'd no longer be human. She'd no longer care about the world above.

She'd be no worse than they, ready to lend her skills to

hurting those she now fought for. And she suspected the Siren Queen knew it.

But curiosity won instead of instant rejection. "How is that even possible?"

The Siren Queen shrugged one colorless shoulder, her scales leaving an exquisite and jagged edge around her throat, trailing down below her arms, leaving them and her shoulders bare. "Exactly how it sounds, huntress. You would then be my representative to your king, and you would better understand our plight and help him understand ours."

Ro couldn't wrap her mind around it. "I can join you, just like that? Become a sirène?"

The Siren Queen grinned, revealing sharp, pointed teeth that looked like they'd been filed down to daggers. Kind of like shark's teeth. Ro blinked. Now that she hadn't been expecting.

The Siren Queen's smile was positively predatory. "Oh absolutely. You just have to agree to it."

Ro didn't miss the pucker that crossed Llyr's face, nor the delighted smile that lit up Merida's. Apparently there was more to it than that.

Wasn't there always?

"Votre Majesté, I beg of you to consider a treaty. Your people no longer harmed by passing ships. Trade agreements with my people. A course of action should any sailors violate the treaty. Other kingdoms following in the English king's footsteps. You can only gain from this."

The Siren Queen smiled, the expression crafty. "And so will you."

Ro nodded, not bothering to deny it. Why should she? "And so will we. No more lives lost, respect for creatures of the sea, our people made aware of your plight. It is advantageous for both our peoples."

The Siren Queen seemed to consider her words. "I'll think on it, huntress."

The queen turned away, her entourage trailing her. Something deep coral poked out of the queen's hair and vanished just as quickly.

Ro jumped. "Wait!" Something teased her memory.

The Siren Queen paused, suddenly facing Ro, though no closer, thank Dieu.

When Ro's eyes connected with Siren Queen's, her memories snapped into place. She was to ask for the combs in exchange for Madame LaChance financing this voyage. And it didn't seem at all odd that she'd just remembered.

"Forgive me, I also have a personal request of you. I've been asked . . . Madame LaChance . . . she said to ask for your comb? Your coral comb?" Ro frowned. "Or was it a set of pearl combs?"

The Siren Queen's entire demeanor changed, but then she gave Ro a wide smile, though Ro got the feeling it cloaked the siren's true feelings. "Well, which is it, huntress? I have both, and believe me, they do vastly different things."

"She mentioned both, I believe. In exchange for something you—she lost in these waters." Ro couldn't bring herself to accuse the siren to her face.

"Ah." The queen eyed her. "You are also authorized to speak for this Madame LaChance?"

"I am." Ro shrugged. "She said one of the ships you sank belonged to her, along with an item she cherished, and she wishes the combs in exchange."

The Siren Queen's jaw tightened for an infinitesimal moment. "I see."

Ro tilted her head. She couldn't help but asking, "What do they do? And why can't you just give the item back?"

She didn't like the smile the Siren Queen gave her. "This Madame LaChance is more cunning than I thought. My dear, if she has not said, then it is not for you to know."

She opened her palm and produced two glimmering, pearlescent combs. As in, one moment her palm was empty, and the next, they rested upon it. Although Ro had not seen them in the siren's hair, she was now aware they were missing from it.

Magic of any kind still startled Ro for some reason, even though she'd seen plenty of it. Even though she *had* it.

Ro squinted against the sheen they picked up and threw into her eyes. They looked like swan wings. "You're just . . . handing them over?"

The Siren Queen laughed. "These? Yes. She is quite right that the above world—her world—needs them far more than I do." She shrugged. "And then my debt to her is paid."

There was a forcefulness to the words that made them feel empty, hollow. Ro got the feeling that no matter what the Siren Queen did, Madame LaChance would never consider her debt paid.

The siren extended her hand, and Ro reached out and lifted them from her fingertips, careful not to touch the siren. She wasn't about to share any more memories with the underwater creature.

Ro looked up after she'd studied them a moment. "And the coral comb? The one that looks like a crown?" Her eyes drifted to the Siren's Queen's head, but it was no longer visible.

The Siren Queen gave a single nod. "I know the one you mean."

"May I have it for Madame LaChance as well?"

"Ah." The Siren Queen's smile held secrets Ro wasn't sure she wanted to know. "Now that, my dear, is not meant for the above world. Not ever." She nodded at the set in Ro's hands. "Take those back to your mistress. She'll have to be satisfied with those alone." She gave Ro a quelling look. "And I would watch myself around someone who wishes to take the power of the sea, huntress, and sends someone else to do it."

Power of the sea? What in all the realms?

Ro tucked the combs deep into her trouser's pocket, tying it closed and grumbling to herself. Not only did she have more questions, her mission from Madame LaChance was not yet fulfilled.

And she was uncertain it should be. Wasn't that just perfect?

Once more, the sirens turned to leave.

"Shall we wait here for your answer?" Ro asked. "I cannot leave your waters without it."

"Go back to your ship, huntress. I will send word." A predatory smile spread across her face. "And do consider my offer, huntress. You would be a considerable asset."

Ro bowed at the waist. "I will keep your offer in mind, votre Majesté, as I beg of you to take mine to heart as well."

When Ro straightened, not a siren was in sight.

30

*R*o turned to the pirates waiting behind her.

Captain Red said, "Well?" She looked a little disgruntled. "What did the creature have to say for herself?"

"Pardon?" Ro blinked. "Didn't you hear her?" They were all standing right behind her for the entire conversation, for goodness' sake.

Captain Red's eyebrows climbed her forehead. "You mean all that mumbo-jumbo of indecipherable sounds and hissing and clicking?"

"It t'wasn't no language I never did heard," another pirate put in, eyes wide.

Ro's mouth hung open. She'd been speaking a language she didn't even know that whole time?

Captain Red just waited.

Ro stuttered out her response. "Oh, well, uh, she said she'd consider my offer, and, um, she said those who have polluted her waters deserve her attacks, and she isn't looking for peace anytime soon. But she'll consider it."

Captain Red didn't blink. "Do we wait?"

Ro shook her head. "Non, she said to go back to our ships. She'll send word."

The pirates slowly scattered, eyes roving the edges of the outcropping, gathering anything they'd brought and heading toward the tied boats.

Captain Red stepped closer. "Think they'll truly consider it?"

Ro scowled. "I don't know. She was rather upset with her sirènes' deaths and the trading of flesh upon these waters, and rightfully so."

The captain nodded, then clapped Ro on the back. "Best update your captain, then."

Ro groaned and stretched her neck from side to side as the setting sun cast brilliant flames of orange across the water. Another long night of rowing. Wonderful.

They came to the tied rowboats, and Ro paused, counting the gathered crew, then eyeing the crafts. "Think we can leave one tied up in case I need it later?"

Ro climbed the netting over the side of the *King's Ransom*— which she still thought was ridiculous to keep on the side of a ship—and allowed herself to be helped aboard.

Every muscle in her body ached. That was the last time she was letting someone keep her from hard labor for months. She needed to be in good shape for every situation.

Ro hardly noticed as they hauled the small craft up behind her. Her eyes were starting to close all on their own.

"Were you successful?"

Ro opened bleary eyes and stared at Captain Montrose, letting his words untwist from utter nonsense until they formed real words.

"Ugh," she grunted.

He looked surprised. "I beg your pardon?"

She swiped a hand down her face. "Food, sleep. Tell you in the morning."

He nodded once, barking a few orders Ro didn't care to untangle. She started toward her cabin. He stopped her with a hand on her arm, and she almost sagged against him. She jerked away. She didn't want to give anyone, especially him, the wrong idea.

"What?" she asked.

"You've got to give me something, huntress. Will we need to defend ourselves?"

She squinted at him a moment before answering. "Now we wait."

He let her go, and she stumbled to her room and her blessed hammock. It cradled her aching body, and she prayed never to row straight through two whole nights ever again, right before sleep claimed her.

Something intruded upon her dreams.

"Nooo," she whined.

She sank deeper into the rough cotton, hoping whatever it was would leave her be.

But the high-pitched squealing that grated on her entire body just wouldn't let up.

"Shut le diable up!" she shouted to no one in particular and covered her ears with her hands. She hurt. Everything hurt. It hurt to be awake.

The squeal came again, reminding her of pigs being slaughtered at the market. But they'd never sounded quite like this.

Her eyes popped open. Wait a second. Something was wrong. The sound came again, and Ro lurched straight up from the utter pain it caused.

The squeal came again, full of pain and misery and death, and Ro fell out of her hammock in her haste, gasping against the pain. She sat up and covered her ears at the physical agony the sound caused her, and her wide eyes fell to the planks below her.

The sound seemed to be traveling through the wood, vibrating through her body, not just her ears. What in all the realms?

When the throbbing eased enough for her to stand, she slipped on her boots and jacket and grabbed her closest weapon, the short sword gifted from the king—habit from years of answering a wolf's cry in the middle of the night—and stumbled out the door.

She came around the edge of her doorframe, and what she saw in the torchlight stopped her cold.

Sirens, four of them, strung up by their arms above their heads. Three were gutted, heads drooping forward, covered in colorless gray scales, center of their bodies hollow, guts spilled all over the ground beneath their limply hanging fins.

The quartermaster was stabbing the fourth at intervals, between the captain demanding answers and not receiving a response. Ro turned and vomited all over the deck. The high-pitched squeals came again to the answering squelch of blade stabbed into flesh, and Ro cried out. The men winced and hunched their shoulders with every cry.

She wondered if they could feel it through the planks as she did.

She spun, wiping her mouth, and darted straight toward the siren, down the short flight of stairs to the lower deck. "Arrête! Mon Dieu, stop!"

The siren picked up her head and looked right at Ro as the captain picked up a scimitar and swiped it through her middle in a U-curve. Everything spilled out, just as when Ro cleaned her prey. Only a creature this magnificent should never be gutted. Not like this.

The life drained from the siren's eyes as Ro's feet carried her too late to the siren's rescue. She stopped before the four hanging forms, bile churning in her mouth, sword clutched in her hands.

A void echoed where their power had vibrated through the deck.

She spun on the captain. "How could you?"

His look said he could not be bothered with a female's delicate constitution, and it took everything Ro had not to hurl him over the edge to any waiting sirens below. He and the surrounding men took plugs of wax from their ears. They faintly glowed and pulsed with an inner white light.

She looked around for Olt or Cen but didn't see them.

The quartermaster spoke first, eyes bright as he looked over his prizes. "Caught 'em watching our ship. Couldn't have 'em singing us to our deaths, now could we? They'll bring a fair price from the king, that's fer sure."

Ro couldn't even fathom how they'd gotten the sirens aboard without setting off a full-fledged attack. Or being entranced by them. Had they used the physician's weapons? Stunned them and carted them aboard?

Her eyes found the captain's. "My job is to negotiate with the sirènes. Find out what they want and stop them from sinking ships. And you think capturing them and killing them before I can do that will help how?"

The captain's look bordered on hostile. "Non, Mademoiselle, your job was to hunt the sirens. Wipe them out entirely so they no longer sink our ships." He shrugged. "It's not my fault you got the idea of negotiating with them stuck in your head. Besides, they were surrounding us. I had to defend my ship."

She gestured wildly to the hanging corpses with one hand, unable to make herself look at them. "So you decide to kill them before I can do my *job*?"

A shaggy eyebrow lifted. "This is your job. Not some namby-pamby attempt at a truce." A hint of a sneer touched his lips.

Ro's hands curled into fists, one strangling the sword's hilt. "Non, Monsieur, you should not assume you know my orders from the king. I am to stop them by any means necessary. And the only way to get them to leave you alone—leave everyone alone—is if they agree to it." She shouted in his face. "Yet before negotiations are complete, you declare war on the entire race! How many ships do you think they're going to sink now?"

His gaze turned colder, and Ro shivered in the matching breeze that danced over the ship. She didn't know if she'd ever feel warm again, not after seeing that.

"I have my orders too, Mademoiselle. I urge you to keep in mind that I do not answer to you."

Ro stepped close, nose to nose, and the men around them shifted. "Let me make myself clear, mon capitaine. You will not harm another sirène while I am onboard this vessel. You will send your deepest apologies to the Sirène Queen, and you will offer whatever gifts she deems worthy to assuage her anger. Can that measly little brain of yours understand that?"

Maybe that was taking it a bit too far, but Ro didn't care. She poked him in the chest with the sword's pommel, causing a charge to light up the air, one whose warning she didn't particularly listen to.

She pointed to the dangling sirens. "You will take those women down, and you will respectfully return their bodies to their families to mourn. Do I make myself clear?"

Fury simmered just under the surface of the captain's visage, and something niggled at Ro that perhaps, maybe, by chance, she'd gone too far, especially with the crew watching. But reason had long since fled, and Ro was in too much of a rage to listen to that little voice of common sense.

"Gerald, Isaac."

Her sword was snatched out of her hands, and two men grabbed her arms.

"Aye, aye, Cap'ain?"

A vein throbbed in his forehead, and his voice was tightly controlled. "I do believe our little huntress needs a reminder of who's in charge. See her to the brig, please."

Grins from several of the men. Again, that part of her brain that had a smidgeon of good sense noticed that several of them looked ashamed of themselves, but that part of her brain was mostly keeping to itself.

They started to drag her away, and Ro's temper exploded.

She pushed off the railing with her feet and did a backflip over both of their arms, wrenching her arms from theirs.

One got an elbow to his gut. Another, an uppercut to his chin. Ro kicked out the knee of another at the same time she elbowed another's solar plexus.

Wrath fueled her on, and she gave herself over to it.

Men dropped around her, several going unconscious when their heads snapped back, some out before they hit the deck, some *when* they hit the deck.

Several were on the ground, crying out or moaning in pain from a now-useless knee or bent-the-wrong-way elbow.

Her sword came at her, and Ro dodged and slammed an axe-cut down on the sailor's wrist. The blade spun away, across the deck.

Someone grabbed her arm, and she closed her hand over his and dropped, to the sound of a nice, loud *crack* of bone.

Part of her was taking vengeance for the callous, casual taking of life. Lives that, oui, had most likely killed before, but had only been curious now, observing the ship after her now-empty promises to their queen. How could she ever make this right?

She jabbed the blade of her hand into a sailor's throat, and he stumbled away, choking. Someone tried to grab her from behind, but she was so in tune with the dance, she simply dropped and shifted her body weight forward, and he sailed over her head and into someone else.

And a part of her was simply enjoying the fight, in a way reminding herself what she could do and how well she did it.

Another man dropped, and she swiped out the legs of another and ducked yet another's swing.

Her sword came at her for a final time, and she leaped into the air, her movement along the blade, out of harm's way, and kicked it out of the man's hand. It clattered overboard.

These men would think twice about sabotaging her mission or harming helpless creatures protected by her ever again.

A small part of her mind got stuck on that word. Helpless. The sirens were far from it. How had they been caught? And why hadn't they fought back or sung the men unconscious? Surely they could've stopped the crew.

But those kinds of thoughts could distract her and get her knocked out in a cold second. So she pushed them away and focused on every swing, every duck, every dance move around each dance partner, making sure she came out on top and not in the brig.

"Enough!" the captain cried out.

Ro suddenly had no one to swing at, and she straightened from her crouch, keeping her senses open to every movement, every sound, every shift of wind.

Captain Montrose was one of the men on the ground, holding his leg.

Her eyesight took the lantern light and turned the deck into the blazing light of day so that she could see every nook and cranny with little effort. It was so bright, she wondered if she should back it off a bit before she was blinded, but she had no idea how to do that.

She still didn't know how she worked.

"Crewman, back away," the captain commanded. "That's an order!"

Ro took in the crewman with a harpoon aimed right at her, and she raised on her tiptoes, ready to spin away when she felt its release coming. She'd snatch it out of mid-air and bury it in his thigh.

She stared at nothing, seeing everything, yet not focusing on any one thing, relying on every thrumming nerve to alert her of changes, to lead her into the instincts she trusted so well, the instincts that had not yet led her wrong.

"Crewman," Captain Montrose growled, struggling to his feet. "Put it down."

After an eternity's hesitation, the harpoon gun's draw was slowly undone, and the shaft of metal slipped to the deck, the sound amplified tenfold in Ro's head, yet not covering any other sound.

"Olt. The lad Cen. Where are they?" Ro demanded.

The captain's lips twisted, though the grimace looked more like pain than anything else. "In the brig. They—protested—the sirens' capture."

Ro nodded once, a part of her deeply satisfied. "Bring them to me."

The captain nodded to the first mate, one of the few uninjured, and he scurried away after shooting her a disgruntled look.

Ro concentrated harder on seeing everything, yet nothing, on feeling every shift of wind on deck.

"Wot's she starin' at?" one of the men said.

"Wot's she starin' at? Who cares? Wot I'd like ta know is why she's a-glowin' like that. Is she a ghost?"

"A spirit?"

"A phantom?" said a sailor with a French accent, one of the few that sounded normal compared to the others with their strange, foreign accents.

"Told ya she was with them sirens," mumbled Hank.

"With the sirens? Have ya ever seen a siren glow like that?"

Hank reluctantly mumbled that he hadn't.

The words should've bothered Ro, but they didn't. Non,

Ro felt herself grow more and more removed from the situation as the moments ticked on, as she waited for Olt and Cen. Who cared if the murmurings on deck grew a little, if the captain himself looked a little paler than he had moments before?

Footsteps. On the stairs. She couldn't let them see her like this—whatever this was. She let go of some of her fierce concentration, returning to a state that felt more natural. More like herself.

The light the lanterns threw at her dimmed just a little, though it still looked like midday to Ro.

The captain limped forward and placed himself between her and his crew.

Ro heard a gasp and peeked toward it. Cen stood there, dirty, scuffed up, one hand over her mouth, tears welling in her eyes, as she stared at the dangling creatures. Olt stood behind her, bloody knuckles and scuffed hands resting on her shoulders, comforting her.

Something inside of Ro pinched, and her control slipped a little more. She scrambled to get it back, but it didn't work that way, and she knew it.

If only she knew how it worked!

It was suddenly dark and nighttime again, the lanterns barely lighting the deck, making Ro feel blind.

Ro nodded at Olt and Cen, pretending a calm she wasn't exactly feeling. She needed to get them out of there before she became shaky with fatigue and weak with regret. She could already feel the wash of exhaustion start to overtake her.

"Olt, lower the rowboat. Cen, go to my cabin and retrieve my things. Please."

They scurried to obey her.

The captain looked genuinely taken aback. "But—where will you go?"

She just looked at him. Pain twisted through her as she realized she'd held him to a high standard because he was everything she'd ever wanted in a père—protective, strong, good-natured, and willing to teach her anything she wished to know about the sea.

And he'd failed her just as her père had.

She didn't answer him. Her gaze landed on one of the crew —she couldn't remember his name—she hadn't harmed. "You. Cut them down." She flicked her chin to the hanging sirens.

The captain nodded his agreement when his crewman looked his way.

Ro tried not to wince with every heavy, wet thud, four times over, but she couldn't quite help herself. It sounded so . . . wrong.

She eyed several other sailors. "Wrap them in extra sails, blankets, anything you can find, not a fin or scale showing, then lower them into my rowboat."

After flicking a glance to the captain, who again nodded, they complied without comment.

The captain swallowed, perhaps realizing what he'd done. At least, Ro could only hope. "Huntress, perhaps we can come to an understanding . . ."

Ro turned back to him, frowning. "An understanding? Explain to me how I'm to explain this to the Sirène Queen. You said they made no move to harm you?"

He nodded, looking he was trying to figure out what Ro was up to.

"That they merely observed the ship, did not attempt to sing or pull anyone overboard?"

"Mademoiselle, please, if they were spies—"

"If? You didn't even bother to find out?" Ro's brows lowered. "You merely assumed and then did more damage than I can possibly undo. How am I supposed to feel safe on this ship, with this crew?"

Ro noted Olt had the rowboat in the water—with the help of the first mate—and Cen had returned with Ro's personal weapons, satchel, and her and Olt's own bundles of posses-sions. She tossed everything but the weapons over, then disappeared over the edge, the bow and several quivers of arrows over her back.

Olt waited for Ro.

Ro's eyes settled on the captain. "They're coming for you, mon capitaine, and I for one will not be here when they tear your ship asunder. I will try to seek a cessation to the hostilities another way. If they'll let me."

She made for the edge of the ship, and the crewmen parted before her, not one of them attempting to stop her.

Ro wasn't exactly looking forward to rowing across the open water with four dead sirens in her easily capsize-able boat and perhaps not enough time for an explanation should any sirens come to investigate.

The sky lightened by degrees in the east, hailing the rising sun about to inch over the horizon. A prickling sensation crawled up her back, and Ro hunched her shoulders against it. She sought the deep shadows of the ship.

No one appeared, and her eyesight did not light up her surroundings, but she was certain she was being watched. And that oily, prickly feeling could only belong to one person: the physician.

When he remained hidden, Ro turned and climbed her way into the waiting boat below, Olt following and then taking up the oars before she could seize them.

Ro turned her gaze to the crew silently watching their departure. Some of their words came back to her now, words that hadn't penetrated the haze she was in earlier.

She'd been glowing? If that were the case, if she'd seen that from one of her shipmates, she'd be scared of her too.

The crew didn't once try to stop her as they rowed away.

Once the ship slipped from view, Ro tried to take the oars from Olt, but he held on.

"Ro, rest. You've been rowing all night and the night before."

Ro sighed and held on, eyeing his bleeding knuckles. "You're hurt. Besides, I'm the one who got us into this mess; I should be the one to take us out."

Olt raised an eyebrow. "What, cause you gutted all those sirens yourself?"

Both girls shushed him at the same time, though Cendre waved her hands around to make up for her silent voice.

Olt winced and dropped his voice. "Désolé. But seriously, you can't blame yourself for their mistakes."

Ro sighed wearily. "But I need to get us out of here. In case they decide to give chase. And you're injured."

"And you're exhausted. Rest."

Ro rubbed her face and sighed. Her whole frame drooped as adrenaline and strength abandoned her at once.

"Just, uh, one more thing."

It took so much effort for Ro to lift her head.

Olt's dimpled grin flashed white against the backdrop of the pre-dawn sea. "Where exactly are we going?"

Ro pulled out her compass from Captain Red.

PART FOUR

Et la petite sirène quitta son jardin et partit vers les tourbillons rugissants derrière lesquels vivait la sorcière de la mer. . . . La petite sirène était terrifiée alors qu'elle se tenait devant la forêt sombre et terrible. Son cœur a battu de peur, et elle a failli faire demi-tour, mais ensuite elle a pensé à son prince et à son espoir d'une âme immortelle, et cela lui a donné du courage. ~Hans Christian Anderson, *La Petite Sirène*

And so the little mermaid left her garden and set off toward the roaring whirlpools behind which the sea witch lived. . . . The little mermaid was terrified as she stood before the dark and terrible forest. Her heart beat with fear, and she nearly turned back, but then she thought of her prince and her hope for an immortal soul, and this gave her courage. ~Hans Christian Anderson, *The Little Mermaid*

31

*T*he pirate who helped Ro aboard looked mildly surprised. "Back so soon, huntress?"

Ro didn't even attempt levity. "I need to see your captain. Right away."

"She's sleeping . . ."

Ro just looked at the female pirate.

"I'll see what I can do."

Ro turned to help Olt and Cen get the rowboat onboard, with its bodies and cargo, but Olt gently pushed her back and wouldn't let her.

She wanted to protest, she really did, but she was just so darn tired. That flare of whatever she'd done on the ship plus the lack of sleep were making it impossible to remain upright. The crew fell silent as the bodies were unloaded and laid out.

Steel rang out as Olt stepped away from the bodies. Ro spun, staggering a little, and blocked Olt.

"Get that bloody man off this ship!" one of them called out. "And send 'im back to where he bloody well came from!"

The other pirates' hearty agreement rang out.

Still no sign of the captain.

Ro eyed her bow leaning against her bag and out of reach

and held her arms out, a feeble attempt to protect the man at her back. "Olt tried to protect the sirènes. His life is forfeit if he goes back."

"What concern is that of mine?" A sword jabbed their way for emphasis. "He'll sink this ship if he's aboard."

Ro gave her fiercest glare, leveling it on each pirate in turn. "This man is under my protection, and I'll not put him adrift until after I've spoken with the captain."

"Huntress?"

Ro lifted bleary eyes as the first mate, Merja, approached, and she sagged in relief.

"The captain will see you in her ready room." She turned her dark gaze on Olt. "Him too."

Ro stumbled after the woman, chanting to herself, *Stay awake, stay awake, stay awake,* with every footfall.

She was running out of options and fast.

Ro hardly noticed when she came into the captain's ready room. She straightened her shoulders and prepared to speak.

Captain Red spoke first. "Good grief, you look like a sleep-walker. Or perhaps one of the zombified men of the southern islands. Doesn't the huntress look awful, Merja?"

Merja didn't respond, and the captain sobered as Olt came in the room.

She turned to Ro. "Tell me everything."

And she did. The greatly abbreviated version.

Captain Red stood over the sirens' bodies, now unwrapped, her hands clasped behind her back. Ro nodded off where she stood between Olt and Cen, trying for all the world to pretend she wasn't as she jerked upright every few seconds.

After an eternity of contemplation, the captain started barking orders, far too loud for this early in the morning, in

Ro's opinion—dawn was only just making itself known, for heaven's sake!

"Unfurl the sails, get away from the outcropping. Strip the sirens of their scales, and prepare the bodies to be returned."

Ro raised an eyebrow. Wouldn't the other sirens notice the missing scales?

Captain Red noticed Ro's look. Without a word, she withdrew a dagger and ran it down the little triangle where tail met fin, along the grain. Clear scales came loose under the sharp blade, and the captain held one up to her guests.

"These are the clear sheaths over their inner scales, the part responsible for their camouflage and the only part useful to us. If we want to live, that is. They only come loose when they shed once a cycle or after a siren's death, when they start to shrivel from exposure to air. We only get about fifteen per siren."

Ro didn't know whether to be impressed or even more sickened. Now she definitely didn't want to share such findings with the crew of the *King's Ransom*.

Ro felt for the little container in her pocket and reminded herself to give one each to Olt and Cen when they were alone. And maybe get rid of the evidence before she saw the Siren Queen again.

The captain went back to barking orders to her crew. "Store the goods belowdecks, and should the sirens ask after them, give them a better bargain than we would've in the first place."

Ro couldn't make sense of any of the words. Goods? Sirens asking for them? It was like the woman was speaking a foreign language.

A yawn nearly split her face.

"And for the love of all that is holy, someone find the huntress and her companions empty hammocks." Her eyes fell on Olt. "We'll decide what to do with you later."

"We could always maroon him, Captain."

Olt tensed, and Ro's head came up. What? What was that? Captain Red's voice gentled, and Ro did *not* like the sultry tones that came purring out. "We'll cross that bridge when we come to it, but crewman, consider your options. We might have to do it. For our safety. They can tear this ship apart with their teeth and bare hands. I've seen it."

Olt didn't look happy about whatever the pirate captain had said in such sexy words, thank Dieu, but Ro was more than happy to stumble after him as he and Cen followed Merja to a large area belowdecks and to the hammocks swinging gently there.

She fell into one, nearly toppling out the other side, and righted herself. She cocooned herself in the scratchy fabric and was almost asleep when she felt someone tugging off her boots.

She peeked at Olt, who winked at her and mouthed, *Go to sleep.*

She winked back before she knew what she was doing and obeyed the moment her feet were tucked safely away.

"We need to wake the huntress now," an urgent voice said.

"No, we need to let her sleep until the last possible moment. Did you see how exhausted she was?" said a particularly masculine and delicious-sounding voice.

Ro made an "Mm" sound and snuggled deeper in the covers. "Keep talking, handsome," she mumbled. "I could listen to you all day."

The woman choked on a laugh, and Olt just choked.

After a few moments, their voices resumed. "The captain would like her help making the decision. She *is* the one who hired this crew, after all."

"She was falling asleep walking yesterday. Literally. Give the woman a break! She needs at least a few hours more to feel herself again."

Ro really wished they'd just be quiet and let her sleep already.

She could hear the smile in the woman's voice. "I can see why you're so protective of her, *handsome*." Her amusement vanished. "But my job is to obey my captain. And my captain said to bring her the huntress, so that's exactly what I'm going to do."

Ro peeked above the roughly woven cloth. Olt raised his hands in a peaceful gesture, blocking the woman trying to advance, and Ro screwed her eyes tightly shut.

"Please just ask the captain if she can get more rest. I'll take all the blame. You won't get in trouble at all."

The woman's voice changed to a low timbre of outrage. "If you think I'm only concerned about getting into *trouble* —"

"No! No, that's not what I meant. I'm just asking you to let me reason with her."

The woman barked another laugh, and Ro winced. "That may take a while with a delicious morsel such as yourself."

Ro's eyes popped open. What le diable?

She popped upright in the hammock, electricity-charged hair springing every which way, and groused, "For the love of St. Margaret, I'm up already."

Olt took one look at her hair and choked back a laugh, then his eyes took in her face, and he laughed outright.

Ro shot him a glare and tumbled right out of the hammock and onto the floor.

The woman just stood there with crossed arms, but Olt scurried over to help her up. Ro pointed a finger at him. "Don't you dare."

He froze.

It was how she got up most every morning, and she wasn't about to look for help now. She had this.

Ro climbed to her feet, using the floor, the bulkhead, and a swinging-too-much-to-be-any-good hammock to move upright before she faced the woman. "Captain wants to see me?"

The woman gave a brief nod before answering. "Aye." She stuck out her hand, which Ro pressed briefly. "Gemma, ma'am." Then she picked up clothing stacked on a barrel and held it out to Ro. "The captain offers you her quarters to clean up in first, then she requests your presence right away."

Ro took the clothes and said, "Just point me in the right direction."

"I'll do ya one better." The woman winked. "I'll take you there meself."

Ro shook her frizzy head. "That isn't necessary, I assure you."

"Isn't necessary?" Gemma laughed and turned to lead the way. "I have a cousin like you, huntress. Doesn't function on little to no sleep, can't form two words before the clock strikes noon. You just follow me, and you won't have to speak to a soul but the captain till you're good and ready."

Ro smiled. This woman was quite possibly the most wonderful person she'd met since leaving France. Ro stumbled after her quite happily.

Not long after a delicious—though hurried—bath, Ro sat in Captain Red's ready room, cradling a strong cup of café and feeling more herself.

Ro blew on the dark liquid and took a small sip. She tried not to shudder as the bitter brew assaulted her tongue. She liked crème and sucre for a reason.

Captain Red got right down to business. "I will take the bodies to the barrier and see if I can smooth things over with the sirens. You'll need to speak to the Siren Queen and explain your side of it. I can't promise anything, but we've had dealings with the sirens in the past. Best case scenario, the sirens understand and we have a respectful burial at sea. Worst case, the sirens tear both ships apart and kill us all."

Nothing like being direct. Ro bought herself some time to mull over the words by taking another sip. Then, "That doesn't sound good, Captain."

Captain Red spread her hands wide. "It's all I've got. I'm sorry, huntress."

"It's not your fault." Ro couldn't help her growl. "It's that imbecile of a captain's fault, and if he doesn't start a full-out war with the sirènes before I complete my mission, I'll eat your hat."

The captain laughed, a deep, rich, full-out belly laugh that had Ro's lips turning up at the corners. "If I've never said so before, huntress, I like you."

"And if I've never said so before, thank you for coming."

Captain Red tilted her head, and her words took on a teasing lilt. "Did you doubt I would?"

Ro took a deep breath and let it out slowly. "I don't know. I didn't know you or your crew, and the first half of the payment was hefty enough, especially once I matched it, that it wouldn't be beyond reason to assume a pirate crew would take the gold and flee." Ro's cheeks burned at the admission. "I apologize for being so blunt."

The captain waved away her words. "Don't ever apologize for being blunt, huntress. I wish more people were as blunt as you. It would save time and useless games." A cat-like smile spread across her lips. "And if we're being completely honest here, I almost didn't come."

Ro's heart dropped to her toes, and she nearly spit café across the desk.

The captain laughed outright. "Oh, don't look so crest-fallen, huntress. I'm here, aren't I? I'm looking forward to the second half of payment, and besides"—she shrugged, her smile teasing—"it's quite an interesting experience to have honest work for once."

This time Ro did choke, not even wanting Captain Red to expound. Ro's reaction must have pleased the pirate captain immensely, because the captain laughed harder as Ro's face flamed brighter. She didn't even want to know how many nights that particular "what if" would keep her wide awake.

Ro tried to rein the conversation back in. "What do you suggest we do?"

"I suggest you take Olt back. To the other ship."

Ro stared at the captain in disbelief. "You can't be serious."

Captain Red just gave her a look.

"What do I tell them? I threatened their lives and took the sirènes' bodies. They'll either shoot me on sight or lock me in the brig. And I don't even want to think of what they'll do to Olt."

The captain leaned forward. "I can't tell you what to do, huntress, but Olt can't stay on this ship. On that I won't budge. After you talk to the Siren Queen, go back to your captain, let him know you've done what you can with the sirens for now, and see if you can continue your mission from the king."

Ro rubbed her temples. "Why can't I just stay with you?"

Captain Red smiled kindly and leaned back, twirling a knife on her desk. "Because the sirens will sink my ship the moment they sense Olt, you know that. We've already had to move far away from the barrier, and I don't know if that will be enough. Unless you have another suggestion?"

Ro snorted. "Besides joining them? We both know that's a bad idea."

"They asked you?" Captain Red took her own sip of café, her eyes intense and on Ro.

Ro nodded miserably. "Apparently the Sirène Queen would love to have the great and mighty huntress as one of her own." Just enough bitterness leaked out that Ro snapped her mouth closed.

"Interesting."

At a noise right outside the open door, Captain Red got up,

looked out, and when she didn't see anything, shut the door and returned to her desk.

Ro desperately tried to think of any other option. "What about the sirène scales? Can't Olt take one of those?"

Captain Red was already shaking her head. "It'll help him resist their pull, but they'll still sense him. Still come after him. They have a grudge against human males that hasn't lessened over time. I can't risk my ship, I'm sorry."

Ro sighed. "Very well. But I don't like it." She looked up. "May I ask what you'll be doing while I'm on the other ship?"

Captain Red drove her knife into the center of a target with a flick of her wrist. "I'll be doing everything I can on my end to back you, to make sure you can complete your mission. But I can't have a man on my ship."

At the look on Ro's face, the captain sighed and continued.

"Because he will get us all killed, huntress, not because it wouldn't be nice to have a man onboard again."

Ro wasn't even going to go there. She wilted a little. "I understand. Merci beaucoup, ma capitaine."

The pirate captain grinned, flashing brilliant-white teeth. "All the thanks I need is gold, huntress. Nothing but gold."

Ro nodded and walked out, not thrilled in the least with what she had to tell Cen and Olt. Would the captain be willing to keep Cen?

She did an about-face and walked back into the captain's ready room. Captain Red glanced up with a mild look. "You should know I don't often change my mind."

"It's not that, ma capitaine. The girl, Cendre. It's not safe for her on the other ship. Will you keep her here with you?"

Now the captain blinked. "Cendre? Here?"

Ro tilted her head. Hadn't the captain seen her come onboard? Of course, Cen had made herself scarce . . . "Oui, she stowed away as a cabin boy. But I don't want her on that ship if I can't protect her. If they find out she's a girl."

The captain considered. "I will talk it over with my first mate and quartermaster."

Ro blinked. "Didn't you offer her a place on this ship once before?"

The captain grinned. "Aye. I did. But she didn't take it. Now supplies will need to be considered, especially since we can't get past the barrier to resupply. Do they know she's a girl?"

"Not yet, but I fear they will soon if they throw us in the brig, and Dieu only knows what a ship full of men will do to a young girl when they discover her."

"Oh, I know exactly what they will do. From experience."

Ro winced and started to say something.

"Don't. I didn't tell you that for your pity. Prepare to depart, and if the girl stays, tell them something about the sirens needing a prisoner for killing their people."

Ro nodded. She didn't care for lying, but she would do it to protect Cen.

"Now go. We haven't much time."

Ro spun and left, and a new worry presented itself. How would Cen react to hearing she was going to be left behind?

Cen crossed her arms and shook her head. Ro was pretty sure she said, "I won't do it. I won't stay," but it was hard to make out with how agitated the girl was.

Ro rolled her eyes as Olt spoke. "It's a good plan, Cen. Then if they kill us on sight, they won't be able to hurt you *or* discover your secret."

She shot him a glare full of vim and shoved him.

Olt snapped his mouth closed, looking mildly surprised.

Cen turned her full glare on Ro, and once again, something about her looked familiar. But, as always, it slipped away. As if Ro were not being *allowed* to remember.

Cen got right in her face and mouthed, "I only came on this voyage for you!"

Ro blinked at that. What in the world? Surely Ro had misread her lips.

"Cen, you can't come, and that's final. I won't be responsible for your death."

Now she was waving her arms and stomping her feet. The girl was throwing a tantrum worthy of Bernadette, Ro's eldest sister.

"I'm going with you!" she tried to force past her lips.

Ro shook her head. "Désolé. You're not. The sirènes are most likely going to sink the ship after what the king's crew did, and I'll not put you in danger." Ro spoke over the girl's attempt at arguing, which wasn't hard to do. "This discussion is over. We need to go." She eyed Cen. "You'll be here when I get back, won't you?"

Cen just crossed her arms and wouldn't answer.

"I hope you will," she said quietly. "I'd like to get to know you too."

Cen deflated a little.

Ro started to turn away, then paused. She dug in her pocket and came up with the two swan-wing combs. She fingered them a moment, then, decision made, held them out to Cen.

Cen just looked at her.

"Will you—hold these for me? In . . . in case I don't make it back, these belong to Madame LaChance. Will you see she gets them?"

Fire lit Cendre's eyes, and she jerked away.

Ro sighed. "Look, I know how you feel about the woman. You won't need to contact her, just send them to her. By post. Or drop them at her boarding school."

Cen gave her such a heated look, Ro resorted to begging.

"Please? It's the last thing I need to do to complete my mission, and well, I'd feel better knowing you have them."

Cendre wavered, then reached out tentative fingers.

Ro let her take them, in her time. "Merci beaucoup, Cendre."

Cendre jerked her chin, but she wouldn't meet Ro's eyes, just stared at the set of pearl combs in her hand.

Ro sighed. Guess she'd have to be happy with that. Hopefully the girl wouldn't hurl them into the sea out of spite. For her or Madame LaChance.

But Ro knew from experience that having a duty, having something to accomplish . . . well, it could only be good for the girl.

"Come on," Ro said to Olt. Olt followed her without a word.

It wasn't until she and Olt were being lowered into the water that the full impact of Cen's words slammed into her. Why had the girl put herself in so much danger just to be near her?

She spun around and looked up at the ship to see Cen peeking over the edge, despair and heartbreak churning in her eyes.

I'm coming back, Ro mouthed, but Cen just glanced away, sullen.

Ro sighed, but there was no other option. She'd promised herself she would protect Cendre, and this was the best way she could do that.

They slipped the oars into place and each took up one, practicing a few swipes until they rowed in tandem. Then they cut through the water, intent for the outcropping, then after that the *King's Ransom* and a very uncomfortable discussion.

And Ro felt the weight of Cen's gaze on her back the whole way.

32

*R*o made sure the rowboat was tightly moored to the outcropping, hidden away from prying eyes. She was pleased to see the one they'd left was still there.

Olt hadn't stopped staring at the barrier. "Incredible. I mean, I can't believe it. It's just so . . . big."

Ro grunted and started to get out. Suddenly, she remembered the scale. "Oh! I almost forgot." She sat back down and dug around in her pockets until she came up with the case Captain Red had given her. She slipped out one of the clear-gray scales and held it out to Olt. "Eat this."

He eyed it dubiously. "What is it?"

"Protection. Against the sirènes." She hoped.

He still looked doubtful, but he slipped it into his mouth. Instantly, his whole face puckered, and he gagged. Ro clamped a hand over his mouth, as much to silence him as to keep it in.

"Look," she whispered, "I've only got one more, and it's for Cen." Which she'd completely forgotten to give her. Hopefully the captain would. "Just swallow. Quickly. The numbness will fade."

Olt shuddered and swallowed, then shuddered some more. Ro started to pull away, but he captured her hand in one smooth, swift motion. "Ro, wait. If anything were to happen to you . . ."

She didn't like the serious way he was staring into her eyes. Or how flustered she suddenly felt. Plus she got the feeling he was about to say something she wasn't ready to hear.

Jerking her hand from his, Ro rolled her eyes to cover her pounding heart. "Oh, calm yourself. Nothing is going to happen to me until I allow it." Ro hopped out of the boat, then offered her hand. "Time to go, sailor."

Olt climbed out after her, still looking like he wanted to say something, but Ro didn't give him a chance. She struck out across the obsidian barrier, and they slipped and slid their way across its slick surface.

They came to a wide-open area, similar to the place she'd met the Siren Queen before.

Olt started to say something, but Ro shushed him. She couldn't believe they hadn't sensed Olt already. Hopefully that meant the scale was working?

Ro bent over and pulled off her boots. Once her bare feet came in contact with the rock, she staggered under its weight. The thrum of a thousand lives under the sea filled her, became a part of her. It was glorious.

Olt reached for her, but she jerked away. She needed to shield him for as long as she could, and his touching her right now would send a beacon to the sirens.

Ro's eyes flew wide. She was shielding him?

Oui, while the magic of the scale eased into him. She grumbled to herself to cover the sudden longing to be trained, the sudden frustration welling up in her at being refused by the Queen of the Fairies to be her student. She needed to learn to wield the fairy magic the queen had given her, not constantly guess how it worked and get it wrong most of the time.

"Experience," she muttered to herself, repeating the Fairy Queen's assurance that she would learn her powers in time. Experience meant nothing if her magic couldn't be found when she reached for it. It seemed to react to instinct, and not when Ro wished it would, either. Yet one more thing to ask the Queen of the Fairies.

But right here, right now, she had another queen to worry about.

She readied herself for a message. Took a deep breath; let it out slowly. Hopefully she did it right.

"Votre Majesté, Queen of the Sirènes, I must speak with you. It is urgent. A matter of life and death."

Olt stilled behind her.

The echo that rumbled around them was Ro's voice magnified tenfold, only felt not heard. The rocks absorbed her message and sent it through the water in trembling waves.

Ro tried again, her voice a deep timbre and the cadence of her words dancing through the waves. "Votre Majesté, Queen of the Sirènes, I come to you with a matter of grave importance. I must speak with you."

Ro could get lost in the power that thrummed through her. But she had to stay focused. Complete her mission. Fight until she'd won.

Although her voice still rippled out in waves, Ro felt no reply. Not a siren moved under the sea. It was as if they'd gone still, listening to her, hoping not to be discovered by the stranger who commandeered their magic and invaded their waters.

She closed her eyes, reaching deep within her to cast her voice farther. "Votre Majesté, Queen of the Sirènes, I must speak with you before all is lost."

This time, there was a stirring of . . . something . . . and she was so focused on it, when Olt touched her arm, she jumped.

Her eyes flew open. Fear of his discovery had a reprimand bubbling to her lips, but her gaze tracked his pointing finger to the water. There, as before, eyes peered just above the waterline. But they weren't the Siren Queen's.

It was Merida, the siren more hostile to humans than the others. The siren she was hoping *not* to see.

"May I speak with your queen?" Ro called out. The rocks under her feet remained silent.

As the figure glided toward her, Ro placed one hand on her bow, though she did not draw it.

The siren stopped not far from her and lifted her face just enough to speak. She sneered. "I can smell your sweat, human. You reek of fear."

Ro didn't let anything but confidence into her voice. "It's hot and humid here. Why shouldn't I sweat?"

Merida's grin, if it could be called that, pulled her lips away from sharpened teeth, and Ro could only think of a shark. One that wanted to eat her.

"That sweat has a different smell. This is nothing but fear. Weak, pathetic fear." She lifted her chin. "What brings you here, human? Queen Zarya could no longer stand your keening and said to silence you." Her grin turned positively feral. "She didn't say how."

"Queen Zarya, you say? She'll very much want to see me. She needs to know—"

While Ro was speaking, Olt shifted a little, and the siren's eyes jerked past her. To Olt. Her eyes widened in surprise, which she quickly covered with another grin.

"And what is this? You bring us a delicious morsel? My, but isn't he tasty."

Olt stiffened, his fingers still wrapped around Ro's arm.

Ro broadened her stance. "He is under my protection, Merida, and I will not allow him to be harmed. More urgently, I must speak with your queen. Right away."

The siren feigned disappointment, but there was something else there. Confusion? Wariness? "Too bad. I would've liked to drag him under." Merida's focus shifted to Ro. "Very well. I can take you to Her Majesty. She will grant an audience this once, but only because you asked so nicely."

The siren's mouth spread in a savage grin, and Ro couldn't help her shudder. She didn't want to go anywhere with that creature. And besides, how would an underwater audience even work?

The siren seemed to read her thoughts. "We have a way to keep you safe in the water, huntress. The queen does not wish you harm."

The sea serpent was lying, she was sure of it. Ro frowned. Wasn't she?

Ro raised an eyebrow. "Or to turn me into one of you against my wishes?"

She felt more than saw Olt's sharp glance.

Again that perfectly lovely yet hideous smile. "Oh, she'd like that very much, but unfortunately for us, you have to agree."

That was never going to happen.

Ro hesitated over going with the siren. But what other way was there? If the Siren Queen would not come to her . . . "Olt is not to be harmed."

Merida turned her cold gaze to Olt, her expression not even thawed a little by the smile she gave him. "Oh, he won't be harmed. No matter how much I may wish it otherwise."

Ro nodded once, decided. "Very wel—"

Olt jerked her to face him. "Don't do it. Don't go with her."

Ro stared up at him, not used to the intensity on his face. "What choice do I have? If the queen will not come to me . . ."

"She's lying."

Ro scowled. "Who? The queen?"

He nodded to the siren still in the water. "She plans to drown you and tell the queen you changed your mind."

Ro's head whipped toward the siren. Her murderous glare confirmed Olt's words—at least, enough for Ro. She eyed Olt. "How could you possibly know that?"

Dusky red crept up Olt's neck, and he had trouble meeting

her eyes. "I just do, all right? Please don't go with her. Please don't trust her. Please."

Ro could hardly say no to him on a normal day. With all this pleading? She didn't stand a chance.

She lowered her voice so hopefully only Olt could hear. "All right, but on one condition."

Olt looked rather skeptical, and for good reason.

"You have to tell me how in all the realms you know that." He opened his mouth, but she pointed a stern finger at him. "And leave nothing out. Promise?"

He hesitated, slid a glance to the siren, then looked back, defeated. "I promise." His eyes moved past her to the siren. "But not in front of her."

"Fair enough." Ro turned back to Merida, startling only a little when Olt took her hand instead of claiming her elbow once more. "Tell your queen I will meet her here as I did before."

"He lies," the siren hissed.

Ro tilted her head. "He hasn't lied to me yet"—she hoped —"and I highly doubt he would do so about this. Go to your queen."

The siren snarled at both of them. "And what makes you think I'm going to do anything you say?"

Ro refused to swallow and lifted her chin instead. "I came here for one goal, sirène, and I do not intend to leave without it."

A wicked gleam entered the siren's all-black eyes, and an excited ripple trembled through her scales. "Mark my words, huntress. When this is over, I'm going to enjoy dragging you to the bottom and watching the life drift from your eyes."

Ro couldn't stop her shudder, but her voice didn't waver. "I think you should hurry, don't you?"

The siren glowered and moved backward in the water, her dark hair fanning out all around her. "I suggest you make yourself comfortable, huntress. My queen shall not be rushed."

Ro held her gaze. "I'm not going anywhere."

Sharp teeth revealed themselves. "You know I'm going to take my time, right?"

Ro's voice took on a dangerous edge, one the barrier echoed. "Go."

Merida startled, then hissed. She shot straight up, tail forming a perfect arc, side fins flaring out, and plunged head-first into the water, her glare promising murder the entire way.

Ro turned to Olt the moment she was gone. "All right, spill. How in all the realms did you know that?"

Olt's entire face was on fire. "Shouldn't you call for the queen again? You know, since you can't trust that one to take her your message?"

Ro just folded her arms. "A spoken word from one of them is a vow. All fey have to keep their bargains or bad things happen to them." A grim expression turned her mouth down at the corners. "Though you never can tell exactly how they plan to keep their word."

Olt tilted his head. "How do you know that?"

Ro rubbed her palm, the one the Fairy's Queen's white rose had sunk into. Fey knowledge pulsed there like a beacon. "I just do. Now, tell me."

Olt shifted uncomfortably and slipped. Ro made him sit and crouched next to him, her eyes not leaving his face.

"Look, if I tell you"—at Ro's harsh look, he amended his words—"*when* I tell you, promise me you won't tell anyone else. And I mean anyone. Not Cen, not your captain, my captain, your sister—no one."

Ro nodded once. "D'accord."

He started running his fingers through his hair, trying to tear it all out all over again. "Look, I can see—colors—around a person."

Ro blinked. Well that wasn't what she was expecting him to say. "Colors."

"Yes, colors. It, well, I can tell what a person is thinking—well, what they intend. By the colors. Over their heads."

Ro just looked at him. "Colors. Over their heads."

She'd kick him off this rock to the sirens below if he was messing with her.

His shoulder-length hair was sticking out all over the place. "That's what I said, isn't it?" He sounded frustrated.

"All right." Ro nodded, trying to sound understanding. "What did you see over the sirène?"

"Black. And green. It tends to mean deception. The green, that is. At least, that shade does."

"And the black?"

He swallowed several times before answering. "Death."

Ro just soaked it in, trying not to blurt anything that would make him even more uncomfortable. She was around magic all the time, wasn't she? She wielded some form of unlearnable magic herself. Why should she disbelieve him?

"You were very specific about the sirène's intentions."

If it were possible, Olt flushed an even deeper shade of rouge. "Intentions are usually pretty clear to me, though I don't always get it right."

Ro thought about it, then nodded once. "All right." She sat back. Mostly to give him space, but also to get comfortable while they waited. "That wasn't so bad, now was it?"

He looked completely drained, no smile in sight. "You try admitting something no one has believed for your entire lifetime."

Ro waved a hand in front of his face. "Allô? Remember who you're talking to? For years I told my family a château in the woods appeared to me one night a year, and not a soul believed me. If anyone knows how you feel, I do."

He offered an apologetic grin. "Désolé, huntress, I'd forgotten."

"De rien." She couldn't help poking just a *little* fun. "Maybe next time, don't hyperventilate quite so much?"

His grin was weak. "Very funny."

She chuckled, and they settled into a comfortable silence.

"Will the Siren Queen come?" Olt finally asked.

"She will come." A few seconds later. "By the way, what did you see over me? You know, that day you told me you knew you could trust me."

He scrubbed a hand through his hair. "Blue. Royal blue. And . . . gold."

"And that means . . . ?"

"Loyalty. That your friendship, once gained, doesn't bend or break easily." A pause. "And great sadness."

Ro sniffed and turned away, pretending unwavering interest in the endless blue surrounding them. "Is that so."

"It is," he said quietly, understandingly.

Ro stared out over the water, jaw ticking. He had no business guessing how she felt. About anything.

৻৶

As before, the sirens glided out of the water without a sound, the queen and her entourage. And a very sullen-looking Merida, sulking at the back of the group.

Ro and Olt got to their feet and did as Captain Red had instructed. They made the sirens' sign of respect: an open hand over one's heart. The gesture was not returned.

The queen didn't banter. "Huntress, I grow weary of being summoned as one would a servant. Your emergency is not mine."

Ro tilted her head. "In this case, it is, votre Majesté."

The Siren Queen just waited, her stare unblinking.

Olt shifted, just a little.

Queen Zarya's gaze immediately went to Olt, showing the

barest hint of surprise, just as Merida had done. "You dare bring a human male to an audience with me?"

Ro bowed, arms spread, not taking her eyes off the danger before them. "I would not have done so had there been any other way."

"There is always another way," the creature hissed. "Tell me quickly, huntress, before I tear his throat out with my teeth."

Ro shot an alarmed glance at Olt, whose hand was still frozen over his heart, his face pale. "Votre Majesté, his life is forfeit for trying to defend your sirènes."

A perfectly sculpted eyebrow rose. "Oh?"

Ro explained as swiftly and respectfully as she could.

The sirens hissed and drew back, fingers arched into claws.

"You dare threaten me and my sisters, huntress?" The Siren Queen's low voice trembled through the rocks under their feet. "Are you truly that stupid?"

"Non! Non, it isn't a threat at all . . ."

Ro's voice trailed off as dark liquid began to thrum through the sirens' veins, standing out in stark relief behind their ash-gray skin. Any visible scales flipped in varying shades of human dress deepened to the darkest of grays, almost impossible to see as their forms began to hum and vibrate, blending in with their surroundings. Black ichor started to drip from their fingernails.

Ro swallowed as the hissing forms advanced. "We've come to beg your forgiveness — to beg your mercy for those who have done such a crime. It was a . . . misunderstanding. A horrible, terrible misunderstanding. We've come to make it right."

A silence filled with rage followed the hollow her words left behind. But at least they stopped advancing.

"Huntress, are these or are these not the very men you brought to my shore?"

"Oui, votre Majesté, but I did not wish any of this. I came to prevent this. I do not wish any harm to your people."

"They are not my people; they are my sisters!" the queen shouted.

Ro flinched.

The queen reined in her anger, though it bubbled just under the surface and leaked into her words. "Are you truly so empty-headed to assume they acted of their own accord? Without the king's orders? That they truly seek *peace*?"

Ro frowned. "The English king asked me to come—we are only to hunt you if I fail. I . . . wasn't told of any other orders."

The siren's voice turned ironic. "Well, of course not. He wouldn't tell anything of import to the mighty huntress, now would he?"

"Votre Majesté, the women I came with—will you accept my negotiations as a part of their crew instead?"

"I would."

Ro swallowed. "And Olt, the only man who defended your sisters—will you spare him and our ship if I take him aboard the"—Ro gulped back the ship's name, the *Siren Hunter*, certain it wouldn't help her cause—"the ship with the female-only crew?"

Queen Zarya's glare for Olt was full of cold fury. "I would not."

Ro spread her hands. "Work with me here, s'il vous plaît. He defended your sisters with honor. I must protect him somehow."

She sneered. "Return him to his ship. I will decide then if I shall be merciful to him and him alone."

"Not a chance," Ro grumbled. Louder, she said, "Captain Red—"

"Already explained the situation and returned my sisters' bodies. She too asked for the sailor's life."

Ro's mouth fell open. She couldn't have mentioned this earlier?

"I am sorry, huntress, but as much as I respect your captain, I cannot condone any male life remaining alive. Not after what they've done and continue to do."

Her look for Olt was so full of hatred, Ro was certain of Olt's fate without her protection.

Ro straightened, throwing off her posturing and taking on a fierce glare. "And Olt is under my protection. Mine. I'll allow no harm to come to him, or you'll answer to *me*."

The Siren Queen's smile was brittle. "At least recall I did warn you. I'll not allow his kind to remain alive upon my waters."

"How are you born, then?" Ro demanded, hoping her sarcasm was well hidden. She had a feeling it wasn't. Her books of lore said the sirens procreated with human males before they drowned them, though now that the words were out of her mouth, she vaguely recalled the Siren Queen saying otherwise.

"We are not born, huntress. We are made." She nodded to a pair of sirens to her right. "And the one who turns you is your mother. Your sister. Your family." Her inhuman, cold eyes settled on Ro. "We could be your family."

Ro closed her eyes. Not this again. She wasn't interested. Not even a little.

Ro's hair swayed in a gust of wind. Olt's fingers dug into her arm and pulled her closer to him. Her eyes popped open.

The Siren Queen was inches from her face. "I could show you. What it would be like. Open your eyes to the world of possibility. You could be so much more, huntress."

The magnetic pull of the siren's all-black eyes had Ro's heart pounding. A part of her wanted to know—the part that had something to prove. The part that drove her to be the best huntress possible. The part that strived to prove to her père that she could fend for herself.

Ro swallowed back her fear, hoping the siren couldn't sense

it, both intrigued and repulsed by the siren's offer. "What . . . exactly would that entail?"

The siren smiled, satisfied, predatory. "You would become one of us. We would be your sisters forever. Your knowledge would pass to us, and ours to you. You would live here, with us, and hunt for us. You would save our lives. Since you know so much of the above world, the way of kings and queens, you could be our spokesperson. Broker peace, trade, and more."

A panicky sort of feeling slithered up Ro's chest to her neck. She didn't want to live underwater. Didn't want to relive her nightmare of drowning over and over.

For some reason, she'd been fine the entire voyage. Nothing about the water had bothered her once, only intrigued her. Even the storm hadn't fazed her.

But here, now, she could only think of her père's sinking ships, the crushing weight of water as it forced them under. Of the men who'd lost their lives. Of all three ships endlessly crushed by the water they'd set out to conquer.

"Would you like a taste?" the Siren Queen purred.

Ro licked her lips, and the Siren Queen's eyes followed the movement. "A taste?" Ro echoed.

"Yes, huntress, a taste. Of everything we can offer and more."

Ro didn't want to live under the ocean. Not at all. But if she could stop the threat to her world . . .

"You must answer, huntress. Either way, you must answer."

"Show me," she whispered, before she could talk herself out of it.

The Siren Queen smiled.

Ro held up a hand, fending off her fear as much as the Siren Queen's advance. "But you only have permission to show me, not turn me."

Olt seemed to panic next to her. "Ro . . ." He grabbed her hand, tried to pull her back.

Ro gently squeezed his hand, released it, and stepped forward. "If it will help me settle this matter, reach a peace with you, and make this right, then show me."

"As you wish." The Siren Queen smiled and touched Ro's temple.

A ball of purple sparks exploded in Ro's vision, bringing with it pain, release, and so much more.

33

Ro closed her eyes and smiled as a rush of bliss poured over her, head to toe. The change was so easy. So painless. And it brought with it everything she'd ever wanted and then some.

Every language, at her disposal. In her heart and on her tongue.

A sense of purpose and belonging.

Power such as she'd never felt, never experienced, ran through her veins and made her feel alive. Nothing like the existence she was drudging through at the moment.

She cut through the ocean, every swipe of her tail propelling her forward with a force that thrummed through her veins. She looked down at her hands. Her stomach.

Sable scales covered everything, yet her upper half was still in the shape of a woman, just like the *King's Ramson's* masthead. Her skin had lost every vestige of color, able to blend in with her surroundings.

Yet she was nothing like a woman. She was so much more —so much more powerful. Her human state was weak. Pathetic. She had no idea why she clung to it so.

Had she known sooner what it was like, she would've shed

her human skin with all readiness. Would've accepted the Siren Queen's bargain right away.

There was no other alternative.

She saw herself standing before kings. Making peace treaties. She saw herself regulating trade. Accepting payment. Hunting. Destroying the men who dared lay a finger on them.

She also saw the sirens' past. How their race had been formed. Every memory of every siren that had existed, passed throughout the race, shared memories to bury deep within each siren and become their own. Her new mind would be able to hold them all.

She saw the first siren, given her powers by a friendly mer to help her find her lost love, who hadn't returned from across the ocean as promised.

They'd agreed to switch places, each to discover each other's worlds. The newly formed mer had found her love across the sea—with his wife and child.

How she'd used her newfound powers, her lovely voice as alluring as any nightingale's, to make him drown himself—then had done the same to the innocent.

How her wicked deed turned the fey magic within her dark and evil, broiled within her voice as something fierce and wild, how after she'd heard the mer calling her name over and over, arranged to have her killed in her weakened human state so she wouldn't have to return the magic in her veins.

How she used her powers to tempt brokenhearted girls over the centuries, changing them into dark creatures who used their newfound magic to right the wrongs done to them.

How after two broken promises, their magic was straining, straining, straining at the threshold, just waiting to break free and destroy the race of creatures it had created. Right the wrong that had been done to it.

And how Ro could use that to her advantage. Such information, just handed to her. And the Siren Queen didn't even realize what she'd just done.

A small part of her mind, the human part of her mind, wished she'd written that story that day in the cabin instead of the ill-fated fairy tale she'd scratched out.

But the siren within quickly snuffed out all human thoughts.

As she would do if Ro gave herself over to it.

She saw so much, all at once. And she couldn't get enough. She wanted more. So much more. She reached for it.

Ro woke up sprawled on the ground, dazed, her mind reeling with all she'd seen.

Olt hovered over her, frantic. "Ro? Ro! Can you hear me?"

She met his gaze, and he sagged.

"Oh, thank God." He swiped a hand over his face. "I couldn't wake you."

Ro struggled to sit up, but he held her in place.

"Don't move. I don't know what she did to you, but they're gone. Just give your head a chance to clear."

Ro nodded and closed her eyes.

Her hands were shaking. Everything she'd seen as a siren —whether a vision or real—kept playing over and over in her mind.

She couldn't make the images stop. The longing stop.

Yet she was terrified of the water. She didn't want to live in it. Did she? She honestly didn't know. Not anymore. And that terrified her more than anything.

She couldn't stand thinking about what she'd seen a moment longer.

Her eyes flew open. "Help me up."

Olt did, and it took Ro a moment to stand on her own.

"What did they say to you?" he asked. "I couldn't understand it. Well, not all of it. I gathered their meaning."

"They don't want peace, and they don't want to extend any grace to you." She looked up at Olt fiercely. "I won't let them have you."

He looked rather pale. "You may not have much of a choice, huntress."

"We'll just see about that."

"What did they do to y—?" Olt began, gently touching her temple.

"Not now. Please." Ro shook her head. "I just—I can't—we need to get back to the ship."

Olt retrieved her boots and slipped an arm around her waist as they made their way to the rowboat. "Which one?"

Ro gritted her teeth and leaned against him. "I have no idea."

In the end, Olt convinced Ro to row back to the *King's Ransom* since the pirates would not let them board—and would most likely shoot him on sight to keep their ship from sinking.

"We have to warn them of the siren's attack," he insisted. "It's the right thing to do."

Ro may or may not have grumbled to herself most of the way to the *King's Ransom*. It was sheer, dumb luck they found it.

They stopped a distance from the ship and eyed the gently rolling water as Olt held his white shirt over his head, draped over an oar. Ro tried desperately not to notice the expanse of tanned, lean, and muscular skin.

"If you ignore me any harder, you're going to pass out."

Ro choked on a laugh even as heat filled her face. "Put your shirt back on, sailor. They're waving us aboard."

He chuckled, dropped the shirt over his head, and rowed toward the ship. Both scanned the water for threats.

"They're not here yet," Olt said.

"I know," Ro said simply. And it bothered her.

They were faster, ruthless, and determined to sink the ship. Giving Ro time to warn the men didn't make sense.

They climbed up the nets on the side of the ship, and the crew pulled their craft aboard after them.

Ro thanked them and turned to Captain Montrose, who stood there watching her.

"Huntress," he said, his tone businesslike.

Ro took a deep breath and blew it out slowly. "Monsieur, we have a problem."

Ro rather enjoyed explaining to the captain and the first mate their situation and the impending attack. Not.

But at least the captain didn't throw them in the brig. Or question the "sirens" taking Cen. It added some weight to their information, in fact.

So far so good.

Captain Montrose nodded once. "Then we haven't a moment to lose. Thank you for the warning."

Ro flicked a glance to Olt. "About Olt . . ."

Olt stiffened.

"As long as he follows my commands, he has a place on my ship." He gave Olt a direct look.

Olt nodded, but Ro noted every muscle in his body was coiled tight, as if ready to fight or grab her hand and flee. "I thank ye fer that, Cap'ain."

Ro couldn't help the sidelong look she gave him as the captain walked away. "Speaking pirate now, are we?" she said in a low voice.

He kept his gaze on the captain, still at attention, but Ro could tell from the twinkle in his eye that a grin wanted to break free.

She tilted her head. He did speak differently around her, didn't he?

Captain Montrose began calling orders to his crew, and the first mate and quartermaster stayed near Olt and Ro as they threw themselves into helping.

Ro fumed as they readied for the sirens' attack. She didn't want to be here. Didn't want to defend these idiots. So why had she allowed herself to be dragged into this foolhardy plan in the first place?

Her eyes caught and held on Olt, accepting a pair of heavy gloves and readying miniature trebuchets just behind the railing, interspersed between the harpoon guns. Sailors near him adjusted the netting on the side of the boat, making sure it covered every centimètre of wood.

Because she had to protect Olt. And Cen. And this was the only way she could see doing both.

She eyed the water, half tempted to take Olt and the rowboat, pick up Cen, and after rowing to the barrier, drag it over on foot and keep rowing. Until they were far away from this mess.

"Cap'ain!"

No one missed the panic in the sailor's voice. A rush of sailors, including Ro, Olt, and Captain Montrose, moved to the port side, just as the call of "Cap'ain!" came from all sides.

Sailors scattered to every available spot along the railing, on all sides of the ship.

Sirens. Hundreds of them. Their eyes just above the water. Surrounding the ship.

Ro's eyes were drawn to one of them, familiar, even if little of her was showing, and her companion. Merida. And Rialta, was it?

Ro blinked. How on earth did she know that? But as she scanned the water, she realized she knew all of their names. All that knowledge . . . Ro swayed under its barrage once more. So very tempting.

Rialta smiled. "Shall we sing to them, Merida?"

Ro startled. She could hear them? From underwater?

Merida hissed a little. "You know we can't do that. We're not close enough to our barricade. We have to give those below more time."

Rialta's voice purred through the water. "We can still try."

Ro looked around her. Was no one else hearing this?

"I say we do what the queen said." Merida smiled. "I say we tear the ship asunder." Her eyes focused on Ro. "But the huntress is mine."

Rialta laughed, the sound like tinkling glass. "I'd like to see you survive that one."

Ro smirked. "Me too," she said without thinking.

Merida startled, then gave Rialta a shove, the first two sirens to move. "She can hear us, seaweed slime! Give the signal."

Ro jumped up on the railing, clasping the rigging. "Sirènes of the Caribbean!"

All eyes homed in on her, razor sharp.

"These men are under my protection. They are not to be harmed."

The men shifted behind Ro, and she could tell they were just as surprised at her words as she.

"They regret their actions and there will be consequences. We come here seeking peace, not war. Forgiveness, not revenge. We want to live in harmony upon these waters, and we will do whatever we can to make it right."

Well, she'd startled Merida and Rialta out of giving the signal, whatever it was, and she held the sirens' rapt attention, though their unblinking, inhuman stare gave no clue of what they were thinking. One thing in her favor, n'est-ce pas?

Ro spread one hand wide. "Has there not been enough death upon these waters? Come, let us reason together. What will you accept in exchange for peace?"

Merida moved just enough to cast her lyrical voice across the water. The low sound traveled so each man could hear it. "Your ship, in pieces on the ocean floor. Your men's bodies, floating in eternal sleep." Merida smiled. "You, one of us."

"Now!" Captain Montrose called. A volley of round globes, popping and hissing with lightning, flew past Ro's head and into the water.

Chaos ensued.

Ro gasped and stumbled off the rail, crouching down as her scalp tingled and her shoulder-length hair started lifting into the air in all directions. Her clothing zapped and popped as she moved.

The sirens' screams hit Ro like a physical blow. She fell to the deck, writhing in pain, control of her body lost to her.

"It's working!" the quartermaster called.

Ro counted in her head. It had been at least three days. The siren scale Captain Red had given her must have worn out. As Ro fought for control of her limbs, she wrested the tiny box out of her pocket and managed to flick it open. Just one scale left.

Clouds converged overhead, dimming the sun by degrees. The wind picked up.

The physician, the creepy, oily man who kept to the shadows, walked into the midst of the mêlée the moment the sun vanished entirely behind a thick bank of clouds, hands clasped behind his back, not even a little affected by the screams.

"Very good," he said calmly. "Another volley, if you will, Captain."

He didn't even raise his voice. He shouldn't have been heard over the chaos, but he was. Captain Montrose nodded, and another round of globes was loosed.

Ro couldn't take her eyes off the physician. She scooted away as he came closer. His eyes dropped to hers after a moment, and he smiled. Ro flinched.

She dropped the scale.

His eyes tracked it as it fluttered to the deck and stuck fast in one of the cracks.

Ro's heart almost stopped.

"Huntress," he said calmly. He extended his hand.

Ro, still shuddering, made herself take it.

Instantly the pain from the siren's cries ceased. Her eyes widened.

He pulled her to her feet. She bent over quickly, pinched

the scale in her fingers, and after a slight hesitation, dropped it into her mouth. She wasn't sure what else to do.

He didn't comment, but his eyes tracked the movement, and Ro could've sworn interest lit his eyes.

Ro pretended it was nothing as the wretched taste lit up her tongue, as she tried not to gag. They looked out over the churning water together, and Ro shuddered for a completely different reason.

"Amazing, isn't it?" the physician asked in his calm, dead voice.

"This isn't right. Why couldn't they have listened?"

His smile made Ro back up a step. "I think you are confusing them with humans, milady. One deserves our pity. A chance at reform. Fey creatures do not. I had hoped—"

A sickening thud interrupted him, followed swiftly by another. Ro grabbed for the railing as the entire ship shuddered. The sirens were hurling themselves at the ship, cracking wood with fleshy impacts. A burning smell met her nose.

The attack abated.

"Fire!" the captain screamed.

Harpoons released to the sound of sickening squelches and ear-splitting screams. Gray smoke poured from wounds as cold iron embedded itself into fey creatures.

Impaled sirens were hauled aboard and dumped in a pile.

The deck trembled as the cannons below roared to life. Just as the reports had said, the sirens dodged the cannonballs neatly, but it gave them one more thing to worry about as other more effective weapons were used.

Before the crew could fire again, sirens—those who hadn't been hit by the lightning spheres—flung themselves out of the water and began latching on to sailors, dragging them into the water.

Ro gasped and pulled out her bow, reaching for a quiver that wasn't there.

Ro's heart plunged. It must still be on the rowboat.

"Huntress, here!"

Ro's head came up, and she caught the quiver filled with double sheaves of arrows. She met the first mate's eyes grate-fully—he nodded back—and she untied the bound arrows.

She had left several crates of her arrows onboard when she'd stormed off, hadn't she? Praise Dieu the first mate had remembered.

She straightened and began flinging arrow after arrow at attacking sirens.

They dodged far more arrows than found their target. Ro gritted her teeth and shot faster, leading each shot a little more and trusting instinct to guide her arrows.

The crew started ducking behind the railing as sirens flew past, giving Ro more clear shots. Still, men plunged overboard. Ro panicked when she couldn't find Olt.

But everything was a mess: water churning, the air filled with sirens and their fins that spread out like wings, men running across the deck, swords flashing, pistols firing, all hands fighting for their lives.

Ro had to trust Olt was all right. She couldn't think of the alternative.

As more and more men thrashed in the water, shark fins began to circle, and it wasn't long till the men bleeding in the water were attacked. Torn apart. To the sound of screams and ripping flesh. Deep-red and pitch-black swirls spiraled out in the water around the ship.

Ro pointed at the sharks and called out to Captain Montrose, who still called orders and fought nearby, sword slashing at any siren that happened to fly within reach. "Quick! Kill one."

He gave her a look that said sharks were the least of his concerns.

Ro didn't have time to explain. She'd read it in one of the beast's books: A captain had observed that when a shark bled in the water, other sharks fled.

"Make it bleed!" she shouted. "It'll scare the others off."

Captain Montrose's eyes widened, then he called out the order. He and the first mate went to work harpooning a shark, while a few others turned their harpoons to the sharks as well.

One of the men successfully harpooned a shark and pulled it aboard.

Soon they'd ripped their knives through it and poured as much blood as they could into the water. The sharks in feeding frenzy seemed to recoil and move away from the *King's Ransom*, circling farther out.

"More!" Ro called.

They didn't hesitate this time.

Rialta screamed, the sound ridiculously high-pitched and painful. "You leave them alone!"

Hands extended, the siren shrieked and flew at the first mate, trying to knock the harpoon from his hands.

Ro's hand found one of the magical arrows in her quiver and let it fly. The powerful shot flung the siren away from the first mate, spinning her in the air and flinging her over the other side of the ship.

The first mate's wide and grateful eyes found Ro, but she was already focusing on the sirens following Rialta.

Ro shot a few more out of the air, their elaborate fins swirling around them and almost looking like wings. Ro couldn't believe how high they could jump, how powerful they were. It almost was like they were flying.

Which made some of the conflicting lore about them make that much more sense.

"Captain!" screamed a man in so much terror, Ro's heart stuttered for a beat.

Heads swiveled toward the man's shout.

Ro cataloged the situation in an instant. A siren was trying to drag a sailor under; he was putting up a valiant fight, clinging to the side of the ship. In an instant, the siren lunged for him and ripped his throat out with her jagged teeth.

Blood sprayed against the side of the ship, and the sailor sank from sight.

Ro could only stare. It was over so fast.

Although the sharks had vanished, the sirens seemed to be starting their own bloodthirsty frenzy.

"Pitch! Get the pitch," called Captain Montrose.

Sailors instantly responded and soon had buckets of pitch in their hands, dumping it over the edge.

An iridescent oil slick spread over the surface of the water, and the sirens moved out further, gasping for breath, trying to wipe it from the gills on their necks and sides.

Several sirens shot away, then rounded on the ship and thrust themselves into the air, clearing the tainted water and resuming their attack on the ship.

Ro steadied herself against the rail and shot arrow after arrow to keep them at bay, giving the crew of the *King's Ransom* a chance to get pulled out of the water.

Where was the bloody captain of the other ship when Ro needed her? Ro dug the compass out of her pocket, flicked it open, and wished there was a way to call Captain Red.

A siren lunged right at her.

Ro dropped the compass and shot the siren out of the air. The creature fell just past her, and Ro had to jump out of the way to keep from getting knocked over.

She looked frantically around for the compass.

The physician stood calmly in the midst of it all, observing, her compass in his hand. He held it out to her. "You really should keep better track of your things, Mademoiselle. Especially such magically powerful objects."

Ro bit back a retort about him trying to hold on to things while shooting arrows and started to shove the compass in her pocket. Suspicion sneaked up on her. Briefly, she flicked open the lid. A slight glow lit up the glass, pulsing in a steady rhythm.

Huh. She didn't know it did that, but at least he hadn't

switched it out with another compass. She shoved it deep in her pocket, relieved.

"I think it's time for another volley," the physician said to the captain, and once again, he was somehow heard above the overwhelming racket of battle.

The captain turned away to relay the order to his men.

But then the physician choked. Ro's eyes flew to his.

One of the harpoons stuck out in the middle of his chest, its tail of rope strung overboard. The physician stared down at it, as if he couldn't even comprehend what was happening. A single drop of pitch-colored blood, just like the ichor that dripped from the siren's fingertips, trailed down his pristine white shirt, and then he was yanked into the water.

Too stunned to move or react or be of any use, Ro could only watch in horror as he disappeared over the edge.

Captain Montrose hadn't seen. He gave the signal, but before the miniature trebuchets could loose another volley of light-filled globes, before more harpoons could be aimed and fired, before Ro could take her hand out of her pocket, Merida's face popped up over the edge of the ship.

"Huntress!" she hissed.

She grabbed Ro's trapped arm and yanked her into the water. Ro's bow clattered to the deck. Ro thrashed to get away, but they hit the water hard and were already diving fast.

Blinding light exploded right next to them.

34

*T*he worst pain Ro had ever felt in her life traveled through her entire body, and Merida let go. Or rather, she could no longer hold on. To anything.

Ro arched her back and screamed underwater, great bubbles billowing from her mouth and floating to the surface.

Pain such as she'd never felt arched through her. Senses reeling, she clawed for the surface, still screaming.

She rose too slowly.

All around her, sirens hung suspended, stunned. Eyes wide, unseeing, their bodies limp and swirling with the sudden cessation of movement.

Ro watched as they floated faster than she did to the surface. Ro reached out, tried to grasp a passing fin, but she couldn't make her body obey.

Those harpooned still had iron-gray smoke billowing from wounds, even underwater, as they were hauled up and out of sight.

Something bumped into her, and Ro wrapped a feeble arm around the body, hooking her hands into the wafting raven hair, trying to find purchase.

The body rose to the surface, taking Ro with it.

Both surfaced. Ro, struggling for feeble breath; the siren, eyes staring, no motion passing her gills. She slowly bobbed in the water, turning to face Ro and then away. It was a siren Ro didn't recognize, though her name teased Ro's memory, just out of reach.

Her eyes screamed for help, but every muscle in Ro's body still locked her in a ridged spasm, leaving her unable to move.

The *whisk* of harpoons sounded all around her, and Ro watched, helpless, as siren after siren was harpooned and dragged aboard, pitch-black blood swirling in the water and smoking in the sky, then smudging up the side of the ship.

"The huntress! Overboard! There, in the water!"

Faces peered over the edge at her right before ropes were lowered and she was pulled upward. She still clung to the siren, so both were dragged aboard at the same time.

"Filthy demon of the sea!" A knife flashed in the sailor's hand.

No, don't! Ro screamed without being able to make a sound.

But it was too late. A deft flick of his wrist, and the siren's pitch-black life force sprayed onto the deck from her throat. Her eyes held Ro's until they were as lifeless as the rest of her.

Ro's muscles began to spasm as she lay on deck, her body jerking uncontrollably, her cheek plastered to the deck, tears rolling down her face as siren after siren was pulled aboard, bloodied, and dumped alongside her.

As Ro watched the bodies pile up around her, she desperately wanted to cry out for Olt, but she couldn't.

Suddenly, she felt someone tugging at her from behind, but it was just . . . wrong. It wasn't Olt's touch. He would never be so rough. Or smell quite so horrible.

She was hauled to her feet and carried between two men, the toes of her boots dragging on the wood planks, toward the infirmary. Her still-paralyzed body wouldn't let her gag on the stench that seemed to be coming from both men or lift her head to see who held her.

Her head lolled, and she could only make little whimpering noises. Not one of them punctured the raging battle on deck.

Whoever it was plopped her in a chair, staying behind her where she couldn't see. One began tying her hands behind her, then her body to the chair, while the other tied her feet together. She still couldn't lift her head.

"So the huntress has returned to warn us of the impending attack," the quartermaster taunted.

Hank sneered. "Bringing hordes of sirens with her. Imagine that."

Great. Two of her favorite people.

Ro made herself focus. She sat strapped to a chair in the infirmary, weak and shaking. She'd never been in so much pain in all her life, and even now, what felt like eons later, she kind of wanted to die.

As control of her body slowly returned, she lifted her head.

The quartermaster raised one filthy eyebrow, crawling with lice. "That's a point right thar, Hank. Perhaps she brought them here to lead the attack herself?"

Ro's eyes flashed to his, and she made a little movement forward. The ropes stopped her. She tried to object, but her mouth still wasn't working.

Hank chortled at the movement.

"Ah. As stubborn as ever." The quartermaster sneered as he flicked a knife in his fingers. "You might be having your orders, but see here, huntress, we be having ours as well."

He leaned forward, his foul breath wafting over Ro and making her gag.

"To see every single one of them little wenches gutted and taken to the king. There's some kind of magic in their blood, you know. Enough of them scientific experiments the good ole doctor does and the like, and we'll know right where the rest of them be. After we use their own power against 'em, o' course."

Ro's eyes widened. She couldn't let that happen.

And . . . they didn't know. Had no one else seen what had happened to the physician?

He gave her a leer she felt down to her toes. "Speaking of experiments, I think we could be doing our own in here, what d'ya say, beautiful?"

Ro spit on him. The quartermaster wiped his face, then drew back his fist. Ro threw herself to the side, her chair tipped, and the door burst open.

"Enough!" Captain Montrose placed himself in front of Ro. "What are you doing here? Return to your posts."

The quartermaster pointed at her with his knife. "She as much as admitted to leading 'em here for revenge, Cap'ain."

Hank's fists were clenched, and he nodded enthusiastically.

The captain's inquisitive eyes shot to hers. Ro stared back, trying to deny it with a look. Excruciating pain made her words hardly effective.

"I would never," she whispered.

The quartermaster advanced. "Why you little —"

Once again, the captain blocked her body with his. "Get. Out."

"But I was just leaving her here for the doc." He sneered at Ro. "You were his payment from the king, you know, for comin' on this trip and doing what you can't."

"Out!"

The quartermaster grumbled but made his way toward the door. Hank eyed the captain, as if sizing up if the two of them could take him.

The captain turned a look on Hank that even had Ro cringing back, and Hank retreated.

Captain Montrose kept his hard look at Hank while he spoke to the quartermaster. "And leave the knife."

Mutinous fury danced all over his face, but he left the knife.

The captain didn't speak again until the door closed behind

them. He retrieved the knife, gently set Ro's chair upright, and began cutting away her bonds.

His hands were shaking.

"I'm to be payment, am I?" Ro asked in a quiet voice.

"I—assure you, huntress. I had no idea about any of that. If it's true, and I doubt it is, I would never have been part of such an arrangement. I apologize for your mistreatment."

Ro drew back a little, staring at him with wide eyes. "My mistreatment? What of the sirènes? They agreed to talk! And you just threw all that out to what, slaughter them and make the killing last longer?"

She couldn't wrap her mind around what the physician could have possibly wanted with her, but she couldn't think about that right now.

He was gone, and the ship was still under attack.

The captain, jaw tight, kept severing Ro's bonds. "You misunderstand. The Siren Queen's nest is here. You led us to her. I had my orders that she was to be brought to the king, alive or no. To wipe out the rest of them. If this muse falls, they all fall." A pause. "I didn't know the rest. I am sorry."

Ro felt sick. "Well, did you get her? Or did you simply kill more of her people, infuriate her, and make peace talks nigh impossible?"

Regret swept the captain's face. "We have not found her yet, no." Then stubborn determination. "But we shall."

Ro rolled her eyes. "Really. Now that you've detonated the weapons and alerted her to your intentions?"

He grunted as he sawed through the ropes at her feet. "We've proven we can finally defend ourselves against the creatures. I thought you'd be happy about that."

Ro shook her head. "There are always two sides of every story, mon capitaine, you know that. And the sirènes have a legitimate grievance with the king. I was here to repair that. Did you truly wish my negotiations to fail?"

His face was stone. "I wish to carry out my orders and to

show the demons of the sea that the king's ships are not to be trifled with."

A lead cannonball sank to the bottom of Ro's stomach. "But why? You could be on your way back to the king, without further loss of life. Yet you chose this?"

The ropes fell free, and he moved to her back. But instead of untying her hands, he gently helped her stand and held on to the ropes.

"I again apologize, huntress, that things did not go according to your plans. I know how frustrating that can be." He walked her toward the door. "But I cannot have you upsetting things here. You shall not be further mistreated, but I must hold you until I can turn you over to the king." He looked troubled. "And I cannot deny that it is suspicious, what with your return and the attack immediately following."

Ro couldn't even believe it. "You mean when I came to *warn* you about the attack? Against my better judgment?"

"Not everyone will see it that way. Placing you in the brig is as much for your safety as it is for ours." He lowered his voice. "I will allow the king to clear up the other matter."

Fear punched Ro in the stomach, and she gasped a breath. And if the king *had* traded her to the physician in exchange for his lightning spheres? "You can't do that!"

If the ship went down . . . Olt . . . Cen . . . drowning . . . she couldn't protect anyone or anything.

The captain's voice was grim as he led her out on deck and toward the hold below. He still looked troubled. "I'm afraid I can and I must. I am truly sorry, huntress. I have enjoyed our talks. I wish things had turned out differently."

As he led her to the stairs belowdecks, a shout momentarily distracted him. It was all Ro needed.

She shoved him hard with her shoulder and bolted for an opening between sailors. They grabbed for her—the captain lunged for her—but she slipped between them and bolted up the stairs that led to the forecastle deck.

"Do not let her escape!" someone called.

Ro gritted her teeth. She knew coming back here was a bad idea.

They clambered after her, but she turned, jumped over their heads onto a barrel, and then leaped onto the railing. As soon as she regained her balance, she shoved off hard, into the ocean, a perfect head-first dive.

Water engulfed her, and she kicked as hard as she could, heading straight down.

She had to get away from the lightning sphere's reach.

Belatedly, she realized she couldn't swim as well with her hands bound behind her and stopped swimming. She started to float upward, but she scrunched herself into a little ball and pulled her hands under her feet and around to the front, twisting her wrists painfully.

Then she pushed herself deep again.

The pressure changed on her ears, and she did everything she could to loosen the ropes around her wrists. She changed her trajectory from straight down and leveled out, readying to push upward as soon as she needed air.

Which would be soon.

Her lungs burned, her head started to feel dizzy, and the pressure on her ears was quickly becoming unbearable. She started to push herself upward, hoping she was far enough out.

Something slammed into her, and she spun sideways. Precious air escaped. She didn't have time to look before something slammed into her again.

This time she screamed.

o came to, breathing fresh, blessed air, gently rocking with the current.

"Oh, good, you're awake!"

Ro's head came up, and she stared into the all-black eyes of Llyr, her springy hair billowing in the oncoming tempest. Ro quickly took in her surroundings. Tied hands in front of her, nothing but water surrounding her. She bobbed on a piece of flotsam, arms hooked over it, feet floating in the water below her.

She sagged on the buoyant, silvery, and rather large piece of driftwood.

An abalone knife flashed, and Ro's hands came unbound.

"What happened?" Ro asked.

"One of our sharks attacked you."

Ro's eyes widened. She'd passed out during a *shark attack*? Her eyes darted all around her. Where was it?

Llyr was quick to add, "Don't worry, I stunned it." She looked embarrassed. "I just happened to stun you as well. I am sorry."

"Sorry? You saved me. You have nothing to apologize for." Ro frowned. "But I don't understand—why did you save me?"

Llyr's eyes shifted to the side. "What my queen asked of you—how your captain betrayed you—" Her eyes met Ro's. "You have a good heart, huntress. That you're here to save life instead of take more of it . . . it's rare in a hunter. Thank you."

Ro barked a bitter laugh. "What good are my intentions if I cannot get anyone to listen to me?"

Llyr grinned. "I just might be able to help you with that. Shall I take you to your other ship to recover?"

Ro sighed and rested her head. "In a moment, s'il vous plaît." She just wanted to relax. Forever.

Llyr leaned close to her face. "Did you learn anything from the human ship? Like what those blasts were? We felt them all the way . . . below."

Ro glanced at her. "Below? In the sirènes' lair, you mean? Was anyone hurt—paralyzed, maybe?"

Llyr shook her head with wide eyes. "Oh, no. It was uncomfortable, to be sure, but that was all. Queen Zarya sent me to find out what happened."

Her eyes looked troubled, like she had so many questions. Questions Ro didn't want to answer. But she had to.

She took a deep breath. "It's a weapon the king sent with the ship I was on."

Mistrust filled the siren's eyes.

"I had no idea, I promise you." She held the Llyr's eyes. "It hurt me too."

"What—what happened?"

Ro went to rub her face, then thought better of it lest she slide off the driftwood so Llyr had to rescue her again. "It paralyzes anything in the water somehow. Fish, mer—"

"We are not mer," Llyr interrupted. She shuddered. "They are flighty, empty-headed things. Like dolphins. And far too colorful for my tastes."

Ro couldn't help but smile, but it was chased away by what else she had to say. She looked steadily at Llyr. "It paralyzed everyone the queen sent to sink the ship."

Llyr's gills starting thrumming even faster. "They're all —gone?"

Ro nodded. "Most of them, oui. Hauled aboard and killed." Ro slumped forward, weak. "I couldn't do anything to stop it this time, either."

Hatred filled Llyr's face. "I'm going to kill them all."

Ro laid her hand on the siren's arm, but the creature flinched away. Ro swallowed and drew back her hand. "Non, please. Let's find a better way."

"A better way?" Llyr laughed, a hollow, hopeless sound. "I have tried my entire existence for a better way, huntress. Look where it has gotten me."

Ro's brow puckered at the sadness in Llyr's voice. She tried to pull up Llyr's memories, but her human mind just couldn't retain all the information the Siren Queen had thrown at her. It was slipping away.

At Ro's questioning look, Llyr expounded, her smile turning sad. "I was on one of those ships, huntress. The slaving ships. My own people captured me, sold me. I was to travel across the great sea and work at a sugar cane plantation in a place called the Bahamas."

Ro's heart broke within her. "Oh, Llyr . . . I am so sorry that happened."

Llyr gave her a ghost of a smile. "As am I. I had been taken above to"—she shuddered—"the reason is no longer important. I had one opportunity, before I was chained again. I took it. I would rather have drowned than live through my nightmare again."

Silent tears tracked down Ro's face.

"My sisters found me, changed me, helped me take down the ship and release the captive humans, those who lived through our destruction, on the nearest uninhabited isles." Llyr shrugged. "I don't even remember my name from that time."

Ro did recall that much. The sirens were renamed when they were changed. Llyr meant, simply, the sea.

"Some of us want to remember everything, to feel everything, to fuel our hurt and our rage. I—I couldn't do that. I wanted to forgive. Forget. Make a better choice, you know?"

Ro nodded, a brief memory of her father selling her to a beast in exchange for his life trying to surface. She pushed it right back down. She, too, tried to forget, though she was quite certain she would never be able to forgive.

She didn't know how Llyr did it.

"Not many agree with me. They think I am—strange. But my people, my sisters, have an example of forgiveness, if nothing else. They may not understand it, but at least they got to taste it."

Ro shook her head. "You're a better—person—than I ever could be, Llyr. Thank you for sharing your story with me."

Llyr smiled. "Oh, huntress, you have such potential deep within. Don't let hate wall it off, grow coral around it and make it impenetrable. You yet have much to do for your people."

Ro tried her own ghost of a smile, but it failed dismally. "Merci, Llyr. I'll take your words to heart." Even if she disagreed.

"But not mine. I'm beginning to agree with my sisters." A hard look—non, an empty look, one completely inhuman, came over Llyr's face. "It's time for you to leave. Go back to your people, huntress, and leave mine alone."

Ro very much felt the same way. "I wish I could, but not all men are bad, Llyr. There are the good ones. Those who fight for what's right. Those are the ones I'm here for. If I could just get your queen to listen to me . . ."

Anger punctuated Llyr's every move, anger born from deep hurt. Something Ro was far too familiar with. "No. We tried it your way, huntress, and now my sisters are dead. Now it's going to be the queen's way. They—maybe they're right, not me. Maybe I should have listened to my sisters."

Ro closed her eyes, tears close, and laid her head on the driftwood. "There's got to be another way."

Llyr hesitated.

Something latched on to Ro's ankles and pulled her straight down.

Ro fought, but whatever had her was *fast*.

Something blurred nearby, and Llyr barreled into the creature at her feet. The moment it released her, Ro swam for the surface.

Then Merida was in her face, teeth bared, gills thrumming, knife in hand. It looked to be made of the same material as the obsidian rocks.

Merida was a bedraggled mess. She must've just barely escaped the battle.

Her knife flashed, and Ro pushed herself back just in time to keep from getting cut.

Merida swung again, her eyes feral. "You! You did this to us. It's all your fault!"

"Merida, don't!" Llyr cried, her voice panicked.

Merida attacked again. Ro tried to dodge, but her movements were slowed by the water. Merida clamped on tight and held the long, glass knife to Ro's throat.

"Don't thrash too much, huntress." The siren grinned, revealing elongated teeth. She clutched the back of Ro's neck and held her steady. "My sharks love it when someone thrashes."

"Merida, stop!" Llyr cried.

A flash of annoyance crossed her face. "And why should I? Our sisters are dead because of her." She hissed the last word at Ro.

"No, she tried to stop it. You know that," Llyr pleaded.

"I suppose that's why her arrows are embedded in so many of us? Oh, yes, I can see exactly how hard she tried to stop it." She spun Ro away from her and spoke close to Ro's ear. "Shall we see how you fend against a shark?"

Ro went still in her arms.

Three sharks circled nearby. Perhaps brought there by Merida. Perhaps attracted to their thrashing.

Ro only knew she was in desperate need of air.

With a sudden, blurring move Ro could hardly see, Merida slashed Ro's forearm with her obsidian blade. Ro screamed. Bubbles billowed in the water, blood swirled out around them, and the first shark barreled right toward her.

Llyr threw herself between Ro and the shark, sending out a blast from her hands, one that stunned all three sharks and sent them drifting away.

Merida shrieked and dove for the sharks, letting go of Ro. She kicked feebly for the surface, lungs burning.

"Llyr! You know they can't breathe if they stop moving. How could you?"

She crooned over them, pushed them forward, tried to revive them. They didn't respond.

Ro kept her eyes on the crazed siren as she desperately reached for life-giving air.

Then Merida's all-black eyes settled on the huntress, and with a shriek Ro felt deep in her bones, Merida came at Ro again.

Ro thrust herself back in the water, but Llyr kept herself between them. She held out her hands, ready to shove more power out. "Don't think I wouldn't do it to you as well, Merida."

Merida pulled up short, teeth bared.

Llyr cast her voice through the water, making herself heard by far more than just those present. "Now hear me, my sisters. The huntress is not to be harmed. She has my word on that, as long as she is in these waters, and it cannot be broken."

Ro arched an eyebrow in surprise, and Merida's mouth fell open. Both stared at Llyr.

"Why in all the seas would you do that, Llyr?" Merida looked beside herself with disgust.

Llyr lifted her chin, not budging an inch. "She saved my life, now I'm saving hers. I owe her as much. Now back away."

With a snarl, Merida complied.

"Now go. See how our sisters fare."

Merida flicked her sable tail at them and snapped herself away, rage in her posture, clenched fists and angry strokes of her tail the last thing Ro saw. She gently herded the sharks away, murmuring to them as she went.

Llyr immediately pulled Ro to the surface. Ro's head poked into the blessed air, and she gasped deep breaths.

Ro started to thank Llyr the moment she could speak.

"Don't," Llyr interrupted. She turned all-black eyes on Ro. "It changes nothing. Go, find your boat and leave us be."

Ro called her back, but Llyr didn't turn once as she swam deep and out of sight.

The siren didn't resurface.

Ro didn't recall saving Llyr's life, but she was thankful to be alive and breathing air, and that wouldn't have happened without the siren's protection. She owed her much.

Even if she didn't understand what had just happened.

The water grew choppier, slapping Ro in the face. The last thing she wanted was to be in the water when the approaching storm struck.

Ro sighed and watched the gash on her arm until it closed. Then she reached into her pocket for her compass. Thankfully it truly was waterproof, and the fleur-de-lis needle swung in its mate's direction.

She tested her limbs, found them all willing to move if a bit shaky, and pushed off for the *Siren Hunter*. She hoped Captain Red was already on her way.

36

*R*o was so focused on taking one stroke after another, when something latched on to the back of her shirt, she took in a mouthful of seawater as she thrashed in the waves.

"Hold still!" said a very grumpy-sounding woman.

Ro allowed herself to be pulled aboard, hacking as they did so, and noticed two pirates in the rowboat—along with Cen. Panic suffused her. Cen couldn't be here! If she were taken . . .

Her thoughts must have been plain on her face, for Cen crossed her arms and glared, clearly daring Ro to say something.

When Ro could speak, she glanced at the pirates. "Thank you for my rescue." She looked directly at Cen. "It is good to see you."

Cen's defiance eased ever so slightly, and she gave Ro a single nod.

The pirates immediately went back to rowing. They quickly cut through the water, toward what Ro could only assume was the *Siren Hunter*.

Ro was surprised when the *King's Ransom* came into view instead.

"We are returning?" Ro questioned, hoping against hope that Olt was their destination.

"For Olt," one of the pirates supplied.

"Ah. Merci."

The cries of battle reached them before the carnage did. It looked even worse from the outside looking in than in the midst of it.

"Your plan for getting him?" one of them grunted at Ro, cutting Cen an annoyed, sidelong glance.

Ro spoke before Cen could try. "I'll get him. If we aren't in the boat in time, get clear, and I'll protect him with my life."

Cen's scrutiny burned the side of her face. Their gazes met and held, and Ro gave a single nod. She would do as she said.

Cen deflated just a little. She looked so young. So scared.

Ro reached over and squeezed her hand, and the pirates quite obviously pretended not to notice.

The *King's Ransom* loomed large on the horizon. Ro's heart dropped. More sirens than before churned in the water, redoubling their attack. Nowhere near as many globes were being hurled into the water. Perhaps they were running out?

The clouds above continued to churn, but they had not yet unleashed their fury.

Cen stood and waved her arms, screaming something unintelligible.

"Sit down!" barked one of the pirates. "You don't want us to tip, do you?"

Cen plopped down and grumbled without a sound.

"Mon Dieu," said one of the pirates. "I've never seen anything like it."

Sirens sprang out of the water, like jumping fish, snatching any sailor within grasp. Ro gaped at the sight, then scanned the ship frantically. Where was Olt?

Cen, obviously distressed, leaned forward as if she could make the boat go faster.

Rage began to build in Ro's chest. If they had harmed him . . .

The sky began to roil above, matching Ro's feelings exactly.

Ro focused on the ship they were barreling toward. The sirens would rue the day Ro had come to their depths if they harmed Olt *or* Cen.

Then they were alongside the *King's Ransom*, and Ro was flinging herself toward it. She clutched the nets and hauled herself aboard.

Most ridiculous thing to have hanging off the side of a ship. Why didn't they just invite the sirens aboard?

"I said sit down! It won't do him any good if we're all in the water without a boat, will it?" Ro heard behind her as she climbed the nets.

Mêlée swamped the deck. King's men hurled fizzing glass globes and harpoons into the sea, and those sirens who weren't paralyzed were flinging themselves across the width of the deck, taking any man they latched on to down to the depths. The cannons and pistols were eerily silent, as if they had run out of balls and shot.

Swords flashed at the attacking sirens.

Ro frowned. Why weren't they singing?

She joined the fight, but they parted like water before her, not willing to engage. Ro found herself immensely thankful for Llyr.

A sailor next to her was taken, and she grabbed him as he sailed by. She needn't have bothered. The siren ripped the sailor from her as if Ro's grasp was that of a newborn babe's. They disappeared over the side in a blink.

A glimmer of light caught Ro's eye. She turned toward it. Her ebony bow, flickering like a beacon, revealed itself to her. She hurried over to it and grabbed it. Someone must have kicked it against these barrels.

Thank goodness no one had kicked it overboard.

She reached for an arrow, but her quiver had emptied itself into the sea.

"Huntress!" one of the pirates called.

Ro's head swiveled toward the shout. Cendre pointed to the lines above as one of the pirates waved her arms and shouted for Ro's attention.

Ro snapped her gaze up. There, Olt hung suspended, near the crow's nest, slashing at sirens who were leaping above the mainmast.

Relief washed over Ro in waves. She hadn't seen him since they'd boarded the ship. She'd begun to fear . . . but she had no time for such thoughts.

Flinging her bow across her back, Ro hauled herself up after him. She could only hope the sirens would leave him alone until she got there.

The sky swirled angrier, and lightning began to flash in earnest all around them.

Curse this storm! Why now of all times? Thank the heavens rain hadn't yet blinded them—it probably wouldn't bother the sirens at all.

"Olt!"

Olt caught sight of her, but his welcoming look morphed into something entirely other. Wide eyes, sword frozen midair, fist clenched white on the line.

"Behind you!" Ro shouted.

A crack of thunder obliterated her words. Still, Olt swung aside just in time to narrowly miss a siren's grasping hands.

An odd sound made Ro glance down.

A siren grabbed the nets draped over the side of the ship. Ro rolled her eyes. But then, smoke and sizzling flesh poured from the siren's hands. With a hiss, she fell back in the water, curled in on herself in pain, and didn't resurface.

Ro blinked. Well. Um. That was rather effective. Probably another trick from the physician. She scowled. She sincerely hoped his body wouldn't be found after the battle.

Ro resumed her climb to the crow's nest, and she couldn't help but feeling very much like a pirate. Or, at least, her idea of a pirate from all the stories she'd read.

An entirely odd thought to have when Olt's life was in the balance.

A buzz lit up her skull, and she flattened herself against the mast, waiting for the lightning strike that was sure to follow.

It didn't come.

Olt clambered into the crow's nest, and she followed.

"What are you doing?" Olt shouted.

Ro couldn't help her grin. "I've come to rescue you!"

He barked a laugh. "Of course you have." He sobered. "I meant the storm! Can you stop it?"

Ro looked at him like he'd lost his mind. "*What?*"

He reached for her but jerked away before he touched her. "Look! Your hands."

"We need to get off this ship, not look at my —"

Certain he'd gone mad, she cast a quick glance down. And did a double take.

" —hands."

Lightning spanned between her fingers, mirroring every lightning strike in the sky.

Or perhaps they were mirroring *her*.

"Can you make it stop?" Olt shouted.

"Make it stop? I don't even know what's happening!" She raised shaking hands, wanting to throw it away from her, certain light couldn't be thrown, no matter how hard she tried.

"The storm! It's reflecting you!" Olt shouted.

Ro flung her hands out. "I don't even know —"

Lightning blasted from the sky with her movement, lighting up the ropes and wood around them, arcing into the water below. Ozone and a burnt odor filled the air.

The sirens trying to dismantle the ship through the torn netting hissed and fell back.

Ro stared, mouth open, dumbfounded. It had happened

once before, in the woods, when she'd fought the Mesdemoiselles of the Mountain, but it hadn't happened since.

"You mean to tell me—"

Ro swung her slack-jawed expression in Olt's direction.

"—that you have all these powers and you don't even know
how to use them?"

Ro snapped her mouth closed. "Pretty much." She grabbed
Olt's arm without thinking. "We have to go."

The terror in his eyes—mirrored in Ro's as she realized
what she'd done—turned to awe. "Whoa," he breathed. "That
feels . . . incredible."

It did. Like a rush of warm air, a current that soothed and
empowered and flowed through both of them. One she only
noticed when she held Olt's arm.

A mighty crack sounded, and her world tilted. The ship
shuddered, and Ro couldn't help gasping as the ship dropped
out from under her just a little, and then rose and fell on a
nudge from underneath.

Another jolt. Another loud crack, and it looked as though
the boards were bending up in the middle of the deck. The
crow's nest tilted even more to the side.

Olt's face went white. "Get clear of the lines!"

He picked her up and bodily shoved her out of the crow's
nest, up toward the very top of the mast. It tilted over the side
of the ship, dangling them both over open water.

"Olt!"

"Keep climbing."

All she wanted to do was hold on, but she obeyed.
Together, they scrambled to the top of the mainmast, away
from the lines, the sails, the heavy wooden beams that could
crush them against the hard slap of water.

The slow tilt halted for a moment. But only a moment.
They clung to the mast.

Olt caught and held her eyes, his hand clasped around
her forearm and hers around his. "Keep your head. When it

gets close to the water, jump clear. Don't look back, just jump."

Ro nodded, but that was all she had time for.

The first few boards splintered.

Ro choked on a scream as her world dropped out from under her, and she plunged toward the sea below.

The sea rushed up at them, and Ro's stomach was flung far away. Her scream stuck in her throat, but then the water was there and she was pushing off the beam with her feet.

The mast slapped the water, throwing Ro clear of the ship's carnage in a somersault.

She slapped the water hard, stunned, and careened in a slow circle under its frothing waves. The lightning traveling up and down her arms winked out.

She fought for control of her limbs. She'd read enough in the beast's library to know if a person didn't get away from a sinking ship in time, the suction from it going down could drag them under and keep them there. Just long enough.

Sirens writhed in the water around her, taking any man who touched the water straight down, never to be seen again. Not one of them touched Ro. Thank goodness for that. And Ro was still underwater. She hadn't taken a deep enough breath. She needed air!

She broke the surface and gasped, getting a mouthful of seawater and spitting the salty fluid right back out. Another wave doused her before she could get a full breath.

Then hands were pulling at her, plucking her from the water. Soon she lay panting in the bottom of a rowboat, anxious faces peering at her.

"Olt!" Ro cried.

But they were already pulling him aboard. Siren hands latched on to Olt—and the side of the rowboat—and started pulling the entire craft straight down into the water.

"Huntress!" one of the pirates cried.

Cen screamed without sound.

Ro instinctively flung herself after Olt, and the sirens dragging him down immediately released him and the vessel.

He flew into the boat, almost upending the craft.

He sagged against Ro, sucking in deep breaths as the two pirates rowed with all their might away from the battle.

More jarring, cracking noises lit up the air, and Ro hauled herself up. Sirens were sacrificing themselves on the nets, flesh sizzling and burning away, as they ripped pieces of net away so others could get to the boards beneath.

And then—and then—the most heart-stopping sound of all. A crack, like a mighty tree splitting in a thunderstorm, like a crack of thunder itself, a crack that spelled doom.

They all jerked toward the noise. The ship, the one she'd traveled across the great sea upon, lurched straight up in the middle and split in two as a spire of obsidian grew right out of the ocean and speared it in half.

A cheer went up from the sirens, the sound grating and physically painful, carrying farther now that they had their stone to cast it.

The halves of the ship didn't even have time to sink as the sirens converged as one, tearing the boards to shreds with their bare hands. Soon, nothing was left. Nothing but debris floating on the water.

Any crewman in the water immediately stopped struggling as the sirens starting singing a haunting melody as one, the stone echoing and harmonizing with their voices, enchanting all who heard it. The men started vanishing, not even bothering to fight as almost-invisible shapes wrapped their arms around them and pulled them straight down.

A few sailors pulled floating ropes out of the water, wrapped the strands tight around their own necks, and sank out of sight, blissful smiles on their faces.

Those in Ro's watercraft clamped their hands over their ears, the music painful, the message clear: *Come to me. Take my hand and sink into the depths. I will take you to our forever home.*

But they were not enchanted. The siren scales were working, praise Dieu.

Ro screamed in frustration as more men disappeared, but no one in the water heard her. They were too busy doing whatever self-inflicted horror the sirens asked of them. Tears slipped down her cheeks.

Sheets of rain began to undulate across the sea, blocking their view of the spire of rock and dismembered ship floating on the crests of choppy waves. Cries began to die out, the singing became muffled, and the pirates picked up their oars.

Their craft moved, untouched, those within silent, somber, and shaken to their cores, to the waiting pirate ship.

"Quickly!" one of the pirates urged when they reached the *Siren Hunter*. "They will turn to us now." She flicked a glance at Olt, and Ro's heart plummeted.

Following the pirates' example, Ro, Olt, and Cen grasped dangling ropes and walked up the ship's side, leaning back to counter their weight, lines slick in the downpour.

The pirates, first to climb, disappeared over the edge.

Ro hauled herself up the long climb, knowing they needed to get away from that precipice as quickly as they could. Who knew what was barreling up under them at this very moment?

Cen kept glancing at Olt, her pace slacking.

Ro shook water out of her eyes. "Eyes up, Cen, or I'll be pulling your sorry hide out of the drink."

Cen's startled eyes met hers, but then she gave a weak grin.

"Now who sounds like a pirate?" Olt grunted, but his voice held a hint of a smile.

Ro chuckled and outpaced them just a little. Almost there . . .

"Cen, nein!" Olt shouted.

Ro jerked around.

A lone siren grabbed for Cen, who was climbing slower than the rest of them because she'd started gasping for air. Olt slid down his rope, kicking the siren away.

A trail of blood painted the rope where his hands had been.

Ro reached down and snagged Cen's shirt, dragging her up the side of the ship and to the waiting hands above.

The stubborn thing kicked and squirmed, and Ro nearly dropped her eight decks into the churning sea and to the sirens below. Raven scales flashed.

She hauled Cen roughly up once more. "Stop it! Are you trying to get us both killed?"

Cendre stopped squirming for half a second—enough time for those above to haul her aboard.

"Curse you!" Cen shouted, making no noise at all, but Ro was already turning back to Olt.

She was too late.

A siren flew out the water, latched on to Olt, and plunged him into the churning water below.

Ro's entire life sank with him into the rain-pocked water, and she couldn't think. Couldn't feel. For a moment, she didn't know what to do.

Time did not reverse itself.

She looped one arm through the rope, then a leg, and let them take her weight. She grabbed for an arrow that placed itself in her hand. She drew the bow, the silver arrow lengthened, and she let go.

It plunged deep, and after a few heartbreaking moments, Olt surfaced.

Ro sagged with relief, then untangled herself from the ropes as he swam toward the ship, just as another pair of arms wrapped around his chest and pulled him straight down.

Ro scrambled for another arrow, but it didn't come.

She jolted into action. Ro dropped the bow, pushed off with her feet, and dove in after him.

Plunging into the water, past grasping hands, she followed his trail of bubbles like a lifeline.

37

*R*o needed air. In fact, she was past needing air.

She strained toward the spot where she'd last seen Olt sinking. It didn't matter; he was no longer in sight. But she had to get to him. She had to.

She kicked again, but it was weak. Paltry. She hadn't much time.

Something shot straight toward her from her left. Ro jerked away and raised her arms to defend herself, but the thing was lightning fast and latched on to her arm. Ro yelled and fought, and precious air bubbles floated out of her mouth and rose to the surface.

The siren gave her a shake and raised her finger to her mouth in a "be quiet" motion. Ro stilled. It was Llyr. She'd come back. Why?

Then the siren held out her hand and blew a large, perfectly formed bubble in her palm. She reached toward Ro's face.

Ro freaked out and started thrashing, even as black spots swam in her vision. Especially because black spots swam in her vision.

Llyr jerked her close and mouthed "be still," and with the

precision of an artist, carefully fitted the bubble around Ro's nose and mouth.

Ro gasped a breath. Paused. Took another.

Her wide eyes shot to the siren's. Llyr grinned, sharp teeth gleaming. Then she winked at Ro, grabbed her hand, and dove deep.

"Curse you," Cendre sobbed out, but Ro was already planting her feet on the side of the ship and kicking off with all her might.

Cendre cursed again and again—something she'd never done before she went on a three-month voyage with sailors—and watched Ro disappear into the water after Olt. She tried to jump in after them, but strong hands held her back.

"Do you want to put the huntress in even more danger?" Merja shouted over the pounding rain. "Make her choose between saving you and saving Olt? Because believe you me, the huntress will choose you. And Olt's blood will be on your hands."

Those words stilled Cen like nothing else could. She watched helplessly as the only two people she cared about disappeared . . . perhaps forever.

As the bubbles lessened and then ceased, the rain lightened until the peak of obsidian that had speared the *King's Ransom* could be seen. The sirens turned away from the ship that was no more and focused as one on the *Siren Hunter*.

Then the pirates holding her were rushing off to save their crew as the first few sirens attacked.

The ship lumbered away from the spot she'd last seen her best friend and her sister, trying to get away from the siren's stone before the rain ceased and the creatures lured them to their deaths.

Cendre backed away from the rail.

Her chest grew tight, and she tried to calm her racing heart, tried to take deep, cleansing breaths. Before her throat closed off completely.

But her mind replayed Olt disappearing. Ro going after him. Then the *King's Ransom* splitting straight up the middle, speared straight through its heart by an obsidian spire of rock. Over and over again.

What kind of power could cause such a whole ship to break in two like that?

Her eyes slid to the planks at her feet.

And would it happen to this ship as well?

Her jaw went tight. Not if she had anything to do about it. She was going to stop the fight before it was too late and all hands were lost. Before they left Ro and Olt behind forever.

Struggling for a deep breath, unable to find one, she glanced to either side. No one was watching her. She slipped behind some barrels to remain unseen, eyes on the spot her family had disappeared, the spot moving steadily away from the ship.

Captain Red ran by, pausing long enough to bark out orders. "Keep this ship moving! They need time to coax the rocks out of the ocean floor. Whatever you do, do not let them becalm the ship!"

Cen attempted a deep breath to calm her racing heart. She had no choice, really. She had to do something. Carefully, she put one foot up on the rail and vaulted herself over the ship's side before she could talk herself out of it—before anyone could stop her.

Her heart nearly flew out of her chest as eight decks rushed past her impossibly fast.

She entered the water feet-first, hardly making a sound over the lingering storm, the battle cries of the pirates, and the thrashing of the sirens.

Water enveloped her, and the pain in her chest eased.

She swam for the closest siren and grabbed her arm. The

thing turned toward her, hissing, then paused, a curious look passing over her face.

Cendre tried to say something but choked. The siren looked pained, like Cendre was a huge inconvenience, but hauled her to the surface anyway.

"Speak quickly, human."

Cendre sputtered and coughed. "Take me to your queen. I must see your queen. Please." She grew desperate as no sound passed her lips.

The siren gave her an annoyed look. "Like I've never heard that before."

Cendre stilled. The siren could understand her?

She started to shake Cendre off, but Cendre held on tight and spoke fast. "Please! She'll want to hear what I have to say." Cendre plunged ahead even as the siren rolled her eyes. "The huntress—she—I—she's my sister."

This got the siren's attention.

Cendre didn't flinch. She'd overheard what Ro had confessed to Captain Red. "I'm willing to take her place."

The siren sneered. "You don't know what you're asking, human."

"I do, and I'm willing."

The siren's expression morphed from disbelieving, to calculating, to downright elated. She grinned. "As you wish."

In a violent move, the siren grabbed Cendre's wrist, her jagged nails piercing her skin and biting deep. Cendre screamed, but no sound erupted from her lips.

A shout came from above. Cendre looked up into several anxious faces from the pirate crew as the siren wrapped unbelievably strong arms around Cendre and dragged her under.

The last thing Cendre saw was blood churning in the water directly above her.

Ro fought not to panic as they traveled deeper and deeper still into darkness below.

All of it came over her, crushing her, its weight reminding her of all it had taken from her family.

It was her biggest fear, come to life. Drowning. Images of the nightmares she'd had after her père's ships sank came back to her, almost choking her.

All those men, dead. Men she'd known. Men who'd roved her père's ships, loaded cargo, been in her père's office, prepping for voyage after voyage. They floated in the water around her, phantoms that wouldn't let her forget.

One brushed her arm as Llyr pulled her deeper and deeper, and a chill trailed down her flesh.

Some of these men had been over to her house for dinner, discussing business with Pére. One of them had a daughter her age.

Those two had older sons who would join her brothers in teasing her. But taken too far, and her brothers were swift to her defense.

They were above her, beside her, in front of her, faces blue, lifeless, hair undulating free and supple. Ship bottom above her, though now it ghosted through her, then littered the ocean floor in pieces.

Three ships, spilling her family's wealth across the ocean floor, the harbinger of the curse that had swept France, bringing destruction and starvation and wolves in its wake.

She had to pull herself from the waking nightmare with all of her strength, reminding herself that it wasn't real.

Llyr's eyes were on her, curious, and Ro offered her a feeble smile.

She would conquer her fear if it killed her. She pushed the phantoms away and focused on her surroundings, but they floated nearby, watching her pass.

Just when Ro was certain they couldn't possibly go any

farther, Llyr kept pulling her down. They were so deep under the ocean. Too deep. Impossibly deep.

Ro shouldn't have been able to bear it, but she could. She shouldn't have been able to see . . . but she could.

From dark blue to darkness so black it was a visceral thing to . . . dark blue again. Then lighter blue. And still it grew lighter.

Ro couldn't believe it.

It should've gotten darker the farther down they went, not brighter.

And yet, after they passed a barrier of kelp, stones covered in something luminous lit their way into a rocky crevice made of the same obsidian as above. The water caressed her in welcome.

Then, something she'd never seen before. Something that shouldn't have been possible.

Blue flame danced in large open clamshells.

Ro blinked. Open flame? Underwater? Impossible.

They swam through a wide tunnel of obsidian, then a cavernous space opened before them. Ro was so in awe of the place teeming with underwater lights—enormous golden globes set far apart in a staggered pattern down into an underwater cavern that tunneled deep into the ocean's floor—she didn't notice where they were headed until it was too late.

Ro backpedaled as Llyr headed straight for one of the lit globes.

Llyr tugged Ro forward with a motion so quick, Ro barely registered it as she was sent hurtling straight for the bubble. Gravity took over once she passed through the slimy surface, and she fell to the concave bottom, sucking in deep breaths of air.

She was covered head to toe, soaked in slimy, glowing-yellow goo that dripped from her entire body. Gross.

"You! What is she doing here?" a deep voice demanded.

Ro scrambled to her feet and pressed her hands against the

wall—tried to push through. Solid like glass, yet still somehow slimy, the bubble's warm yellow light made it hard to see through to the sirens beyond. And even though the solid surface gave a little under her hand, stretching as a bubble might, it wouldn't let her pass.

"She's here about the prisoner who was just brought in," Llyr replied.

Ro squinted through the light to see the other siren—fierce-looking with an ebony tail and ebony scales that went up to her neck and onto her face, though her arms were bare with gray flesh. Her dark hair fanned out behind her like an open shell.

The creature flashed a grin of sharp teeth. "Which one? We have many prisoners."

Llyr looked at Ro. "The one who is friends with the huntress."

The warrior siren, the only thing Ro could think to call her with her fierce looks and soldier-like demeanor, blanched a little—a few of the ombré scales on her face turning light gray before flipping back over to ebony—and flicked a glance at Ro.

"I will inform the queen." She shot away with a powerful flick of her tail. It looked effortless, but the current of water pushed against the globe and rocked it.

Ro scrambled to hold on, but the sides were slick, and she nearly face-planted.

She tested the globe again. It gave under her hands, but she couldn't push through it. "Am I a prisoner too?"

Llyr swam close. "You can hear me?" Her lips didn't move. Something Ro realized with a jolt.

Ro spoke normally. "I can. How?"

Llyr flashed a grin, made even more terrifying by the yellow glow on the sharpened points. "I was hoping it would work."

Ro raised an eyebrow. "And that would be . . ."

"Oh. My apologies. You are not a prisoner, no, but these

are our prison cells. It allows our prisoners to hear us when put on trial for their crimes."

Ro rubbed her forehead, giving it a nice thick coating of goo. "Trial . . ." she said weakly. So that's what the sirens did with the men they took.

"Yes. You see, we aren't the monsters your tales make us out to be. We don't just drag men into the ocean and drown them. We put them here, in these holding cells, where they await trial until the battle is over."

"But you do drown them."

Llyr shifted and glanced away. "Well, yes, but only after they have been given a fair trial and their crimes made clear to them."

Ro barked a laugh. "A fair trial," she said drily. "Tell me, have any of your captives been found innocent? Set free?"

The siren stared at her, didn't answer.

Ro grunted. "Thought so." She tried to wipe the slime from her face, but she just managed to spread it around more.

The water swirled at someone's approach, and Llyr turned and bowed. "The mighty huntress, my queen."

The massive queen came right up to the Ro's prison and stopped. Her tail hung far below the bubble as she towered above Ro. She was easily twice Ro's height, if not more. She looked completely different than on land.

On land she'd been beautiful, delicate—as disguised as a human as an otherworldly creature could be. Here, muscle corded her body, power pulsed from her, and all of her features stuck out in sharp relief, as if her scales had been sucked tight to her bones, giving her a skeletal look.

Scales the color of pitch covered her entire body, and the scales on her face and hands changed to pale gray so Ro could see them. "Huntress, this is a most inconvenient time." A dark eyebrow rose. "Unless you have come to join us?"

Ro fought to keep her temper in check. "I am here for the

one called Olt." Never had the ridiculous name been more dear to her.

The siren raised both eyebrows as more shadowy scales receded, her porcelain skin icy-pale in the blue flame and yellow glow. "You came here—risked your life and my wrath —for a human male?"

Ro lifted her chin. "Not all men are the monsters you make them out to be."

The Siren Queen laughed, the sound like gravel grinding under a horse's hoof. Which only made Ro miss her horse, Fairweather, all the more. "Oh, really? Name five."

Ro blinked. "Five what?"

"Five men who are not monsters."

Ro didn't hesitate. "My brothers, Claude and Pascal, Trêve, Liam, and Olt."

The Siren Queen rolled her eyes. "And your father too, no doubt."

Ro's jaw tightened. "Non, I would not name my père." The admission cost her, but Ro kept speaking. "But there are good men in the world, and I am here for one of them."

"I see." The Siren Queen regarded her coldly. "I am not in the habit of letting my prisoners go, huntress, and I am pressed for time." She started to turn away.

Ro raised her chin. "I can offer gold."

The Siren Queen laughed, throwing her head back with the gesture. She spread her hands wide. "And what need have I for gold, huntress? Does it not sit in piles around me? Can I not take it any time I choose from any ship I want?"

"Not without loss of life."

"Oh, but that is all I want, huntress. Many, many lives lost, till all humans fear crossing my waters. Till they *stop* crossing my waters. Not gold."

Ro's felt sick. She gave a firm shake of her head. "Absolutely not. My mission is to save lives. Is there nothing you would barter instead?"

The siren regarded her a moment before answering. "No, huntress. Nothing. Just you."

Ro's temper flared. She couldn't give them that. It was too tempting. "And you would risk your sisters? Because believe me, Queen Zarya, if we cannot come to an agreement, the English king will send more hunters, men with harpoons and nets and hooks and those lightning orb things, to wipe out as many of you as he can. You've already seen the cost from one battle. And those weapons were experimental."

The queen sneered. "Do you really think men are a threat to me? That they can fight underwater? That we cannot paralyze them with song and sink their ships before they come close to us?"

Ro took a step forward and pressed herself against the sloping side of the globe. "Sirène, I know my fellow huntsmen well. They will not stop, they will not rest, until they bring your sisters gutted and hanging for the king's ransom he will offer, I promise you."

At the mention of what had already happened to four of their sisters, most of the sirens surrounding her grew still or growled, and fury danced in the queen's eyes.

Ro lowered her voice. "I would not wish that on any of you."

Anger morphed into surprise.

Ro felt its shift and pressed ahead. "I truly regret what happened, but it is but a precursor of things to come if these waters are flooded with huntsmen." She lowered her voice even more, trying for a reasonable tone, praying to the Creator with everything within her that they would listen. "In my land, when the curse fell, wolves flooded my kingdom and threatened my people. Gautier, he was leader at the time—"

"A king?" the Siren Queen interrupted.

"Non, votre Majesté. The true king was dead and the crown prince placed under a curse that made it impossible for him to lead."

She nodded once. "Go on."

"This Gautier, a steward in the king's stead, hired huntsmen and paid them well to wipe out the wolves threatening my people. I cannot tell you how many huntsmen flooded our realm. How many *became* huntsmen. How many wolf pelts they brought in, and how much useless gold was handed out in payment."

"Useless? What do you mean, useless gold?"

Ro shrugged. "No food grew in my kingdom. What good is gold if it cannot be used for sustenance?"

The queen nodded thoughtfully. "And what is your point in telling this particular tale?"

"My point, votre Majesté, is that even though there were few huntsmen in my kingdom, once gold became involved, the number of huntsmen surged. Everyone brought Gautier wolves. Even if they didn't know what they were doing, they found a way. They hunted." She made sure she had the queen's rapt attention before uttering her next words. "Even me."

"Ah." The queen sank just a little, a relaxed stance, her gills thrumming and her fins undulating in the current, though she still towered above Ro. "So *you* can be bought with gold."

Ro shook her head. "Non, I did it to provide food for my family. To be able to buy food from the Mesdemoiselles of the Mountain."

The queen rubbed her forehead. "I'm assuming if I ask you about these mysterious Mesdemoiselles' involvement, you will tell me, but to be frank, huntress, I don't care. It has nothing to do with me, and I tire of your stories."

Nothing new there. Her family hadn't particularly cared when she shared stories either.

"My point," Ro growled, "is that you are putting your people in unnecessary danger. That you are plunging headfirst into a fight that need not be fought. That you and I can, right here, right now, prevent a war between the world of men and the world of sirènes. We can live peaceably, perhaps even separately."

The siren seemed to be considering her words, so Ro plunged ahead, hoping she could keep the delicate balance of interest and consideration.

"You've said you dislike being above water. That even when your scales turn to skin, the air chafes you. That you can't be above long without starting to dry out."

Ro strained forward, though she couldn't take another step, and adjusted both hands against the side of the sphere.

"Why not live separately? You can disappear. Slip into legend. No one need know you exist, and you and they shall not be harmed. Surely one of these options is agreeable to you." Ro paused. "Or perhaps you have another solution?"

The thrum of the tide, the sway of underwater plants, and the gentle stroking of fins and gills against the current—they all kept Ro company, heightened, as she waited.

Amazing how such a stressful moment, a possible turn in the tide of history, could be so peaceful. Moments before war could cease or intensify.

Because no matter what King Wilhelm called the hunt, that's what it was. War. Slaughter. The king wanted to wipe out an entire race, and Ro couldn't let that happen.

No matter that they'd attacked her ship.

"There are those of us who want peace and would leave you and your world alone, votre Majesté. I ask only for your consideration."

"As I have asked for yours, huntress. Several times." The queen drifted higher over Ro. "I will ask you once more, and once more only. Will you become one of us?"

Although she hated herself for it, overwhelming fear swamped her. A lifetime underwater . . . not even the proffered power could tempt her, not after the phantoms had reminded her of what she so hated about the sea. A lifetime of seeing their forms float through the current, forever dead. Forever reminding her of the life she'd lost.

She swallowed hard, tried to keep the bile at bay. "Non, I . . . can't. I'm needed above. I just can't." Ro shuddered. "About Olt . . ."

The Siren Queen's smile was brittle. "I'm afraid I have no prisoner by that name. Now if you'll excuse me, I have another ship to bring down."

Panic threatened to strangle Ro. "But I thought you didn't hunt women!" Ro shouted, trying to bring reason back to her.

The queen pulled back, considering. "You know, you're right. Not all women are to be trusted, just as some men are. It looks like I'll have to amend my philosophy." She raised her arms above her head and shouted. "We attack any who seek to harm us in these waters! We offer no shelter, no quarter, and no mercy. To anyone."

A gasp came from a few of the other sirens. The one who looked to be her captain of the guard came close and spoke low. "Your Majesty, are you certain? We have never harmed womankind before. They are our ancestors, our protectors, after all."

Ro tilted her head. Protectors?

The Siren Queen sneered, eyes on Ro. "They are nothing like us. They are sniveling, whining creatures, coming to their men's aid and defending them, and I no longer have any respect for them."

Ro felt the jab like a physical slam to her pride.

"There are good men!" Ro shouted. "Not all, I give you that, but the good ones love us and protect us and fight for what's right. Of course we will fight for them. Die for them, even. Would you kill them too?"

Another siren spoke up. "She's right, Your Majesty. What of the one who let Llyr go? And the one who set Rialta free after she'd been captured? There are a few." The siren's all-black eyes swung toward Ro, sending a chill skittering across

Ro's skin in the warm bubble. "Precious few, but they do exist."

"More than that," Ro countered. "Why not defend yourselves against only the ones who hurt you? Why not make a bargain with the English king that you will not harm his subjects except for those who harm yours?"

The Siren Queen pretended to consider what her sirens and Ro had said, but Ro could tell it was all pretense. Her mind was made up. Her sharp teeth flashed white-blue in the glow of the blue flames.

"Your women declared war on us, huntress, when they came to your other ship's defense. When you and they wiped out most of my sirens above. What course have we but to fight?" She turned away, raising her voice. "Prepare for war!"

After a startled moment, the sirens echoed their queen: "To war!"

Though a few exchanged glances, a mighty cheer rose in the cave, rattling the walls, setting the blue flames to dancing, the globe to rocking. Ro's heart trembled with the sound.

As though a tidal wave swept through the sirens, their scales on their arms, face, and shoulders turned from creamy pale-blue to the color of pitch with a little flipping motion, and panic threatened to sweep Ro under its tide.

She could barely see them in the murky gloom of the dark water.

About half of them swam to the bioluminescent algae and smeared it like war paint on their cheeks, their tails, up their sides, while the others did not. In a great rush, most of them swam away, and the Siren Queen turned back to Ro and addressed Llyr.

"Take the huntress back to the surface and see to it that she is not harmed while in your keeping." She fixed a cold smile on Ro, her pointed teeth absolutely terrifying. "And after that, well, anything could happen."

38

*O*nce again, the air bubble was fixed around Ro's mouth after Llyr pulled her through the giant slimy bubble. Ro barely noticed. She was in shock. She didn't know what to do.

"I am so sorry," Llyr said.

Ro grabbed her arm. "Then help me free him. You know. You told me you know. Not all men deserve this. Some, but not all. Not Olt."

Her eyes widened. "You can hear me? Outside the bubble?" She flicked a glance at the glowing yellow bubble behind them.

"I can."

"But—how?"

"I don't know, and it doesn't matter. I need your help. Please. You know him to be kind."

The siren hesitated.

"Please," Ro whispered.

Llyr moved closer and dropped her not-voice. "Are you prepared to face the consequences? If you are caught."

Ro tried to answer, but she couldn't. Emotion swamped

her, and she fought back tears. She choked out, "Anything. I'll do anything."

And she meant every word. Except hand the power she'd been given over to the sirens for them to kill more people.

Llyr nodded once, decided. "Follow me."

They swam deep into the Siren Queen's lair, keeping to the wall. The same bubbles Ro had been in were scattered all over the cave. They came to a stop behind a pile of rocks, not far from one of the prison cells. It was stuffed full of prisoners.

Olt was inside, lying limp on the bottom.

Ro jumped when Llyr's voice spoke close and low.

"I'll distract the guards. You pull him out."

"How? It became solid glass when I was inside. Well, slimy, bendy glass."

The siren grinned at her. "Then don't go all the way inside."

Llyr swam away, toward the sirens guarding this particular globe. Ro gazed at all the men from her hidden spot. So many. Her eyes drifted to the other globes closest to her, and her eyes widened when she caught sight of one particular prisoner. The captain.

Images of him gutting the sirens came to mind, and Ro wanted to gag. She almost felt he deserved his prison cell. Almost.

"Sisters! Have you news of the fight above?" Llyr asked.

The sirens guarding Olt's cell turned away from Ro, facing Llyr. Ro left her hiding place, feeling like she was a beacon shouting her location to every siren, and swam cautiously toward the cell. Almost there, she moved until the globe was between her and the few sirens in the chamber.

Olt's back was to her as he lay unconscious in the globe. Ro slipped her arms in, not liking the coating of goo they received, slowly wrapped her arms around him, and tugged. He started to slip through the wall.

One of the other prisoners saw what was happening and started to protest. Ro shook her head furiously, unable to put her finger to her lips.

"I will come back for you," she mouthed.

It didn't help.

By then, she had the other prisoners' attention, and they grabbed for Olt. Ro hauled him out of the cell before anyone could stop her.

She dragged him back to her hiding place. He floated easily enough in the water, but his dead weight drifted too close to the ocean's floor, dragging up a cloudy mix of sand.

Thankfully, the guards' attention was pulled to the riled up men in the globe, not to her. One of the sirens lowered the spear shaft she held and shoved it against the bubble. Electricity flowed from it, and the men flailed inside.

Ro couldn't get back to her hiding place fast enough.

Olt remained unconscious, but to make matters worse, he started to thrash when he could no longer breathe. Ro's eyes widened, and she looked around frantically for Llyr. She was still talking to the guards as they laughed at the writhing men's pain.

Desperately, Ro shoved her face close to Olt's and forced her bubble over his nose and mouth.

He sucked in several breaths, calming a little, but Ro couldn't move away. She had to sit there, trying to watch for danger out of the corners of her eyes, sharing her oxygen with Olt.

Her eyes fell on his lips. It wouldn't take much—just shifting forward a fraction—and she could kiss him. She blinked, and it took everything in her not to jerk back.

For the love of all the saints, would such thoughts leave her alone?

Ro tried not to squirm. Could Llyr come back already? And what if someone else found them first?

The water shifted near her, and then Llyr was tugging her away, forming another bubble around Olt's nose and mouth.

"When I say so, head for the surface as quickly as you possibly can."

Ro nodded.

"All right, then. Follow me."

They eased away from the rocky outcropping, and as they got closer to the cave tunnel, Ro felt hope threaten. They might actually get away with this.

A shout. Ro rocked forward with the push of sound from behind, then whipped around, her hair swirling in her face. She tugged the just-long-enough-to-be-bothersome strands away, and her heart dropped. They'd been spotted.

Llyr shoved an unconscious Olt at Ro. "Go!"

Ro grabbed him and kicked off. It wasn't fast enough.

"Hurry!" Llyr called. "Before they—oh, fish scales." The siren grabbed both of them and shot toward the surface.

The siren painfully clamped tight to Cendre's still-bleeding wrist and tugged her into a cave lit from within, with glowing rocks and blue fire and yellow globes. Cendre's mind spun from the sudden plunge into blackness deeper than any she'd felt before, and now from the lights that accosted her senses, lights that should've been impossible.

How were the rocks glowing? And why was the fire blue *and* underwater? The yellow spheres looked like little suns— Cendre had never seen such beautiful things in her life.

"Your Majesty!"

Cen cringed against the siren's strident voice. It seemed to echo in her head, and it definitely brought on a headache. And since the noise was within, she couldn't even rub her ears to make it feel better.

They rounded a yellow, glowing orb that Cen was having trouble taking her eyes off of onto a scene that chilled Cen to her very core.

Sirens, entirely covered in dark scales, glowed like the rocks in stripes all over them. They held spear-like weapons, only with three prongs, above their heads and gathered around the biggest and most powerful of the sirens, elaborate coral crown perched atop her head.

The Siren Queen.

It sounded like the queen was giving out orders of some kind. "You, lead the frontal charge. Distract them while you and you lead a surprise attack. Come up on both sides, but don't breach until it's too late for them to defend themselves."

Cen's siren called again, "Your Majesty!"

As the massive siren turned toward them with a scowl and a flash of sharp teeth, Cen tried to backpedal. Her siren wouldn't let her.

She dragged Cen toward the sirens who looked like they were getting ready to kill something. Lots of somethings.

The siren jerked Cendre's arm above her head, dangling the girl before them like some kind of meal. "This one needs to speak with you."

"Now isn't the time," the Siren Queen hissed through jagged teeth, her scales flashing in irritation.

The other siren didn't back down. She grinned, in fact. "Oh, you're going to like this, sister. It will be well worth your while."

The Siren Queen's eyes roved over Cendre with interest, as did many of the other sirens'. "Oh?"

Cendre just wanted to shrink back and disappear, but her wish wasn't immediately granted as it often was above. If anything, the sirens grew more interested as the thought flew through her mind.

In fact, the sirens communicated in a series of clicks and sound pulses, and even though Cendre realized this on some level, she understood them perfectly. Just as she understood she had become far more of a curiosity to them for some reason.

"Interesting," the Siren Queen mused. "Well, go on, girl. Speak. I have places to be, humans to kill. What is it that you want?"

Water stung Ro's face, the bubble flattened against her face, and the pressure on her ears was almost unbearable as Llyr sprinted for the surface. Nothing like last time. They burst through the surface of the water and hurled in a perfect arc in the air, straight for an outcropping of obsidian rocks.

One many ships had crashed upon, evidenced by their skeletons everywhere.

Something Ro could only see because they hurdled high through the air.

Llyr landed lightly on her feet and took off running—on her glistening gray-pale *feet*, Ro noticed through a haze—with Olt under one arm and Ro under the other.

By all the realms, the sirens were so incredibly strong and fast and changed form so quickly!

A horde of the sirens appeared behind them. Their scales changed from water-hued to gray skin tones as they came after them. Llyr kept running, outpacing her sisters, but barely.

Llyr came to the top of the highest stones, and Ro saw at the same time, with her heart dropping, that sirens were coming up the other way too. And from both sides. They were surrounded.

Llyr spun and yelled, "Stop!"

The other sirens paused, but there was murder in their eyes and vicious smiles on their lips.

"They are mine! I can do with them what I will."

One of the leading sirens grinned. Ro tried to remember her name. But it was gone. "Oh, but they aren't, and you can't."

"That one's still on trial!" another called, pointing at Olt. "Justice needs to be done."

Llyr shook her head, her wet hair slapping her shoulders. "He has done nothing to harm us. Nothing! In fact, he tried to save our sisters."

Ro wriggled free, and Llyr set a slumped-over and still-unconscious Olt next to her on a flattened piece of rock nearby. Llyr perched on her spire, yet somehow seemed to widen her stance, making herself as threatening as possible.

"Are you prepared to fight us, sister?" another siren asked in a sultry tone, amusement strong in her voice.

Llyr didn't hesitate. "For the huntress and her friend, yes."

Amusement vanished, and the sirens all growled deep in their throats.

Ro groaned. "Llyr, non . . ."

Her head whipped in Ro's direction. "Do not question me on this, huntress!"

Ro snapped her mouth closed.

The sirens inched forward, Llyr readied to fight—Ro tried to see past her own stringy, tangled hair—and tension mounted.

Time seemed to slow, and as one, the sirens rushed them. They blurred and clambered over rocks, leaving no room to escape, and started tearing Llyr and Ro apart, faster than should have been possible. The last thing Ro saw was one of them dragging Olt into the water . . .

Time reversed itself, and the sirens surrounded them once more, straining forward, ready to make their move.

Ro immediately threw her hands wide. "Stop!"

A few of them jumped, and instead of the well-orchestrated

attack she'd just seen, they faltered, came at them hesitantly, not all at once. But they came nonetheless.

And were forced to stop not far from them. No matter how hard they tried, not one of them could get close. Some kind of invisible barrier stopped them.

Llyr spun on her, eyes wide. "What are you doing? *How* are you doing that?"

A bead of sweat, or perhaps water, slid between Ro's shoulder blades. She grunted, concentrating too hard to answer. Not that she could have.

Then the sirens all paused as one, tilting their heads slightly. Llyr paled, then stared at Ro in horror. Panic started mounting inside of Ro.

What did they know that she didn't?

⚓

Cendre couldn't answer the Siren Queen. What was she even doing here? She wasn't brave; she wasn't a hero. She'd only come on this journey to find the family she'd been searching so long for. She'd just wanted a home. A place to belong.

Fear wracked her body, and her breathing started to tighten.

"Let me guess," the Siren Queen said in an unimpressed voice. "You wish to join us, use your newfound powers to exact revenge. A lover who scorned you, perhaps. Believe you me, I have heard it all a thousand times." She flicked an elegant hand, the jagged nails tipped with flecks of ichor. "But I haven't the time to oversee a changeling right now. Perhaps another time."

She turned away, and the slight bolstered Cendre's temper and drove away her fear. Cendre strained forward a little and shouted through the bubble over her mouth and nose. "Non! You will listen to me."

The Siren Queen turned back with dangerous eyes. "Careful, little human morsel. It would not take much to snap your neck."

The sirens surrounding them laughed, the sound physically grating, and the one still holding Cen dangling from her wrist laughed right along with them and shook her a little. Cen swayed in the water.

Cen's gaze was challenging. "Your siren is right. There is something about me you will very much want to hear."

The Siren Queen's voice was dry. "I doubt that very much."

Cen straightened, something incredibly hard to do with the weight of the water on her and the current that made her drift to and fro. "I am the huntress's sister, and I have come to take her place."

The Siren Queen's full attention snapped to her, and every siren near them went completely still.

"I will join you, but I demand you release the men you have not yet killed and release my sister from ever being pressured to become one of you—one of us—ever again."

The Siren Queen opened her mouth, but Cen kept talking.

"And furthermore, I demand you release Olt."

She hadn't meant for her voice to tremble when she said his name, but there it was. Her heart, bared for all to see.

The Siren Queen smiled, the thing of beauty monstrous to behold. "Ah. You love him."

Cen raised her chin. "It doesn't matter. My sister's life does. And she wants the rest of the men free, including Olt."

"Very well," the Siren Queen said with a smile that terrified Cen to her toes. "We are happy for you to join us. Now this will hurt very much."

Cen couldn't help it. She writhed backward, but two long, muscular sirens came up on either side and held her steady, taking over for the siren that held her.

The Siren Queen smiled as she advanced. "Once you have promised yourself to us, it cannot be undone, little one."

Cen shook her head, hating the fear that was close to making her lose control. "That's not it," she gasped.

"Oh?" The Siren Queen bent her head nearer and nearer to the poor, frightened girl.

"Non," she gasped again. "I wish to say goodbye. As myself. I must."

The Siren Queen regarded her a moment. "I tend to grant only three wishes, not four." She seemed to struggle for just a moment. "I am only obliged to give three."

Cen had no idea why she offered that little tidbit, and by the look on the Siren Queen's face, she didn't either. Cen pressed on before panic tightened her lungs and made it impossible to breathe. She could already hear the slight wheeze to her voice.

"I have only asked for three."

The Siren Queen raised an eyebrow.

"Yes," Cen gasped out, panic squeezing her throat tighter and tighter. "One: the men freed, including Olt. Two: my life for the huntress's. Three: to say goodbye. As myself."

She shrugged. "Well, when you put it that way . . ."

The Siren Queen dove forward and bit into Cendre's neck. Cendre screamed and thrashed, but the siren held on tight, drinking deep of Cendre's life force until she felt faint.

It came in waves. Cendre stopped thrashing. Her body slumped, unable to fight any longer. Her head lolled to the side. Intense cold eased into Cen's entire body.

Just as her eyes started to close, just as she noticed how pale, how gray her arm looked, the Siren Queen grabbed Cendre's wrist and sank her fingernails deep into her skin.

Ice-cold sensation flooded Cendre's arm and climbed into her shoulder. Cen looked down to see ichor flooding her body, being pushed from the siren's nails into Cen's veins.

Cendre screamed, the air bubble popping. She sucked in water without meaning to, and it felt like her lungs were being crushed.

The Siren Queen frowned and squeezed Cen's wrist harder, forcing the poison to flood her system faster.

Veins stark against pale skin, Cen couldn't stop staring at the dark color flooding her body. The ice freezing her system.

She knew the moment it hit her heart and shot into the rest of her body from there.

Instant relief eased the pressure on her lungs.

Blessed respite flooded in and out with every breath. She looked down at her body to see the darkness spreading rapidly, her skin going gray ever faster. The tones camouflaged them under the water perfectly. As soon as it touched her sides and neck, gills split open in slits of fire, moving gently with the current. The pain receded.

She took a deep breath. Then another. She could breathe!

She pulled her shirt free of her trousers to check. The gills undulated with the current, opening and closing with every breath she took.

Cendre could breathe for the first time in her life. It didn't hurt. It wasn't difficult. The ocean rested in a comfortable weight on her, the temperature absolutely perfect.

Her eyes fell on her trousers.

Her trousers. She still had legs. Why did she still have legs?

The Siren Queen's voice came to her, distinct and clear. "Take her to the transformation chamber. She needs time to grow her scales and her fin." The Siren Queen sighed, her voice disappointed. "And call off the attack on the huntress."

39

It chose that moment to fall over. Ro lunged to catch him before his head bashed against the rocks or he slid down the precipice. Magic slid away from Ro's fingertips.

She jerked her head up, but the sirens were no longer moving toward them.

A few of the sirens edged away, looking reluctant, but one took a step forward. "Merida!" another hissed. "We have our orders."

Merida hissed and moved away slowest as the rest of the sirens plunged one by one into the water. One motioned for Llyr.

"Sister, come. You heard our orders." Her eyes shifted to Ro, and she stared at the huntress with something like awe in her expression.

Llyr still stared at Ro, her face distraught. "I am sorry. I am so, so sorry."

Ro couldn't help feeling her entire world had just changed, but she didn't know how. "Llyr, what's going on?"

Llyr didn't answer. Ro got the feeling she couldn't, but that didn't make any sense.

The siren called for Llyr again. "Sister, are you coming?"

She backed away from Ro and Olt, turmoil churning in her eyes.

Ro vacillated between holding Olt upright, keeping her eye on Merida, and begging Llyr to tell her what was wrong.

Before she could ask, Llyr mouthed "I'm sorry" one more time and jumped into the water with the rest of the sirens.

All but one disappeared: Merida, who still looked like she wanted to tear them to pieces. She tried to take a step toward Ro, winced, and then edged away, as if any other motion caused pain. She finally bared her jagged teeth and dove under.

Ro felt something warm trickle out of her ears and dabbed at it. Her fingers came away with blood and water mixed together. Huh. She'd read that could happen if she dove too deep too quickly—or resurfaced the same way. She must've burst her eardrums.

But no other symptoms seemed to be forthcoming.

Ro looked down at Olt, still unconscious, still all muscle, still far too handsome, and still very much someone she had to carry.

She scanned their surroundings, realizing they were near where she'd stashed a rowboat. Praise Dieu.

She leaned over Olt and roughly pulled him up, bending to sling him over her shoulder. She staggered under his limp, muscled weight and starting picking her way toward the cove where they'd hidden the rowboat.

Hopefully the sirens hadn't found it and ripped it apart.

She didn't know what had happened with the sirens, but she had a feeling she wouldn't like it. But they needed to get to the pirate ship before the sirens came back.

If only Olt would wake up and carry his own dead weight.

Ro grumbled at him the whole way to distract herself from her worry.

Why wasn't he waking up?

❧

Cendre's eyes started to slide closed as bliss invaded her, but a voice invaded her mind before she could give herself entirely over to sleep.

"Which chamber, Your Majesty?"

"Put her in my transformation chamber. It will take some time for this one to be ready to join us. Oh, and introduce her as Cordelia once she is ready."

"Cordelia, my queen?" Cendre could hear the hesitation in the siren's voice. Isla.

Although Queen Zarya's voice was sharp, a note of weariness tinged it that hadn't been there before. "Yes, Cordelia."

"But, Your Majesty, forgive me, why Cordelia?"

The answer, when it came, was softly spoken. "Now she is the daughter of the sea. My daughter. Now go."

Cendre felt herself being lifted and drifting away, and one of the sirens spoke, just so her companion could hear. But Cendre could hear it too.

"Did you see that? Queen Zarya turned her herself. She's never done that before. Not since . . . well. You know."

Cendre glanced up, her head lolling pleasantly, as the other siren, Kai, replied.

"And naming her Cordelia? She must want the huntress's blood in the royal line quite badly."

Cendre looked from siren to siren. Their names came to her as each spoke, wafted on the cusp of her memory, then drifted away, to be replaced by other names, other memories.

They took her into a small cave, bioluminescent sea urchins dotting the room in an attractive pattern. It was small, warm, and comforting.

Cendre instantly liked the place.

They settled her on a natural-looking rock formation that created a sort of a bed, then covered her with weighted blankets of what looked like netting from a ship.

The edges of the blanket snapped into grooves in the rocks with hooks, holding her tight to the rock.

"Will she be all right?" Kai fretted.

Isla snorted. "Since when have you cared when a human turned into a siren?"

"Since it was me and I almost died!" Kai snapped.

Isla sighed with what sounded like great patience. "The queen turned her. She bears the huntresses' blood in her veins. Do you see her thrashing? No, she is sleeping as peacefully as a babe. Now, let's go. We have men to return."

The last words were most definitely said grumpily.

They moved out of the room together, rolling a stone in front of the mouth of the little cavern.

"Do you think the queen will actually give the men back and call off the attack?" was the last thing Cendre heard before she closed her eyes and gave herself over to the most delicious sensations of rest and belonging and *breathing* she'd ever felt in her life.

※

Ro was barely onboard, Olt being carried to the infirmary, when the shout came.

"Captain! Man overboard!"

Ro followed the captain's steady footsteps to the port side of the ship.

"Lower the ropes!" Captain Red shouted. "Get a craft in the water and get that man aboard before the sirens find him."

The rowboat settled into the water with two occupants as another call came.

"Captain! Another one to starboard. It's Mary, ma'am."

The captain groaned. "Is the other craft repaired yet?" At a few "ayes," she continued. "Lower it starboard. Continue on your course."

Her crew scurried to obey.

Captain Red rested concerned eyes on Ro. "You made it."

Ro nodded, too tired for words.

"Your sailor, too."

Ro shot her a look, but again, the fight drained out of her before it had begun.

Captain Red grinned. "Glad to see you've still some spunk in you."

"Men overboard!"

Ro jumped toward the voice, but the captain was already moving to the side of the ship where the cry had most of the crew hanging over the railing. Ro joined them.

Ro gasped as, one by one, heads popped up in the water. Men who'd been imprisoned below. The crew in the first rowboat pulled in as many as the craft could carry.

"Pull them aboard, then meet up with us!" the captain shouted.

The second rowboat joined the first, Mary safely onboard.

Ro caught the captain's eye. Captain Red flashed a quick grin. "If we stop now, we might just head straight to the bottom." She shrugged. "Or we might not be able to get her going again." The captain worried her lip. "I hope you found a way to get us past that barrier."

Ro followed her gaze to the tattered sails overhead, siren-sized holes ripped through them as the remains snapped in the breeze.

Goodness gracious, the sirens had been able to leap that high?

Ro ventured a question at the risk of sounding clueless. She was so *tired*. "But aren't we moving too fast for them to catch up?"

The captain barked a laugh. "They call it limping for a reason, huntress."

She turned away and bit out a few more orders as the crew swiftly loaded the rowboats with the few survivors and headed toward the ship, rowing hard to catch up to the slowly moving vessel.

The men were pulled aboard, and Ro helped identify them. Eleven. There were only eleven left. Ro dropped her head as grief swamped her.

So many lost.

"Hurry! This one needs help right away. Take him directly to Anika."

Captain Montrose was carried by, along with another sailor she'd seen but never spoken to. Ro followed. They plopped the captain on a table in the ship's infirmary.

A quick glance revealed Olt being carried to another cabin nearby.

"If we don't stop the bleeding . . ." Anika, the ship's physician, muttered to herself.

Ro stepped up. "What do you need me to do?"

"Tourniquet," barked Gemma, the ship's chef, assisting the overwhelmed physician.

Ro whipped off her belt and handed it to her. She didn't even look up, just took it and wrapped it around the captain's leg.

"How many?" rasped Captain Montrose. "How many of my men are left?"

The pirate didn't bother answering, working steadily to save the captain's life, leaving the answer to Ro.

She swallowed. "Ten." Her voice cracked. "Only ten, besides yourself. Well, and Olt." She flicked a glance at the man the chef had been working on before the captain had been brought in. He didn't look good at all. "Perhaps."

The captain's head fell back, and a tear slipped down his cheek, startling Ro. "So few."

"Oui. I am sorry, mon capitaine. I am so sorry."

After a moment of grieving, a hard look came over the captain's face. "They need to pay."

The words chilled Ro to her core, the sensation followed swiftly by disbelief. "Surely you don't mean that."

"I do."

Ro slammed her fist on the table, jarring instruments. "It was your own doing! Gutting them like fish while I was trying to make peace? Driving them to sink your ship? They let you *go*, Captain. They didn't have to do that. In fact, I don't think they would've had they known what you'd done! That it was *you*."

Ro was shouting now, but she didn't care. Gemma tried to shush her to no avail. The man in the corner didn't even stir.

"How could you? I was brokering peace! Trying to end their hunting of men. You've made all my efforts worthless."

He turned away from her, his face to the wall.

Ro dropped her voice and leaned close. "I am going to win in spite of you, Captain. Know that. You will not harm any more of them. Not for the rest of your career. Do you understand?"

The captain didn't respond.

She slammed her fist once more on the table, the rattling instruments more than satisfactory. "I said, do you understand?"

The captain jumped, then barely nodded, his face white.

"Your word, Captain. Give it to me."

"You have it," he rasped.

Relief flooded Ro in places not filled with fury, which were admittedly few, but doubt soon chased it away. Could she even trust him?

Ro felt the hardness come over her. Resolution. It didn't matter. She was *going* to win in spite of him.

She leaned close and dropped her voice to a deadly calm. "Bon. Because if you do not keep it, I will throw you to the sirènes myself, and I'll not stop a single thing they do to you."

Ro spun on her heel and stomped out of the makeshift little hospital that had spilled out of the original infirmary.

MICHELE ISRAEL HARPER

Captain Red stood in the doorway, face stoic, eyes troubled.

Ro brushed past her, but she didn't try to stop Ro, and she didn't say anything.

Ro couldn't possibly care less. She was the one who would have to explain to the king why most of his men hadn't come back from this voyage, when she could've prevented it. When she thought she *had* prevented it.

All because of a stupid, selfish, and stubborn captain. Not to mention the bloodthirsty and equally stubborn Siren Queen.

And now she had to figure out how to undo everything he'd done. How to make the sirens listen. Before things got worse. She had not come all this way simply to admit defeat and limp home.

Ro went over to the railing and grasped it, looking down into the water so far below her.

"Captain!" one of the crew shouted, not far from Ro.

Ro turned as the captain walked up. "Yes?"

Merja came up to Captain Red and saluted. "That seems to be all of them, ma'am."

"And what of the girl?" Captain Red asked. "Any sign of her?"

Merja flicked a quick glance to Ro then lowered her gaze. She shook her head once.

Captain Red's jaw firmed. "Then take a rowboat out and circle again."

Stunned, eyes wide, heart dropping to her toes, Ro stood there with her mouth open. "Non," she whispered. "Cendre?"

The captain took a deep breath and turned to her. "Huntress . . ."

"Non!" Ro shouted. She didn't even know she had one leg over the railing until hands were hauling her back and pinning her to the deck. She fought with all she had to get back to the rail, back to the water—back to the girl she'd promised to protect.

Every effort of hers seemed wasted, like she couldn't find that dance to make her fight untouchable.

"Take her to the brig!" the captain ordered. She huffed in disgust. "I can't be watching her and taking care of my ship and crew and prisoners at the same time. Bah."

She waved Ro away and stalked off, and it took four of them to drag Ro beneath the decks and cast her behind bars.

Ro screamed and rattled them, but nothing she did budged them, not even the magic she tried to access but stayed just out of reach. No one checked on her, no matter how much she shouted. Ro sagged to the straw-strewn floor, still holding the bars, and sobbed.

She'd failed. Again.

And it had cost her Cen's life.

༄

Hours later—as the ship headed for the barrier and the rowboats gave up roving the waters near the battle, looking for survivors—the door to the brig swung open. "Cap'ain says you can come out."

Ro didn't move, elbows propped on knees, hands clasped, eyes staring at nothing.

The crewwoman shrugged. "Makes no difference to me, mind you, but I sure wouldn't want ta be sittin' down here for much longer. Especially since we haven't scrubbed the place out yet."

After another long pause, one in which Ro had no idea how much time passed, shadows shifted, and Ro looked up at the open door.

No one was there.

Ro started to climb to her feet, when something hummed and touched her hand. She paused and looked down.

Her bow, just as lovely as before, sat next to her with one remaining arrow.

She touched it, drew strength from it. Then she shrugged the bow over her shoulder and tucked the remaining arrow in her belt.

Ro climbed to her feet, clasped the bars, and started dragging herself out. She had to pause at the doorway and wait for one foot to wake up. She rotated her foot a few times to make sure she could move, then marched with resolute steps upstairs to the deck.

She stopped by her hammock long enough to grab her red cape, left behind when she'd changed clothes.

She paid no mind to the open stares that crawled all over her back and shoulders as she made her way to one of the rowboats and started freeing it from its bindings.

"What are you doing?"

She didn't pay attention to who'd said it, but it didn't matter. "I have need of it."

The other person grunted. "Captain know you're doing this?"

Ro didn't answer, still maneuvering the heavy boat over the edge to lower it into the water below.

The other person gave a disgusted snort and started helping her. "Best not get me marooned, huntress."

It was enough to clear Ro's fog for just a moment. A wry smile lifted one side of Ro's mouth, and she turned to the woman helping her. "Then why help me?"

Merja shrugged. "You can't do it on your own. Simple as that. Besides, I've lost those I love as well. And although I don't think you're thinking clearly"—she gave Ro a stern look—"you don't have the look of someone about to drown themselves. I hope."

Ro's smile turned sad. "Non, I do not wish to die."

"But you might?" she asked.

"Aye," Ro said softly. "I might."

They worked together wordlessly to get the boat into the water. Once there, with sweat streaming down Ro's face, neck, and shirt, the crew on deck watched Ro climb eight stories down into the boat, release the ropes, and start rowing away, alone. Ro looked up, wondering if this was the last time she'd see the ship, and her eyes rested on the captain watching her out of her port window.

Their gazes held for a long moment before the captain turned and stalked from view. Ro pulled harder, and the small boat cut through the water.

Hours later, she heard a voice say, ***Stop***.

She didn't bother to drop anchor. The boat would be where she needed it when she needed it. She stood, untied her red cape, and let it slag into the bottom of the boat.

Instantly, doubt assaulted her. Fear, terror, uncertainty. The feeling rocked her back on her heels, and she sat down hard. She eyed the red cape. Tied it back on. And the feeling abated. In fact, it felt as though Mère eased an arm around her shoulders and whispered, "You can do this. You were born to do this."

Tears filled her eyes, and she flicked them away. Oui, she could.

Ro held her bow like a staff and readied herself to jump in. She stared into the water, dark and threatening and full of cold promises. A cold that reached up and vowed to squeeze the life out of her.

She stepped over the edge and entered the water with barely a splash.

The bow dragged her down, a heavy weight in her hand, and she sank fast. The water seemed to part from her as if it wanted to get away from the bow as quickly as possible. And this time, the swift pressure change didn't bother her in the least.

Her feet touched the sandy bottom, her cloak billowing behind her.

Just as she'd seen the siren do, she spread her hands and

willed a bubble to form over her mouth. She didn't doubt. She couldn't. Or it wouldn't work.

Water fled, and the space around her filled with air. Blessed, fresh, clean air that reminded her of a spring day after a cleansing rain.

She didn't question the magic, just demanded it obey her. And it did. For once.

Then she concentrated, and the bubble expanded until it enveloped her entire being. Then it hardened, snapped closed, became impenetrable to any who wished her harm. Yet it still undulated gently with the underwater current.

Incroyable.

The sand at her feet remained just wet enough that it packed down when she stepped, like the rim of a beach. Ro began her steady trek along the ocean floor.

She'd come to silence a siren, and she wouldn't leave until she had.

40

*R*o's feet led her to a cavern she hadn't been to
before, one deep in their realm and full of understated elegance, crafted from underwater elements and
obsidian.

Pure-white sand covered the floor, which declined to the
back of the room in steps. Burning fire-orange columns made
of coral supported a roof almost too high to see. Blue flame
undulated in open, magenta clamshells spaced evenly
throughout the room, drifting with the current.

Ropes of pearls, hung as decorations on the obsidian walls,
swooped down into the room, lining theater-type boxes on the
walls, reminding Ro of billowing curtains in the French opera
houses. And giant pearls were spaced evenly on the steps,
giving innumerable sirens a place to sit, evidenced by the many
sirens lounging upon them.

All sightlines drew the eye to the back of the room, to the
throne there, midway up the wall on a deep shelf. Ro could
barely make out a tunnel opening just behind it.

A throne room.

"I demand an audience with the Sirène Queen!" Ro's voice

bounced around the entirety of the underwater chamber, and all eyes swung her way.

A moment's pause like a skipped heartbeat, then motion exploded.

Sirens hissed and swam toward her, reaching, grasping, teeth bared.

The first one hit her bubble and flew back, the reaction like lightning and fireworks all at once. A few more slammed into it before they could stop, or perhaps before they saw what had happened to their sister, and the same thing happened.

Wild lighting arched and popped, an impossible feat underwater, and multicolored fireworks exploded in every direction. Not one of them penetrated her pocket of air.

But the bolts were drawn to the fire in the open clamshells, which swelled halfway up the cavernous wall before settling into mere pinpricks of light, leaving behind blistering scorch marks and cracks in the obsidian.

The struck sirens floated in stunned silence, spinning away, as the others in the room dared not move.

Ro took a step deeper into the cavern, bow clutched in her fist, her bubble moving with her in liquid-smooth motion.

"I would speak to the Sirène Queen!"

Though their eyes were still dark, though they still hissed through bared, pointed teeth, the sirens drew back and looked at each other as if uncertain what to do.

Ro's eyesight illuminated their ebony scales, making the sirens visible in the low blue light of the cavern.

Ro yelled it a third time, the space filling with her voice, going out from her in waves.

"I demand to speak to the Sirène Queen!"

A heavy sigh came from the front of the room, near the hidden tunnel's entrance. "Stop your wailing, huntress. It does not become you."

As the water cleared of churning sirens, the queen settled

upon the scalloped, abalone-lined throne, a stark contrast to the obsidian wall behind it.

"Speak quickly. You are not welcome here." The creature's smile was strained.

Ro blinked. The Siren Queen looked—older. A tad shriveled. What had happened to her? Ro shook off the thought. She had a job to do, and she couldn't afford to get distracted.

Besides, the queen had to stay there until Ro had her say.

If only there was a manual for her magic, not just this vague sense of knowing. One thing was for sure, if she ever found such a manual, she was going to memorize every single blasted word.

As Ro gathered her words, she settled her bow in the sand before her. Although the queen did not move, Ro felt her draw away from the bow as though she'd done so physically.

Ro casually held its tip. "Votre Majesté, you took something from me, something precious."

A perfect, raven-scaled eyebrow rose. "Oh?"

"Does Cendre live?"

A wholly satisfied look crossed the queen's face, pointed teeth glistening in her wide smile, ropes of hair floating around her like an octopus's tentacles. "No."

Although Ro knew that would be her answer, her heart crashed to the sandy soil, and it was all she could do to keep her voice steady.

She nodded. She'd known. Somehow. But she'd wanted to make sure.

"Will you sign the treaty and accept my final offer to leave me and mine alone?"

Again, that eyebrow rose. "As you've accepted mine, huntress?"

With one swift move, Ro reached into her red cape, withdrew the single silver arrow, and drew it into her bow, thumb steady on her cheekbone, pointed at the Siren Queen's heart.

Lightning startled to crackle out from Ro's hands, writhe

across her arms, and leap onto the orb she was in, lighting it up like one of the physician's spheres.

The sirens hissed and recoiled, and the Siren Queen's face went white. "How *dare* you bring such a weapon into my throne room! Into my home."

Ro's gaze was like flint. "How dare you kill the men and women I swore to protect. How dare you kill Cendre and hurt Olt!"

The Siren Queen didn't say anything, and not a siren moved. No one wanted to startle the huntress or cause her to release the enchanted weapon. To create even more blue lightning so deep in the ocean, so far into a realm that used blue flame for light.

Blue flame that fed off the same power as the lightning orbs, power that would quickly connect and heighten the blast. The resulting explosion would raze the cavern and roast all within.

Ro stilled. Now how on earth did she know that?

Her palm throbbed, where the Fairy Queen's white rose had melted into her palm, and Ro's eyes widened.

The power within the enchanted rose spoke to her in whispers, giving her knowledge she didn't have before, as though the Queen of the Fairies was standing at her elbow.

Ro forced her focus back on the Siren Queen. "One of us is not leaving this cavern until she has what she wants. And I guarantee that won't be you."

The Siren Queen couldn't mask the fear on her face. "You do realize if you detonate the weapon"—her eyes were on the globe surrounding Ro—"you will not escape either?"

Ro couldn't help her feral smile. "Does it look like I care?"

The Siren Queen swallowed. "Perhaps you would consider joining us . . ."

Ro jaw tightened. "I will not join you, and you will not ask again. My life is above the sea. My job, my mission, is to stop the king's ships from being sunk, his men from being killed, and trade from being halted. Now, the king prefers I kill you all"—a sound like a kitten's purring, growling, and hissing filled the space around Ro, only it was the most terrifying thing she'd ever heard—"but I prefer to reach an agreement."

She just wasn't above threatening them to make it happen. Not anymore.

She released the arrow's draw, slipped it away, and withdrew the waterproofed parchment she'd carefully stored in wax paper. She held it up for all to see.

"The king signed this before I left"—*the only thing he did that I asked*, she thought wryly—"and you're going to sign it as well."

"Oh, really?" The queen sneered. "And what good will that do? Do you truly think a treaty will hold that I've been forced to sign?"

In reaction to her rising temper, the bubble around Ro started to pulse and grow in size, just a little, and blue flame sizzled the water next to it in a slow boil.

"I am going to do my job, queen, one way or another. I'd prefer to negotiate, not spill blood. But make no mistake that I will. That I have."

The queen bared her teeth at Ro and hissed. "You dare come into my seat of power and threaten me?"

Ro kept the bow cradled in her hand, in the sight of all. "Think of it more as a warning, Queen Zarya. You *will* be hunted and you *will* be stopped. I'd just prefer you be a part of the decision." Her voice lowered. "I'd prefer your beautiful people not be wiped out, as you tried to do with mine."

The Siren Queen blinked and snapped her mouth closed, mid-retort. She eyed Ro to gauge her sincerity, and Ro held her gaze. How many times would she have to say it before the queen believed her?

The queen straightened. "Did you truly negotiate an option where we will remain unharmed by your king and his people? After all that has happened?"

Ro nodded once, not bothering to correct her. King Wilhelm was not her king. "Oh, yes. You see"—she stepped forward a little, as if sharing a secret, her grin a little wild —"because you're going to agree never to interact with humans again. Not one of your sisters will be seen or heard from, not ever again."

PART FIVE

<< Nous avons donné nos cheveux à la sorcière de la mer en échange de son aide. . . . Elle nous a donné un couteau. . . . Avant que le soleil se lève, tu dois le plonger dans le cœur du prince, et lorsque son sang chaud touche tes pieds, ils grandiront ensemble dans la queue d'un poisson, et tu redeviendras une sirène. . . . Hâte-toi ! L'un de vous doit mourir avant l'aurore. >>
~Hans Christian Anderson, *La Petite Sirène*

"We gave our hair to the sea witch in return for her help. . . . She has given us a knife. . . . Before the sun rises, you must plunge it into the prince's heart, and when his warm blood touches your feet, they will grow together into a fish's tail, and you will become a mermaid again. . . . Make haste! One of you must die before the sun rises."
~Hans Christian Anderson, *The Little Mermaid*

41

The queen half rose out of her chair, her face white with rage. "How dare you."

"Oui, I dare, votre Majesté. You will disappear. Go into legend. You will never, ever surface or bother anyone above the sea. As far as mankind is concerned, you will no longer exist."

The Siren Queen's jaw ticked, and Ro held up the thick, heavy parchment once more. Yet one more thing to be grateful to Madame LaChance for. The craftsman had promised it would hold up underwater, that the ink wouldn't bleed.

She was about to find out.

Ro held it out and waited, not giving an inch. She was done bargaining, asking for something she couldn't reach. Now she was the one in charge, and *they* would do what *she* demanded. Or she'd destroy them all, including herself, right here, right now.

The Siren Queen flicked a finger at one of her sirens. "Bring it to me."

Ro allowed the lightning to mostly wink out and the flames to dim. She held it outside the bubble. The siren snatched it from her, careful not to touch her or her bubble, and swam it over to the queen on her throne. Seething, the queen held open the contract and pretended to read it. But then she scowled.

The Siren Queen lifted dangerous eyes to Ro. "Our voices will not work above water?"

Ro nodded once. "You'll never take free will from a human, not ever again."

Fury boiled in the Siren Queen's eyes. "I can't say I like those terms."

"Didn't expect you to."

The queen allowed the parchment to drift away. "Then why would I agree to abide by them?"

Ro's smile was more of a threat. "Because you lost the right to bargain when you attacked my ship. When you killed the girl I swore to protect."

The queen twitched at that, but she said nothing.

"You lost the right to bargain when you hurt my friends. My colleagues. You have lost every right in this situation, dear queen, and the only way to ensure this ends well for your people is to stay in your world while my people stay in mine. I will have your agreement, one way or another."

The Queen of the Sirens held Ro's gaze, her inhuman, unblinking stare more than a little unnerving. The queen broke their gaze first. "I see."

She picked up something resting on the arm of her throne and twirled it. It flashed silver in the cave's dim light.

"And what of stopping the trade of human cargo?" Her grin displayed her pointed teeth and made her parchment-thin skin stretch tight against the bones of her face. "That will be rather hard to do if we are not allowed to surface."

And rather easy for the new weapons to be used on the sirens, for more ships to be sunk, for things to spiral right back to where they'd started.

Ro sighed. As much as she wanted each of those ships resting on the bottom of the ocean—cargo safe in the lands they were taken from—if she caved on this, the sirens would insist every ship they saw needed to be inspected. Better not touch it.

"Allow us to monitor our people, and you monitor yours."

Queen Zarya rolled her eyes. "Oh yes, because that's worked so well for you in the past."

Ro couldn't deny that. Yet another thing about which to have a word with King Wilhelm.

"No," the queen said decisively. "I will not sign it without the cessation of human cargo upon my waters. On that I will not budge, huntress. Too many of my girls have come to me from such ships, and I cannot allow such atrocities to continue." After a moment, "I hold all of their memories." Her all-black eyes settled heavily on Ro. "The things you humans do to each other."

Ro bowed her head, unable to deny it. But would the king allow it? She stilled. You know what? He'd sent her to negotiate, and she wanted nothing more than to ensure people—all people—had their freedom.

She raised her head, nodded, and held out her hand for the contract.

While the other siren returned it, Ro squinted at the blade the queen twirled in her fingers. It looked familiar. Was it a ruby-encrusted dagger like Madame LaChance's? And Captain Red's? And . . . someone else's . . .

It teased her memory, but the siren held out the contract, and Ro was distracted.

Ro made the change, initialed it, and sent it back to the queen. "Please sign next to it as well, votre Majesté, so the English king can see the change we agreed upon."

Queen Zarya raised an eyebrow but did it. She continued reading. "It seems to have some advantages for my people as well."

Ro kept herself from rolling her eyes. But of course it did. "Such as not being slaughtered?"

"That too. It's true that your air does not agree with us."

She shrugged a powerful blue-gray shoulder, her iridescent sable scales ending just at her collarbone. "I guess it won't be much of a hardship."

Ro's mind spun. To change her mind so quickly—the queen must be hiding something.

"What of the underwater weapon," the queen continued. "Will you stop its use as well?"

Ro swallowed. The only part of the plan she had no control over. She nodded at the contract the Siren Queen still clutched. "The king has already signed it. Once you sign, you will both be bound by your word."

Ro raised her voice a little, in case any of the other sirens had the same concern.

"You know the blast cannot reach this deep. If you stay in your world, any rogue users of the weapon will have no chance of reaching you."

The queen sighed, deep and heavy, the sound like a throbbing pulse. "Very well, then. I will sign." Ichor converged in her veins and began to pulse with every beat of her heart. The poison dripped from her fingernails. She flicked a few drops into the water surrounding her. "Back away from the huntress, please."

As the sirens obeyed their queen, she offered Ro a fake smile.

"No more killing. Well. It seems I find myself in your debt once more, huntress. How shall I ever repay you?"

Ro blinked at how swiftly she'd changed her mind. "Just sign it and abide by what you sign. That is all the repayment I need. Our worlds need not collide, unless harmonious coexisting is one day achieved."

The queen flipped to the beginning of the document and reread every word. Slowly.

After an eternity, she huffed and signed it with her finger, the poison sinking into the page and staining it, as she grumbled a little under her breath.

Ro couldn't help the thought that popped into her head. That wasn't very ladylike, according to Cosette.

An ache filled her heart, and all she wanted to do was see her sister. Hug her. Tell her everything. It was all she could do to push her longing away and focus on the danger before her.

A crack like thunder sounded and echoed in Ro's ears the moment the siren finished signing. Ro smiled. The Siren Queen and her people were now bound by the magical laws of the contract, something Ro had been careful to add.

Something that could destroy the entire race if broken.

The Siren Queen raised an eyebrow. "And what of my copy of the contract?"

Ro withdrew another from within her red cape. She unfurled it for the queen to see. Matching signatures rested there: Ro's, King Wilhelm's, and now Queen Zarya's. "Your copy. I must have the original, I'm afraid."

The queen nodded, a calculating look in her eye.

Ro decided to head off that little mischief before it went anywhere. "It cannot be undone, votre Majesté. You know the laws of the fey."

The queen gave her a smile that wasn't, then handed her signed parchment to the siren at her side.

The siren brought the signed document back, but she stopped a little too far away. Ro waited, eyeing the siren and the queen in turn. The queen gave a heavy sigh and waved a hand.

The siren moved just a little closer and held it out, close to the bubble, but shying away as if afraid of it. Ro reached out and grasped it, and the siren flicked a jagged fingernail under Ro's wrist.

Ro hissed and jerked her hand back, holding her throbbing wrist.

A few droplets of blood drifted away in the water, then dripped down her arm. Tension crackled in the room. A brief, wicked smile touched the siren's face.

Ro tried not to panic. They'd all just gotten a taste of her blood. Could it be used against her? To track her somehow?

The queen pretended not to see, but Ro didn't miss the quick, pleased look she gave her siren.

As soon as the bleeding stopped, Ro straightened and poked the signed copy back through the bubble, careful not to let any part of her outside of the bubble again. The siren snatched it away, her grin exultant, and returned to the queen's side.

"If that is all . . ." the queen began.

"It isn't."

Ro could've made a fuss—she had every right to: blood spilled while brokering peace was practically declaring war—but she was here to prevent that. And the sirens knew it.

"My third and final question."

The Siren Queen froze, giving Ro a look that said she was hoping Ro had forgotten she had one question more.

"May I have Cendre's body to give her a proper burial at sea?"

The Siren Queen's eyebrow rose. "What, to dump her into my waters to pollute them? As much as it pains me to decline, she has already been laid to rest. By our methods."

Ro's mouth tightened. "I see." Disappointment tried to overflow in tears. "How did she—how did she die?"

The siren's smile was cold. "I do believe you have run out of questions. Leave my domain, huntress, and do not ever come back."

Ro nodded and gave their sign of respect, even though she really, really didn't want to. "Thank you for your cooperation, votre Majesté."

A quick smile spread across the Siren Queen's face, and she dove at Ro's bubble faster than Ro could see. Ro jerked away on instinct, but that was all she had time for.

The Siren Queen pulled up, just inches from the bubble. "Listen to me and listen well, little huntress. If your king breaks his word, just once, all of humankind that crosses my waters will be mine, and there's nothing you can do to stop it."

Rage flashed in Ro's chest. She leaned close. "Let me make myself clear. One broken promise changed you. The next cursed you. Another will wipe you out. Consider your next move carefully."

The Siren Queen twitched a little, a flicker of surprise at Ro's knowledge of her people's story, knowledge that she herself had handed Ro, covered quickly.

To emphasize her words, lightning began to crawl out of Ro's hands again and onto her bubble.

As the Siren Queen's enraged, horrified expression riveted on Ro's hands, something in the siren's hair caught Ro's eye. Like a mirage becoming reality, a pink-orange crown wavered to life upon her head.

The coral comb Madame LaChance had said was hers.

As if the swan-wing combs weren't enough. The combs — Cendre had on her person. Ro's eyes widened. She couldn't return empty-handed.

Without really thinking about it, Ro plucked it from the Siren Queen's hair, lightning fast. It slid through the silky, free-floating locks without a tangle.

Her hand was back through before the Siren Queen could react. Ro could only imagine she'd done something so unlikely, so unexpected, the siren was stunned just long enough. She had no other explanation for matching the siren's speed.

The creature shrieked in rage, first grabbing for her head belatedly and then lunging for Ro. Her jagged, ichor-stained nails hit the barrier with a *clack*, and Ro couldn't help the terror that swept through her.

To cover her fear, Ro held up the crown and snarled. "I believe this belongs to someone else, Queen Zarya. You shouldn't take things that don't belong to you." *Like Cendre,* she didn't add. But she wanted to.

The Siren Queen seemed to age right before Ro's eyes,

though her rage didn't dim in the slightest. "Huntress," she said, sounding somewhat strangled. "You have no idea what you've just done."

Ro was too furious to care. "Oh, I know exactly what I'm doing." Ro shoved a finger her way. "You and your descendants are bound by the contract you just signed, votre Majesté, and I suggest you take my words to heart. Or I'll be back, and not one of your creatures will survive me."

Ro spun and stalked away.

A part of her hoped the Siren Queen *would* dare, just so Ro could do something about all the pent-up anger. Her bow was the perfect weight in her hands, her arrow, within easy reach.

She'd lost too much to be messed with.

It wasn't until she reached the spot where she knew her boat was waiting above that weariness swamped her. She staggered under its weight, and her bubble flexed around her.

Ro's eyes flew wide. She couldn't give in to fear, couldn't give up yet—or her magic would fail her and she would drown.

Whispering surrounded her, and the melted flower pulsed in her palm, infusing her with instructions.

Swallowing hard, she lifted her darkwood recurve bow and poked it gently through the bubble. Part of the bubble caught and held on the bow's curvy end, and she felt herself being tugged upward. As the Fairy Queen's flower had instructed her to do.

Her eyes drifted to the wrist above her head. Although it was no longer bleeding, it hadn't healed. It was still an angry red, gash deep, a pulse of black below, spider-webbing out.

What had the siren done to her?

42

*R*o's head breached the water's surface, right next to her craft. She tossed in the bow and tried to ignore the ache in her wrist as she pulled herself aboard.

It wasn't until she'd clambered into the boat and lay panting in its bottom that she let the events of the last few days crash over her.

She'd done it. She had her peace treaty. France would have her trade agreement with the English king, something they desperately needed to rebuild their commerce after the curse. Madame LaChance would have at least one of her combs.

All at the very high cost of a ship, most of its crew, and one young girl's life.

Ro choked on a sob. After a moment of almost paralyzing grief, Ro swiped a hand over her damp face, shoved her feelings deep inside, and sat up. She got out her compass and watched the fleur-de-lis arrow swivel toward the *Siren Hunter*.

The hunt may not have gone how she'd wanted, but thank Dieu it was over.

She'd just taken up her oars when a head raised slowly out of the water, like a predator's. Ro's eyes riveted on the lone figure. Merida. The siren who'd tried hardest to kill them all, but specifically, Ro. Who had murder in her eyes right now.

Ro went cold.

Merida came close and smiled, though it could hardly be called that. "I made you a promise, huntress. A promise to drag you to the depths and watch your body float lifeless under my hands."

Ro withdrew the signed contract, unfolded it, and scanned it. "Oh?"

The siren visibly paled, which was quite a feat with colorless skin. Then her all-black eyes flashed a deeper color, if that were even possible. "I suggest you row quickly, huntress. There are many . . . things . . . in this water. Things that are attracted to small watercraft piloted by measly humans."

Ro held her gaze. "And I have my promise from your queen. Safe passage."

Merida's smile grew. "From my queen, not me."

Ro scowled harder to keep her fear at bay. "If you attack me, Merida, you are no longer under the treaty. I have every right to defend myself, and your sisters can do nothing."

A slight hiss was her only warning.

Merida lunged at Ro, but as soon as she got within a few feet of the boat, Ro whipped up her oar and slammed it into the side of Merida's head, swatting her from the air and into the water. Merida arched in pain and fell back. The oar followed her into the ocean.

Ro snatched up her bow and aimed the final silver arrow at Merida's chest the moment she resurfaced. "I'll not say it again, Merida. Back away."

The creature snarled.

"Merida, don't."

The siren swam for the boat, eyes boring into Ro with every stroke. Ro let her arrow fly at the correct moment.

It zipped right around the siren and plunged deep into the water.

Ro stared after it, mouth ajar, frozen in a deadly second of immobility. Whatever happened to the blasted thing never missing its mark?

Merida grinned, her hatred full of delight, and lunged straight out of the water and for the huntress. Ro flinched away, raising her bow to fend her off too late. Seconds before the creature slammed into her, something pummeled Merida out of the air sideways and took her deep into the water. All Ro saw was a pair of ebony fins flared out.

The boat rocked, the ripples slowed, and the sirens did not resurface.

Ro leaned out over the water, straining for the oar, but she couldn't reach. With a heavy sigh, she slipped into the water and swam for the paddle, holding the rope to the craft so it wouldn't get away from her.

Her fingers had just closed around the oar when something came up under her and lifted her into the boat. Ro sprawled, dripping wet, red cloak up and over her head.

She fought it off and looked all around, but nothing. The creature was gone.

Ro wasted no time dropping the oars in their grooves and cutting through the water. She just hoped she was going in the right direction. But far away from Merida was good enough for now.

Ro was pulling hard on the oars when her senses heightened. She popped up, stance wide, wielding an oar like a weapon as the rowboat rocked, and scanned the water. Nothing. No sirens.

Movement caught her eye.

She spun toward it and found eyes watching her in the dusk. Ro clutched the oar tighter, ready to swing. Was it Merida? Was she back to finish her off?

The head went under, and seconds later, Llyr popped out of the water, right next to the boat.

Ro yelped and nearly fell overboard. "Llyr! You startled me."

Llyr gave an apologetic smile. "That was not my intent."

Ro looked all around her. "Merida. She—"

"Will never bother you again."

Ro could only stare at the siren, mouth open. That's when she noticed the ragged rake of nails across her face, small chunks of gray flesh between her teeth, and several tears in the fins flaring out below her in the water.

Before she could say anything, Llyr held out her hand. "I know where your ship is. I can take you there."

"But if you're hurt . . ."

"I'm fine." Llyr smiled slightly. "Hand me the rope, huntress. These waters are not safe for you."

Ro scrambled to grab it. "Merci beaucoup, Llyr. I don't know how to thank you properly."

"It is enough, huntress, that you and the boy live."

Ro shook her head. "I don't understand. Why are you helping me?"

Llyr glanced away and hesitated, as though she wasn't going to answer.

Ro was done with mystery. "Tell me," she demanded, a bit too harshly. She took a deep breath to calm her ragged nerves. "And Olt . . . why did you help him?"

Llyr flipped to her back and started swimming, looking perfectly at ease and still as beautiful as the first time Ro had seen her, wounds notwithstanding. They cut through the water at a remarkable speed.

Dripping wet, clothes stiff with saltwater, hair clinging to her face, Ro was sure she looked like a drowned rat. Nowhere near as glamorous as the strikingly perfect siren who'd rescued her. Again.

The siren looked like she wasn't quite so sure why she'd helped Ro either. "It was something you said. About not all men being bad."

Ro squinted at her.

Llyr shrugged. "It's true. A man once helped me escape my captors. He thought he was in love with me, sure, but he set me free when he could have kept me for himself. And Olt . . ."

Ro swallowed, hard, gratefulness filling every pore.

"He sacrificed himself for that girl. It was probably the only reason he was captured."

Ro's glance was sharp. "What do you mean?"

The siren's smile was small and quick. "I don't know if you noticed, huntress, but none of my sisters were willing to take you on after I claimed you, even though our queen gave us permission. Well, except Merida. I don't think they would've touched Olt had he not been separated from you."

Ro frowned, the pain of losing Cen hitting her all over again. "I don't understand. Why were they willing to listen to you? Why did you—claim me?"

Llyr's smile grew mysterious. "Ah, but I cannot tell you all of our secrets. You will have to join us for that."

Ro barked a laugh. "Non, merci."

The siren's smile dimmed at her words, her iridescent scales and hair shimmering in the deepening light. "I thought you might say that. It's a shame. I would have liked to know you better."

Ro had to smile at that. "I have to admit, I would've liked that too. Who knows? Maybe I'll come back one day."

"You won't."

Ro blinked at the certainty in the siren's words.

"You will not be back here in your lifetime, and you will not stand before our queen again." A speculative look came over her face. "Though she may yet stand in front of you."

Ro had heard some strange things in her time, but . . . "How in all the realms could you possibly know that?"

The siren shrugged one shoulder, the movement very French. "I have seen it. And I have not yet been wrong."

"Oh. Well, oh." Ro still couldn't get over one thing. "But—

I still don't understand why you helped us. You hate humans. You wanted to kill us all."

The siren paused, stilling the quickly moving boat with one touch. The water rippled around them.

Llyr pointed to a shape in the distance. "Your ship is there, huntress. Fare thee well."

Ro blinked at how quickly they'd arrived. "Llyr, please." The siren turned back to Ro. "Help me understand. Not much of this voyage makes sense. I need something to make sense."

Llyr came close to her, peered deeply into her eyes, and cupped her cheek. "You have our Darya's eyes. How could I not aid you?"

Ro couldn't even come up with a response to *that*.

"Goodbye, huntress. I hope your lover makes a full recovery."

"He's not my"—the siren slipped into the water without a sound, leaving barely a ripple in her wake—"lover."

Ro huffed out a sigh. Of course she would leave right then.

She patted her pocket to reassure herself the contract was safely tucked away.

The fey were bound by the contracts they signed, with disastrous results if broken. Even if Ro drowned on the crossing back to England and the contract followed her to the bottom of the ocean—which she sincerely hoped wouldn't happen—the sirens would still be forever bound by the contract King Wilhelm and Queen Zarya and the French huntress Ro LeFèvre had signed.

And the king had his own signed copy, tucked safely away in his palace. He would know the moment she succeeded.

She picked up both oars, weary to her core, and headed straight for the *Siren Hunter*. She needed to see how Olt fared.

Now if only all fairy creatures would leave her in peace.

43

*C*aptain Red was waiting for her.

Ro helped pull the boat on deck and secure it before facing the formidable woman. Her mind was swirling with what she'd say—what excuse she could give about why she had to leave—when she opened her mouth.

The pirate captain beat her to it. "Did you do what you needed to?"

Ro snapped her mouth closed. She wasn't expecting that. Not to have to explain. "I did."

Captain Red nodded once. "Good." And she walked away.

Ro blinked, her unneeded explanations churning within her with no place to go.

"Oh, um," she said to no one in particular. "I guess I'll go to my hammock?"

But no one answered, and no one made her go below. Ro eased herself out of the way, just waiting to be told to go away, to hide herself. No one did.

The nearest crewmember offered a smile, and Ro returned it. The journey may not have gone as she'd hoped, but she had a signed agreement, and no one else would have to die. It was something, at least. And Olt . . .

Ro turned and made her way to the infirmary.

She passed the captain's ready room. "Oh, huntress?"

Ro stopped in the doorway. "Oui?"

"We'll be arriving at the Ring of Death soon. Might you be on deck when we do?"

Ro nodded solemnly. "But of course."

"I take it we'll be able to get through?"

Ro froze. "I —" That hadn't specifically come up, but surely the sirens would know her intent? "I believe so," she choked out, suddenly feeling very foolish.

In all their talks, Ro had said nothing about the barrier. Her mind scrambled through what she could remember of the contract. Had King Wilhelm included access to his colonies? Surely he had.

Captain Red nodded absently and tapped the map she was pouring over. "There are so many unexplored islands here, so much unexplored water. I wonder how the locals fare."

Ro nodded respectfully, her mind elsewhere. "Has Olt woken up yet?"

"He hasn't." A smile lifted the captain's mouth even as she kept her gaze lowered, as if she just knew Ro was dying to ask.

Ro edged toward the infirmary. "I think I'll just —"

The captain barked a laugh. She winked and said in her raspy, sultry voice, "I'll have Gemma send something edible your way."

Ro nodded gratefully and hurried belowdecks to Olt's side. As she picked her way through the room, she took in the men and few women resting there. The occupants moaned, had trouble moving their legs, or had buckets of vomit next to them that the crew were keeping emptied and rinsed as quickly as possible.

Being held in the underwater chambers apparently had very unpleasant effects.

But none of them were unconscious like Olt.

Ro settled by his side and took in every inch of him. He looked the same as when she'd left. As she held his hand in hers, she couldn't help her worry.

Would he just wake up already?

"Huntress."

Ro jerked awake and sat up quickly, trying to pretend exhaustion hadn't just knocked her out.

Gemma smiled, holding out a bowl of exotic fruit. "Eat up, huntress. Cap'ain wants you on deck after."

Ro nodded blearily and rubbed her eyes, then reached for the bowl.

Gemma held it out of reach. "Any nausea, lower backache, numbness in your arms or legs, ringing ears, head or neck pain?"

Ro rubbed her neck, her brain trying to catch up with the words. "I don't think so . . ."

"Uh-huh. What's my name?"

Ro's eyebrows raised. "Gemma?"

"And yours?"

Ro scowled. "I think I know my own name. Will you give me the fruit already?"

Gemma passed it over with a grin. "Just checking. I wasn't looking forward to cleaning it up later."

Ro attacked the fruit like a wild dog, only speaking after most of the bowl was gone—in a few seconds. "Gemma, my gracious, merci. Where did you get this? It's delicious."

Gemma took back the empty bowl as Ro swiped juice off her chin and onto her trousers. "We were able to trade for it before all the craziness with the battle. Anyway, we'd like to get through to get some more and to repair the ship, so if you wouldn't mind?"

She gestured toward the stairs. Ro nodded and bounced to her feet, pausing long enough to squeeze Olt's hand.

He didn't respond.

Heart in her throat, Ro climbed the stairs, and her eyes riveted on the obsidian barrier. It looked as solid as ever.

They traveled along its length, seeking a way through, and the only sounds heard on deck were the wind snapping the sails, the creak of lines, and the slap of waves against the hull. But the tension was a visceral thing.

With a heavy sigh, Captain Red moved to Ro's side. "See anything I don't, huntress?"

Swallowing hard, Ro shook her head.

"Very well." The pirate captain turned away and started barking orders. "Continue repairs. Keep an eye out for survivors, just in case. Helmsman, keep searching for a way through. The moment you find something promising, report to me."

Captain Red walked away, and Ro stayed at the rail until the sun dipped below the horizon, hoping beyond hope they'd find a way through.

It had been two days. Two days and nothing.

Olt hadn't so much as twitched in all that time. Ro was still in the overflow infirmary, at his side, not bothering to look at Captain Montrose, who'd steadily regained his health.

He now leaned on a cane and looked like he was departing. To another room, perhaps? They still hadn't gotten past the barrier.

"Huntress."

Ro didn't look at the tall man. The man she'd once looked up to. Her gaze remained steadily on Olt.

He took a fortifying breath. "I'm truly sorry for all the trouble I caused you. That was never my intent. My intent was to save lives, to follow my king's orders. I cannot apologize for that."

Ro didn't acknowledge that she'd heard him.

"But I can and do apologize for the hardship I caused you."

Ro jerked her head in a brief nod.

Captain Montrose let out a whoosh of breath, as if he'd been holding it. "What will you do?"

Ro felt he didn't need to know.

"I will seek passage with the rest of my crew," the captain continued. "You are welcome to join us."

Ro kept her gaze on the man held underwater too long, this man the captain had put in danger, this man . . . who'd become a friend. A dear friend.

And her only link to Cen. Whom the captain had as good as killed himself.

"Non, merci," she choked out.

A pause. "I thought as much. Fare thee well, huntress. Shall we meet again, I pray it will be on better terms."

"As do I."

Ro looked up just as he stepped through the door and settled his hat on his head, his tall, fatherly figure leaning heavily on his cane.

And just like her father, he had deceived her, betrayed her, and left her.

"I forgive you," she said, Llyr's words echoing in her head.

Captain Montrose froze, his shoulders tense, but then he seemed to deflate. He didn't look at her, but he gave a single nod and left.

A feeling of peace swept over her, and Ro took a deep breath, letting out tension with a stream of air. It hadn't solved everything—of course it hadn't—but she felt lighter inside. Maybe Llyr was right.

Because no matter how angry she was at him, she didn't have the strength to hold on to that feeling. Not again.

She took Olt's hand in hers and dropped her forehead on

their clasped hands. "Please wake up. Please. Tease me, berate me. Something. I need . . . you. To talk to you."

Tears dripped onto their joined hands as Ro sent desperate prayers into the heavens. She couldn't lose someone else. Not one more person.

Especially someone who meant so much to her.

44

endre opened her eyes. She instinctively knew she wasn't Cendre anymore; she was wholly something else.

And it had never felt more right.

She started to get up, but netting held her fast to the stone shelf. She strained forward, just a little, and it snapped like brittle, rotted ropes. She felt one. They were practically new.

She made her way around the little chamber, her all-black eyes taking in everything at a glance. She'd never seen anything like the bioluminescent creatures placed in patterns all over the walls, and she found them fascinating.

Then she came to the door and the stone rolled in front of it. It was not meant to open from the inside, but she did so anyway.

Just a small push did the trick.

Wide eyes met her calm ones as the heavy stone came crashing down and split apart. She eyed them all. As she looked at each one, she instinctively knew each of their names.

They greeted her. "Welcome, Cordelia."

That's right. Her name was Cordelia.

She nodded to each in turn as she came out, her powerful tail making every movement effortless.

"Where is my queen?" she asked them without speaking. It hurt to talk underwater, but they did so whenever humans were present. Now they could talk as they were meant to: through little impulses of sound.

The others all looked at each other.

One finally dared to speak, but Cordelia did not understand their fear, though she felt it pulsing, throbbing, under the surface of everything they said and did.

"She said you would come to her once you said your goodbyes."

Cordelia tilted her head. Goodbyes? Ah, yes. The human wanted closure before she gave herself fully to the siren.

Cordelia could just snuff her out. End her now. Go the Siren Queen and begin her new life under the sea.

But that was not the bargain.

Cordelia sighed, feeling phantom longings stir in her breast as Cendre awakened. She shoved the human creature back down. She would be given rise once more, but for now, she had no place here.

And then as soon as she was done with her, she would disappear entirely.

As every human should.

Cordelia eyed the sirens surrounding her, her new sisters, then her gaze settled on the one who'd spoken. Isla.

"Show me my new home."

Isla rushed to comply, and Cordelia found she quite enjoyed every whim of hers being obeyed. Though she didn't yet understand why they did so.

Cordelia took it all in, the vastness of the underwater kingdom, the thousands of sirens, as her guide unveiled their secrets to her, awakening memories in her breast.

"How long was I asleep?" Cordelia interrupted.

There was a startled silence from Isla, the siren showing

her around the ocean's floor. Their hunting grounds. Their gathering grounds. Where messages were sent. Where dolphins and orcas and sharks and other creatures could be persuaded to let them ride for traversing long distances.

"Three days, milady."

"And why are you doing that? Why are you acting the way you do around me?"

Isla blinked rapidly and glanced at the other sirens in their little entourage—five in all—but none of them came to her rescue.

Isla bowed her head. "My lady, forgive me, but it is not for me to say."

Cordelia turned all-black eyes on the siren, and although she instinctively knew their eyes matched but for a swirl of something Cordelia couldn't identify, it seemed her glance terrified the older siren.

Isla quaked a little as she continued. "I truly cannot say, my lady. Please know all will be revealed in time."

Cordelia nodded. She wasn't happy with that, but she would accept it. For now. "Very well, then. Show me more."

They started to turn away, but a rush of water announced the arrival of another siren.

She bowed low to Cordelia. Cordelia's eyes drifted over the siren. More wild than the rest. Willing to take more risks. An air of danger around her. Merida.

"Merida. Rise."

The siren did so with a slight wince, though it did nothing to dim her savage grin. "I trust you are enjoying learning of your new world?"

Cordelia glanced past her. She hadn't expected small talk. Disappointing. "I haven't time for niceties that mean nothing."

That response seemed to please Merida. "I would speak to you alone."

Cordelia nodded, and the others scattered. They almost seemed relieved to be away from her.

Once they'd gone, Merida limped forward in the water and held out a ruby-encrusted dagger. "A gift. From the Siren Queen."

She moved carefully, as if hiding great pain. The skin at her throat was all jagged and raw, wounds rippled across scales in several places, and a few of her fins were torn, trailing behind her like limp sails.

Cordelia wondered briefly what had happened to her before she decided she didn't care. The memories would come as soon as the human creature within stopped taking up so much space. She couldn't wait to rid herself of Cendre.

"Oh?" Cordelia smiled and slipped it from her sister's grasp, suddenly fascinated by the lovely weapon from the above world. "How beautiful! It's not even a little rusted."

Merida just looked impatient. "Uh-huh. Right. Anyway, she said you can have your sister back. Here. With you. All that ties her to the above world is the human, Olt. Once he is no longer in the way, well, she can return with you."

"How is that possible? The huntress never gave her consent."

Merida grinned. "She has already been turned. It's only a matter of time."

Cendre rose to the surface, just a little, and both asked, "How?"

Merida looked startled for half a heartbeat. "Our blood flows through her veins. Our poison now taints her. All that is left is for you to kill her lover, Olt, and bring her here to live with you." Merida tilted her head, her expression turning coy. "Or you can consider my solution."

"And that is?" Cordelia alone asked.

Merida's grin widened. "You can have your human life back. One with Olt in it."

Both Cen and Cordelia stilled at that. "Why would I want that?" asked Cordelia as Cendre asked at the same time, "Could I? Really? But how?"

Merida drifted back a few lengths, startled eyes wide, as what came out was unintelligible.

Cordelia closed her eyes and forcefully pushed Cendre down and held her there. She opened her eyes when she had control and asked again, "Why would I possibly want that?"

Merida bowed her head. "I speak to the human, Cendre."

Cendre pushed her way free.

Merida's eyes met hers. "You can return to the above world, with Olt as your lover, if you but kill the huntress."

Cendre cried out, but Cordelia kept it from breaking free from her lips, just barely. Cordelia stared at the other siren coldly. "If you want the huntress dead so badly, you do it. You kill her."

Rage was quickly covered with a deferential bent of her head. "I no longer can, milady." She touched her throat, just briefly. "My . . . ability . . . to rise to the surface was torn out. If I don't stay deep, I will suffocate. I can no longer regulate my air to either rise or dive from our queendom."

Cordelia couldn't have cared less. "Again, I ask you. I see the advantage of the huntress becoming one of us, but once the human creature has said her goodbyes and been snuffed out, why would I possibly want to give up this life for one above the sea?"

Merida's glance slid to the side, as if checking to see if they were still alone. "Because the human part of you will never truly be snuffed out. Not really. The ghost of your past self will always be with you, whispering hopes and dreams and rage and terror, and it will never, ever shut up. No matter how much you beg it to." She shrugged. "But if you kill the huntress, I can show you how to put the human in her form. Rid yourself of her forever."

Cendre recoiled, but Cordelia smiled. "Oh, really?"

It'd been three days, and Olt still hadn't woken up. They'd moved him into a private room, away from those steadily regaining their health, the one right next to Gemma's. Ro hadn't left his side unless forced away. She took all her meals right next to him and slept in the wooden chair the captain let her borrow from her ready room.

Her entire body felt like one giant bruise.

Ro couldn't wait for him to wake up and tease her. What was wrong that made him sleep so long?

Gemma bore her questions patiently, probably realizing Ro needed to worry *with* someone instead of getting answers the interim doctor didn't have. They wouldn't know anything till he regained consciousness.

Ro didn't know if she could take it much longer.

"Huntress, go do something active. Now."

Ro looked up, bleary eyed, and it took her a moment to realize the pirate captain was speaking to her.

Captain Red chuckled. "I mean it. Take a walk around the deck. Shoot some arrows. Scratch that. Save any weaponry until after you've slept awhile. But please, your mind will be the better for it."

Ro looked back at Olt.

"I will stay with Olt."

Ro gave the captain a look, and she hadn't realized she'd expressed exactly what she was thinking until the captain burst into laughter. Ro jumped a little, the loud noise ringing in her head.

And she couldn't help but notice Olt didn't have any reaction at all.

"Do not worry, huntress. Anyone can see he has eyes only for you. Though you can't blame a girl for trying, not with a morsel that delicious."

Ro was one thousand percent horrified at the captain's observation, and the captain knew it, what with her continued and breathless laughter.

"Oh, huntress, you should see your face! Go. I promise I'll send for you if he wakes."

Ro rubbed a hand down her face and stumbled from the room to walk the rim of the deck a few times.

And she'd never been more thankful for the captain making her. The warm, tropical air cleared her head, and the mild activity worked out a few kinks.

"Huntress!"

Ro's head whipped up at Merja's call. She met the first mate halfway and felt her own excitement rise—for the first time in three days—at the excitement on her face.

"What is it? Is Olt awake?" Ro blurted.

Her expression dimmed a little, and Ro felt like she'd been punched. What was she so blasted excited about, then?

"No, I'm sorry, but he has responded to something—"

Ro was already walking toward the chamber. "What was it?"

She didn't miss the sly look Merja slid her way. "The captain mentioned your name, and he moaned a little, tried to open his eyes."

Ro's heart jumped into her throat, and her footsteps sped up.

"I don't have to tell you the captain found that absolutely hilarious."

"And made several jokes, no doubt," Ro muttered.

The first mate chuckled. "Oh, most certainly."

Ro nearly ran the captain over as she barreled into Olt's room.

Captain Red laughed, of course. "Thought that might get you in here."

But Ro was only half paying attention. She went to Olt's side and took his hand, studying his face. "Olt?" she whispered.

Nothing. No response. In fact, he looked a little paler. A little worse. Ro frowned.

After a moment, the captain said quietly, "Gem, keep me updated?"

"Of course, Captain," Gemma replied.

Ro held Olt's hand tightly. "Come on, Olt, wake up. You're scaring me here."

The captain chuckled, but it was a little more subdued. "And tell that one he'll be just fine."

"I've been trying to, Captain."

Ro grumbled a little. He'd be just *fine* when he finally woke up.

She took her place by his side and watched every rise and fall of his chest.

45

*C*endre searched for the ship, thrilled that Cordelia had finally released her to say her goodbyes, cutting through the water with such speed it amazed her. She'd never felt so alive. Never been able to breathe so deeply.

And she had her voice back. Finally.

Cendre found the ship easily, its echo bouncing back to her from the barrier. Moored not far from it, the *Siren Hunter* rocked gently in the waves. Cen categorized everything in a brief glance.

They'd never make it across the great sea without extensive repairs.

She could feel the emotions from those onboard bleed into the waves. Hope that they would find a way through. Despair that they hadn't yet. Loss and heartbreak—throbbing loudest from a room a few decks from the top, coming from the huntress.

Cen's heart leapt in response to finding her sister.

She raised her head out of the water, watching the late-night movement on deck, a few deckhands keeping an eye on things. In seconds, she'd learned their pattern and how best to avoid them.

She lowered her head into the water, took a deep breath through her gills, and with a powerful swipe of her ebony tail, popped up again next to the ship. She crawled eight decks up the side, not really thinking about how easily she did so.

She slid onto the deck, drying herself with a flick of her scales, and delighted herself with the breeze that danced across her perfect skin. Her hair had turned from blonde to a delicious midnight black in the transformation chamber, and she was certain she'd never looked more beautiful.

She opened her mouth to sing everyone onboard asleep, but nothing happened. She grabbed her throat. Her voice!

Realization dawned. Taken away by whatever treaty the Siren Queen had signed with the huntress. She could see the document in her mind's eye as if she'd read it herself.

Their voices would no longer work above the waves so that they couldn't take away a human's free will. Cendre was disappointed she hadn't gotten the chance to hear her new voice above the waves, but she understood. At least her voice below was beyond compare.

Cordelia spat at her in disgust, full of outrage at her quiet acceptance of their fate.

Cendre shushed her. She had no voice here, now. It was Cendre's time to speak.

She used the magic deep within her, the magic that turned people away from noticing her, the magic that made her so easily find an unquestioned place aboard the king's ship, and sent it out in a little wave.

Most everyone resting onboard drifted into a deeper sleep, and the watch moved to other parts of the ship, lulled into safety.

And the exhausted soul below her feet fell into the deepest sleep of all.

She made her way down toward the room where Ro was. Cendre paused and looked down at herself. Well this would never do.

Even though she knew her sister wouldn't wake, not until Cen was back in the water and wanted her to do so, an inkling of humanity trickled into her thoughts.

Ro would be mortified if Cen went in there looking like this —perfection.

With barely a conscious thought, she shifted the color of her scales from gray flesh tones to iridescent midnight and clothed her human-looking body. With another slight shift, she softened the color to blend in with the ship. She shrugged. It still wasn't proper attire for the above world, by any means, but it would do.

As she passed through the ship, her scales shifted to match its color.

She made her way into the room in which Ro sat slumped over Olt's too-still form.

Cendre startled. She didn't know Olt was in here. She hadn't sensed anything from him. Odd. She circled them a few times, her heart breaking.

Regret clawed its way up her throat. She thought she'd have plenty of time to get to know them.

Apparently bringing up a little humanity opened the floodgates. All of her hopes and dreams, as they were before she'd become a siren, came flooding back.

As did her human voice, thanks to her promise from the Siren Queen.

Cendre stood over the sleeping couple, tears streaming down her face, dropping to the floor as little round pearls. Had she known she'd never again speak to her sister, she would've asked her questions. Not pushed her away. She would've made herself be brave. She would've told her the truth.

And the last thing she'd said to Ro was, "Curse you."

Cendre bent down and placed a fervent kiss on her sister's brow. "I love you. I'm so sorry. I wish I'd taken the time to tell you. To ask about our parents. Our siblings. To warn you about grandmère." A wry smile lifted her lips. "Now you'll have to find out about her all on your own."

Ro didn't stir.

Cendre ran her fingers through her sister's dark-brown hair, brushing some strands off her forehead. "I would never wish you cursed, dear sister. I wish you so many blessings, such great happiness, that your life cannot contain it all."

Cendre turned to the prince. Her prince. Yet, hers no longer.

She rested her hand on his head, then sucked a breath.

He was dying. In fact, he wouldn't last the night.

Her jaw tightened. She'd just have to do something about that.

Cendre moved her hand to his forehead, felt around inside for what was wrong, what was sucking out his lifeforce. She found it, worked on repairing it. His brain wasn't getting enough oxygen. It was shutting down.

Fatigue swamped her, but she didn't give up. She worked on repairing the damage, on returning his memories. She sagged the moment she'd done all she could.

Now it was up to his body to repair itself.

Olt took a full, shuddering breath, then settled into a deep, restful sleep.

Cendre smiled, kissed his forehead. Took a moment to run her fingers through his hair.

"Oh, Olt, you'll never know how I feel about you. How much I love you. How much I want to be with you. Someone who showed me kindness, gladdened my heart, made me want to discover things I didn't know were possible."

Her eyes flitted over the pair.

"But I can see you love her, and she loves you—even if she doesn't know it yet. Don't give up on her. She needs you so."

He shifted in his sleep, and Cendre knew he'd heard her on some level and had agreed. Having that kind of power still baffled her.

She allowed herself one last brief touch, and ran her fingers through the hair fallen over his forehead. Brushed it back. Watched it fall into place.

A frown flitted across his face, and she snatched her hand back.

She almost feared they'd wake, but she had her promise. She could say goodbye. As herself. Without their knowledge.

"And now you have each other, as it should be." Her smile was sad. "I only wish I could've been a part of your lives just a little longer."

Cendre stroked Ro's right hand, and her eyes caught and held on a trail of darkness snaking its way over her wrist.

Cendre frowned and turned over her sister's hand. The gash was deep and bright red, puckered and angry looking. Shadows veined out from the injury in all directions, and Cendre knew it was only a matter of time until Ro felt its effects. Until the sea started calling her too.

Until she could no longer push it away.

"Oh, my love, what have they done to you?"

Her siren blood screamed at her to remember who she was, that this was a good thing, that she should want the huntress as one of them, but she pushed it gently back. That was the creature within talking, not her.

And she would not be rushed.

A pulse of light caught her eye. She lifted her sister's other hand and uncurled her fingers. There, in her palm, pure-white light flickered in time with her heartbeat. The light trailed up her arm through her veins, and Cendre followed it.

It led her back to the other wrist.

This time, she could see it. The Fairy Queen's magic fought with the Siren Queen's, a silent, raging battle, unseen by mortal eyes. The shimmering glimmers would disintegrate the inky ichor, then the murky tendrils would entwine around the glittering strands and strangle them out of existence.

Cendre flipped over her own wrist and held it next to Ro's, comparing the matching marks.

She couldn't help her mild curse. The magic infused in Ro's human blood fought valiantly. It had stemmed the flow enough that it would be some time before she turned.

But she would be turned.

Cendre's transformation was nearly complete, but the huntress had not agreed to it as she had. And the sirens were never allowed to turn someone without their permission. It could unravel their magic, make the sirens susceptible to other creatures. Especially to, say, a huntress who specialized in defending humans against the fey.

She had to help her sisters. All of them, including the one before her.

Cendre lifted Ro's wrist to her lips and bit down gently. Black and red blood flowed, along with the fairy magic, which scorched her lips and burned her tongue. Still, Cendre sucked out the poison, and she didn't stop until it was gone.

It was the last gift she could give her sister.

She hurried to a porthole and spit it into the water, waiting to return until the pain was more manageable.

Cendre examined Ro's wrist once more. It no longer bled, no longer had any murky tendrils, and as if exhausted, the fairy magic throbbed dimmer and dimmer until it winked out. But an angry gash remained, so she ran her finger across the mark, urging it to close. Urging it to return to normal.

She frowned when she took her finger away.

The wound had closed, but the skin was still puckered, now raised in an ugly, pinkish welt. She must've used most of her store of magic on Olt. She couldn't make herself regret that. Now it was up to Ro's body to heal itself as well.

"I love you both."

She turned to go, heart breaking that she'd see neither of them again, when she remembered. "Oh."

She slipped off the seaweed satchel she'd wrapped around

her shoulders and reached for the pearl combs within, but her hand came out with the dagger instead.

As if she'd been waiting for the right moment, Cordelia surged forward and seized her wrists. Cen watched in horror as her joined hands raised, dagger fisted in them, over the sleeping pair.

I'll let you choose, a voice said. *But I suggest you do so quickly, or I will.*

Cen's gaze darted between the two. She couldn't do that. She couldn't kill either of them.

Yet . . . her eyes settled on Olt. She could be with him. The sister she hadn't known existed had stolen him from her, ignored her, discarded her. She could make a new life with him. Create a new family. A safe place.

But he wasn't blood.

Her gaze drifted to her sister. They could dance through the waves. Teasing, exploring, playing. Learning everything about each other and more. She wanted that so badly she could taste it.

All she had to do was kill Olt.

Cendre's hand trembled, and her eyes slid to Olt. Then Ro.

The pull to use it was so strong, she quaked under the onslaught.

Do it, a voice urged. *You know sisters should be together. Forever. You know you want to be with him. Either way, choose.*

If she killed Olt, she could take Ro underwater with her. Right now. She could be turned again. Cen could do it herself, now that the fairy magic was out of her system.

If she killed her sister, Creator forbid, then she would shed her siren skin and have the life with Olt she'd wanted since he first stepped foot in her tavern. And Cordelia could go back to the sea. Without her.

Her eyes slid over the sleeping pair.

Do it, Cordelia urged. *Kill the boy. He chose her over you. He deserves it. Take the huntress, take her deep, and reveal who you are. I will allow it.*

Desperate laughter bubbled up inside of Cendre and spilled over. *You have much to learn of me, siren, if you think I'm going to kill my sister or my friend.*

For a split second, Cendre wrested back control of the dagger, aimed it at her own chest, and thrust it straight at her heart.

Cordelia screamed and threw the dagger out the porthole at the last second. A slash of fire lit up Cendre's chest as the tip scraped a furrow in her scaled skin. Cendre cried out, but her eyes were drawn to the flash of red light outside.

The moment the dagger touched the sea, the place where it fell broiled and turned a brilliant shade of crimson. Cendre turned away as soon as the red light winked out.

Cordelia's screams of rage faded as Cendre shut a door on her and locked it. Cordelia wasn't saying or doing *anything* else until Cendre said so.

Cendre tried to heal the wound leaking inky-dark ichor, but she couldn't. She'd poured herself out for Ro and Olt, and now she'd have to wait to heal till the magic came back. If it came back.

She pushed away her fear.

Pressing her fingers to her wound, she once again dug around in her satchel. She pulled out the pearl combs with shaking hands and held them out to Ro.

"For you. But promise me you'll not give them to Madame LaChance."

Head still propped on her arms, Ro nodded slightly, her agreement as ironclad as if she'd spoken.

Cendre smiled, still shaken to her core by what had just happened. "Bon." She leaned down and kissed Ro's forehead for the last time. "You will always be the sister of my heart, but don't be sad for me. I now have an entire ocean of sisters, and they protect their own. I will be well cared for."

She hesitated. She had one thing more to say, but the words struggled past her lips.

"And . . . can you do something for me?"

Ro nodded, though still fast asleep.

"When you see Grandmère"—she frowned—"please tell her I am happy. Please tell her I am loved. Please tell her that I"—*love her*—"that I am well cared for."

She deflated a little as the words she truly wanted to say would not come. But the feeling didn't last long. Something on Ro's person called to her, whispered to come near, that it had secrets to tell her.

When Cendre slipped the pearl combs into Ro's pocket, something within brushed her hand. Something she immediately seized. She withdrew a coral comb and held it up to the light. The wedge of coral shaped like a small crown glowed with an inner beauty, and it sang to Cendre, enticing her to cradle it close.

Her wound closed, and she pulled her fingers away in surprise. Still, a deep furrow of a scar remained, as if to remind her of her choice.

"I am sorry, sister, but this is something you cannot have. Its power is too great for even you."

Her gaze reluctantly left the bauble and lovingly caressed her sister's face.

"One day you'll understand, I promise."

She slipped the comb into her hair. The power of the sea filled her. She closed her eyes. Took a deep breath. Enjoyed the rush thrumming through her.

The Siren Queen's song danced through her and tugged her toward the ocean. She let the song drench her. Soothe her. It felt like raindrops and the gentle rocking of currents, a wild tempest underneath.

Excitement filled her.

Something had always been missing. Something she'd craved more than she knew what to do with. She'd always thought something was wrong with her, but that was a lie. Something had been drawing her this entire time.

A life under the ocean.

No longer focused on the sleeping pair, she followed the call. Without another word, she left the small room and passed unseen through the hall and up the staircase. She stepped onto the edge of the boat.

And plunged into the water without a sound.

Once there, the comb shot power away from her in a wave, then came back and traveled over her entire body. She smiled and touched the piece of jewelry once before diving deep.

She was no longer Cendre, the cinder girl, but Cordelia, the daughter of the sea.

46

*R*o opened her eyes and sat up. Where was she? What day was it?

Her eyes fell on Olt's sleeping form, his chest gently rising and falling under the sheets. It was always the first thing she looked for.

Ro groaned and dropped her head, rubbing her sleep-encrusted eyes. Another night come and gone, and Olt still lost to sleep. How long had it been?

"Hey, beautiful. Did ya miss me?"

Ro's head jerked up.

His gorgeous, gold-flecked brown eyes and heart-stopping grin were aimed right at her.

"Olt!" Ro jumped up, knocking over her chair, and flung her arms around him. "You're awake. Oh, praise Dieu, you're awake!"

He made an "oof" sound, but he started to return her embrace.

She pulled back, beside herself. "The doctor! I'll get the doctor. Do you need anything? Water? Food? Water?"

She was already turning away, but Olt caught her hand. "Hey."

Ro paused, tears brimming, smile threatening to split her face.

"I just need you."

Ro's smile froze, her entire body stiffening.

He tugged on her hand. "To help me up. I feel like I've been sleeping for weeks and could swab an entire deck by myself."

Ro let out her breath and eyed him suspiciously. He didn't look like he could walk to the galley, much less swab a deck. When he started to struggle upright, she placed a hand on his chest, not letting him go anywhere. "If the doctor says you can get up, then you can get up. Not before then."

Her brain registered that there was a firm, muscular chest under her hand, and she snatched it away.

"I shall return."

Ro turned and something crunched underfoot. She bent down to get a closer look. Little seed pearls littered the floor, spread out like someone had kicked over a container of them.

"What is it?" Olt asked.

She flicked a glance at Olt. "Nothing. I'll be right back."

Still, Ro scooped up a few without thought and practically ran from the room to get some help, shoving them deep in her pocket on her way.

Cendre dove deep and dove fast. She still didn't understand how everything worked, but she knew the Siren Queen was waiting for her. Knew that she was ready to talk.

And Cendre couldn't wait to hear what she had to say. She was ready to begin her new life under the sea.

She swam straight toward the throne, anticipation making her giddy. She didn't know what to expect, but she couldn't wait to find out why she'd been summoned.

She pulled up right in front of the throne and gasped. The

Siren Queen was old. Decrepit. Barely hanging on to her thousands of years of life. Draped across the throne, her powerful form diminished.

"Why, whatever happened to you!" Cendre cried.

The Siren Queen looked up and startled. "You! What are you doing here?"

Cendre blinked away her confusion. "I—my—what do you mean?"

The Siren Queen snarled and reached out a feeble, gnarled hand. "Get that human out of my sight!"

No one moved to obey. They all stared at Cendre, fear pulsing throughout the throne room.

Cendre wanted to cry, but she didn't want to shed pearls for the entire room to see. "What have I done to offend you? Why are you angry with me?"

The Siren Queen recoiled when Cendre swam closer. "You are not Cordelia! I demand to speak to Cordelia!"

Cendre felt the siren try to push her way to the surface, but Cen pushed her right back down and held her there. She would confront her sometime, decide what to do with her, but that would not be today. For now, she was in control.

Cendre gave the queen a mild look, giddiness over her power giving way to composed assurance, as if she'd been draped with a warm current. "Calm yourself, my queen. Hysterics do not become one of your station."

"Why you insolent little guppy." The Siren Queen surged forward, then her eyes riveted on the coral crown in Cendre's hair. "Where did you get that? Give it to me!"

She swiped for it, but Cendre easily caught the weakened siren's wrists and held them in a vise-like grip. The queen slammed her tail into Cen's side, but in her weakened state, it barely rocked Cen in the current.

That just made the Siren Queen thrash all the more, rage overtaking her features. "How dare you! I will not give my throne to a human."

Cendre smiled, the expression cold, even for her, and pushed the queen away, who stumbled back into her throne. Maybe Cordelia wasn't as repressed as she'd thought. "Oh, but you will. You already have, in fact." She turned her wrist, just enough for the queen to see the dark veins webbing out under her skin. "You have given me the tools to take what I want, and not one of your sisters will stop me."

At that, the queen's guards, who had been frozen until that moment, made an uncertain move forward. Cen's eyes flicked to them, and they halted.

Queen Zarya hissed, swiped up something red and glittering from the arm of her throne, and lunged at Cendre, using all of her strength for a killing blow.

As if it had been waiting for the perfect moment, an arrow zipped through the water and pierced her side, throwing off her attack.

The ruby knife wafted to the floor and winked out of existence.

The sirens in the room held their tridents aloft, looking all around them for the threat, some shooting off in the direction the arrow had come from.

The Siren Queen held her side and drifted in the current, her entire being shuddering with pain. Sizzling smoke broiled out of the wound, and the enchanted silver arrow hummed a warning for Cendre to stay away.

Cendre smiled, as if the arrow wasn't the least bit unexpected, and came close to the Siren Queen. "Tell me what you wanted to quickly, for you haven't much time."

"I hate you," the Siren Queen hissed. "I will always hate you. Just as I hated your ancestor, my first sister, for leaving us, I will hate you with my dying breath. You are not fit to rule. I gave my throne to Cordelia, not you."

"I know." Cendre swam upright, her siren body lithe and strong and beautiful, and grasped the Siren Queen's weak head in her hands, forcing her to curl her tail under her and shy away. "But you no longer have any say in the matter. Now, this will hurt very much."

Then she drew the life out of the Siren Queen like taking a draught of water.

It tasted delicious. Like power and eternity and life essence. She drew in the siren's life force even faster, thousands of years, of knowledge, pouring into her.

Soon the Siren Queen lay there like a dried husk, no more left of her than the skin of a molten sea cucumber, the bones of a ship, and the scales of a seadragon.

Cendre turned to the sirens nearest her. "Please remove her body, and see to it that she receives a proper burial."

The sirens moved quickly to comply, fear evident in their faces and their jerky motions.

Cendre addressed the room. "Send messengers far and wide. The hunters the former queen sent out are to be recalled. Any humans still imprisoned will be returned. We will honor our agreement with the human king, and not one of my people will attack one of the huntress's people, not unless we are acting in self-defense. We will recede to our world and leave them to theirs. Do I make myself clear?"

"Abundantly, my queen." The room echoed as the sirens answered as one.

"And will you follow my proclamations?"

"But of course, my queen."

"And will you follow me as your queen, until I choose another to replace me?"

"With all of our hearts, my queen."

And with the third answered question, her queenship stretched tight and snapped around her—like a second skin.

She would be their queen until she gave her rule to another, just as the last Siren Queen had done.

At that Cendre swam the last few lengths to the throne— her throne—and turned. She made eye contact with everyone in the room before she sat regally on the throne, claiming it as her own.

All the sirens cheered until it shook the cave and Cen felt a niggling fear that the cave would fall down around their heads.

Cordelia quite promptly squashed that fear and told her to act like the queen she was.

Cen smiled. She had a feeling she and Cordelia would get along just fine.

Cordelia snarled at the idea.

ঙ

Ro looked out over the ocean, trying to think of a way to get past the barrier. Her enchanted bow had melted away after using the final silver arrow, leaving the plain ash bow in its wake. Returning to the sirens was out of the question.

Olt came up beside her, still moving slowly and carefully, and watched the barrier drift by for a bit.

"It's hard to believe a barricade can be that big, isn't it?"

Ro nodded without comment.

He glanced around the ship. "So . . . um . . . I'm glad you had a backup plan." He smiled when her eyes met his.

Ro couldn't return his smile. "That plan didn't include losing Cen. We were supposed to go home. All of us."

Her words chased away the smile on Olt's face. "Aye," he said quietly. "I miss her too."

Ro couldn't answer past the burn in her throat. They turned together back to the sunset. It slipped away in layers of citron, rouge, and then burnt orange.

Olt spoke first. "Captain said she's holding a service tonight. For the crew lost."

"I know."

"Including the English crew."

Ro did a double take. "That's generous of her."

424

"Yeah." He looked down at his hands. "Would you care to go with me?"

Ro turned her gaze away from the setting sun and studied Olt. "I had planned on attending."

Olt met her gaze. "I know. I'd like you to attend with me. Together. Cendre, well, she meant a lot to both of us . . ."

The suspicion slid away from Ro's heart. She covered his hand with hers. "But of course I will."

Olt took it, threading his fingers through hers. "Merci, Fräulein."

Ro kept herself from sucking in a harsh breath, not allowing him to know what a friendly, mere brush of skin did to her. He didn't mean it that way.

Ro gently withdrew her hand. "Those aren't the same *langues*, you know."

He bolstered his smile to cover what looked like disappointment. "I know."

Suddenly, the darkening, empty corner of the ship seemed too . . . intimate. Ro moved away. "See you tonight?"

He nodded, his smile gone, a wistful look on his face. "Tonight."

Ro headed belowdecks to splash her face with water. She needed to get ahold of herself before the service in just a few short hours.

The service was beautiful. The night was dark, so dark, without a moon, that nothing could be seen past the light of the torches. Someone read a portion of Scripture, then floating lanterns were lowered into the water, one by one, as crewmembers' names were read aloud.

Captain Montrose's deep baritone rumbled out each of his missing crewmembers' names, and Captain Red interspersed her rich, full voice with his. Until she fell silent.

And he kept reading.

Sniffles were heard throughout their joined reading, but once Captain Montrose took over, his list far longer than hers, a deathly silence overtook the ship.

There were so many. So many lives lost.

Ro dropped her head as the list went on and on . . . and on.

Olt placed a hand on her shoulder, and she clasped it. Desperately.

There was a pause before the captains read the last name together. "Cen."

Captain Montrose still didn't know Cen's secret, but he had honored Captain Red's request anyway. If he wondered—anything—he was smart enough to keep it to himself. He understood the lad had meant something to the huntress, and he left it at that.

Olt and Ro lowered the last lantern together, and silence shrouded the ship. One by one, the crew drifted away, and several helped Captain Montrose back to the infirmary.

Ro felt Olt's eyes on her, but she refused to look his way. Her gaze was on the final lantern, falling behind the rest, as it drifted away.

Cen's life, so short, so unnoticed, and she'd only come aboard because Ro had asked her to. Because there was something about the huntress the girl had wanted to know. It was Ro's fault she was dead.

Ro slipped out from under Olt's grasp and moved to a dark section of railing. She needed to be alone. To think. To mourn. To . . .

Ro slammed her fist on the banister.

Cendre was in her care—her care!—and now she was dead.

It didn't matter that the fool girl had jumped into the water after them. It didn't matter that Ro had known nothing about it. It didn't matter that the battle was complete chaos and there were many losses on both sides.

Cendre was her responsibility.

Ro gripped the banister, wringing the smooth wood in her hands.

The one good thing that had come from it? That happened in spite of it? She'd made the sirens listen to her. She had her peace. Her silence. The human world would never hear from the sirens again.

Yet Cendre was still dead.

"There's nothing you could have done."

Ro gripped the railing harder. "I am going to punch the next person who says that to me."

Olt took a decided step back. "Even though it's true?"

Ro gave a shake of her head. She couldn't even respond. True or not, it didn't help. It simply made her want to throttle the closest person. And grieve to the depths of her soul.

"Ro, please." A long pause. "I lost her too."

That got Ro's attention. Her head came around, and she searched his eyes. "I'm sorry."

He gave her a phantom of a smile. "Me too."

Hesitant, unsure, slow enough to stop should Ro object, Olt stepped up to her and slipped one arm around her waist, then the other.

Ro sucked in a breath and stiffened. Olt just stayed there, holding her gently, giving her plenty of time to walk away.

A tear slipped down Ro's cheek. Then another. Olt's arms around her tightened.

Ro laid her head on his shoulder and let her heartbreak overflow in tears.

47

The next day, Ro peeked over her cards at Olt, worrying her lip. They hadn't talked about what had happened the other night, and they'd gone back to their normal banter after she'd dried her face.

Ro couldn't have been more thankful.

But why she'd agreed to play cards with him, she'd never know.

That wasn't true—she was allowing him to distract her. She couldn't spend another moment wondering what she could've done differently to save Cendre.

At least it was much more enjoyable than the last time she'd played cards—to win her and Cosette's freedom from Gautier.

Ro flicked a glance at the jagged rocks to the starboard side.

They were so close to their destination, right on the other side of the barrier, but they just couldn't reach it. The ship floated next to the solid obsidian barrier while the captain tried to decide on the next course of action.

"You gonna play, or are you trying to delay the inevitable?" Olt taunted.

Ro laid down what she hoped would be the winning card.

Olt crowed his triumph, hurled down his winning card, and did the most ridiculous victory dance Ro had seen in her life. It reminded her of her brothers.

Gemma and Merja, both working nearby, exchanged a glance and a smirk.

Ro dropped her cards on the plank-and-barrel impromptu table and crossed her arms, trying not to smile. "Very mature of you."

The wind picked up a card and hurled it overboard. Ro scrambled to snatch up the rest of them.

He dropped onto his barrel and leaned back, arms behind his head. "And that, my Mademoiselle, is how it's done."

Ro just rolled her eyes and started stacking cards, a small grin making an appearance. She most certainly was not his Mademoiselle.

"So," Olt said, "back to what I was saying earlier. I don't think—"

A shout from one of the crew interrupted him.

"Captain! Captain! Come quickly!"

Someone else called at the same time, "Man overboard!"

Ro and Olt jumped up and followed Captain Red, who barreled out of her ready room and nearly bowled them over in her haste.

Ro leaned over the side of the ship, not believing what she was seeing. One by one, heads starting bobbing above the water as dark shapes deposited them at the surface and winked out of sight.

"Pull them aboard! Quickly!" Captain Red called out.

"But, but—that's not possible," one of the crew said. "It's been four days!"

Ro couldn't count them all, but by the time they'd been hauled aboard, she was close to thirty-five. Ro smiled. It wasn't the fifty-plus they'd left with, but it was so much better than the eleven rescued before.

A few of Captain Red's crew popped up as well, leaving her

with a full crew.

Well, except Cen.

"Captain, siren sighted!"

Ro followed Captain Red to the other side of the ship. A lone siren bobbed far out in the water. Ro wasn't sure which one.

"Is that all of them?" the pirate captain called.

The siren lowered her head, held an open hand over her heart—their sign of honor—and slipped under the rolling waves.

And even more incredible than that? Portions of the Ring of Death slowly sank out of sight, leaving huge gaps for ships to cross.

The captain nodded, satisfied, then started calling out orders. The moment everyone in the water was onboard, the ship lumbered to life and slipped past the barrier. Then the captain sent rowboats to search for a safe harbor to repair the ship.

Injured were quickly seen to, and the rest were stuffed belowdecks. Hank, the quartermaster, the physician, and the first mate from the *King's Ransom* were not among them.

"I can't wait till they're off this ship," one of the crew-women grumbled.

Ro couldn't agree. She could stand before the English king with over half of his crew. This day was looking up.

Ro took in the ocean past the barrier.

It was now an aqua blue, vibrant in color and so much clearer. They were finally in the warmer, balmier, and bluer Caribbean waters, limping to the closest port. Hopefully one that catered to pirates.

Although . . . the English hadn't exactly been able to send king's men here for quite some time . . . who knew what the closed-off world was like now?

After the bustle died down, Captain Red walked up to Ro.

Ro glanced at her. "The men?"

"In the brig."

Ro's eyes widened.

The captain gave her a look. "King's men on a pirate ship? What else could I do?"

Ro couldn't argue. "I think they'll be thankful you saved their lives."

The captain smirked. "One would think that."

"I take it transporting them back to Angleterre is out of the question?"

"Absolutely."

Ro sighed. "I thought as much. Do you think they'll be able to find passage?"

The pirate captain just shrugged. "I'll leave them wherever we dock to repair the ship, but finding their way home might be difficult."

Ro tilted her head, her question unspoken.

The pirate captain gave a full-fledged smile. She was gorgeous. Had Olt noticed? Ro couldn't help sneaking a glance at Olt.

But non, he was glaring at the pirate captain as he always did. *Why*, he wouldn't tell her, no matter how hard she tried to pull the information from him.

But at least he was glaring. And she hated that it pleased her to no end.

"Because the sirens have made travel nearly impossible between the Americas and Europe. They'll be lucky to find a ship willing to cross the barrier."

Ro's eyes widened. "In that case, are you sure you won't take them?"

The pirate captain winked. "Oh, quite sure, huntress." She leaned on the rail next to Ro, and Ro couldn't help but notice the long look she gave Olt, more come hither than anything, and she didn't like the little hitch her heart gave.

But Olt's glare deepened, easing away some of the tension threatening to strangle Ro. Then a thought occurred to her.

She cast a nervous glance at the captain. "But you'll take Olt back, right?"

This time the captain gave Olt a speculative look. "Perhaps."

Ro's head reared back. "Perhaps?"

But Captain Red had already pushed off the rail and was walking away.

Ro spun to Olt. "She'll take you, won't she?"

He looked grim. "I don't know. Honestly? I doubt it. I'm still a danger, if, you know, any sirens ignore the treaty."

"Well she'd better take you. Or we're finding passage elsewhere. Together." Her face burned. "Well, not *together* together. And only if you want to . . ."

Her voice trailed off as Olt grabbed his chest and staggered back a little. "Why, huntress, I had no idea you cared!"

Ro snapped her mouth closed, face flaming brighter, unable to say one coherent word. Olt just laughed. Then he dropped his voice and leaned close.

"I wouldn't want to cross the great sea without you, either."

Then he kissed her cheek.

Olt sauntered off as though her entire world hadn't just tilted off its axis.

She stared after his swaggering form, mouth parted. What was wrong with him? And worse, what was wrong with her? She kept hoping he meant every word, every action, instead of taking his teasing for what it was. Ugh.

Her brothers had teased her mercilessly, yet every time she tried to convince herself he was just teasing her as a brother would, he had to go off and do some fool thing like *kiss her cheek*.

Ro's fingertips found the spot that craved more of his touch, and she wished with all her heart she didn't. Romance complicated everything, and then when it was ripped away?

Ro's heart gave a pang.

Well, she couldn't take that again. Not ever.

48

They'd been weeks at the harbor, outfitting the ship to Captain Red's specifications. Specifications Ro thought were excessive. And time wasting.

"Are we ever going to leave?" Ro grumbled.

Olt voice right next to her made her jump. "Well, you could always go ashore with me. Get a warm meal, take a walk along the shore, swim in the surf, I don't know, actually have some *fun*."

Ro continued coiling rope, thankful calluses had started replacing blisters. At least this captain let her work. She shook her head. "I need to be here. For when we leave."

Olt started to protest, then seemed to think better of it. His tone took on that teasing lilt that made her want to throw caution to the wind and go along with whatever he said. "Oh, come now. We can have a grand adventure. Sign on to another ship—one that won't be fired upon on sight, I might add—and work as part of the crew the whole way back to England. You'd like that, wouldn't you?"

Ro shot him a look. "I'm happy right here, thank you very much."

Captain Red's voice cut through their conversation. "Huntress, crewman, in my ready room, now."

Olt looked disgruntled as he watched Captain Red sweep past, but Ro finished coiling her length of rope and followed, a bounce in her step.

The captain must have news! Perhaps they were setting sail.

Olt took his time, silently protesting with dragging steps. Ro rolled her eyes at him. She couldn't wait to hear what the captain had to say.

Captain Red was already at her desk, hands folded atop it. "Close the door."

Ro peeked over her shoulder—Olt moved to obey, though he didn't look happy about it—and then Ro leaned across the desk, hands splayed in its surface.

"Well? Have you news? Do we set sail soon? Tomorrow, perhaps?" Ro bit her lip to keep a further barrage of questions at bay.

The captain swiped a match on her desk and took her time lighting a cheroot and smoking a few puffs before answering. The rasp of her voice matched the rasp of the matchstick. "I've decided we aren't going back to England."

Ro's hand slipped, and she nearly face-planted on the captain's desk. "Not go back to Angleterre?"

Ro looked to Olt for support, but his arms were crossed, brows lowered, as he glared the captain's way. Pretty much his constant pose when she was around, and Ro had no idea why. No help from that quarter.

She turned back to the captain. "But why? What about the other half of the gold?"

Captain Red waved her hand, setting the smoke to swirling. "I find I like it here much better. Warmer clime, not as many king's men on the hunt for us pirates, and ports that don't even blink an eye when a pirate ship comes in to be outfitted." She belched. "The rum is quite good too."

Ro could only stare. She'd never heard of a pirate turning down gold!

Olt spoke, his voice quiet and hard. "How do you expect us to get home?"

Captain Red shot him a smile, eyes dancing. It seemed to please her to no end that Olt disliked her so. "Not my problem."

She turned back to Ro, who was still having trouble speaking. Coherent words just wouldn't come together in her mind.

"I will give you two days to vacate my ship"—her eyebrows rose as she leaned forward—"unless you wish to become a member of my crew . . . ?"

"Never," Olt spat out.

The captain's eyes stayed on Ro. "I wasn't asking you, crewman."

Ro shook her head. "I have to get home. Right away. My sis—"

"Yes, yes, your sister." She waved her hand and sat back. "We all know you have to get back to your sister."

Ro cocked her head. She didn't talk about her sister that much . . . did she?

"Very well, then. As I said, you have two days to vacate my ship."

Ro choked out, "But—but—what are we to do?"

"I don't know, and I don't really care. Find another ship and crew to set sail to England, or Angleterre, as you call it." A wicked smile found its way to her lips. "Although most ships won't set sail until spring, if any are brave enough to do so at all, what with the remains of the sirens' barrier. It's nearly winter, after all."

Ro's fists clenched. "How could you? You said you'd take us back." She'd thought they were friends. Well, more than acquaintances. Well, at the very least, business partners.

The captain shrugged. "I changed my mind."

Ro tried to answer, to come up with something to convince her, but the captain spoke first.

"That is all. You may go."

Olt grunted and turned to go, but Ro had to know. "If you do not return us to Angleterre, our bargain is off. You will not receive the rest of the gold, not now, not ever."

The captain's eyes stayed on hers. She looked amused. "I know."

The back of Ro's throat burned. "Why? Please, just tell me why."

Captain Red looked out the open window, sweet breezes sweeping through the room and whisking stagnant air away. "Crewman, you may go."

Olt hesitated. "Ro?"

"Just go," Ro ground out. She couldn't decide if the burn in her throat was tears or anger or betrayal. Or a terrifying mix of the three.

"Yes, but will you be safe?" Olt asked.

Ro shot him a glare that said how utterly ridiculous his question was, and he raised his hands and backed out of the room, one last stone-cold look directed the captain's way. Ro waited till the door closed to turn back.

"I am not in the habit of explaining myself, huntress, but thanks to you, I have a full crew and a floating vessel instead of a shipwreck." After a somber moment, her eyes set to twinkling. "Are you sure you'll not join us?"

Ro didn't bother answering.

The captain shrugged. "Your loss. Ours as well." Her eyes sought the beach, palm trees bent over sand, swaying gently in the breeze. "I do not mind telling you I've found a place I belong. I always hated the cold and the dangers it presented, and I never realized how delicious it would be without the English king's presence—and others—dogging our every step." She grinned. "Not that I mind adventure, mind you. I'm just overly tired of conducting funerals for my girls." Her eyes sought Ro's. "Something I think you can understand, non?"

Ro's heart panged, but she gave a single nod. "Oui." Ro gentled her tone. "But what I can't understand is why you cannot simply return us, collect your fee, and come back here."

A dark look flashed across the pirate captain's face. "Do you remember what I told you about Wilhelm? Long ago?"

Ro nodded.

"My sister and I knew him. As children. In fact, my sister married him."

Ro startled. But—she didn't know he had a queen! Why had she never met her? Why had no one spoken of her?

The pirate captain collected herself. "She died, huntress. Poison."

Ro's heart skipped a beat. Suddenly, any lingering hurt about Cosette not being her real sister evaporated. She didn't know what she'd do if she lost Cosette. "My deepest condolences."

Captain Red waved off the words, puffing on the glowing nub. "Wilhelm refused to investigate. Believed his mad witch of a stepmother that it was just 'one of those things.'" Her gaze was out the window, on something much farther away than the surf and trees. "He put her in a glass coffin, perfectly preserved, so he could look at her—talk to her—whenever he wanted."

Ro's eyes went wide. *He what now?*

Captain Red chuckled without humor when she saw the look Ro tried to mask.

"My thoughts exactly. I saw it precisely once before I was thrown out for raving at the madness of it all."

The silence stretched between them. Ro didn't know what to say.

"I can't go back, huntress. No matter how many times I ready myself, I just can't do it."

"I don't understand."

Captain Red blinked and sat back, her eyes on Ro. "Well, I wasn't expecting that reaction from you of all people."

Ro slashed a hand, her thoughts whirling. "Non, I mean, perfectly preserved? Not allowed to see her? Could it be magic?"

The captain rubbed one hand down her face. "Ro . . ."

"Non, I mean it. What if she isn't dead? What if they're hiding something? What if magic is only keeping her asleep—?"

"Arrête! Stop!" The captain was on her feet, a wild look to her eyes. "Don't. You. Dare."

"But I only—"

"No. I cannot go down that path again. I will not."

Ro pressed her lips together, trying so hard not to object. Things were not always as they seemed. She'd learned that much with the beast.

Captain Red paced madly behind her desk. "I thought the same. I investigated. Got thrown out of the palace, put in the stocks, even spent several freezing nights in the tower. And then I met with the embalmer."

Ro felt like she'd been slapped. "Oh."

"Oh. 'Oh,' she says. Exactly." Fresh wounds lay bare and bleeding in the captain's eyes. "I will not return to that land ruled by a mad king. One who would not even afford my sister —his wife—a proper Christian burial. Where he allows no one to speak of her." A sneer curled her lips. "Where he gazes at her lifeless corpse and talks to it and lays out dresses for it. I can't do it, and I won't."

Disgust curled in Ro's belly. At the king, not Captain Red. She straightened. "I understand, ma capitaine. I am so sorry I caused you unnecessary pain."

The captain laughed as she ground out her cheroot and began lighting another with shaking hands. "Now *there's* the response I was expecting." Once she'd taken several long drags of smoke, she looked up at Ro. "I expect you to disembark and find another ship. Quickly."

Ro couldn't find it within her to object, no matter how inconvenient it was. "As you wish, ma capitaine. Merci beaucoup for your assistance, and I wish you the best in your new life. A fresh start. Healing. And hope."

The captain nodded, her wavering smile fixed on Ro.

Ro couldn't say later what madness overtook her in that moment, but she walked around the desk—the barrier the captain had placed between them—and wrapped the tall woman in a firm hug.

The captain took one shuddering breath, then another, then slowly returned the hug.

Ro stepped back. "If you need anything, you need only ask."

The captain's smirk was still wobbly. "Pirating and all?"

Ro couldn't help her wry smile. "Assistance from one friend to another."

Captain Red gave her a solid nod. "Aye." She offered her hand. "My friends call me Rose."

Ro paused. "Rose—Red?"

Captain Red laughed, a bit self consciously. "Heard of me, aye?"

"But—but that would mean your sister—your sister is—"

Captain Rose Red rolled her eyes. "Snow White. I know. Names that plagued us both throughout the years. Our elderly mother was a bit . . . eccentric, to put it mildly." She fluffed her hair in an exaggerated movement. "Hair as red as roses and a temper to match." She grinned. "But mine serves me well now, non?"

Plagued her? More like made her infamous. Even Ro had heard the tragic tale of the two sisters in curse-ridden France. In fact, they were from France. She'd just missed the part about Rose Red becoming a dreaded pirate and Snow White becoming the queen of Angleterre.

The compass! That meant . . . its match had belonged to Snow White. No wonder Captain Red wanted hers back. Ro pulled it from an inner pocket and held it out. "I believe this is yours."

The captain stared at it awhile, then reached out and closed Ro's hands over it. "Keep it. In case you have need of me one day." She nodded at it. "Press on the glass, and it will call to me."

Ro's eyes widened. So that's why the glass had lit up when she'd accidentally pressed it during the battle. She looked at the lovely compass in awe. "Merci."

Captain Rose Red's smile was genuine. "It is an honor to know you, huntress."

"It has been a pleasure, ma capitaine. Rose." Ro stuck out her hand.

Captain Red shook it firmly.

Ro turned and strode from the room. She had to see Cosette so badly she could taste it.

Olt wasted no time collecting his few belongings and stalking from the ship.

Ro didn't exactly want to get left behind. She grabbed the weapons that had made it through the fight, her red cloak, and her satchel with her odd mermaid story and clothing from the Canaries.

She was just glad Cen had the foresight to move their stuff from the *King's Ransom* to the *Siren Hunter*.

She grabbed the lines on either side of the plank leading down to the pier, and something red and angry caught her eye.

Ro paused, her eyes on her wrist. Where had that scar come from? It was so slight, she'd almost missed it, but surely it hadn't been there before.

Yet . . . she could've sworn inky tendrils trailed up her arm, causing pain, making it difficult to grasp things, making the sea throb and say dark things to her . . .

A wisp of a memory threatened to land in her mind, but it flitted away before she could grasp it. The scar on her wrist was now as familiar to her as the rest of her scars. She'd gotten it while fighting the sirens, and that was that.

She shrugged and followed Olt off the *Siren Hunter*.

Now to find a ship that would take them past the Ring of Death and back to Angleterre.

49

*R*o straightened, back aching. She never, ever thought this would be the case, but she might actually be thankful Captain Montrose had never listened to her and allowed her to swab the deck.

It was the most disgusting thing she'd ever done. By the end of the day, it turned into a thick black sludge that reeked of all kinds of nasty things.

And these sailors only used a mix of water and something mild to scrape the saltwater buildup away.

She twisted her back to relieve it, then took a moment to scan the ocean.

This time, the sliver of land on the port side had been the Americas, yet another land she had to sail past without experiencing. Now they were cutting deep into the Atlantic, straight for the Ring of Death.

Ro couldn't believe how long it had taken to find a ship willing to cross the Ring of Death. They'd been months in the Caribbean—months—and winter had eased up just enough up north that a ship was willing to set sail.

She and Olt had signed on immediately as deckhands.

Ro felt Olt's eyes upon her and peeked.

Yep, he was laughing at her.

She jerked her head away and bent over her task.

Rope-burned, blistered, bleeding hands, and a new fear of heights when she was sent to the crow's nest for lookout duty —that was entirely new. She hated the feeling. She supposed a crow's nest falling out from under her while a ship was speared in half from underneath could do that to a person.

Thank goodness her exceptional eyesight made her the best lookout on the ship, so she could experience the feeling of terror when she was sent to the crow's nest again and again.

That's complete sarcasm, in case anyone is wondering, Ro grumbled to herself.

"Deckhand."

Ro turned toward the voice, not willing to be struck again. What could she say? She wasn't used to being called that, and she wasn't about to let Olt be thrown in the brig as he'd almost been when he'd come to her defense.

Apparently smooth, fast talking was a strength of hers when someone she loved was in danger.

Loved?

She blinked, snapping the thought off at its source. She wasn't going there.

The quartermaster wasn't his usual cocky self. "Cap'ain's requesting you as lookout. We're about to go over."

Ro nodded once, knowing exactly what he meant. He handed her the spyglass, which she tucked in her belt, even though her eyesight was far better than the paltry thing, and began the arduous climb.

All she could think of was the world dropping out from under her as the *King's Ransom* had gone down. Fear clutched at her heart, leaving her breathless, shaky, palms sweaty. *Not* ideal for climbing miles upon miles of lines to the crow's nest.

And then all that water below her feet . . .

She made it to the top and breathed her thanks to the Creator that she was still alive and hadn't experienced that horrible plunging feeling once more. Although her stomach reminded her of it quite convincingly.

She scanned the horizon, just fine as long as she looked out, not down. Ice-cold wind whipped at her this far north.

The captain called up to her, the wind grasping the words and trying to bat them away. "Report anything, anything at all, deckhand."

Ro nodded. "Aye, aye, mon capitaine."

The captain paced below her for a long while before joining the pilot at the helm. All hands were alert, on deck, staring out to sea. Ro couldn't help but thinking the tension was as thick as crème brûlée.

Something she could not *wait* to experience again once she got home.

Her gaze roved the sea, alert for dark shapes in the water. She didn't know how much good she'd be without her weapons, but the captain was firm they were to be stored until she left the ship, and Ro didn't want to raise more questions of why she had such extensive hunting gear in the first place.

She was not the huntress right now, much as she wanted to be.

Ahead, the rock-like barrier, now riddled with huge gaps between the jutting stones for ships to pass, announced they would soon cross the Ring of Death.

Tension mounted, and Ro rolled out her shoulders, trying to relieve its pressure. To ready herself. As she scanned the rocks, Ro's breath caught.

There, on the rocks, blending in, lining them as far as the eye could see. Sirens.

Ro's hands tightened on the rim of the crow's nest. "Sirènes sighted, Monsieur!"

The crew were already in position, so no panic or bustle ensued, though tension mounted to an excruciating degree.

The sirens sat motionless, bottom half fins of all-dark

scales, top half a mixture of scales and gray, colorless skin, all with midnight hair, all with midnight eyes, all watching Ro.

They passed the women-like creatures without incident, and Ro held as many gazes as she could.

I protect this ship. I keep my word. She willed them to hear her thoughts. To heed her warning. To remember her words.

The echo of their silence came back to her.

The ship passed unharmed, the warning that they were still there, still watching, taken to heart by Ro. She would pass it along to the king. The English king. The French king. And every other kingdom to which the warning would be sent, her signature attached.

One of them gave a signal — the sign of honor — and Ro did a double take. Was that Llyr? Non, but she looked familiar . . .

Of course, they all did, thanks to her fading memories from when she was, briefly, one of them.

The rest of the sirens copied the sign — Ro returned it — then in groups of twos and threes, the sirens dove into the water, hopefully never to be seen by mankind again.

As soon as the barrier crept from view on the horizon behind them, the crew let out a whooping and hollering that shook the vessel.

The crow's nest trembled under her feet — something she was less than thrilled about — but Ro couldn't help her smile as the men at her feet danced and cheered. One of them took up a fiddle for an impromptu celebration, and Ro leaned on her elbows and enjoyed watching from afar.

She didn't come down until dusk fell, making sure she hadn't given them false hope. But not a siren bothered them for the rest of the voyage.

Ro took a deep breath and let it out slowly as she looked out over the endless carpet of blue and the burnt-orange sky. She'd done it. She'd silenced the sirens.

And she was on her way home.

50

*R*o scrambled out of the hold, her bag flung over her shoulder, and gripped the rail till her knuckles turned white. Her eyes soaked in the expanse of fresh green, herald of spring. Angleterre. She'd never been so happy to see land.

As they slid through the channel and into port, then waited their turn to dock, impatience flooded Ro.

The Port of London really needed a better system of docking to accommodate all the ships. An eternity passed before they were allowed a spot alongside the wharf.

Once the plank was extended, she beelined across the busy deck and scrambled down the plank. They only had so much time to unload before another ship claimed their spot.

A flash of red caught her eye. Ro paused right before she stepped off the plank. Another, and then another, woman in a red cloak walked by.

She stared with her mouth hanging open.

Olt came up behind her and whistled. "Well, would you lookie there, huntress. You've started a trend."

Ro flushed and wrapped her mère's red cloak tighter around her, beyond thankful she hadn't lost it to the voyage.

"Why anyone would want to copy me"—now a little girl walked by in a red cloak—"much less half the women in Angleterre, is beyond me."

Olt shouldered his bag and grinned at her. "I told you you were well liked."

Ro sniffed and adjusted her own bag. "Nonsense."

Her mind spun with everything she needed to do. She needed to see Madame LaChance, right after she gave her report to the king. And then find out how her sister fared. Write her a letter. Non—go see her. That got her moving again.

Ro stepped off the merchant vessel's plank and onto the wharf. Even reeking of fish and shrouded in fog, she could've knelt and kissed the ground.

But first things first.

She took off for a hack but staggered madly before she'd gone three steps.

"Whoa, there, huntress." Olt's fingers closed around her arm. "Give your sea legs time to wear off."

Ro wrenched away and tried to take another step. She bumped into a stranger, who shoved her and gave her a dirty look. "You can't be serious. I didn't have this much trouble in the Caribbean!"

Olt chuckled. "Ah, but you did stumble around a bit, remember?"

She tried to walk on her own again but was rather unsuccessful.

"Careful. You don't want to end up in prison for being drunk."

Ro gritted her teeth. "They. Wouldn't. Dare."

Olt shrugged. "Perhaps. But there might be king's guards in London who don't know you."

Ro spun on him and promptly fell into him, whatever she was about to say thrown to the ether.

His roguish grin was back, and he held her a smidge tighter

than was absolutely necessary. "I have to admit, I really am enjoying your throwing yourself at me like this."

She scrambled to get away from him. "Don't get used to it."

Olt offered his arm again, and Ro took it, teeth grinding. He grinned and started whistling. Cheerfully. Like everything else he did.

Olt's firm, warm arm cradled hers, and Ro found herself relaxing. So she scowled at it. How could a single touch from him bring such peace? His arms felt like safety.

Ro blushed, hotly, and tried to stomp away. Yet hanging on to Olt's arm was the only thing keeping her out of a drunkard's jail, so she kept it.

They staggered around for a while—all right, it was only Ro—as she tugged him toward a hack. She had to find out if she had any letters from Cosette.

Olt matched her steps. "Where are we going again?"

"I am going to the palais to update the king and retrieve my lettres." *Then I'm going home. Maybe,* she didn't say.

"Oh, good, then. I'll go with you."

Ro steeled herself and lengthened her strides. He could leave now. Find another vessel to sail away upon. Why he was sticking with her, she had no idea.

Also things she didn't say.

She wasn't going to let a minor inconvenience—such as someone who smiled entirely too much, only saw the good in everything and everyone, and was perpetually cheerful no matter the circumstances—spoil how glad she was to be home.

She only hoped Cosette and Trêve were well.

Olt allowed himself to be hauled away, whistling cheerily the entire time. He hailed a hackney and placed her inside before giving directions to the king's palais and settling himself beside her. He changed the subject. "That wasn't so bad, now was it?"

Ro stared out her window. Yeah, right. He might as well say "I told you so" and be done with it.

"And we made it, just like you said."

Barely. That was the worst crossing in the history of crossings. Frigid air, ice that threatened to snap sails and lines, storm after storm after storm, and more iceberg sightings than she cared to remember.

All because they'd taken the first ship eager to get across the great sea at the end of a long and hard winter. She *hated* being cold.

"Hey." He bumped her shoulder, jolting her out of reliving the worst crossing in the history of mankind. "A livre for your thoughts?"

Ro sighed, deep and weary. "I never wrote to my sister before I left." She cast him a sidelong glance, not sure why she was telling him this. "She must be mad with worry."

He looked as if he cared about every word she spoke. "She'll understand. And as soon as you're done reporting to King Wilhelm, you'll see her before you know it."

Ro offered him a small smile, grateful he was kind to her no matter how prickly she was. She only hoped he was right. "Thank you for that, Olt."

After one of the most awkward and maddening confrontations of her life, Ro sighed and sank onto the stiff English settee, thankful to be done explaining herself to King Wilhelm and his advisors—for the hundredth time.

Was it so hard for them to believe the details of her voyage? Why did they keep staring at her like she was some scientific specimen to be dissected? What was wrong with everyone since she'd gotten back? Anyone she merely glanced at turned awkward, stuttering, gawking.

Or subjected her to a round of questioning akin to torture.

At least she hadn't brought up the little matter of King

Wilhelm's dead wife in a glass coffin. *That* would've gone over well.

Ro growled and pulled a pillow over her face.

She hated to admit it, but she missed Olt. She hadn't seen him in a few days, and she hadn't realized how much she'd come to rely on his teasing and carefree manner.

She pulled the pillow away and sat up. Well, then. She'd just have to come up with a reason to see him. If he was still here, that is.

A pile of letters, ones she hadn't noticed when she'd stumbled in the room, sat on the little desk next to Ro's settee. Finally! It'd taken them long enough to locate them.

She reached over to pluck them off the table.

Someone knocked on her door. Ro hesitated, hand hovering over the letters. Should she just ignore it and hope whoever it was went away? Surely she'd been through enough already today.

No sooner had she thought it than the knock came again.

"Urgent message for Huntress Ro LeFèvre!"

Ro sighed, dropped her hand, and called, "Entrez, s'il vous plaît!"

The door swung open to a pair of guards outside her door, courtesy of some namby-pamby idea from the king to keep her safe—or to keep track of her—to a sharp-looking messenger marching into her room with all the emotion of a leaf.

Ro idly wondered if he'd trained to look that dull on purpose and grasped her letters, idly flipping through them, silently urging him to go away.

The door swung closed behind him.

He clicked his heels and snapped to attention. "Urgent message from Madame LaChance to the huntress, Mademoiselle Ro LeFèvre."

Magnifique. Another person to subject her to a round of questioning.

Ro tried to keep annoyance out of her tone and failed. "So

you said. What has she to say?" Was being left in peace for the remainder of the evening too much to ask?

He delivered his message without an ounce of inflection. "Madame LaChance congratulates you on a successful voyage and wishes to hear the details from your own lips. She also speaks to an unspecified matter of unfinished business between you and wishes to conclude that matter with you in person. Shall I send your reply? Huntress? Did you hear me? Huntress?"

Ro stared, frozen, at the sender of her letters. She flipped through them, slowly at first, then picking up speed. Cosette . . . Cosette . . . Cosette—they were all from Cosette! Jagged writing, distress in every line, most pages discolored from rain or—tears.

She ripped one of them open. And the next. Till she'd gone through them all.

Holding the most recent letter in trembling hands, Ro frowned at it, the rest scattered around her feet.

"Huntress, really, I—"

She shushed the messenger and focused on her sister's words.

My dearest Rosette,

Please, come at once! I am begging you. My daughter—Have you received any of my letters? I've written so many, but I haven't heard from you!—Beau and I have a daughter now. Can you believe it?

(I am writing as though my other letters have been lost, because what else can I think? You were supposed to be back years ago, though Beau keeps assuring me your voyage will be long and difficult, what with the task the English king has bestowed upon you. But surely not this long? I worry so. Please return to us soon, my darling. I cannot bear to lose you both.)

Where was I? Oh, yes, my daughter! She is but three years old, and the dearest thing of my heart.

But what is so urgent—what I can scarcely believe has happened

—our daughter—your niece—has fallen into an enchanted sleep, and we cannot wake her.

Mon Dieu, we cannot wake her!

(Please forgive the tear-splashed pages, but you can imagine the depths of my grief-stricken heart. Oh, my darling little girl! She is everything to me. You are everything to me. Please come home safely.)

We don't know what to do! Please help us, dearest Rosette, please. If anyone knows what to do, it's you.

I love you. I miss you.

With all my heart, I await your return.

Your Cosette

Your Cosette. With those words, something clicked firmly into place in her mind. Cosette was her sister, no matter whether blood bond or fey bond or no bond at all connected them, and Ro would give her life for her. No matter what.

And that sister needed her help.

"Have you no reply for Madame LaChance?"

Ro's head jerked up. She'd forgotten the messenger was even there. "Pardon?"

"A reply. For Madame LaChance?" At least a hint of emotion colored his voice, even if it was exasperation.

Ro shook her head and shooed him out. "Non. Now out. Go. I must away at once."

Now he looked distressed, like he didn't know what to do with himself. "I fear Madame LaChance demanded—er, *requested* a response immediately. In person. I am not to leave without it. Your carriage awaits, Mademoiselle. Please, I must insist."

An inkling of a thought nagged her. What if she offended Madame LaChance?

The beast's words came back to her. *Madame LaChance is not to be trusted.*

Marvelous. Magnifique. Superb. She was about to offend

the financier of her voyage, but what else could she do? Her sister needed her.

And still the messenger wouldn't leave her be.

When he didn't budge, Ro huffed a breath and began shoving him toward the door.

"My lady, this is most unusual . . ."

She pushed him over the threshold, said, "Bonsoir, Monsieur," and shut the door in his face.

"Milady!" he called through the door. "Madame, er, my employer was most insistent that you see her right away."

Ro's brow knitted. Something teased at her memory, something Madame LaChance had very much wanted.

Suddenly, she remembered the combs in her pocket. Digging deep, shocked that she hadn't thought of them once since the Siren Queen had given them to her, she pulled them out and stared at the two pearlescent swan-wing combs, even more glorious than the last time she'd seen them.

Ro frowned at her hand. That wasn't right.

She'd given the swan-wing combs to Cen. She should be holding the singular coral comb, the one the Siren Queen wore as a crown, the one Ro had plucked from the Siren Queen's hair.

Why were the details so fuzzy?

Whatever the reason, Ro still only had a portion of what Madame LaChance had asked for, with no way to acquire the other comb.

Ro groaned and shoved them back in her pocket. She looked forward to explaining that little mix up to Madame LaChance. Honestly, she didn't think she could.

And the messenger was waiting . . . her eyes settled on her letters.

Cosette came first.

"Tell her—tell her—an urgent matter calls me away. That I will see her as soon as I return," Ro called absently, her mind already on the letter in her hands, her unknown promise to Cendre diverting her thoughts from the combs.

The messenger on the other side of the door huffed and stomped away.

It just didn't make sense. How could Cosette have a three-year-old daughter? Ro had only been gone a little over a year, even with all the delays.

Her mind scrambled to count the seasons. She'd left France near the end of spring, and it was almost summer again. Even with her and Olt's extended stay in the Caribbean, how could three years have passed?

Ro glanced at the date on Cosette's letter. And did a double take.

"Non," she whispered. "It can't be."

Ro jumped to her feet and ran from the room. She had to see Olt.

Flinging open her chamber door, she ran right into Olt's firm chest, his hand raised to knock. She took a deep breath. No one smelled quite like him . . .

She cut herself off in the middle of another deep breath and stepped back, hoping he wouldn't tease her for the heat on her face. Hoping the guards who were quite obviously looking away wouldn't notice. "Olt!"

He was still holding her arms. "Right?"

"I know!"

His eyes were dancing merrily. "But how—?"

"I have no idea!" She made her way back into the room, snatching up one of Cosette's letters. She shoved it under his nose. "Three years. Three! Can you explain it?"

He shook his head and took it, scanning the letter's contents.

Ro flushed and snatched it back. "How did you find out?"

He didn't look embarrassed, though Ro certainly was. She'd just handed him her letter, filled with all kinds of personal, private things she wasn't ready to share with him yet. If ever.

"Chambermaid."

Ro's jaw went hard without conscious thought.

He gave her a mild look. "Not like that. She was sprucing up a room for me and went on and on about how long the huntress had been missing and how she couldn't believe you'd come back after all that time. When I could get a word in, I asked how long it had been. She wasted no time telling me."

Embarrassment flooded Ro. Could she possibly be more insecure?

"But three years!" Ro sank into her armchair, staring at the letter without seeing it. "Cosette must think I've abandoned her."

"I take it you need to see her? Right away?"

Ro nodded absently.

"When do we leave?"

Ro looked up at him, surprised. "We?"

He grinned. "Of course. I'm coming with you."

She barked a laugh. "Merci, but non. I'm going to help my sister."

"Of course you are. And I'm going with you."

Ro's eyebrows climbed her forehead. "Excusez-moi? You're not."

"Sure I am."

Ro snapped her mouth closed, biting off each word. "I am going alone."

He shook his head and pointed to the letter. "Something tells me you might need my help. Besides, a grand adventure? A princess in need of rescue? Count me in."

It wasn't worth arguing over. He wanted to come? Fine. It meant nothing to her. "You'd better be at the stables by the time I saddle my horse. I'm not waiting for you."

Olt pulled her to her feet, looped his arm through hers, and escorted her to the door. "I wouldn't expect you to. Besides, my room's on the way. I'll meet you there." He winked. "I won't be two shakes of a lamb's tail."

Ro gave him a look. She'd never get used to his English sayings. How like Olt to adapt to whatever culture he was in.

Her thoughts spun as Olt kissed her cheek and hurried out of her room. How would he adapt to her culture? What would he think of her family?

And more importantly, what would they think of him?

She shook her head and hurried to pack. It didn't matter, because they were business partners—or something. Nothing more. Why was he coming with her again?

She packed her things tightly into her bag and did a quick sweep to make sure she hadn't left anything of import, then headed for the stables. Olt could find her there. She needed to see to Fairweather.

At least the king had kept her horse for her. That horse was the last link to the rest of her family, the last of her père's stock.

Hopefully Fairweather would be so thankful to see her, he wouldn't mind the return crossing to France as much as he had on the way here.

Ro flung open the stable door. Someone stood just on the other side.

"Olt!" Ro didn't mean to scream in his face, she really didn't, but ça alors, he'd scared her. Again.

He just grinned and checked the sky. "About time, huntress. I've been waiting for ages."

Ro just rolled her eyes and elbowed past him. "Vraiment? Really? Three seconds, more like." He must've run if he'd beaten her here.

Olt's carefree manner swaggered out with his grin. "And here I thought you were excited about another grand adventure with your trusty sidekick and couldn't wait—"

Fairweather stuck his head over his stall door, and Ro's breath stalled in her throat. "Fairweather!"

He was already straining over the stall door, whickering in greeting, and Ro ran to him and threw her arms around him, completely forgetting there was a witness to watch her melt all over her horse.

"Oh, my boy. My big, gorgeous boy. Did you miss me, huh?"

He nosed her pockets for the carrots she'd picked up in the kitchen, and she quite happily handed them over. She smoothed the few gray hairs his coat had picked up in her absence.

Olt came up and said, quite solemnly, to the horse, "Think I can get her to talk to me like that one day, huh?"

The horse snorted, as if to say, "You wish," and Ro elbowed him quite severely in his side. Olt, not Fairweather.

Heat washed over every inch of her body. Olt was never going to let her forget this. "For the love—hand me that tack."

Olt grabbed his chest and tried to look wounded. "See how she treats me?" The horse didn't look impressed. Olt turned his big brown puppy-dog eyes on Ro. "What about my own horse and tack?"

Ro just rolled her eyes. "I think we can both manage our own saddles and bridles, n'est-ce pas?"

"Oh, no. I wouldn't dream of not helping my Mademoiselle."

He turned to grab her bridle and started whistling cheerily even as a pang slammed into Ro's chest. As much as he might wish it otherwise, as much as he kept hinting at it, she would never be his Mademoiselle.

Fairweather stared at her with far-too-intelligent eyes, and Ro brushed him off. "Oh, I'm fine," she said under her breath.

He clearly did not believe her.

She kept stealing little glances at Olt as he first helped Ro with her tack and then started working on his own. He caught her staring and sent a wink her way.

Ro bristled and adjusted Fairweather's saddle a little harder than necessary.

Olt wanted to come with her? Fine. He wanted to flirt with her and tease her and pursue her across kingdoms and continents? Fine.

But she would by no means be an easy conquest.

THE END

Ro's story continues in

Quell the Nightingale

Book Three of the Beast Hunters.

Coming Soon from L2L2 Publishing.

ACKNOWLEDGMENTS

There are so many wonderful people to thank!

To my critique partners, the reason this book exists: I cannot thank you enough for creating such a tight-knit group to keep us all accountable. Thank you for helping me with this book! I treasure each of you more than I can possibly say.

To my amazing beta readers: Cathrine, Alex, Barbie, Aaron, Nicole, Laura, Alicia, Cam. You suggested so many things to make the story tighter, more succinct, more tension filled. I cherish your comments! (If I forgot anyone, please know I am great at keeping notes but terrible at finding them again.)

To my Dream Big Writer's Group: I have loved weaving this story at your side, amid writing sprints and laughter and intense brainstorming when my plot gets away from me once again. I am so grateful for this writing group!

To everyone who endorsed this book or gave me valuable feedback: Hope, Julie, Derrick, Becky, Laura VAB, Merrie, Heidi, and Laura G., oh my goodness! It is terrifying to ask for endorsements, and the fact that you gave me such lovely ones made me cry. Seriously. Thank you from the bottom of my heart for such kind words! I will treasure them always.

To my Realmies: I have never loved being a part of a writing community more. Thank you for being a safe haven in the storm, and thank you, Scott and Becky, for creating such a fun and safe space for Christian sci-fi and fantasy writers. You guys are my favorite.

Sara, this cover! Thank you for capturing my ideas so perfectly, and thank you for the many kind emails. I am so grateful for you! (And so happy for you! Squee!) :D

Thank you, Savannah Grace, for your amazing edits on this story. You made it so much better, and I loved squealing with you over Olt and our darlings, Cen and Ro. I love your edits so much! (And cannot *wait* to hear what you think of *QtN*!)

Laura Hollingsworth, I cannot tell you how much I adore your illustrations! Thank you for bringing Ro, Olt, Cen, the Siren Queen, and Captain Red to life. I am blown away by your talent and skill and that you were willing to work with me to make this dream come true. You are amazing!

Ben, I can't tell you how happy I am that you love to cook. I have enjoyed your creations so much, and it takes such a huge weight off when you give me that extra time to write.

Blaze, Maverick, and Gwenivere: I love each one of you so much. Thank you for being so excited that I write books, and thank you for being gracious when I took time to finish this story when you so badly wanted me to write all five books in your series at once. Now on to *Diamond Unicorn Kingdom*! I love you all more than I can possibly say. You are my heart.

Thank you, dear reader, for spending your valuable time on my stories! It means the world. I can't wait to hear what you think of it. (Excuse me while I go hyperventilate . . .)

And most importantly, I must thank my precious Savior for dying for this stubborn, insecure, and sometimes frustrating daughter of the King. May I live my life how You created it to be—may I do my best, write my best, for You.

With all my heart,

~Michele Israel Harper

ABOUT THE AUTHOR

Michele Israel Harper spends her days as an acquisitions editor for L2L2 Publishing and her nights spinning her own tales. Sleep? Sometimes . . .

She has her Bachelor of Arts in history, is slightly obsessed with all things French—including Jeanne d'Arc and *La Belle et la Bête*—and loves curling up with a good book more than just about anything else.

Author of over eight novels (and more on the way), Michele prays her involvement in writing, editing, and publishing will touch many lives in the years to come.

Visit www.MicheleIsraelHarper.com or www.L2L2Publishing.com to keep in touch or to learn more about her!

About the Author

Michele loves to hear from her readers! Follow her on social media, check out her website, or drop her a line to let her know what you thought of Silence the Siren. *Happy reading!*

www.MicheleIsraelHarper.com
Facebook: @MicheleIsraelHarper
Twitter: @MicheleIHarper
Instagram: @Michele_Israel_Harper

REVIEWS

Did you know reviews skyrocket a book's career? Instead of fizzling into nothing, a book will be suggested by Amazon, shared by Goodreads, or showcased by Barnes & Noble. Plus, authors treasure reviews! (And read them over and over and over . . .)

Whether you enjoyed this book or not, would you consider leaving a review on:

- Amazon
- Barnes & Noble
- Goodreads

. . . or perhaps even your personal blog or website or fave social media account? Thank you so much!

— The L2L2 Publishing Team

FRENCH GUIDE

Below is a quick guide to the French words I used in this book. I tried to ensure they were self-explanatory in the story, but if you have questions, the meaning should be explained here. It was so hard not to use more!

I adore absolutely everything French, and I hope my love for this exquisite language and beautiful country and lovely people came through at least a little. Bon voyage!

- Oui: Yes
- Non: No
- Bon: Good
- Arrête: Stop
- Allô: Hello
- Bonjour: Good morning or hello
- Désolé: Sorry
- Pardon: Pardon me
- Excusez-moi: Excuse me
- Quoi: What?
- Magnifique: Magnificent
- Merci: Thank you
- Merci beaucoup: Thank you very much

- Rien: Nothing
- De rien: You're welcome or it is nothing
- S'il vous plaît: Please—literally, "if you please"
- N'est-ce pas: Is it not? Isn't it so?
- C'est comme ça: It is what it is
- Au revoir: Goodbye/until we meet again
- Très bon: Very good
- D'accord: Okay (But since "okay" wasn't around in the 18th century, it means "all right" here.)
- Mademoiselle: Miss
- Mesdemoiselles: Miss, plural
- Madame: Ma'am
- Monsieur: Sir
- Mère: Mother
- Père: Father
- Grandmère: Grandmother*
- Votre Majesté: Your Majesty
- Mon Roi: My King
- Mon Prince: My Prince
- Mon Dieu: My God
- Mon chou: My darling—literally "my cabbage" (It's a term of endearment, I swear!)
- Ma chère: My dear
- Ma chérie: My darling
- Mon ami(e): My friend
- Mon amour: My love
- Mon capitaine: My captain, masculine
- Ma capitaine: My captain, feminine**
- Boîte de Jeu: Game box, specifically used for the game l'Hombre, or Quadrille, from which the English game Whist was derived
- Livre: French money
- Château: Castle
- Palais: Palace
- Sirène: Siren or Mermaid

*Note: Technically, it should be "grand-mère" in French, but in all honestly, I just don't like how it looks. Since English is closed construction, I took the liberty of using "grandmère" in this series. I hope you will forgive my changing it to match my preference!

**Note: At the time of this writing, not all occupations have both masculine and feminine forms in French, including the occupation of captain. Many in France are pushing for equal terms, which for a gender-specific language, means that there be both feminine- and masculine-specific nouns. I thought I would add my support and perhaps in my own small way move for greater equality by including the feminine form of "ma capitaine" for Captain Red.

(Plus, I mean, it just looks so beautiful, am I right?)

More from L2L2 Publishing

If you enjoyed this book, you may also enjoy:

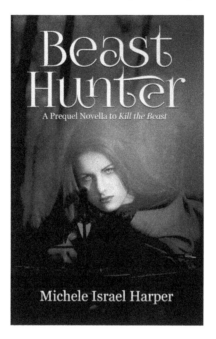

Ro's people are starving. A curse has overtaken her land, blackening the soil, wiping out crops, and bringing ruin to all. She doesn't know what to do. The only people who thrive are the huntsmen, brought in by the mysterious Gautier to stem the flow of ravenous creatures looking for food. When Ro accidentally kills a wolf, an idea begins to form. Could she become a huntress? Earn enough livres to feed her family? But her world is shattered when her father promises her to a beast in exchange for his own life. If she doesn't go, a curse will fall on her family worse than the one destroying their land. But Ro is determined to save her family another way. Will Ro have the courage to seek her own fate instead of the one pressed upon her?

.

More from L2L2 Publishing

If you enjoyed this book, you may also enjoy:

Huntress Ro LeFèvre races back to France with one thought on her mind: get there before her niece succumbs to a sleeping curse—a niece she didn't even know she had. Ro must use all her skills as a huntress to find the enchantress responsible before the child reaches the point of no return, before she is crushed by the curse's power and never wakes again. Thanks to her extended time fighting the sirens, she hasn't much time. Trapped in a tower with a feisty girl who is far too protective of her pet swans and her enormous coils of hair, Ro's heart is shattered when the mysterious empress known only as the Nightingale keeps Ro from her goal, toying with her as though she has all the time in the world to waste. Where is the blasted Queen of the Fairies when Ro needs her most?

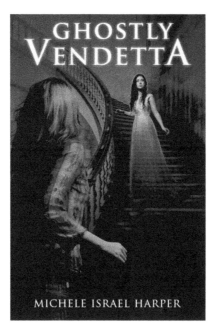

WHERE WILL WE TAKE YOU NEXT?

Discover *Beast Hunter,*
Hunt with *Kill the Beast,*
Anticipate *Quell the Nightingale,*
Shiver with *Ghostly Vendetta,*
and Devour *Zombie Takeover.*

All at
www.love2readlove2writepublishing.com/bookstore
or your local or online retailer.

Happy Reading!
~The L2L2 Publishing Team

ABOUT L2L2 PUBLISHING

Love2ReadLove2Write Publishing, LLC is a small traditional press, dedicated to clean or Christian speculative fiction.

Speculative genres include but are not limited to: Fantasy, Science Fiction, Fairy-Tale Fantasy, Time Travel, Alternate History, Space Opera, Steampunk, Light Horror, Superhero Fiction, Near Future, Supernatural, Paranormal, Magical Realism, Urban Fantasy, Utopian or Dystopian, etc., or a mixture of any of the previous.

We seek stunning tales masterfully told, and we strive to create an exquisite publishing experience for our authors and to produce quality fiction for our readers.

Silence the Siren is at the heart of what we publish: a fabulous fairy tale with speculative elements to delight our readers.

All of our titles can be found or requested at your favorite online book retailer, local bookstore, or favorite local library.

Visit www.L2L2Publishing.com to view our submissions guidelines, find our other titles, or learn more about us.

And if you love our books, please leave a review!

Happy Reading!

~The L2L2 Publishing Team

Lightning Source UK Ltd.
Milton Keynes UK
UKHW010208240821
389362UK00001B/205